ALSO BY WILLIAM SAFIRE

FICTION
Freedom
Full Disclosure

LANGUAGE
In Love with Norma Loquendi
Quoth the Maven
Coming to Terms
Fumblerules
Language Maven Strikes Again
You Could Look It Up
Take My Word for It
I Stand Corrected
What's the Good Word?
On Language
Safire's New Political Dictionary

POLITICS
The First Dissident
Safire's Washington
Before the Fall
Plunging into Politics
The Relations Explosion

ANTHOLOGIES
Lend Me Your Ears: Great Speeches in History

(WITH LEONARD SAFIR)
Good Advice on Writing
Leadership
Words of Wisdom
Good Advice

SLEEPER SPY

SLEEPER SPY

William Safire

RANDOM HOUSE NEW YORK

Copyright © 1995 by The Cobbett Corporation

All rights reserved under International and Pan-American Copyright
Conventions. Published in the United States by Random House, Inc.,
New York, and simultaneously in Canada by Random House
of Canada Limited, Toronto.

Library of Congress Cataloging-in-Publication Data
Safire, William.
Sleeper spy / William Safire.—1st ed.
p.   cm.
ISBN 0-679-43447-X
I. Title.
PS3569.A283S54   1995
813'.54—dc20   95-8482

Manufactured in the United States of America

24689753

FIRST EDITION

Book design by Carole Lowenstein

Homage to
E. Phillips Oppenheim
and
James Jesus Angleton

PART ONE

The Searchers

Prologue

BARBADOS

He was free.

Never before in his long career, first in the KGB and now in the Russian Federation's Security Ministry, had the control agent felt himself beyond the reach of Moscow's arm.

But now the document freeing him lay on the coffee table of a bungalow on the leeward side of the island. From the porch, looking west into the sunset, he could see the landing lights and faintly hear the approach of the evening flight from America. Berensky, the sleeper agent now acting under his direction, would be at the bungalow within an hour.

"Tragic crash near Odessa has taken the lives of the chief of the Fifth Directorate and his deputy," read the decoded fax message. He had been ordered to return to Yasenovo, on the outskirts of Moscow, for urgent consultations. A new economic intelligence chief would have to be appointed and briefed.

Control had a good idea who the new man at the top of the Fifth was likely to be: one of the brilliant young academics, all good looks and meager experience, brought in by the reformers after Yeltsin put down the old guard's attempt at a coup. Their youth did not bother Control; he was a veteran agent; Aleksandr Shelepin himself, the KGB chief who had led the "anti-Party plot" to oust Khrushchev in the old days, was not yet forty when he took over at KGB headquarters in Dzerzhinsky Square. What troubled Control was the ready recognizability of their faces.

Nikolai Davidov's face, for example. Davidov was the most probable choice to take over as director of economic intelligence. He had the dark good looks and square jaw of an American television anchorman. What kind of face was that for a spymaster? Control thought the best face for espionage should exhibit a bland forgettability, much like Control's own visage: professionally nondescript, a scowl not especially threatening, a countenance easily overlooked. A face to put people to sleep.

He ran the tip of his tongue along the thin lips of that face, savoring the delicious fact that not one of the new crowd in Moscow knew what Control knew: the identity of the sleeper agent who had been planted a generation ago in America. Someone in the bureaucracy surely had a general idea of Berensky's work from Control's guarded reports, and a few of the old-timers with long memories of Shelepin's day might even know the sleeper's Russian background. A banker in Bern and an economist in Helsinki who were in on the launch of the sleeper's activation and assignment—to invest the assets of the KGB—might know, though they dealt through Control and only indirectly with the sleeper. But nobody now alive at headquarters in Yasenovo had had, up to now, any need to know the sleeper's American identity. The current name and address of the sleeper was the best-kept secret in the KGB.

Now, with the old Fifth director and his deputy both dead in the crash, and with all files on Aleksandr Berensky long ago deliberately destroyed to prevent his discovery by CIA penetrators, only Control and one other Russian agent were aware of the sleeper's name and whereabouts, his mode of operation, and the scope of his assignment. Control allowed himself to savor the miserly pleasure that comes to political insiders, secretive scientists, art thieves, enterprising journalists, and professional spies: the sense of early, exclusive possession of invaluable information.

He walked inside the bungalow to one of the two bedrooms, opened his suitcase, and felt gingerly for the two old record albums he had obtained as soon as he received the news of the crash and Moscow's order that he return.

He asked himself: Who else knew who the sleeper was? In the field, one other Russian agent knew Berensky's American name and legend. But that agent, who had penetrated the U.S. government and was supplying information to fuel the sleeper's financial engine, was also Control's responsibility. The two men, sleeper and mole, reported only to Control. He was certain neither had any other point of contact with the KGB. He wished now that he had never let the two get into contact with each other, but that had been unavoidable; the sleeper needed to have immediate access to financial data from the mole, and Control could not always be available as go-between.

For four years, Control had been given no other assignment than to run these two agents. The sharp focus of this assignment was unusual at a time of tightened budgets at the Kremlin, but was a measure of how vital to the Russian state the directorate deemed the success of the sleeper's unprecedented operation.

The album covers were between his shirts. The Bruch Second Violin Concerto played by David Oistrakh and "Songs for Swingin' Lovers" by Frank Sinatra. He reached inside each album cover and extracted the two flat, round sheets of plastic explosive.

The material was not Semtex, manufactured in the Czech Republic and retailed by Libyan middlemen to terrorists; Control wanted no part of such a provenance. This was Composition D, made in the U.S. for military use, said to be more malleable and reliable.

From his wallet, he took out an instruction sheet on how to mold the plastic explosive, install the detonation device and its timer, and fix it in place. This was not properly Control's line of work, but he was certain it should not be beyond the capability of a resourceful agent, even one long once-removed from direct operations. He reread the instructions and followed the first step to stretch and mold the two pieces of black plastic into the single two-foot length he desired.

Would Berensky want to join him in taking advantage of the deaths at the top of the Fifth Directorate? Would he agree to redirect the plan? Holding the plastic in both hands, Control paused to ponder. Even before Berensky was given a huge stake in gold and had begun to receive closely held financial information a few years ago, the sleeper had become a successful banker in America; he understood the mysteries of money; he moved vast sums of other people's assets around in lightning trades.

On the other hand, Berensky—Control thought of him in his Russian, not his American identity—was the dedicated disciple of his father, a KGB chief who was such a stern ideologue that he had sent his son to live a lifelong lie behind enemy lines a generation ago. It troubled Control that the sleeper might be afflicted with notions of loyalty to the new regime now in power, or—even worse—with dreams of supplanting that regime with the old KGB faction once headed by his father.

If Berensky refused to take the money and go into private business with Control, there was always the banker in Bern to fall back on for his expertise. But Berensky would be better.

Control now wished he had taken the time to know the sleeper better. Belatedly, he judged himself deficient in tradecraft for not being able to determine the motivation of an agent given such trust. But Aleks Berensky had never been a confiding soul; in all their meetings over the five years after Aleks was activated, the tall, heavyset man had seldom smiled, had rarely grown openly angry. He remained unperturbed, as a gambler or a banker should, even in those rare cases when the economic intelligence Control provided him was mistaken and caused him serious losses.

Following the directions on the sheet, Control pressed the detonator shaft into the plastic explosive. Berensky was the name given to the bastard son of the KGB director Shelepin, but the sleeper was his father's son. Berensky was a Shelepin to the bone. Purposeful above all.

What else would possess a young man to leave his pregnant wife behind forever, to train for years in the KGB's American Village to pass for an American, and then to insinuate himself into an alien society, never revealing himself until called upon to betray the trust he had built up for a generation? Control had run spies that were in the business for the money—by far the most reliable motivation—or for the thrill, or were driven by some burning theology, or because they had been entrapped and turned. But all those spies had the comfort of continuity of contact; steadying their psyches was the reassurance of a regular series of transactions, made personal by the lifelong security of their own control agents.

Not the sleeper. For nearly twenty years, he had been all alone and unreached-for. He had never been called upon for any espionage and was not permitted to contact his motherland for advice or encouragement. His permanent home was in the enemy's house. A sleeper was an intelligence agency's longest-term investment, never to be risked for transitory gains. This particular sleeper was like a time bomb attached to a generational calendar rather than a clock.

Control reminded himself that the explosive detonator in his hand was to be attached to the small quartz-driven clock in the kit. He consulted the instruction sheet again, clicked the timer into the detonator, and checked the hour against his own watch: 7:00 P.M. He set the clock for 11:00 P.M. and pressed the assembled device into the lengthened plastic. It drooped in the middle when he held it in both hands, but he found the answer to that in the instruction sheet: mold the plastic to the object to be exploded.

He went through the bathroom to the bedroom that did not have his suitcase on the bed. The last time they met on this island, Berensky had expressed a desire for the room with the view of the nearby hotel casino rather than of the ocean, and was asleep by ten. He would have his favorite room again.

Control slid on his back under the bed and pressed the length of the Composition D around the rod stabilizing the innerspring mattress. He jiggled the detonator and clock to make sure they were wedged in securely. As a fail-safe, as the instruction sheet suggested, he rigged the switch so that he would have to come into the room and reach under the bed to activate the timer. He would do that during a break in their meeting, only if the sleeper failed to grasp the private financial opportunity that lay before the two of them. If Berensky would not be his partner, the sleeper would lie down on his well-wired mattress for his final sleep. And then Control would take a long walk on the beach, in a safe position to observe the fireworks.

The sleeper paid off the taxi at the entrance to the hotel, waited for it to drive away, and did not enter the lobby to check in. He hefted his garment bag and chose to walk the five hundred yards down a dark gravel road to the farthest guest cabin.

Berensky did and did not enjoy his meetings with Control. The wiry little man was the point of contact with his authentic existence; that was good, after the long two decades of operating totally detached from his roots. Control was the place to put questions to the KGB mole in Washington—what would the Commerce Department announce was the GNP deflator on Friday?—and through him, as cutout, to an agent he did not know in New York—what commodity price was the Federal Reserve most closely watching this month? Control was the conduit for answers that would determine his investments of the fortune, in coming weeks. And he was the veteran agent who had slipped outside

KGB channels to bring Berensky a personal farewell from the sleeper's natural father, Shelepin, before that giant of espionage had died in obscurity and disgrace.

The part Berensky did not enjoy was systematically deceiving the new leadership of the KGB. Not that Berensky was afflicted with scruples; with his bloodline, he was aware that deception was bred in the bone. But if Control were to learn the actual size of the fortune he had amassed in the past five years, that intelligence would surely cause the Kremlin—in desperate need of hard currency—to trigger a premature conclusion to his enterprise.

Berensky felt the time was not yet ripe to cash in; the political forces within Russia had not come to a decisive turn. A challenge to the Moscow regime was imminent; an underground organization, which might better serve Berensky's political purpose, was spreading and strengthening. Because the sleeper could not yet be sure which faction he would support—government or underground—he kept a separate set of books with low, yet credible, figures. That is what he had in a section of his garment bag, to show Control.

"Good evening, Mr. Seymour." Control changed his code name on the tenth day of every month, going down the list of New York State governors. He was up to Horatio Seymour. The system struck Berensky as silly, but it was not for him to criticize the tradecraft of longtime operatives. He did not know Control's real name, and when they were together, preferred to call him Control rather than that month's gubernatorial code name.

"I have news for you, Aleks."

"The Fed's interest rate decision?" He walked into his bedroom and threw the garment bag on the bed. He flicked on the light in the adjoining bathroom, peed, splashed water on his face, and brought the towel back into the living room, rubbing his face dry. "I could make a killing with that."

"Bigger news. This." The veteran agent, a polo shirt over his bony frame, leaned across the coffee table and handed Berensky the printout of a fax message.

Berensky read the news of the plane crash and shrugged. "They come and they go. Too bad. Bomb aboard?"

"No, I think this was a genuine accident. It will affect you and me, but I will come to that in a moment. Your report, please."

Berensky handed over the one-page summary of the trading done by a portion of his network of brokers. It showed a fortune that had grown to $13 billion.

"Bottom line, we made a profit of six hundred million dollars in the past quarter. It's in the Antilles bank, and we're using it to buy oil tankers."

"Not good enough. You're slowing down."

Berensky let himself seem to bridle, but did not argue; his actual profit in the quarter had been $2 billion on a real fortune of $30 billion. "I'm only as good as the information you get me. You have the data I asked for last time?"

Control nodded but did not hand anything over. "Let me see the disposition of the present assets."

Berensky showed him the placement of the $13 billion he was prepared to show the KGB: banks, account numbers, holding companies, corporate fronts, all accessible only to the sleeper and the lone person he reported to.

Control rose and put that in his briefcase, then went to the kitchenette for coffee. "You want a shot of rum in your coffee? It's the local custom."

The sleeper disliked rum, but went along. Control apparently had something on his mind beyond the normal information exchange.

He set down the coffee cups. "Aleks, the significance of the message from Moscow is that you are now a complete mystery to the KGB."

"You are the KGB," Berensky countered.

"True, for the time being. But except for me, nobody in the organization knows who you are. Nobody knows what the size of the fortune is, and frankly, I have been conservative in my reports." He made a gesture with his hands as if removing handcuffs. "You are an independent operative. Do you have any idea what that means?"

"You're suggesting we abscond with the money."

Control looked pained. "That would be foolish. They would find me and kill me, after getting your name from me. And it would be—" he searched for the word—"dishonest."

Berensky remained silent, awaiting the proposal.

"You were entrusted, years ago, with three billion dollars in gold bullion," the veteran began. "This was the money in the treasury of the KGB, along with certain overseas holdings of high members of the

Party." He sipped his rum and coffee. "I suggest we return to the Russian Federation a return of one hundred percent on its investment—six billion in dollars, which is about what they think it is today. They will be ecstatic. You will be a hero."

"And what's to be done with the rest?"

"You are familiar with the Feliks *organizatsiya?*"

Berensky knew that many of the ousted apparatchiks, along with hard-liners in the KGB forced out after the coup attempt, had formed a loose alliance with the new-rich Russian mafiya and Chechen and Ingush patriot-hooligans. When these groups fell in with the longtime underworld—the *vorovskoy mir*, "society of thieves," that had operated before and after Bolshevism—the amalgam of criminals, corrupt bureaucrats, and crooked entrepreneurs had chosen the name "Feliks" after Feliks Dzerzhinsky, founder of the Cheka, the predecessor of the KGB. What Berensky did not know was whether the purpose of the new community of crime was simple greed or the ultimate seizure of political power.

"No," he lied.

"You're out of touch with what's happening in Russia, Aleks. Many of the new businessmen, and many of your father's old friends from the days he stood up to Khrushchev, are working together to restore the glory of the Soviet Union, or so they say. The Feliks people know about the three billion sent to you. They think it belongs to them."

"To some extent, it does, I suppose."

"So let's give it back to them. Three billion to the Feliks organization. Their money was kept safe. Nobody gets interest on gold. We'll be heroes to them, too."

"That leaves four billion," said the banker.

"For you and me. We should cut in our junior partner in Washington to some extent, with a little left over for my contacts in Bern and Helsinki, and a tip to the agent in the New York Fed. You could effectively conceal our assets. Everybody rich, everybody happy." Control paused. "What do you say?"

Berensky felt nothing but revulsion for this man and his scheme to carve up the fortune he had so creatively amassed, and with it the political power it represented; the handler was downgrading it, as if the fortune were spoils, to be shared by political fixers. If he took up

Control's invitation to corruption, the sacrifice of twenty years of his life would be rendered meaningless. The varied centers of talent brought to bear on building up the world's largest unknown fortune would see their joint effort reduced to a grand swindle.

"Lot to think about," he said mildly. "You're not in a rush, I hope." Above all, he did not want to cut off his flow of highest-level economic intelligence, which gave him an advantage over every other major investor in the world.

"Your father had a saying, Aleks. 'The house is burning and the clock is ticking.' "

Berensky nodded; he could hear his father, Shelepin, using that proverb to express urgency in his Lubyanka office before his arrest in what was called the anti-Party plot.

"The new chief of the Fifth Directorate will want an accounting immediately," Control said.

"Maybe you can put him off."

"There can be no delay. There is some sort of crisis at the Treasury and they are desperate for hard currency. I'm disappointed in you, Aleks. You think about it while I go to the john."

"I'll do a refill on the rum coffee," Berensky said. As Control headed through the bedroom, Berensky picked up their cups and went to the kitchenette. He was not going to be stampeded. Control needed slowing down. The sleeper kept a strong sedative in a small packet in his wallet; he took it out, tore it open, and spiked his colleague's coffee and rum. The rogue control would get drowsy soon and ultimately pass out. Berensky would then decide what course to take: to wait until the clear light of morning to suggest a plan to delay the conclusion of their mission, or to take him out on the beach that night and let him accidentally drown in the surf.

After the sound of much flushing, Control came back through the door to his bedroom, his look of irritation gone, and joined Berensky in sipping the coffee.

"I noticed a couple of old record albums in my room," Berensky said to make conversation. "I suppose they still use phonographs down here."

"Probably just the covers," Control said, sipping. "They use them for wall decorations. I have the answers you wanted." He took a paper out of his pocket. "Gold production figures in Russia and the estimate of the winter wheat crop. And the news to be announced next week about our oil consortium with the Japanese."

Berensky looked over the insider information from the KGB about Russian plans. His traders in Chicago could act on that. But nothing from within the U.S. government; was the mole inactive? Perhaps Control was holding back that end of the intelligence until he had a reaction to his scheme to divide the fortune and vitiate its potential to stage or prevent a coup.

"Have you decided, Aleks?"

The sleeper stalled. "Let's go back over those figures again. And tell me about the new man, Davidov."

Within five minutes, the sedative took sudden effect—unfortunately, a drastic effect, perhaps brought on by the mixture with the hot rum. Berensky was alarmed to see Control try to rise, and find no feeling in his legs. The little gray man slumped back in his chair, a look of horror on his face, trying to say something but getting nothing out but a piti-ful gurgle, gesticulating toward the bedroom door. In a moment, the man was unconscious.

That was not at all the reaction that Berensky had planned. Had he miscalculated the dosage? Was Control especially susceptible to seda-tion, or allergic to this drug? He tried to awaken the agent by slapping him and then with cold water on his head, with no success. The man would have to sleep it off. He lifted the light body and carried it in his arms into the closer bedroom, momentarily forgetting it was his own; then, rather than maneuver the limp Control through the small bath-room, the big man kicked away the garment bag and laid him down on Berensky's own bed.

Irritated with himself for the miscalculation, he went out on the porch, sat on the steps to the sand, and took in the mild, starlit Caribbean night. He resolved never again to use any kind of drug on anybody until he had first studied the literature. In this case, the unex-pected reaction was not a major problem; if Berensky decided against any extreme measure, Control would get up in the morning with a headache and feel sheepish about drinking too much and passing out.

He looked at his watch; past ten-thirty. He decided to take a walk along the beach to think through the crisis posed by the death of the directorate chief. The music and lights of the casino attracted him for a few moments; he looked from the outside, then started to walk back slowly. He needed only a month's delay, to make a series of deals that would mushroom the fortune to a size that could be decisive to one or the other of the forces that would direct his motherland; surely Control could be talked into a month. The secondary decision about Control's fate then made itself: Berensky would let him sleep it off.

The explosion ripped the roof off the cabin and lit up the night sky. Even at a distance down the beach, Berensky felt the shock and then the heat. Heart racing at the realization of the fiery end that had been meant for him, he folded his arms across his chest and watched the blaze destroy what was left of the bungalow and the bits of body in it. He had to admire the impeccable tradecraft: Control had prepared the elimination of Berensky in a way that permitted no successful investigation.

He had no further business in Barbados. The sleeper spent most of the rest of the moonlit night walking to the airport.

Chapter 1

The pedestal remained in the center of the former Dzerzhinsky Square like a great unfilled tooth. The statue that had stood atop it, of Feliks Edmundovich Dzerzhinsky, "Iron Feliks," the founder of Stalin's secret police, had been toppled and dragged away in the heady days following Gorbachev's downfall and the failed coup of 1989.

"That must have been a sight. Were you here, right at this window, to see it? How did it make you feel?"

The questions popping out of the American agent drew a studied smile from the Russian just installed as head of the Fifth Directorate of the Federal Security Ministry, called the Cheka in Feliks Dzerzhinsky's long-ago day.

"I would hardly have been here in Lubyanka," Nikolai Davidov countered, "unless as a prisoner in the torture cells downstairs. I was an academician at the time, something of a dissident." He was exaggerating; he had been a reformer, perhaps even an oppositionist within the Party when that took some courage, but could hardly claim to have been one of those hardy souls who lived in constant fear of the Gulag. But agents, especially Americans, preferred Manichaean clarity to the shadowy ambiguities of life in the Soviet era.

"I was down there in the square just after the attempted coup," Davidov recounted, "helping affix the cables to the statue so that the mob, the people, could pull it down." In fact, the mob with its ropes could not manage the feat; Davidov had had to send for a government crane. But shading the truth, whether for dramatic effect or for more serious disinformation purposes, came as second nature to him.

The agent—an American literary agent, not a member of the intelligence community—looked at him sharply. "You don't strike me as the sort of person to be a high official in an organization like this."

That pleased Davidov even as he frowned. The mustachioed Russian was tieless; his black leather jacket was draped casually over an office chair. He knew his easy demeanor and youthful good looks were the opposite of what Americans would expect in a high official of what they still called the KGB, especially the head of the directorate responsible for foreign economic intelligence.

"And what do you expect us to look like?"

"Fat and evil, like Beria in Stalin's day. You don't fit the stereotype. You're out of character."

"Ah, Ace—may I call you that?"

"You may not," said the agent. "My name is Matthew McFarland. My lifelong friends call me Matt, and there aren't many of them left, because I've had a very long life. My business associates and clients, one of which you may be lucky enough to become, call me Mr. McFarland. The only people who call me by that odious nickname 'Ace' "—the supremely confident American spat out the word—"are my competitors and the rude or uninformed."

The Russian held up his hands, palms out, to ward off the burst of irritation. Davidov had been made aware of this sensitivity of the man universally called Ace—it was detailed with gusto in the published profiles—but wanted to present a naiveté about American literary agents.

The KGB had something to sell: its secret files. Not files it had any need to keep confidential, of course; only those that would reflect discredit on the bad old days and rehabilitate victims of Stalin's purges whose example would be useful today. More to the point, Davidov's assignment was to sell files created by the KGB's newly reinstated disinformation section to reveal secrets that never were. In the headquarters regrouping, old scores remained to be settled all over the world: selected foreign helpers had to be rewarded with silence, while expendable and expensive agents could be usefully burned.

The pose Davidov intended to strike for his agency was a genteel poverty. Here was the once-mighty Soviet security and espionage apparat, now come on hard budgetary times, reduced to peddling its innermost "family jewels," as its CIA counterparts like to call the deepest secrets, turning to capitalist publishers for sustenance. It was illusory, of course—internal security and foreign intelligence remained as well financed as before—but out of this illusion of weakness came a devious strength.

The charade required Western literary agents, especially the American superagents. Those middlemen conferred enough credibility on Russian writers, and on KGB documents, to persuade Western publishers to market the memoirs most useful to Russia today. Under the agents' eager aegis, political reputations would be made and destroyed, historical myths demolished, and new fantasies created, to serve the purposes Nikolai Davidov and his colleagues had in mind. Best-sellers could be created, accompanied by much Western media attention, with the label "exposé." Lenin once said the capitalists would sell the rope to hang themselves; now that Russia had embraced capitalism, the sale of memoirs and secret documents was a nice variation on the Leninist theme. And it would generate some hard currency, always desirable for the directorate concerned with foreign economic intelligence.

"I withdraw the Ace. Mr. McFarland, then. Let us put aside this suspicion, rooted in a bygone age." The Russian indicated a chair at a small table in front of his desk and took a chair opposite. Davidov picked up the brown glass ashtray and looked the question about smoking at his visitor; McFarland shook his head in distaste. The Russian sighed to himself and made ready to suffer through another meeting with an American who preferred an environment called "non." He put aside the ashtray and took up a manila folder.

"The Kirov file," he announced. "One of the great mysteries of the early Stalin era—"

"Not interested in ballet," snapped Ace. "Not the Bolshoi, much less the Kirov. Never sell. People who like dancing don't like books."

Davidov did not respond right away. Did the American not know about the murder of Stalin's rival, Kirov, the mayor of Leningrad, by one of the assassins working for Iron Feliks? Was Ace playing the fool? Of course, the St. Petersburg ballet school was named after the beloved mayor, and Rudolf Nureyev had made the name synonymous in the West with ballet rather than with Stalin's treachery. But surely an American literary agent would know of the earlier, sinister meaning of the Kirov affair. An eminent Kremlinologist at Harvard had concocted a novel about Stalin's murder of his popular rival: Ace must know that. Davidov concluded that McFarland was pretending to be ignorant of

Soviet history to the point of boorishness, thereby establishing a position of patronization. His estimation of his interlocutor rose a notch.

"Perhaps you have a particular secret in mind," he inquired.

"Your Lee Harvey Oswald file was the obvious first choice," said McFarland, "with the surveillance of Kennedy's assassin when he was here. But you already gave that one away."

Davidov let himself look pained. "Gave it away? We sold the literary rights, and then made a separate deal with Unimedia for the television rights. Maybe we could have gotten more, but that was last winter and we were desperate—"

"Babes in the woods, you were. No guaranteed paperback, no first serial sold beforehand, no percentage of the gross on movie rights, electronic rights never even mentioned in the contract—don't you people know about CD-ROM or on-line publishing?" The agent slumped back in disgust. "No wonder you lost the Cold War. You don't know the first thing about negotiation."

Davidov did not respond to the American's provocation, which he assumed was a negotiating ploy. He silently recalled SALT negotiations in which the Americans had been trapped into strategic disadvantage for decades, and the negotiations for agricultural purchases at the 1972 summit, which the Americans later indignantly called "the great grain robbery." But what the literary agent said was troubling. If the Oswald file looked like a giveaway, it would lack credibility; only what was paid for dearly would be believed.

"On the other hand," Ace went on, "you stripped that Kennedy file clean before you sold it. You probably have the real file for sale later. I can handle that for you, if you permit debriefings of the handlers that are still alive."

Davidov shifted in his chair. Not one of the handlers in that case was alive; fortunately, the deposed apparatchiks had seen to that long ago.

A discreet knock and his aide, Yelena, entered with a written message. She was reformist and reliable; his predecessor had years before rescued her from the ranks of "swallows" assigned to seduce foreign diplomats and trained her to be an analyst. The note she handed him read: "Feliks visitors asking archivist for follow-up file. Cooperate or delay?"

"Cooperate, by all means," he told her, flashing a grin, and as she left he tossed out a thought to the literary agent: "How about our man in

FDR's Oval Office? We knew about Einstein's letter that started the Manhattan Project before your President did."

"Your guy who hit Trotsky sold that already, fingering Oppenheimer and Fermi. Sold pretty well, but the KGB man couldn't produce the smoking gun, and you can't get the scientific establishment riled up twice."

Davidov refrained from pointing out that Stalin's legendary hit man Sudaplatov, in his recent memoirs, had not revealed the identity of the mole in FDR's Oval Office. He suspected that McFarland had been sent to see him with a specific project in mind, and this was preliminary sparring. "The Cuban missile crisis?"

"Never sell, after Dobrynin's memoirs, and he got an up-front advance that guaranteed a first printing of a hundred thousand copies. Twelve-city book tour, the works. I could have done better for him, but the agent selling it was capable." The dapper American leaned forward, tapping a large ring on the table for emphasis. "C'mon, Davidov, ante up—something big, an oh-shit story."

"I am unfamiliar with that expression."

"An oh-shit story. It's a plot that makes the reader clap his hands to his cheeks—like this—and say, 'Oh-shit!' It's what every publisher dreams about."

"Like—"

"Like wiretaps of Castro and Kennedy and Marilyn Monroe all involved together. Or a mole high up in the CIA. You could bring the guy out and have him write a book, *I Was Aldrich Ames's Handler.*"

"But there is no second mole." Davidov had to be careful.

Ace waved that aside. "You have to say that to me, but of course there is. And a Third Man, and a Fourth Man, same as the British. Instead of waiting for them all to get caught by the FBI, you could bring 'em in from the cold."

"Perhaps you should assign that story to a novelist."

"Nope, gotta be the real thing," Ace snapped. "There's real interest in an American Philby, somebody up high who was protecting your mole that we caught. And a bundle if it involves some American politician or diplomat who's well known."

When Davidov remained impassive, McFarland tried another tack: "Or some big-shot media right-winger who worked for you all along, which would satisfy the souls of liberals, who buy books, and want to get even for your guy who fingered Oppenheimer. Something to flabbergast the world into saying, 'Oh-shit!' Didn't you guys do anything you're proud of?"

The Russian stood, taking that as an insult. "Some operations will never be for sale," he said. But he knew the literary middleman could be useful. "On the other hand, we might be able to come up with a revelation or two that causes the world to say—to react in the way you want."

The agent went to the window for a last look at the empty pedestal in the square that had returned to its pre-Soviet name. "Who do you suppose they're going to put on that pedestal now?"

"Nobody," Davidov said firmly. "I spoke to the head of the First Chief Directorate himself about it this morning because some churchmen had a plan afoot to put an Orthodox cross there. We're going to cart away the pedestal and plant flowers."

"Some pretty terrible things must have taken place right here," Ace observed, his mood shifting perceptibly.

"Mainly against Russians. We are not proud of those terrible times at all." Davidov's new office, on the square, was provided to him mainly for show; its location in downtown Moscow, its view of the Kremlin, and its marrow-chilling history of atrocities especially impressed foreign visitors. He did his real work "in the woods," as the headquarters at Yasenovo, in a park beyond the outer ring road, was called. Davidov sensed that the American was coming around to the central purpose of his visit.

The literary agent, channel to publishers in the West, contemplated the line of Kazakh vendors selling food and souvenirs in the square below, now renamed Lubyanka; Feliks Dzerzhinsky's memory was being expunged from the city in every way possible.

"If you run into any of Feliks's people," Ace McFarland said in a low voice that would be difficult for recorders to pick up, "I have a client who happens to be a great reporter."

Davidov said nothing to indicate he caught a reference to the Feliks people. He awaited the follow-up probe.

"This fellow is not asleep," the agent said, accentuating the last word. "Irving Fein is his name, the great reporter—you may have heard of him."

Davidov took that to be an oblique allusion to a sleeper agent.

Though his heartbeat sped, he chose to ignore that probe as well. He wondered who McFarland represented in this and how much the client knew, but was not about to ask, in a room where their conversation could be so easily monitored by some of his colleagues who did not wish him well. He nodded a polite goodbye.

"Irving's good," Ace put in, all innocence. "Never sleeps on the job. You ought to meet him."

The directorate chief escorted his visitor to the anteroom and turned him over to the tour guide for a look at the old cells.

Chapter 2

The smoked-glass walls of the Park Avenue reception room of "M. McFarland, Literary Representation" reflected the black looks of authors kept waiting.

Irving Fein picked up, looked over, and put down each of the recent best-sellers of Ace's clients that were spread all over the huge coffee table. He fidgeted at the wait and burned at the undeserved success of the formula freaks. Romances by hacks with slavish "followings" cozied up to how-to books by quack cosmetologists; musings of charlatan shrinks nestled among memoirs of former Presidents on paper that "bulked up" to doorstop thickness, leaning against horror novels that raced their screenplays to the public view.

All those books, with the exception of the slim volumes of suicidal poetry by soulful wastrels that Ace took on as clients for the cachet, had what none of Irving Fein's books ever had: "legs."

"Legs" were the result of the driving force of prose narrative and televisable personality that made a published product march smartly off the shelf into the buyer's arms. Irving took from the table a spy novel by a guy he knew who used to be a good reporter and put it in his brief-case, as beat-up and disheveled as its owner. He felt no guilt at stealing a book; Ace probably had cartons of them.

He squinted at himself in the expensively darkened glass and saw a raging *flop d'estime*. For a journalist who had started out so fast—a Pulitzer before he was thirty for a newspaper series on terrorists, a near miss on a National Book Award for his worst-selling tome on arms merchants—Irving Fein found himself kicking around the media, respected by peers but seen as trouble by editors, potent in print but unable to capitalize on what he wrote by touting it effectively on television. Maximum energy, zero synergy. His sources, secure in his protection, had stuck with him; no reporter alive had better-placed, more trusting sources, developed over years of manipulator-manipulatee symbiosis. But editors, younger and more remotely British every year, were slower to return his calls.

Fein laid what he considered his personal curse on all of them—they should get beaten to a big story by a talk-show host with deep pockets. He reserved a special spot in his Media Hell for the tight-assed bookers of the television news-feature shows whose airy decisions about panelists and guests made all the difference in getting lucrative lecture dates. These well-bred young nepots—Irving was certain they were all related to big shots somewhere—kept telling him he had a "hot-personality" problem. Why was that? he asked himself, because the answer pleased him: the reason Fein came across as permanently angry was that he knew so much about what he knew, he found it hard to edit himself down to a zingy sound bite. That was why the roundtable shows shunned him. "When you go on," one of the TV types had instructed him, "you mustn't go on and on."

The media world was a year-round garden party, which was fine for the vendors of strawberries and cream but was hell for someone known to be the perennial skunk at the garden party. Whatever Fein wrote made the media-certified good guys look bad, which caused all sorts of media self-flagellation and earned him dirty looks from the clean and wholesome. Why was this? he asked himself in a long-running internal dialogue. He was ready with the answer: His stories were replete with villains and hypocrites, hollow hotshots and moral cowards, but never any heroes. Readers liked heroes, or at least villains with redeeming features, but this reporter made his targets look bad clear through.

Irving Fein, resolutely independent operative, a free man with his own lance, could poke his head into any newsroom in town or bureau in Washington and get a wary welcome, but it had been a long time since he had had a major score, and everyone knew it.

Now he had a lead on a big one. Like an oenologist sniffing an uncharted vintage before the first cases of wine got off the boat, Fein felt the thrill of knowing he was the first to tell that this one would develop mightily in time.

The week before, he had received a blind tip on his answering machine about "the Feliks people" in Russia searching for a sleeper spy operating in America. He had tried this slim lead on a counterterrorism source at the CIA: Walter Clauson, last of the crowd brought in more than a generation before by the Agency's legendary molehunter, James Jesus Angleton. Clauson had survived the Halloween Massacre of CIA hard-liners in the Carter years as well as the more recent post-Ames purge.

"Mr. Clauson, this is Irving Fein. You've probably been reading my series on the Agency."

"I don't like to get calls at home this early, Mr. Fein. Perhaps you can call me later at Langley."

Irving knew he had to get it all out in one breath. "I'm told you're the one who tried to talk the FBI out of investigating the U.S. banker in Nairobi who was fronting for Iran in the Libyan tanker deal."

Clauson had slammed down the phone. Irving counted to twenty-six, his lucky number, and redialed; at the opening expostulation, he said, "Don't hang up, I have something you want to know." That usually stopped the intelligence types. "First I want you to know I respect you. It takes a lot of guts to hang up on Irving Fein, knowing what I can do to your career at the Company, and my hat is off to you."

He let the guy apologize at that point for having been testy at being awakened with an accusation of malfeasance. "Next let me tell you something you may or may not know: not everybody in the little house on F Street wishes you well." The F Street property was a few steps from the Old Executive Office Building, near the White House, where Bill Casey, as Director of Central Intelligence, had liked to hole up in the Reagan era. Fein assumed Clauson was working at the F Street building, and if his guess was off, no harm done, because most of the spooks at the Langley headquarters in Virginia thought the presidential ass-kissers of the F Street gang were undermining the cause of unpoliticized intelligence estimates.

To the no-longer-sleepy counterspy's izzatso, Fein responded: "I'd go further—these guys were on the phone to me this morning stabbing you in the back about—" He flicked the button in the phone cradle rapidly to break up his voice and said, "Maybe I shouldn't be talking this way. How about a cup of coffee at the Mayflower in an hour?"

The reporter knew his spook had been hooked. Like most other bureaucrats, deskbound spymasters suspected some other department competing for their budget was dumping on their work. The suggested meeting time was too soon to set up serious surveillance, in case Clauson thought his phone was tapped and he would have to mislead the sweat merchants at his next scheduled fluttering.

They designated a spot and met. Fein trolled at first with a sampling of all he knew about CIA politics, especially a deal between the new Director of Central Intelligence and the Justice Department to turn all the rest of counterintelligence over to the FBI. Nothing spooked the old spooks more than the thought of losing the counterspy operation worldwide to another agency.

Then Irving did some serious fishing. The Russian mafiya—with a *y*, distinct from the Sicilian variety—was well known and its ties to officialdom had been long suspected, but who were "the Feliks people"? And what was this about their search for a lost or defected agent in America, who supposedly had the key to some vast fortune?

All the reporter had to start with was the blind tip about a "sleeper"—an agent planted in America by the KGB long ago and never activated—plus a notion that it had to do with serious money being socked away for later Russian use. No more than the outline of a story, devoid of detail. The voice-mail message told him to contact "one of the old Angleton types" at the Agency to find out more, which pretty much narrowed the field down to Walter Clauson. Irving Fein acted as if he knew much more, of course; he was aware that spooks always preferred to confirm or amplify rather than to hand over something new.

He got little out of Clauson; the man was a pro, searching to find out how much the reporter knew, trading his ability to confirm for the revelation of what cards the reporter held in his hand. Irving bluffed, pretending to withhold information about what he knew lest Clauson pass that along to a friendlier reporter, more easily controllable.

He waited for questions from the CIA man, and derived a little nourishment from the counterspy's probe about who in the Agency had suggested that Clauson might be knowledgeable about a sleeper agent. That could mean that Clauson could not be sure of containing the story within the Agency, or it could mean Clauson had told one of his agents to tip Fein and was being smart now in covering that up. Of those two possibilities, Irving was inclined to believe the first—that

Clauson did not know Irving's initial source, a disembodied voice with no credibility at all. If that judgment was correct, then it followed that Clauson was willing to engage with Fein for a good reason: to control, contain, or at least monitor the reporter's investigation.

That's what Bill Casey had done with Bob Woodward, at least at the start, but the reporter had later prevailed on the superspook to open up more. Then Woodward had parlayed leads dug out of Casey into detailed responses from others in the Agency who didn't like the Director. The trick was to fool the would-be container of the story, and Irving Fein was certain he now played that game better than anybody. Just to begin to play it again gave him his much-needed news hit—that rush of hunger to the heart piqued by the scent of an exclusive that would peel the onion of post–Cold War espionage down to where the tears were.

Clicking high heels snapped the ruminating Fein back to the present. He was in a superagent's reception room, not on a park bench trying to milk an intelligence official.

The woman had a familiar face, atop a long, endangered-species coat, followed by a couple of breathless sycophants. She appeared in the dark mirror, on the way to the elevator. He swung his eyes over from the referent to the real thing—a woman with almost regular features and hair that was so naturally sandy-blond and casually combed it had to have taken hours to create. Fein almost said, "Don't I know you?"—which meant she was a television regular, not an anchorperson but a featured performer, and he remembered that he liked this one. She seemed to have a measure of *gravitas* on the air, some crispness of assurance that other pretty faces lacked. The name escaped him; she was still a personality, not yet a celebrity—a face, not yet a name.

Standing at the elevator, she jabbed compulsively at the button already lit; she looked back at him with eyes that struck the reporter slumped on the couch as registering a lack of interest bordering on distaste.

Fuck you too, lady, and the horse you rode in on, he said to himself. Irving determined that his first question to her, if she came over to him and tried to make conversation, would be "Do you have any idea how many leopards, the fastest animal alive in a short dash, died to make that coat that some network muckeymuck probably paid for?" That would not merely wipe off the expression of mild disdain but rattle her teeth, which he judged too perfect not to be capped.

His opportunity did not arise. The elevator arrived and the young woman and her retinue marched into it. Not so young, reckoned Irving; mid-thirtyish. On second thought, to those who are late-forty-ish, mid-thirtyish is young; mid-thirtyish is what people who called themselves thirtysomething wished they were. His spirits sunk further. She was not too young for that coat, which she probably paid for herself, because performers in that business pulled down ten times what they were worth as journalists. So what if it was a leopard? He didn't like cats.

The nickel dropped; actually, it was a quarter now. Her name was Viveca something; he could hear a voice saying, "Newsbreak, Viveca something reporting."

"Saw Viveca out there," he told never-call-me-Ace when he finally got into the agent's office. "Good kid. She could make it."

"You know her?" At Irving's shrug, McFarland assumed a worried-about-my-client pose. "I worry about that girl. So much talent, such a great future, yet so vulnerable."

She hadn't seemed so vulnerable to the reporter. "Armor-plated" would have been his choice of an adjective. "You going into television agenting, Matt? At your age?"

"I will soon be an octogenarian," said the agent with pride, contemplating his well-shined shoes, placed on the footstool because his feet did not reach the floor. Fein thought of buying him a set of spats, if they still made spats; that would fit the image Ace cultivated of the intellectual dandy. "But no, like the proverbial shoemaker, I will stick to my last, that of literary representative. I lived by the written word, I will die enhancing the value of the written word."

"So what's with you and Miss Talking Head?"

"As you might deduce, intrepid investigator that you are, Viveca Farr is considering writing a book. I am encouraging her. A substantive book would add depth to her reputation as a newsperson. It would dissuade journalists like yourself, Irving, from thinking of her as just another pretty face."

A title for her book leaped to the reporter's mind—*Dancing on the Glass Ceiling*—but he had his own fish to fry and didn't want to waste time on someone else's. He drew his chair close to Ace and lowered his voice. "You got into Lubyanka? Did you see the new guy, Davidov?"

"The chief of the Fifth Directorate received me, yes. He is interested in using my services in bringing some of the files to public view."

"Did he offer any hot stuff—moles, traitors, real news? The Second Man?"

Ace shook his head. "So far all that's on the table is stale historical files. The only surprise was the man himself. Never thought someone so high up in Russian security would be such a combination of intellectual and matinee idol."

"But a goniff at heart. You gave him the little zinger about the Feliks people?"

"I did, in precisely the words you suggested. 'If you run into any of Feliks's people,' I said, 'I have a client who happens to be a great reporter.'"

"And how did he react to that?"

"No reaction. Stone face."

"Balls!" Irving got up and started pacing, smacking the walls in the space between famous clients' pictures. "You used the word 'asleep'?"

"Yes, as you instructed. 'This fellow is not asleep,' I said about you. Again no reaction. Then again, 'Never sleeps on the job.' Frankly, it sounded a bit heavy-handed, saying it twice."

"And he didn't rise to it? Not even a flicker?"

"I don't know if the Russians have a word for 'poker face,' but that was his expression."

Irving stopped abruptly as a thought began to form. "Absolutely no reaction is a reaction. If he knew nothing about the friends of Feliks, the KGB man would have said something like 'sure' or 'maybe, one of these days.' But if Davidov just went blank, then he's hiding what he knows about them, and maybe about a sleeper." He drew back his lips in a kind of smile. "Lousy poker player. Doesn't belong in that job."

"Perhaps I could be of greater assistance, Irving, if you took me into your confidence. I am aware only that 'Iron Feliks' Dzerzhinsky was a presence that struck fear into Russians right up to our times. When freedom came to Moscow, his statue was ripped off the pedestal in the square in front of the former prison. You have not vouchsafed to me the significance of 'Feliks's friends,' or of the need to impress the KGB with your lack of sleep."

"Ah, the old vouchsafecracker at work." Irving put out of his mind Ace's inability so far to get him a decent book contract. "Can't tell you yet. But now I can go back to my sources—having put a probe right into that goddam yellow building—and gotten a panicked reaction from the smoothie who's fronting for them."

"Director Davidov didn't exactly panic. He just didn't pick up on your phrase."

"He froze, the sumbitch froze. I can use that." The reporter saw how he could exaggerate to his source the Davidov nonresponse, trading that for a next step into the story. "Lookit, I know we've got a big one here. Not ancient history about who stuck the ice pick into Trotsky, but stuff going on right now, heavy sleeping."

Ace blinked; Irving did not want to speculate further about sleeper agents in place, or whom they worked for, or what their mission was. He didn't know much himself beyond the slender leads. But the reporter could feel the questions bubbling up, the sort of questions that created a vacuum into which answers rushed. Who planted the sleeper? Who has been controlling him, the new KGB or the old apparatchiks who make up part of the Feliks people? What triggered his activation? Does he have a network within the U.S. government? What is his assignment, and if it is to steal economic secrets, how successful has he been? How big are the bucks involved? Who are the sources of Irving's tips, and what is their motive for getting him on the trail? Those were for starters.

"I hope you have the big one at last. I'll go on representing you for old times' sake, Irving, but frankly, you're becoming a stain on my firm's escutcheon."

"Mark my words, Ace, the first serial rights on this story will be a newsmagazine cover." When the agent looked skeptical, the reporter felt pressured into tipping a little more of his hand. "What we've got here is some kind of financial mastermind operating underground in America, with megabucks from the old KGB, out of the reach of the law. He's maybe got access to all the intelligence resources of the KGB to give him insider stuff all around the world." Now Irving was guessing. "And he's been building up a pile of dough big enough to cause a financial panic, destabilize the government in Moscow, and help the mafiya and the old commies take over and start grabbing back the old empire."

Now Ace looked suitably alarmed. Irving thought he could put it across with a happy-ending possibility: "Or—if the stash gets big enough and is used right—he could use those assets to help the Russian people make it under capitalism. A whole lot of the future of the world hangs on finding this guy, and making sure he delivers his bundle to the right people."

"Or giving it back to the investors he stole it from," Ace amended.

"Nah, this is bigger than cops and robbers. Ace, for crissake, open your eyes." Irving, flying on hunch alone at this point, took the agent to the mountaintop. "This is a story about, first, the corruption of the world financial markets to build up a fortune; and second, about the struggle between the good and evil elements in Russia to find and use those assets. By digging out the first story, of how the sleeper does it, I can have an impact on how the second story comes out. If I can get the news, then I can make the news. Don't you see?" Until that moment, Fein himself had not quite seen it that way; talking it through had helped. Had he sold Ace?

"I recall the story of Moses leading his people out of Egypt," said the agent, "and telling his scribe of his plan to miraculously part the Red Sea."

Irving beat him to the punchline: " 'If you can bring that off, Moses, I can get you four pages in the Old Testament.' You'll see, Ace. There's a huge story here, and I can dig it out if you can get me a good advance without tipping it."

He rushed out past the smoked mirrors to the elevator, irritation with Ace mingling with a perfumed sense of a woman's recent presence and the tingling in his fingertips he got when he was on to something.

He touched the arrow that summoned the down elevator; it did not light up. He hated that sort of thing, because it made him feel impotent. He jabbed at it again, as Viveca Farr had done earlier, and wondered if the unlit button stirred her hidden anxieties as well. Third time, the light came on; the damn machine in Ace's fancy office building needed fixing.

Chapter 3

NEW YORK

Six minutes to air. She took her position at the anchor desk this early to get over the willies that had afflicted her since she began on-air work five years before. She was certain that red-light fright would never leave her even when she sharp-elbowed her way onto the anchor desk of the evening news.

The newsbreak, one word, was perfect for Viveca Farr: sky-highlights short enough to make an impression and not so long as to get boring about any subject. The prime of prime time, between entertainment shows at 9:00 P.M. EST, reaching thirty million viewers, did not arouse envy among the network news anchorpeople because it ruined dinner right though the week; besides, the slot was usually filled by a newcomer not seeming to be competition for them. But as Viveca saw it, the newsbreak was her own show; the camera never left her face, even with film running over her shoulder on the screen. She was the forty-five-second star.

She shot a glance at her head on the monitor. The highlights on her blond hair attested to the teamwork of hairdresser and lighting man: not brassy, not like the surface of a glazed doughnut, but not too softly feminine either; rather, a sensible hairdo for a woman doing serious work. The makeup person was on her side, too: eyeshadow that seemed heavy in the flesh came across with just enough emphasis on the screen. The one attribute she could not see on the monitor, slightly off to the side, was what her favorite reviewer said was unique to Viveca Farr: a direct look into the camera with cool deep-blue eyes that riveted the viewer.

Nodding curtly to the stage manager, she told the prompter operator, "From the top," and started to run through her lines. She came to a word she didn't like in a line about the President's appearance that evening: "The President praised her indomitable will . . ." She knew she would fluff "indomitable."

"Give me another word for 'indomitable,' " she told the producer in the booth.

Through her earphones, she could hear the wiseguy's voice: "You pronounced it perfectly, Viveca, and that's the word the President used."

"Let's not argue. I want another word, if you know one."

"How's 'indefatigable'?" She could hear the snickering in the booth and on the set.

"I want another word or I want another producer," she snapped. "Get professional." She could see her lip glistening in the monitor, and motioned for makeup. "Who writes this stuff, anyway?"

"Sometimes the on-air reporters have been known to write their own news," the producer said sweetly. That stung; Viveca knew she could not write well and resented the fact that everybody else knew it. Her talent for communication was oral and visual, not bound to a word processor. A stagehand attaching the microphone to her blouse fumbled and brushed the lapel of her jacket; she recoiled, hating to be touched by the stage help, and would have done it herself but for the union rules. Her assistant, placing the water glass under the table out of camera range, picked up the newscaster's nervousness and spilled some. "Mop it up, for crissake!" Viveca hissed at her, then, "Never mind, wasn't your fault," because she did not want the reputation of driving her aides to tears.

The stage manager languidly held up four fingers. "I like to hear it," she said, because the guy sometimes held his hand in such a way as to make the finger count unreadable. He dutifully said, "Four minutes to air," adding, "Actually two to first commercial, three to second commercial, three-fifty to local promo," to annoy her. This was the guy who had saddled her with the sobriquet "Ice Maiden"; better that than the opposite reputation.

She picked up the reading copy, shuffled the pages together, tapped them on the table to straighten out the tops, and then muddled them up again. That's what the pages were for; not to be read but to be held, to be looked at in a pretense that no prompter was causing the script to be crawled on a screen directly in front of the camera, and finally to be gathered up in a pretense of tidiness to convey an illusion of finality at the end of the telecast. Show business. It galled her how the news types made much of their profound knowledge of what they were reading even as they played the game of make-believe, holding the pages of a script never meant to be read.

Her hairdresser came on for the final touch-up with spray and comb. Viveca was glad she had put having her own hairdresser into her contract, along with her own makeup person, even though her television agent said it looked un-newswomanlike. That agent wouldn't like her going to Matthew McFarland to help her create a book, either, but she wanted the best literary rep around to handle her debut in the bookstores. Her publicist had told her that the slob sitting on his spine in Matt's reception room was some big-name print journalist, made to cool his heels while her potential best-seller was being discussed; Viveca liked that.

A book was a ticket to seriousness; a well-received book said you mattered. Her mentor back in Nashville used to say the world was divided into people who wrote books and people who said they were going to write a book someday. She wished she had him in the control room right now instead of that smart-ass who wanted her to fluff the word.

"Would somebody please bring me a dictionary?" she requested through perfect teeth.

"We have your synonym for 'indomitable,' Viveca," said the producer in her ear. "It's being put on the prompter now: 'steadfast.' "

She nodded and consented to a read-through. Three seconds short; no need to add anything, she had an internal clock that knew how to stretch. Would her old mentor be watching this? Probably; no reason why not, most television-watchers did, and after he got over his rejection as she moved on and up, he had built himself a nice little family. You're not talking to a friend, he used to tell her, pointing at the red light on the camera, you're talking to a judge, stern but fair-minded; and you're being judged every minute. What the judges want from you is credibility, and what you want from them is respect, not gee-isn't-she-cute. She thought of the bag of potato chips he would give to her before every show back in Nashville so long ago: "Crisp," he said. "Think crisp."

The self-assured newscaster dressed crisply and spoke crisply. She knew her greatest strength was her command presence; in person, she was short, but on the screen she sat tall. Dominant but not domineering; in firm control of herself and of her topic, whether she knew the subject or not.

She straightened her spine, closed and opened her eyes, tightened her sphincter as if she were fooling a polygraph, leaned forward and lifted her chin. Inhale. The red light came on and she felt her surge of authority thrust aside all nervousness. "Newsbreak, Viveca Farr reporting. We have a new Director of Central Intelligence, the first woman ever to hold the post. In naming Dorothy Barclay, the President praised her steadfast will . . ."

Chapter 4

NEW YORK

"We're coming to a tunnel," the literary agent announced from his car phone. "If I fade out, I'll get back to you."

Ace McFarland's vintage Rolls was nowhere near a tunnel. He always took the bridge to Manhattan. But he liked to make his calls short and authoritative, leaving the impression of busyness even on a slow day, and he had found this a good way to break off calls with drama but not insult.

"Viveca, I've been thinking about your book," he said. "Your initial reluctance about writing your memoirs was right—you're too young to do an autobiography. It would seem pretentious and invite criticism, especially from the envious. Your memoirs would undoubtedly sell, considering there'd be a book tour and it'd be easy to get you on the best talk shows in every major market. But in the long run it would be criticized as presumptuous, and I don't want you exposed to any vilification by the 'shock jocks.' "

When she had suggested a book about her life, Viveca had raised that concern about the appearance of pretension only as a minor caveat. Ace judged he could get a paltry $50,000 advance against royalties for the book; most of that would go to an as-told-to ghost. His own 17 percent commission, taken off the gross and the highest in the field, would hardly be worth his time. No movie or miniseries would be likely from a Viveca Farr memoir, which meant the value of the paperback would be less. The project would be seen for what it was: a blatant promotion of her as a personality, enabling her to appear on other networks and local stations flogging her book. It would probably help her lecture fees, but her literary agent had no part of those. And the

selling thing about a memoir was that you actually had to have memories of memorable events, unless you were a household name, in which
case you had to have memories of formative details. No; it was too early
in Viveca's rise to semicelebrity for a memoir. Ace had a better idea.

"You should be doing something more substantive," he advised.
"Something you can get your reportorial teeth into." She had perfect,
gleaming teeth, he realized, perhaps not reportorial; no matter.
"Perhaps there's a major subject that you could do in conjunction with
a television special." That would move a book off the shelves; even
books on the English language grew legs when given the impetus of a
TV series.

"Matt, do you have a subject in mind?" Viveca sounded disappointed; her heart had undoubtedly been set on a biography of herself
that she could control, one that would block any unfriendly biography
from the market. Ace knew she was thinking of the blurbs about her
talent from has-been colleagues of hers, or from famous clients of his,
that would be used in advertising the hardcover, and of the hundreds
of thousands of paperback copies that would carry those avidly
solicited, smarmy encomia on the cover. He was not certain that blurbs
sold any book, but he was sure that the prospect of blurbs sold some
celebrities on writing books.

"I have the germ of an idea," he said. "It would be perfect for someone with your skills. Hello? Can you hear me?" He cut himself off,
ostensibly going through the tunnel. Long association with Irving Fein
had taught him a few communications tricks. He had stopped going
through tunnels at the first suggestion that they might be targets of
terrorists. Ace McFarland could see himself being blown gloriously off
a bridge, never buried in a tunnel.

He stepped off the elevator into his waiting room, assessed his appearance in the darkened glass opposite, and hailed Irving Fein, seated all
over the couch. He would not remonstrate with Irving about stealing
the books on the coffee table; that's what the books were there for, to
be stolen and replaced at publishers' expense. He led his client down
the long hall to his corner office, chirruping greetings to his associates
and their assistants on the way.

"I want a huge advance for a book," said Irving, plopping himself down in the designer chair with the nubby fabric, then getting up, grabbing a couple of oversized throw cushions that were sticking into his back, and throwing them onto another chair. "I'll invest it all in the research, which is gonna be a bitch."

Ace looked at him in weary fondness. "Presumably you are speaking of a six-figure advance," he said. "Years ago, I was able to get that for you."

"Whatsamatter you can't anymore? Losing a step?"

"Times have changed, Irving. Publishers' budgets have tightened, the number of blockbusters has grown smaller. Your own position has changed because of the smaller sales of your last book—which I personally thought was excellent, despite the reviews, and despite that unfortunate episode on your tour." Fein had appeared in the Green Room moments before airtime for an interview, had refused to sign the standard release form because of its boilerplate waiver of libel protection, and had been pushed aside for a cookbook author.

"I never waive my rights. The publicity dame knows that. Years ago, I was sitting in a Green Room with Edward Bennett Williams—we were guests on some show—and the producer's sweetie comes in with the paper to sign. Williams, the great lawyer, showed me what to do. Where it says 'hereby agree to hold harmless,' he made a little caret after the 'hereby' and wrote in 'do not' and then signed it. The kid only knows from get the thing signed. But my luck, this time in L.A., the producer reads it and kicks me off. Fuck 'im. Besides, the books weren't even in the stores yet in that town, so the whole thing would have been a waste of time."

"We all know," the agent agreed with only a touch of irony, "how publishers conspire against authors to prevent the sale of their books."

"And they never advertise until it's too late," Fein added. "And the first printing is always too small, so when a buyer walks in they're out of stock. Jeez, you wonder why my last book died."

"A significant first serial sale would have helped," Ace reminded him gently; he did not add that magazines from *Time* to *The New Yorker* to *Reader's Digest* had turned down Irving Fein's book about international arms dealers. Though the book was based on solid and original reporting, its subject was behind the topical-interest power curve.

"They stole the ideas and assigned their own reporters," Fein muttered. "Never again. We publish in secret."

"But not secret from me." The agent let him have a glimpse of reality. "Irving, I love you. In my considered opinion, you are the greatest reporter alive today. Bar none. And many others agree, albeit reluctantly."

"Here comes the 'but.' "

"Nobody has your sources, and nobody has ever milked them for more exclusive information. But your books do not sell. Maybe it's your lack of exposure on television, or whatever, but a six-figure advance is not in the cards." Ace let that sink in. "Unless, of course, you can convince me you have a world beat that will scare the hell out of everybody." As a seeming afterthought, he threw in: "Or unless we can figure a way to team you up with somebody who remedies your weakness in sales."

"I have the world beat, I think. At least a good lead on it." Fein was dispirited by the bad news about the advance and seemed not to have heard the suggestion about a collaborator. "But it's gonna take a hell of a lot of digging, and I can't afford it."

The agent knew when to wait.

"The communists back in the Nixon days, the era of détente, beat us on some grain deal. They concealed a big shortage, bought from us cheap, saved a bundle."

"*The Great Grain Robbery,*" the agent said, recalling the book on the subject. "Not mine. Didn't sell."

"The KGB realized the need for big-time economic espionage later on." Irving leaned forward, intensity in his voice and body. "They planted an agent here—maybe recruited him here, in some college—and let him work his way up in the banking business. Never used him, never put him at risk. They figured they'd want him for something big one day. It's not done often, takes a lot of restraint. The agent is called a 'sleeper.' "

"That's why you had me emphasize the word 'sleep' twice in my conversation with Davidov. Glad you told me. I thought I was being a hypnotist."

"You were better off not knowing when you went in there," Fein said, not apologetically. "And the way our KGB smoothie clammed up tells me he's sensitive to a hunt for the sleeper."

"And it turns out," said Ace, anticipating the plot, "this Rip Van Winkle agent has become the head of the Chase Bank, or Chairman of the Federal Reserve, or maybe even Vice President of the United States, and you're going to expose him." The agent thought quickly: "We'd better get a libel lawyer in at the start."

"More to it than that, Ace." Fein's face took on its tradecrafty, vulpine look. "Came the late eighties, the Party's over. Ahead is the collapse of communism, the breakup of the Soviet Union. The Party has all these assets—not just buildings and famous paintings, they're not hidable, but liquid assets in banks and safe deposits around the world. In gold, diamonds, who knows what else. Billions, which the old boys are not about to turn over to the new bunch."

"And the sleeper agent in the U.S. is the man they choose to assemble and conceal the assets," the agent assumed. The yarn was getting better. "He becomes the trustee, in effect, for all the wealth of the Communist Party."

Fein looked at him with new respect. "You got it. How'd you get it so fast?"

The agent had seized the idea so quickly because the plot was familiar to him. "*The Odessa File,* by Frederick Forsyth. Big best-seller back in the seventies, movie, huge paperback. Nazis hid the money at the end of the war to finance the comeback of Hitler or somebody like him. Great plot. Enough time has gone by for a freshening-up."

Fein moved from his deep couch to lean across the agent's desk, elbows on the blotter, and glare directly into his face. "Ace, this is no novel. It's not 'virtual reality,' even. This is real life, in real time. People could get killed for this, including even reporters. And literary agents who know too much."

"Why?"

"Heavy money. Vicious people. Big political stakes."

The prospect of personal danger did not trouble Matthew McFarland; at his age, such spice added to the piquancy of life. He met the reporter's gaze and replied levelly: "Nonfiction would get you two bites at the apple. The actual facts first, in book and serial and on-line form, and the television dramatization later."

Irving Fein shook that off. "Now here's the problem. The old-timers at the top were killed in an accident recently. I hear the sleeper's control agent has disappeared, gone off the scope. That means the new guys at the head of the KGB may not know who his own sleeper agent in America is."

"Surely there must be some record. An old address, a name—"

Irving shook his head delightedly. "The antireformers still in the KGB may know where the file is buried, or may not. There's an amorphous bunch of gangstercrats who call themselves the 'Feliks people,' after your friend Dzerzhinsky, inside and out of the KGB. They may or may not know. Could be misfiled in the Lubyanka stacks, maybe deliberately, or could be it fell between the cracks—"

Ace raised a finger. "Through the cracks. Between the stools."

"Whatever. And nobody in Russia knows. And that leaves this one agent in the deepest cover sitting on top of all this money and power. He may be out of control. Or he and his control may be going into business for themselves."

"That's a good twist."

"It's not a goddam plot twist, Ace, for crissake—it's what's happening! If the wrongos in Russia glom onto the fortune, they could finance the ultranationalists, build more bridges to the new mafiya. They could lead a movement to save the 'near abroad' and bring back the old Soviet Union." He started waving his arms. "A return to imperialism, Cold War Three, a new arms race, huge American defense budgets— you get some idea of it?"

"That's the danger," Ace nodded, drawing him on, "and the opportunity?" Happy endings were important.

"If the right guys get the fortune, they have real capital—a leg up on reform and democracy and all them good things. I mean, this isn't penny-ante stuff we're talking about. Or just money. The political stakes are as big as they get."

Evidently exhausted from his pitch, Irving turned and pulled a pair of pillows off the couch and lay down atop them on the floor, twisting his neck back and forth. Ace knew it to be an exercise done to relieve back stress.

"And what, my supine friend, do your friends across the river say?" The agent was aware that Irving must have developed at least part of this story with his many sources at the CIA.

"Across what river?" Irving was rolling his head back and forth across the nubby pillow. "I got no friends in New Jersey."

"The Potomac. I am told that 'across the river' is a term of art in the world of espionage, meaning the CIA. John le Carré uses 'across the pond.' "

"David coined the term 'mole,' too, Ace." The agent noted that Irving instantly used le Carré's real name, David Cornwell, to show he knew him, and was on a real-first-name basis. Irving was quick. "And they never call a penetration agent a mole at Langley," he instructed. "They say that's novelese. Think nonfiction, Ace."

"I take it you will not vouchsafe—that you do not want to tell me how much our government knows about this?"

"I think they want to use me to help them find out. Doesn't bother me, long as I get the story first. But I have to cover my nut."

The "nut," McFarland knew, would be rather large: the expense of an extensive investigation. "I can get you a substantial advance, Irving, only if I can assure a publisher that the end product can be promoted with great panache."

The reporter sat up. "I promise to work with an editor this time, if they get me a good one. Not some tight-ass broad fresh out of Wellesley who never heard of James Jesus Angleton."

"Think bigger. Think best-seller. Think of a collaborator with the ability to ensure a television dimension. That's what gives a book legs. Think of a full partner who could help, at your direction, to open doors in the banking world."

"Don't need a partner. I work alone, except for a researcher."

Ace gave him a dash of cold water: "Alone, this idea is worth seventy-five thousand tops. Less my seventeen percent commission."

Irving arched his back three times; this was stress. "You have another of your clients in mind, I can tell. How much with him?"

"With her. With her, I feel confident I could get two hundred and fifty thousand, fifteen percent royalty from book one, with a seventy-thirty split on paperback and a hell of a miniseries sale."

"Her?"

"Viveca Farr."

Chapter 5

LANGLEY, VIRGINIA

The new Director of Central Intelligence was the first acknowledged homosexual appointed to that post, and the first woman. Dorothy Barclay was determined to conduct the nation's new era of espionage in a manner that would be unassailable by historians: no dirty tricks, no assassinations of foreign leaders, no backdated findings, no fancy office buildings hidden from oversight, no brutish informants, no feuds with the FBI about cooperation in finding potential penetration agents. Covert action would be undertaken only with the approval of the designated members of the relevant committees of Congress. Notification "in a timely fashion," as the agreement between the Agency and Congress specified, would no longer be interpreted loosely; "timely" meant within a hard-and-fast twenty-four hours.

Her two primary missions had been defined by the President in their initial meeting. One was to correct the Agency's most glaring weakness by infiltrating terrorist groups with human agents. Plenty of money would be available for such "humint." The budget was tighter for the satellite surveillance of signal intelligence, "sigint," but those facilities had to be maintained and focused to support the other mission: to rebuild the network of agents within the Russian Federation that had been rolled up during the disastrous eighties. Of course, Moscow was an ally of sorts today, but precautions had to be taken for the future.

"You're going to tell me about the family jewels," she said to Walter Clauson, who had asked to see her. She used that expression to show her familiarity with the in-house term for the Agency's most intimate secrets.

Clauson was known to the new intelligence community as the Last of the Mohicans; he had made plain his discomfort with both the downsizing of the CIA and the near abdication of counterintelligence, leaving all that tracking of Russian and Chinese agents to the FBI. She planned to ease him out quietly, but because his record included a written warning to his superiors in the early nineties to fire Aldrich Ames for drunkenness, the old hand could not be ousted without repercussions in Congress. The previous DCI had promoted Clauson to chief of counterintelligence, even as the retiring executive snatched away most of that discredited section's responsibilities.

"Your predecessor in this office already reviewed those 'family jewels' matters with you," the counterintelligence chief said in his gentle—she thought oily—voice.

"You're certain we have no other mole?"

"With the exception of Ames and one Chinese agent, nobody has ever penetrated the Agency at a middle level, or been what novelists call a mole. And nobody has ever penetrated at the Philby level, near the top." Clauson put in a cautious afterthought: "Or at least our ambassador in Moscow was so assured by Nikolai Davidov soon after that young man took over the Fifth Directorate."

"You trust Davidov?"

"I don't even trust you, Madam Director, much less the academician they think so much of at what we used to call the KGB."

"What's the matter, Clauson, you can't handle the idea of lesbian-Americans?" She let him have that right in the choppers to see how he would react.

He reacted like a pro. "Your sexual preference, being public, is not a security risk. My institutional loyalty to whoever serves as DCI is unstinting. Personal trust is something to be earned over time. I hope to earn yours."

Unlikely. She let him make the next move; he had asked for the meeting.

"One family jewel, Director Barclay, is current and troubling. You have been briefed on the sleeper agent somewhere in our midst?"

She nodded. "I was briefed and cannot say I like your approach. Why bring in a reporter?"

"Mr. Fein brought himself in with his intriguing questions," Clauson said. "We were presented with a choice: either we let him print a sketchy story about a Russian sleeper agent in the U.S.—thereby driving the threat further underground, not to mention embarrassing our friendly rivals in Moscow. Or we cooperate with the reporter to some extent in the hope of helping him help us flush the sleeper out."

"This sounds like FBI work, counterintelligence," she told him, knowing he would hate the thought. He probably knew that the FBI considered the threat from a sleeper far-fetched.

"Mr. Fein's journalistic goal," he pressed, "is to expose the sleeper and disclose his assets. He thinks those assets may be considerable. Our goal is parallel but goes beyond mere revelation. It is to seize those assets. At the least, it is to make certain a huge fortune that could destabilize a government does not get into the wrong hands in Russia. To that end, I propose that we deal with Mr. Fein rather creatively."

Barclay knew Irving Fein's skill at manipulating manipulators. She decided to build a firewall between herself and Clauson's involvement in this one. It would be impolitic within the Agency to stop his inquiry, but she was determined to keep him unaware of a larger picture. The Deputy Director for Operations would oversee and limit Clauson's poking-about, and close it down after he was retired in an Agency-wide reduction in force.

"Do I need to know all these details?"

"Your need to know," said Clauson formally, "is limited to this: an American citizen, a banker of repute, will be approached by Mr. Fein. He will be asked by Fein to impersonate the Russian sleeper agent."

She did not want to appear to be drawn in. "How do we know this?"

"The reporter told me that was his plan. He asked us to suggest a credible impersonator, someone with banking experience, a conspiratorial bent, and a willingness to undertake a dangerous mission."

"Why does Fein need our help? Why doesn't he find his own ringer?" She could hear the FBI Director, as well as the chairman of the House Intelligence Committee, asking her the same question.

"Whoever he enlists will undoubtedly come to us to verify what national service Mr. Fein claims to be performing. Both the banker and the reporter will want to have the coloration of law in their project."

"That's not ours to hand out."

"A private effort to find the sleeper, if one exists, is certainly in the public interest," the counterspy said. "I think we should give Fein, and the banker he selects to flush him out, our sanction."

"I nonconcur." She chose that verb because it had more bureaucratic resonance than "disagree." Barclay wanted Clauson to know she disapproved of a loose-cannon operative, especially one under the control of a reporter. She knew Irving Fein well, from their student days at City College in New York, a bit of data she was not about to share with this old espionage hand. Irving had protected her on a story when she badly needed a journalistic guardian, and she owed him one. But this was not necessarily the one.

She knew that Clauson's suspicion about a sleeper building a fortune in the United States for KGB use had been indulged by her predecessor in his final weeks; if she flatly denied this request for tacit support of an off-the-books probe, it might invite criticism later. But she did not want any sleeper hunt to compromise one of her primary missions, and Dorothy Barclay would be damned if she would let Clauson's cooperation with Fein get out of hand.

"If this Irving Fein person," she said, "who has been hostile to some of the Agency's covert actions in the past, wants to hire an impersonator, that's strictly his business. We're not involved. We cannot recommend one of our contract employees. If they do anything illegal, or get themselves hurt trying to get a big story, it's their responsibility."

She would lock this in with a memo to the DDO, who had expressed a worry about Clauson's compromising his own indirect monitoring of the sleeper rumor. "All you're authorized to do," she told the veteran operative, "is to stay in touch with Fein to see what he comes up with. Your role is strictly passive." She drove it home: "Which means if some banker calls us to see if an impersonation has our approval, the CIA has no position. Not yes, not no. Understood?"

Clauson sighed. "Your order to monitor passively is understood, Madam Director. If developments warrant," he added, "I may ask for a reclama."

She had been warned about those reclamas. They were time-consuming appeals to executive decisions that permitted counterintelligence to prevent an executive decision from being recognized as permanent. "Forget the damn reclama, Walter. You should have plenty of other things to do."

So did she. As he nodded curtly at his dismissal and left, she consulted a budget summary: $4 billion was being cut out of the intelligence community this year. She was determined the cuts not come out of antiterrorism. Counterintelligence was a likely target for the budget-cutters, with its function basically having been moved across the river to FBI headquarters on 9th Street. The vestigial CIA mole-hunters had failed to come up with the "Second Man" protecting Ames; as a result, operatives like Clauson were scorned at the Bureau and in the oversight committees.

Dorothy Barclay was not going to resist Congressional demands for an Agency less mean and more lean. Time for a major Reduction in Force: she had read that in the seventies one such bureaucratic blood-letting was called the Halloween Massacre. It occurred to her that an appropriate time for another major riffing would be in the coming month, on St. Valentine's Day.

Chapter 6

CHICAGO

As he left the Mercantile Exchange for his studio apartment in Marina Towers, the saying that stuck in Berensky's mind was "The house is burning and the clock is ticking."

With the nonpublic information provided by the KGB over the past four years, he had multiplied the original stake of $3 billion by ten. He estimated it would take $100 billion in equity to finance a destabilization and takeover of the Russian Federation, if that was the political purpose of the Feliks people. He would judge their character and goals later. Now he was under pressure to make major trades to run up the fortune quickly, before his moment of independent action ended.

The Fifth Directorate had been decapitated by an airline accident. The only remaining member of the KGB hierarchy who knew the sleeper agent's American identity—his longtime control agent—had blown himself up in Barbados. He presumed the KGB must now be turning itself inside out to reestablish contact with him.

Berensky further assumed that the CIA had penetrated the KGB enough to determine that a sleeper was using the former Party assets and current KGB intelligence to amass a fortune. He did not believe U.S. newspaper accounts of the CIA's handing over counterintelligence to the FBI; that was almost certainly disinformation of the sort that Shelepin pioneered in the fifties.

That meant that both the Russian and American espionage services were looking for him and trying to trace the fortune. In addition, the Feliks people—who knew of his existence, and whose money had formed his original stake—were surely using all their underworld contacts to find him. Sooner rather than later, the sleeper was certain, one of these organizations would break through the complex series of cutouts and fronts he had established to hide and leverage the assets; at that point, his historic decision of what to do with the money might be wrested from his hands. That was why he felt an urgency to make big money in the coming quarter.

The final intelligence from Control about Russia's oil consortium with Japan had been useful; it meant an increase in the supply of oil, and augured a small dip that day in the world price. Through a series of investments in financial derivatives based on oil futures, he had made a couple of hundred million dollars. The gold production figures were more valuable; his London gold broker relied on the likelihood of a shortfall in Russian production to take a strong position.

But this was relatively small potatoes. Inside information about Russian dealings would not permit dramatic gains, even when leveraged as heavily as Berensky now could manage. For major moves, he needed to get key figures from the KGB sources inside the U.S. government. Then he could play currencies, the most concealable major form of speculation.

Control's death made that more difficult: the mole in Washington did not want to be contacted, and he would have to wait; the agent at the Federal Reserve in New York was unknown to him, and passed along information only through the Washington man.

In retrospect, the sleeper knew he had erred in not taking Control's unconscious body out and drowning him. Of course, his lack of firmness had turned out to be fortunate: if he had killed the greedy handler, Berensky would have gone back to sleep in the bungalow and been blown up. But he could not count on that luck in the future. He vowed to act with more vigor next time a confederate showed signs of crossing him.

Where was he most vulnerable? In Bern and in Helsinki. The banker in Bern was the longtime contact of, and probably partner of, the faithless Control. The banker had on deposit only the first $3 billion in gold—the original Communist Party stake—but it was likely that he shared Control's plans to seize the entire fortune. Berensky would be safer if the banker died.

The economist in Helsinki had an idea of the sleeper's identity and could be a source of blackmail. She was connected to too many agencies: certainly Stasi in Germany, probably the KGB or Russian Foreign

Intelligence, possibly his Washington contact. The sleeper was more inclined to trust her, however; there was a simple way to put her loyalty to the test.

He dialed her direct extension at the Econometric Institute in Helsinki and recognized the voice that answered the phone.

"This is Dr. Gold," he announced briskly. "The veterinarian in North Carolina. Your vet in Davos sent the slides of your Bernese mountain dog's lung to my laboratory."

"Of course," she said. "How good of you to call so promptly. What's to become of my Berner Sennenhund?" She used the Swiss name of the breed; Berensky admired her quick take of an unrehearsed code.

"The prognosis is not good. Your Berner has a form of cancer that is a genetic fault of the breed. I have to advise you to put him down."

A pause. "That saddens me. The Berner has been a faithful companion."

"You owe it to him, then, to put the animal to sleep before the onset of great pain."

"I understand, Doctor. How long do I have?"

"Three or four days. No longer than a week. I feel for you, ma'am—I lost one of my own not a couple of weeks ago. It's sad, but necessary."

"You're right, of course. I will do what a responsible pet owner must do."

Chapter 7

POUND RIDGE, NEW YORK

Viveca Farr confronted herself with a direct question: What does a legendary reporter drink? Irving Fein was coming to see her, at Matt's instigation. She decided he'd probably drink Scotch.

She checked the bar in the den; plenty of Scotch. No bourbon; she had finished the bourbon herself the other night. White wine? She was ready to bet Irving Fein would never ask for white wine. Maybe red wine. She hesitated, then pulled down a bottle of the cheaper stuff, sank the screw in the cork, and deftly opened it. "Breathe," she told it, and poured herself a glass.

Matt had suggested this first meeting be held in his office, but Viveca didn't want the agent to act as her chaperon; she wanted to handle the world's greatest investigative reporter, as he liked to bill himself, all by herself. She could have had him come to her apartment on Central Park West, near the studio, but that was decorated in whites and silks and Man Ray photos; even so, now that she thought of it, that might have been better. Living in a storied stone house in Pound Ridge—Tudor-style, eighteen rooms, on four landscaped acres—was as pretentious, in its way, as calling yourself the world's greatest reporter.

She could hear him saying "What a goddam palace" and thinking of her as some kind of princess complaining about a pea under the mattress. Impressing him that way was a mistake, but this is where she came to escape from the television crowd on weekends when all its Manhattan members traipsed out to the Hamptons as one impenetrable mass. She could explain how rich she was not, what a regular person she was, if that turned out to be important to him; she suspected that it would. From that one glimpse of him in Matt's waiting room, the journalist struck her as one of those prestigious smart-asses who resented success in others whom they considered lightweights, success they assumed was too easily gained.

She was fearful he would see through her in a minute. She couldn't write; she could ask a list of questions with fervor, but she lived in dread of a surprise answer that required a follow-up. Who needed this?

It wasn't that she was dumb, or not naturally curious, but there had been little time to become a policy wonk on the way to television news celebrityhood; by the time your brain became convoluted enough to understand the nuances of foreign affairs and economic dreariness, your face was too wrinkled to attract an audience. All the producers who brought her along too fast later criticized her for coming up too fast, for not "paying her dues." One year she was running copy, the next year she was on the air, station managers pushing her for their ratings, viewers taking her every word so seriously. The reviewers all used the same word to describe her delivery: "crisp." Would Irving Fein be hungry? She put out the potato chips.

Waiting for her potential new collaborator, Viveca looked in the bar mirror; the slight worry line between her eyes added to the illusion of authority. Her makeup was understated for this occasion, the blond hair mid-length, carefully casual, no spray glazing her head the way it had to be on camera. Her face's saving grace, she knew, was its slightly crooked nose; the imperfection added character. Nobody wanted a fashion model doing the news. What was wanted—sought desperately, by producers and advertisers—was mastery without age, good looks without glamour, *gravitas* without weight. On the air, she had the rare ability to transmute attractiveness to authority, and she knew it.

That confidence faded when the camera's red light went off. What if Fein asked her about the Kurdish tribes in Iraq or the black gangs in L.A.? In that case, she would turn the question back on him; men so handled invariably spun out their answers. But what if this one really wanted to know what she thought? He was a reporter; he was, if not great, certainly good; he would not be put off. Her schedule did not include time to develop any of the wide knowledge he would probably demand.

The hell with him. What she brought to this marriage was the beginning of fame—potential stardom—and the art of presentation. He could do the digging and the thinking and the writing. As Matt had explained, selling her on this notion, the television dimension provided synergy to the story and sales to the book. And what the hell did "synergy" mean? What if she used that word and Fein asked her what it meant? He was sure to judge her, as they all did; suddenly Viveca was afflicted with the sinking feeling that this might not work. The moment he started hitting on her professionally, she would threaten to throw him out; Matt had confided that, commercially, he needed her more than she needed him.

A gray station wagon crunched up the driveway, and she went out to meet it, her glass of wine in hand, hospitable in a defiant way. His car, as she had feared, was a disgrace to the neighborhood. The dilapidated state of the vehicle, despite its "no radio" sign for burglars, was a statement that he was poor and honest and proud and would make putting her down part of his life's work.

"Where's the butler to park the car? Thanks, I can use it." He took the drink from her hand, knocked it back, went, "Yecch—haven't you got a decent bottle of wine?" and led the way into her house. "Goddam palace," he said.

"I knew you'd say that."

"Pretty run-down, though." He touched the leaves of a plant. "Fake. Good fake, though."

She would have to disabuse him promptly of the idea that she was wealthy. "The house is a white elephant," she said. "Half the rooms are closed off permanently. My family used to own it, and I was a girl here, before my father lost it all and went to jail and died. I bought it back after the market dropped at a foreclosure auction." She caught herself beginning to talk too fast; jabbering was always a giveaway. She didn't say the rest—that the house was too much for one maid to clean and she didn't make enough money to keep up the grounds properly, other than to have the front lawn mowed.

He fitted the description she'd heard of a newspaperman, as looking like an unmade bed. She kicked herself for not having worn jeans; here she was, in a skirt and blouse and Donna Karan cotton cardigan, while he was wearing wrinkled chinos and a loud red shirt, all understated Ralph Lauren without reaching for it.

She got out the Château Talbot, showed him the label.

He gave a pretty-impressed look. "Good stuff, Cordier's second-best. Eighty-four is over the hill, but let's give it a shot."

She shrugged and handed him the bottle, eased out of her shoes, and sat on her feet on the couch. She stripped the cellophane off a new pack of cigarettes and lit one.

"Mind if I smoke?" he said.

That threw her. "You mean—smoking bothers you?" Real writers still smoked, didn't they? She smoked because it gave her something to do with her hands. And it was associated with hard newsmen, and bothered most people on the set.

"I love to smoke," he said with some nostalgia. "I gave it up. It kills me to see somebody enjoying a good, long drag. Go ahead if you really need to."

She thought it over, stubbed it out. "Tell me about this sleeper spy."

"Big fella, loner, high-stakes player, megabucks stashed away. Dedicated commie from year one, maybe did a little wet work along the way. Your kind of guy."

Viveca wondered what "wet work" was, and if any of what Fein said was true. She used her best question on him: a direct look and a whispered "Really?"

He didn't go for it. "First let's figure out how to work together. I never had a collaborator, I'm a born loner. Two divorces."

"I've never been married," she said. "Either."

He stopped to weigh her last word. "That's good, the 'either.' I'm a good reporter—nobody's better, to tell the truth—but a lousy writer. You a good writer? A decent writer? Any kind of writer?"

She pointed to his two books, flatteringly stacked on the lamp table. "Those are well written."

"Well rewritten, you mean. The copy editor couldn't handle it. They had to hire someone who worked cheap to rewrite long stretches, punch up all the chapter leads. You can't write, huh? Either?"

She was not prepared to admit that. "I write most of my own scripts. You probably saw the smart-ass stories that accused me of being a 'rip-and-read' announcer. That's not true. Lot of mean and jealous people in my business."

"Forty-five seconds is how many words?"

She reached for her pack of cigarettes and lit one in silence. He had caught her in a lie and was enjoying it.

"Look, kid, the Ace says you're my meal ticket, so I'm for you. If you can't write, we'll find something else for you to do. You can wheedle information out of guys?"

"I have been doing on-air interviews for nearly seven years," she snapped. "Heads of state. Candidates. Raped women. Great reporters."

"I hurt your feelings." After a moment, it occurred to her that Irving Fein, the great questioner, wasn't going to say anything until she did. She took an ostentatious, unsatisfying drag on her cigarette and inhaled deeply. The expression on his face was sympathetic, which she found infuriating. By being sorry for her for having to be so defensive, he was dominating their first meeting. And still he didn't say anything.

"If you don't want to tell me about the fantastic story you're supposed to have," she said finally, "we're not going to get very far."

"You don't have to fill up silence," he said. "You could have outwaited me, and I would have had to blurt something out. You lost that one."

"Journalism 101?"

"Hell no, this is postgraduate stuff. Learn, it wouldn't kill you. I'm secure. We're not competing."

"If you're so secure, why can't you get a book published by yourself? Why do you need a girl like me as a crutch?"

"I like that, shows a little spirit. But why do you call yourself a girl? You're thirty-three, I looked it up."

"Your source is wrong, I'm thirty-two. That makes our average age over forty." He was probably sensitive about his age, pushing fifty; age was one of the things she was just beginning to get sensitive about. She could zing him on his developing paunch, his furtive slump, his general air of determined messiness; the only thing possibly attractive to her about him was his intensity, a quality she never looked for in men but might be useful in a collaborator. That and his reputation within his trade. The trick to handling him was not to show secret vulnerability—that worked best with network executives—but to keep him off balance by not deigning to treat him as an equal. So he'd written a couple of books and won a bunch of prizes; big deal. She had an audience a thousand times the size of his and made ten times his income.

"Come on now, Irving, cut the fencing." She did not rise, but crossed her legs and put her bare feet on the coffee table. She had reason to be proud of her legs, not long, but perfectly proportioned. "Do you have a story or a lot of talk?"

"How could you tell the difference?"

"Don't patronize me. You're not the one to judge a reporter in my business."

"Oh. Your business is different. You deal in pictures, in sound bites. We printniks are grubbing after hard facts about real scandals, and the fuzzy new electronic world leaves us suckin' hind teat."

She had him off balance and, carefully scratching an ankle with one manicured toe, pressed her advantage. "If you have something worth working on, I'll know."

"I don't know how much Ace told you, but it's a big one."

"Matt McFarland doesn't like to be called Ace. You'll have to learn to be nice to your agent. He can make it all happen for you."

He gave her an unbelieving squint. "Look, kid, Ace loves to be known as the Ace. He tells people not to call him Ace who don't know him from Adam. The Ace is his shtick, his up-from-the-street attitude. It's the handle that separates him from the literary types who made agent the easy way with three-hour lunches in ritzy bistros." He put his heavy shoes on the edge of her coffee table. "The nickname Ace is that little touch that tips the scales to editors who assign profiles. Pretending not to like it is his pose. Don't fall for poses. Deal with reality, and people will begin to respect you."

"You know all about poses. Yours is media biggie, strike terror into the hearts of wrongdoers, darling of journalism schools." He was probably right about Ace; she hadn't thought of that, and she was beginning to enjoy dueling with this so-secure character. "But there you sit, with your clodhoppers on my good coffee table, in a pose of your own." He didn't move them.

"You're afraid you're over the hill," she pressed, "and you're in debt." She was guessing, but was sure she was right. "You need one big hit to get back in stride, and you hate having to share it with somebody younger and more hip and much more attractive than you. And you can cut out the 'kid' business. I'm thirty-two years old—not thirty-three—and I've been on my own since I was sixteen making a damn sight more money than you ever made."

He drained his glass, set it down, and rose. "Give me my hat, I'm leaving." She had pushed him too far; she did not want to lose him; it could be he wasn't as tough as she thought he was.

"I hurt your feelings," she mimicked. She poured them both another glass, coming close, then drawing back.

"That was your best line so far," he said, sitting down again, "and it was the one I wrote. But you delivered it well."

"And you don't have a hat."

"I wasn't leaving yet. The database says you started as a cocktail waitress at sixteen."

"You learn a lot fast about men that way."

"You learn how to belt down that booze, too. No?"

"Let's see, now. You don't like my smoking or my drinking. Is there anything else I do that doesn't please you?"

"I used to be a drunk, too, when I was your age. Very popular in the newspaper business. You either straighten out or you self-pity yourself into oblivion."

That was a thrust Viveca did not appreciate at all. She had been drinking more than before, but she was sure it was not a problem, and she held it down at dinner before airtime. There was a world of difference between a drinker and a drunk; he needed a zing back.

"If we do this book together," she said slowly, "and I say *if* we do it, we are going to keep the hell out of each other's private life. That's rule number one. You can pad your expense accounts and go whoring around all you like, the way the database says you do—that's none of my business—so long as you move the story along."

"Never missed a deadline in my life. And the expression in the journalism field is to 'advance the story.' "

"Your problem isn't deadlines, it's assignments. You can't get them. And that's why you need me."

The muscles in his cheeks worked. "I don't take assignments. I get stories on my own that force assignments from editors. And I don't just sit there and look pretty and read."

"You used to be a big name," she stayed on the attack, "a power in the news business—how did you make it, anyway?"

"I didn't make it on my back."

"You prick!" she yelled, and threw the cigarette at him. She had not slept with anybody to get a job for years and bitterly resented the charge. But she regretted the loss of control immediately; it gave him the upper hand.

He picked the burning butt off the carpet and looked at it. Sighing at his weakness, he took a puff, inhaled, and coughed before dropping it in her wine, which she had been looking forward to finishing more than she was ready to admit. "So you're not the Ice Maiden after all."

"Which is it, then—Ice Maiden, untouchable, iron pants—or the girl who screws her way to the top?" Both reputations had plagued her. "You can't have both. One or the other," she said.

He weighed that. "Not necessarily. You can coldly calculate whose bed it's profitable to sleep in."

She saw red. The sexist charge of sex use was untrue, at least since she fought her way onto the air, and it was the classic put-down that men she outdid so often used to steal the pleasure out of her success. "What do you know," she lashed at him, "about what an attractive woman has to go through every day on the set?"

"And don't give me this phony feminist shit, either." He picked up one of his books and dropped it in her lap. "I wrote the series on sexual harassment years ago that damn near busted up the Business Council, and you never gave the woman's movement more than the back of your hand."

"Here's your hat," she said, crossing her arms. This was not going to work out.

"Don't get up," he agreed. "I'll let myself out."

Chapter 8

WASHINGTON

Irving Fein waited until ten in the morning, flashed a phony ID that said he was over sixty-two, and bought a senior citizen's fare ticket on the Delta shuttle to Washington. He remembered how he used to do that with the youth fare until he was twenty-five and couldn't get away with it anymore. He asked himself: Should a reasonably healthy man of forty-eight be able to pass for sixty-two? His face was creased, not wrinkled; hair was messy, not missing. He chalked up to experience his look of knocked-about maturity. The time would come soon enough, he realized with rue, when he wouldn't have to fake senior status at all.

He could finesse the hotel expense in expensive Washington by sleeping on the couch of a reporter he'd once helped. Figuring the four airline snacks (two for the round trip, two more he could always get by complaining to the stew about the other ones) and what was in his friend's fridge, the bus to La Guardia and the Metro to D.C., and breakfast at the McDonald's on the site of the old Sans Souci, he could do the whole trip for under $150. His accountant, Mike Shu, could write that off against a royalty, if he had any royalties coming; lately, his sales never ate up the advance.

He did not feel bad about having to scrimp in a way that most salaried correspondents thought demeaning. No matter how lavish the expense account, Irving Fein would ostentatiously continue to move about on the cheap. Frugality in travel was the way of the transgressor, as Negly Farson, his journalistic predecessor, used to claim. When a newspaper or magazine popped with an assignment, or a producer romancing Vera Similitude hired him as a consultant, Irving would charge top dollar for meals and transportation and pocket the difference. To fussbudget administrators who asked for verifying bills on travel and entertainment, he gave the excuse of the harried free-lance too busy with genuine oh-shit stories to worry about bits of paper, not to mention his need to protect his sources from the prying eyes of the politicized IRS. It was not merely that he was cheap, he insisted to himself—though he was profoundly cheap—nor that he would brook a breach of ethics; his enterprising approach to T&E was a good habit gained in youth and carried with pride into maturity, like beating up on airline ticket agents who conspired to seat him in the middle of a row.

The pictorial memory of level gray eyes and manicured bare feet traveled with him, enlivening his reverie as he fastened the seat belt that he still called his safety belt. Whatever protective network executive or guitar-humping rock star was shtupping Viveca Farr was one fortunate fellow. Size six shoe, he judged; size six dress; nothing out of the ordinary front and back, but legs curved stunningly to perfect ankles; the ankle, he was certain, would just fit in the circle of his thumb and middle finger, a method of measuring ankle perfection with which he was blessed. Curious that Viveca Farr never showed her legs on television; the only time he had seen her full-length was on a morning interview show, and she was wearing slacks. Presumably, great legs did not lend themselves to the persona of crisp authority.

And she was about five feet four, which made him feel tall.

Pity she was such a hifalutin sourpuss. Would it have been worth it, teaching her how to pump a source, how to extract a new fact and then walk back the cat to see what had been misleading and who never again to trust? Irving shook his head and said, "Uh-uh, fuhget it," out loud, drawing a look from his shuttle seatmates on either side. He had tried that tender pedagogy a few times in his life, and the girls had always fallen for him until that moment of stupendous stupidity when he fell for them, at which point everything fell apart—the affair and the story and the job and what the psychobabblers called the self-esteem. Why did the greatest teachers have to be the worst lovers?

Still, he could have used her as a come-on and a front, as Ace suggested; on this trip alone, he would have made a few hundred on expenses. Viveca was a scrapper, to her credit, and verbally gave almost as good as she got, but Irving sensed she just didn't have the killer instinct. It wasn't enough to be a bitch; you had to have an innate talent in order to elevate insult and innuendo and irritation into a knack for control.

April in the inherently Southern city of Washington always lifted his spirits. Not the cherry trees around the basin near the memorials; he scowled at the hordes of Japanese visitors with their Japanese cameras snapping pictures of their Japanese kids in front of the long-ago gift from Japan. He had once rented a house here with a flowering cherry tree in the front yard and in April put out a "Remember Pearl Harbor" lawn sign just to stir up the tourists.

What the reporter liked was the leakiness of the capital in the springtime. For no apparent reason, the lips of sources who would clam up in the winter would open up like the petals of flowers in spring. Clandestine meetings in the parks were warmly natural, never frigidly furtive. His favorite spot was in Lafayette Park, across Pennsylvania Avenue from the White House, near the central statue of Andy Jackson waving his cocked hat. The bench had a plaque next to it: THE BERNARD M. BARUCH BENCH OF INSPIRATION. It was where the elder statesman had liked to sit and receive administration visitors in the Truman years, despite the irritation of the President, who never appreciated Baruch's too-well-publicized advice.

Fein sat on Barney's bench for a while, killing time; he had a date soon at the nearby McDonald's with the CIA source. He used the moment to relive his scene at Viveca Farr's house, spicing his repartee with should-have-saids and slipping in a hint of a come-on that he wished she had flashed. He would have spurned it; his philosophy was never to mix business with pleasure unless a really worthwhile opportunity presented itself. He was no fetishist, but those small feet stuck in his mind. Did she manicure and polish the nails of her own toes? A person could slip a disk that way.

Facing the White House on that bench, he thought of the story of Lincoln shining his shoes and being asked, "Mr. President, do you black your own boots?" Lincoln had answered, "Whose shoes did you think I blacked?" But it was just one of those Lincoln stories; no source. He rose from the bench, mildly inspired, and strolled over to the fast-foodery.

"I admire your selection of a rendezvous," Walter Clauson said, in line for an Egg McMuffin. "Nobody would ever look for me here, and yet the location has historic resonance."

One block from the White House on 17th Street, on the site of the Sans Souci restaurant that had carelessly ruled and failed decades ago, the yellow arches marked a place of noisy privacy. Clauson picked up his tray and paid the tab for both of them. At the table, Irving laid two dollars down to pay his share, less to establish his independence than to suggest that he had a publishing patron.

"Who's subsidizing you?" the intelligence official asked, pocketing the bills.

"Book publisher together with a television producer," Fein lied. "Ace is making a helluva deal for me. I'll find the sleeper, make a bundle, and retire. What do you know about him?" Irving made it a practice never to end a response to a source without a question of his own.

"You don't reveal your sources and methods, we don't reveal ours." Having established that, the Agency veteran took a sip of coffee and confided: "The mention of a hearing impairment of his left ear was on a military conscription report in the KGB's Berensky file."

"Who's Berensky?"

"The older Berensky, who died in 1980, was the man chosen to be the ostensible father of the illegitimate son of Aleksandr Shelepin."

Irving knew that name; Shelepin was the young KGB chief who developed the disinformation department in the fifties.

"And what happened to the little bastard?"

"Under the name of Aleksandr Berensky, born in 1950, the man you are looking for transferred to duty abroad at age twenty-two—that's the sleeper whose American name and address we do not know."

"Anything else about him? Cross-eyed, flat feet, whatever?"

"Big, like a linebacker. Six foot four, two hundred pounds back then, must be two-fifty or so now, in his mid-forties. The only other information is about his mental acumen: he led his class at the Leningrad Academy, with special aptitude in mathematics. Unless he's been dulled by life in America, the sleeper is smart."

"If he's smart, he should be making great piles of dough with all the money they've been stashing with him." Irving wound up and gave him the big question: "So how many six-foot-four guys that emigrated from Russia in 1972, and are bankers who have been raking it in lately, can there be? Don't you guys have an in to the American Bankers Association?"

"Ah, but he's not a traceable Russian immigrant. The KGB trained him in their American Village and slipped him in with a prepared identity, no accent, and a 'memory' of an American childhood—schools, camps, recollections of a suburban paper route."

"The whole legend."

Clauson nodded. "All that leaves us with is that he's physically big and tall, in his forties. He could have had his hearing fixed. And probable training at a bank or business school. A fairly large cohort."

Irving made that the end of a page in his mind and started a new mental page of notes. The picture in his mind would be recallable for about an hour after the meeting, during which time he would transcribe his mental notes.

The reporter got up and got them both refills of their coffee. "So Berensky was the name the sleeper had in Russia before he got tapped for this job." He thought of Ace talking with Davidov about the extensive KGB records and files. "Have any of your agents or assets looked for that name in the KGB files?"

"No, because their archivists are alerted to report on anyone who asks about that family. The KGB then follows the searcher to his or her source."

"So that's why Nikolai Davidov lets people poke around the files in Lubyanka?"

"To find out who wants to know what, including about the sleeper," said Clauson, "or better still, who knows what file to search for him. Maybe one of the searchers has a clue to the identity and location of the sleeper agent that the new generation of KGB officials doesn't know about."

Fein started a new page of notes in his head. "Who besides the KGB wants to know?"

"The Russian anti-KGB, in this case. The *nomenklatura* capitalists; the four hundred or so *vorovskoy* godfathers; the unreconstructed communists; the KGB hardest-liners who were shoved aside in the early nineties—a motley crew that some of us put under the general rubric of 'Feliks people.' You and I talked about this already—why are you wasting time?"

"Because your time isn't valuable, brother Clauson." Irving was cheery about it. "You're about to get your ass kicked out into the Old Spook Retirement Home, according to my contacts—who, by the way,

really despise you. You must have upset a lot of people in your day."
He knew how to ingratiate himself perversely with the beleaguered
Clauson, who nodded grim agreement. "Your purpose in meeting me
here, and in filling me in on these details," Irving told him, "is less to
help me than to find out what I know and don't know. Right?"

Clauson did not nod or not nod.

"I am now about to lay on you my plan to find the sleeper," the
reporter announced. "Its daring concept will astound you, because you
guys don't think big anymore. And your knowledge of it will make you
a hero with your new Director, because you can run back to her to say
how closely you are monitoring my efforts."

"You will put some sort of price on your revelations, I presume."

Irving brushed that aside. He thought of the cartoon of the two
prison inmates manacled to the walls of a dungeon with one saying to
the other: "Here's my plan."

"Here's my plan to find the sleeper in a hurry, at low cost, without
a whole bureaucracy tied up for years running taps and polys and filing
reclamas and fluttering each other and all that shit." He had Clauson's
full attention. "I'll make the sleeper come to me."

"That certainly would save time, Mr. Fein. And how do you propose
to induce this experienced agent, who has imbedded himself in American society for a generation, and has been running money on a scale
far beyond the normal dreams of avarice, to meekly give himself up to
you?"

"I'm gonna create an impostor. I'm going to tie up with a banker
who knows how to run big money in a way that's hard to trace—
futures, derivatives, swaps, whatever. And he and a little team I'm
setting up are gonna walk back the cat on the big financial killings that
the real sleeper has been making. By tracing them back, I'll find him."

Irving knew the CIA man knew what he meant by "walking back the
cat": looking critically at the past's activities through the present's eyes.
Counterintelligence did that every time a defector's bona fides were
accepted and the spy debriefed: interrogators could walk back the cat
to past events and apply the new information to see who had to know
what about old operations.

"The Feliks people are going to hear about my boy," said the
reporter. "Same with the KGB, or whatever the hell initials they use
now. And because the real sleeper has his lines into both of those

outfits, he'll find out about this 'other' sleeper. Of course, Berensky will know it's an impostor, and he'll want to find out how close my banker, operating in parallel, is getting to him. And he'll come after us."

"Ingenious," Clauson said promptly. "Dangerous, too."

"What's dangerous? This guy came over here as a kid, never been in trouble. He's a goddam banker, doesn't know from wet work. And he doesn't have any KGB connections, except maybe his one handler, right?" It was important to get confirmation of that.

"As far as we know," said Clauson.

Irving relaxed a little. "So what's the danger?"

"Berensky—under whatever name he goes by here—is the custodian of great wealth, perhaps the largest agglomeration of privately held assets in the world by now. He and his clients have a great deal to lose. Not only the political object of his long-term assignment, but real money as well. I think the term is 'megabucks.' "

Irving turned that over. "He's the richest man in the world."

"Except that it's not his money," Clauson cautioned. "He could protect his hoard, and himself, with non-KGB personnel."

"The Russian mafiya, with its underworld connections over here." Irving had heard they were sharing turf with Italian mobsters in Brooklyn's Brighton Beach.

The agency man nodded. "Or the real sleeper could come after the impostor himself. Violence is usually in the character of a sleeper agent. This one would think nothing of arranging for somebody's death."

"If it gets to that, I can come to you, right? The Agency wants to find him, too, no?"

"You might be better off calling your local sheriff," said Clauson. "But I may be able to help if you're successful." A thin smile of admiration appeared on his face. "If I were the real sleeper, and my contacts back home or in the financial markets alerted me to the fake sleeper's operation, I'd want to engage somehow. He just might, as you say, come to you."

At least Irving could be sure that the Feliks organization, and probably Davidov at the KGB, would be tracking down his impostor; the Americans, too, if the FBI and CIA were on the ball. "The trick is to become a player in this," said Irving, "not just a goddam observer. If my guy's any good, he'll attract all the spooks looking for the real sleeper. The KGB and the Feliks types over there, and your buddies at the FBI here."

That would give Irving some information to trade. You had to have some chips to put down on the table in these big stories before you could rake any other chips in; if he could get some intelligence traction with his fake sleeper, he could play these other outfits the way he was playing Clauson of the CIA. Other reporters "cultivated" sources at agencies, hoping to get dribbles of information; Irving Fein got the agencies to cultivate him because he found out things they wanted to know, which became the currency to buy other secrets.

"You'd need a really smart banker," Clauson observed, a little too coolly. Irving surmised he had a candidate in mind.

"Who is also a big guy and good actor," the reporter said. "And willing to take some risks. He may have to fool some of the real sleeper's relatives back in the old country before it's over."

"Even the wife he left behind, if she's alive. That may be quite a challenge."

"Aah, twenty years, people change, people forget." That was a weakness in his plan, and Irving wanted to slip past it.

"Who do you have in mind to impersonate the sleeper?"

Irving turned the query back on the questioner. "Need your help on that. Maybe somebody you've dealt with before." It would help to have one of the many global bankers who had done chores for the Agency, maybe on contract, to give this impersonation the coloration of legality in case some regulatory agency got too curious. Also, someone who had shown an inclination toward espionage; though Irving did not want to exaggerate the danger, things could get a little messy for the phony sleeper at the moment of confrontation. He waved himself off that worry; surely the ringer could be extricated in time, and he'd be the star of the story, be a hero to the banking world, make a bundle in psychic income lecturing on the basis of the best-seller. Irving knew a White House aide who would put the successful impersonator up for the Medal of Freedom. "Who's your candidate for the job?"

"You want a choice of three?"

Irving could not see himself running around the country interviewing heavyset bankers six foot four or taller and spreading the story of a secret Russian controlling billions of dollars in assets of the defunct

Communist Party. *The Wall Street Journal* would print the rumor in a week and the competition would be baying and treading all over the trail. He told the counterspy to recommend the best of the bunch.

Clauson held half of a cinnamon-raisin bagel in front of his mouth, which Irving presumed was to absorb the sound, or prevent lip-reading from outside, or whatever other surveillance the spooks fantasized about. "I have a friend in the marble halls of 21st Street. Might have a suggestion."

Irving took a fast mental walk up and down 21st Street in the nation's capital. Not the State Department, on 23rd. The F Street Club? Brick, and on 20th. Finally the quarter dropped: the Federal Reserve buildings, both white marble. As casually as he could, Irving said, "If the Fed doesn't know a banker who could fill the bill, nobody does. When can I see him?"

"My friend might not want to see you. But I can be your conduit." Clauson was keeping control, the first element of counterintelligence tradecraft. "You think he'll have a linebacker-banker on tap who's a little hard of hearing?"

"You can always fake a little deafness," the CIA man replied, lowering the bagel.

"What's that you say?"

Chapter 9

MOSCOW

The archivist had standing instructions to alert Nikolai Davidov, new chief of the KGB's Fifth Directorate, if anybody—no matter what the authorization, no matter how powerful the countersigner—asked for any of the files even remotely touching on Aleksandr Shelepin, or any of that former KGB chief's relatives or intimates.

He looked up from the requisition in his hand at the man and woman behind the counter. The aging fellow wore the jacket of what had been a uniform, now bereft of insignia, a sign of a Red Army veteran in dignified financial distress. The striking young woman with him, her dark hair chopped too short, might have been his daughter.

"This requisition is in good order," the archivist said in a friendly way. Davidov had ordered him to adopt a cooperative demeanor whenever this circumstance arose, as it had before. All who came were taken to the correct cabinet in the right room, were left alone, were secretly videotaped as they looked in vain and left in frustration. Their requisitions, along with a photocopy of their identity papers and a transcript of their visit conversation, created a new file in a cabinet upstairs labeled "Shelepin searchers." That one was fattening nicely, into its fourth drawer in a second cabinet, but nobody except the Deputy Director himself and a few of the KGB old-timers had access to it. When the archivist dared to suggest that the file be one of those entered into the new computer, he had been told it was not intended for easy recall. He wondered why Shelepin, the apostle of deception and disinformation who had been ousted by the Khrushchev reformers, was suddenly of such interest, but the archivist knew better than to ask his superiors.

"The purpose of your research?"

"Family history," the man said.

"I think an uncle of mine may have been related by marriage to someone in the Shelepin family," the young woman explained. "I am a television journalist. It might make an interesting reportage."

The archivist nodded encouragingly, as if accepting all that. Her identity papers, in which the requisition was folded, showed her to be a Latvian—but a Russian Latvian, one of the "near abroad," those waiting to be made citizens of the broken-away republic. Her television station, if he recollected correctly, broadcast in Russian, and was probably unpopular with native Latvians, who wanted the Russian-speakers out. Yet she had a Latvian name: Liana Krumins.

Rather than let his curiosity show, he waved over his assistant and told him to accompany them to the stacks. When the trio were out of earshot, the archivist turned on the taping system and brought the picture of his visitors up on his monitor.

"Is this where the files have always been?" he could hear the woman with the chopped-short hair ask the attendant.

"You are in Lubyanka," the guide answered. "Up to three years ago the rooms on this floor were prison cells."

"This is where the torture went on?" the man in the civilianized uniform asked. The archivist turned from the monitor and reached for the man's internal passport: Arkady Volkovich, sixty-six, Russian from St. Petersburg. The stamping showed he had been to Riga four times this year.

"All you have heard is true," the guide was saying to them. "This was the central spot for all the evil that was inflicted on the Soviet peoples for seventy years."

He opened the door to a cell and pointed, with perverse pride, to a wall with manacles still attached, an identifying sign beneath it. "It was felt that this was the most suitable place for the records of those years when the old KGB oppressed us. God knows, it's secure enough." Farther on, he touched another door: "This is where Wallenberg was executed. The Swedes were never told."

The archivist, watching from his station, switched to a camera in the room where searchers for these particular files were led. The man and young woman entered, were shown the drawer and given a work table. The guide said, "When you're finished, call for me down the hall. Please be neat with the files, and bring what you want for photocopying. It's five thousand rubles a page this month, or one dollar, or one mark. I should warn you, you may be searched afterward, because we don't want to lose any original material." He left them to the privacy of their monitored search.

It seemed to the archivist, who had observed much idle rummaging since the files were half-opened to the public, that the man, who was leading the young woman through the search, knew the particular file he was looking for. He opened one drawer, checked the headings of the musty records, then went to another. In the third cabinet, he came across what he was apparently seeking, wrenched the file out of the tightly packed drawer, and placed it on the table. Before plunging in, the veteran looked at the three-inch-thick accordion-pleated file in its entirety.

"It's been sanitized," he told the woman.

"How can you tell?"

He showed her the broken pleats that revealed an old file, once stuffed, now slimmed by gleaning; the strings that tied it were worn at their outer edges where they had once held the bulging contents. "But let's go through it systematically," Arkady said, emptying the contents on the table in an orderly fashion. "They may have missed a clue to the whereabouts of the son."

After turning over each page, he handed it to the young woman, who tidily replaced it in the folder. He stopped at a newspaper clipping. "The obituary of Shelepin's brother. Make a list of these survivors." She started to write down the names, but he stopped her. He shook his head in wonderment. "Must have been a hundred people go through this file, but they didn't know how to look for the boy. Here—take this and this, and this, for the photocopier."

"Not the clipping? I want the clipping."

"Can't draw attention to it." He held it for a moment, apparently weighing the risks in stealing it. The archivist, watching the monitor screen, hoped he would, but the man returned it to the folder. "Now, do we dare ask for the file on—" He dropped his voice, lest the room was bugged, but the archivist could read his lips forming a "B."

"We're here, why not?" The young woman was impulsive, perhaps daring; the observing archivist hoped it would lead her into trouble. "They can't put us in jail for asking. It's not as if he's a nonperson anymore. This is not the old days."

"It's not the new days either. You ask them," he said, "after I leave. You're the journalist."

Chapter 10

RIGA, LATVIA

The man in the khaki jacket with the insignia removed, Arkady Volkovich, insisted to his superiors in the Feliks *organizatsiya* that he had not made a mistake in letting Liana Krumins press ahead to the next file.

"She is a journalist, a real one. It is not a cover," Arkady explained. "I gave her a name to look up. Following it to the next file was the natural thing for her to do."

"Did it alert the archivist?" The question came from a former high official in the KGB, ousted as soon as the Yeltsin reformers took over, who had found a hard-liner's home in the Feliks organization's power goals and investigative techniques.

"If it did, he gave no sign." As Liana had gone off with the guide to the next filing room, Arkady had chatted up the apparatchik in charge, a drone more interested in his television set than his work. The Red Army veteran had told the archivist the file had been picked apart over the years and contained little of family interest. But the woman was a reporter, he added, and had to impress everyone with her thoroughness. Chopped her hair short to look like a man; never any makeup, not even to cover a pimple; furrowed brow, pursed lips—you know how they get. The archivist had acknowledged that with a grunt and presented no bureaucratic obstacles to Liana Krumins's quest for the file on the survivor at Shelepin's brother's funeral.

A heavyset woman with iron-gray hair at the middle of the table wanted to know what had happened after Arkady left Liana behind at Lubyanka. She spoke with authority. The veteran saw how everyone in the stark basement room, including the former high official of the KGB, deferred to her.

"I waited across the square, as she and I had agreed," he began. "At the bazaar where the Kazakhs sell their copper pots and pans. After about an hour and a half, she came out. You can't cross the square because of the traffic going around the pedestal, so she turned left and walked down Mysnitskaya Ulitsa to the bookstore."

"Was she followed?"

"No, Madame Nina. I would have seen."

"Were you followed?"

"If so, they were very good." The sauciness of that remark did not seem to please the woman at the center. Her impassive cross-examination troubled him. He knew her only by her first name, which was a diminutive at that; her hair was drawn back in a tight bun. In a matronly dress and a heavy cardigan sweater, she peered at him through thick glasses.

Arkady was not fearful of the former KGB man, or of the Chechen hooligan with the assault weapon standing against the wall. As a courier in various branches of Internal Security, he had come across more than his share of those. But Madame Nina gave him the impression she could see through him, which troubled a man with much to hide.

He had learned that after the breakup of the Bratsky Krug, or Circle of Brothers, in the early 1990s, a new criminal politburo had been formed. Seven *avtoritety*, authorities, controlled the major population centers from Petersburg to Vladivostok, each with its representatives from the new capitalist mafiya, the old *vory* underworld, the former KGB, the Caucasian enforcers. The summit meetings of the inner *avtoritet* were held in Riga, capital of newly free Latvia, out of reach of the new KGB and with easy air access to the West.

All this heralded the post-communist era of institutionalized corruption, but Madame Nina's presence gave an old-Soviet Lubyanka quality to every meeting of the organization. Arkady tried again, this time with no hint of disrespect. "She was the one who pushed on to asking for the Berensky file. I don't think either of us was followed afterward. These days they don't have so many people to follow everybody around."

"You are certain of that."

She evidently didn't believe him; he knew better than to profess his loyalty, because that would further erode his credibility. "There was ice and snow that night all over the sidewalks outside Lubyanka," he offered. "In the old days of the KGB, there was not a snowflake that fell that was not swept away immediately, from the front door all the way past the bookshop down to the all-night café for the drivers. But the sign on the door now says 'Federal Security Ministry' and it seems the new KGB doesn't have the budget anymore to sweep the street or follow every suspect. I doubled back to see if any tracks in the snow had followed hers. She was not followed."

"And after she came out of Lubyanka, when you made contact again with our journalist asset," the woman with the pale, hard face asked, "what did she report?"

That was the difficult part for Arkady. "She had been told there was some trouble getting the Berensky family dossier, Madame Nina. They told her it might have been misfiled in the transfer of papers. She did not see it."

"Does that sound plausible to you?"

He had to be careful here. "No. I suppose the archivist wanted to send the file she requested to Nikolai Davidov first. She said they told her to come back in a week."

Madame Nina waited. When he added nothing, she asked, "To be told that took her an hour and a half inside?"

"That worried me, too, Madame. This Krumins girl is not one of us, of course. I do not know why she was chosen to help us in the search for Berensky." At Madame Nina's glare, he added hastily, "Nor do I have any need to know. But her purpose is not our purpose. She is in this only to feed the curiosity of her television viewers."

"Our purposes run parallel," the woman in authority said, "at least for now. Is she aware of the risk to herself in this search?"

To Arkady, who had come to admire Liana Krumins, that was the maddening part. "She has no way of knowing she is running any risk at all. We led her to a story about a missing agent for her television program, and now she assumes she is off on her own. That is how journalists think."

He would not say so, but he had begun to worry about the short-haired young woman's safety. Liana was independent-minded. She had sided with the Latvians against the Russians before independence, which had taken great courage and had cost her time in jail; then she had sided with the Russians on human-rights grounds when the Latvians tried to push Stalin's colonialists out. Liana's politics were passionately against whatever was the popular grain; soon after Independence Day, her intensity in front of a camera and her willingness to touch on controversy had made her the most avidly watched television reporter in Riga. She seemed to relish taking risks on the air, much as she had put her own freedom at risk when the Baltics were under Soviet rule. Arkady suspected there was more danger to her in pursuing this story than he or she knew.

The Feliks people's idea—which Arkady considered a sound one, given her journalist's credentials—was to set her on the sleeper's trail and then follow her. But the *avtoritet* had no guarantee she would let them follow. Nor could the Feliks people be sure that the new men at the KGB would not follow her, too.

Arkady had picked up a rumor that of all those searching for the sleeper, Liana Krumins of Riga television would be the one that the unknown spy would choose to contact. He did not know why and was too cautious to ask; he was not yet among the most trusted. It was unfortunate that the inquisitive young woman did not know the risk she was running, perhaps acting as both hound and bait, but she struck him as someone who if she knew would probably run the risk anyway.

Madame Nina seemed to read his thoughts: "Does she suspect why she was chosen to be given this information?"

"I guess she thinks we think she is a good investigator." That was safe to say. He would ask nothing further about the organization's interest in her but would keep his ears open. It would be interesting and perhaps profitable to learn why she, of all the journalists in the former Soviet republics, had been selected by the Feliks people to lead the search back to Berensky in his American identity.

Over a beer in the little all-night café down the street from Lubyanka, Arkady had told Liana to stay in close touch with her initial contact—himself—and urged her not to trust others among the Feliks people or to go off on her own. He hoped she had taken his advice to heart. The veteran in the demilitarized jacket said nothing to the committee of this unauthorized warning. He found Madame Nina to be more menacing, in her command presence and her ingrained doubt about those she interrogated, than most of the security apparatchiks had been in the old days.

After informing Arkady that someone else would follow Liana back to Lubyanka next week, the impassive woman at the center of the table formally dismissed him. Arkady suspected that Madame Nina, first among equals in the tightening alliance of old apparatchiks and new capitalists, of resentful nationalists and outright gangsters, did not trust anyone to associate with Liana Krumins for too long.

Chapter 11

NEW YORK

Ace McFarland's slim cellular phone was in his jacket breast pocket. A wire ran to small receivers over his ears and a tiny microphone held in place in front of his mouth. He knew the setup made him look like an extraterrestrial being, but it granted him total mobility. He liked to pace as he worked his instrument of deal-making, and his call from his television news star client had him walking and talking across his office, down the hallway, across to the executive john, back to his office.

"Viveca, I'm chagrined at his exhibition of boorishness." He let her go on reciting the details of her tempestuous encounter with Irving Fein, clucking and groaning at the proper intervals. "You are right, there is simply no excuse for that. I feel awful that I was the one responsible for subjecting you to that. No, no, I should have known the chemistry would never take. My fault, entirely. How could Irving have been so—so unprofessional? As of this moment, he's not my client anymore. Which means he may never get another book published as long as he lives."

"Well, wait a minute, I'm not out to ruin the guy." The agent's escalation of her sounding-off caused the newswoman to back away a bit, as he had hoped it would. "I just won't work with him, ever, under any circumstances. But if it got out that it was my fault you dropped him as a client, all his friends—who think he's such a hotshot reporter—they'd come at me. They're a mafia."

"You're absolutely right, of course, Viveca. I'll find some other collaborator for him on this story, which will not be difficult at all, because it's developing into something bigger than I thought. You just forget the whole project. Forgive me for inflicting such an experience on you. He may well be the greatest reporter in the world, as his peers seem to think, but he's a lout. Totally insensitive." She broke in with an "And that's not all," but he kept overriding her complaints with his fervent agreement. "Yes, yes, insulting—no, I don't want to hear it. Sexual favors? You? Last straw."

He let her build toward a second peak of indignation, held her there a few moments, then let her taper off.

After she wound down, there was a pause, and she said: "What did you mean when you said it was developing into something bigger than you thought? You thought his story was pretty big last week."

"Oh, Irving said he hit pay dirt with a source in Washington this morning, but he tends to exaggerate." He had not yet returned the call from the reporter, whose book would be a difficult sell, but that was because he wanted to get a report from Viveca first. "I'll team him up with someone in your industry who's insensitive to the point of being numb, and they'll win all kinds of awards, and more power to them. Not for you. You need someone who can show some decent respect for your talent and your proven record of success. I'll find him, or her, you'll see. May take a little time, but—"

"You spoke to him? Did he tell you about our awful meeting in Pound Ridge?"

Ace paused for effect. "He said something about having acted like a jerk, and seemed a little sheepish about it. But he didn't give me any of the details as you just did. I'll bet he was plenty ashamed of himself, as he certainly should be. Nerve of the guy, and then to mislead me into thinking he just made a few minor faux pas. If I had known the truth when I talked to him, I would have told him to take his world beat, and all the professional acclaim that goes with it, and stick it in his ear. Viveca, you'll have to believe me, I've been in this business forty-five years and this has never happened to me before."

"He said he acted like a jerk? Those were the words he used?"

"Something like that. I'm not like you newspeople, I don't make notes, all I make is superagent history. Viveca!" Clients, he'd learned long ago, liked to hear agents shout out their names. "He's a proud man, and let's face it, he's insecure in a lot of ways, but I could tell he knew he overstepped in trying to browbeat you."

"He felt bad about it?"

"He'll feel a lot worse when I tell him I have to find someone else to make his 'global exclusive,' as he calls it, salable." He pushed a button on his desk that made a loud buzz. "Viveca, that's an overseas call I placed before, and it's hell getting through to Beijing—can I call you right back? Again, I'm terribly sorry, but the hell with him, we'll find someone that's right for you to work with. Be right back to you."

He took off his earphones, went to the door, and told his secretary to return the call Irving Fein had placed from a phone booth in Washington.

"Irving, sorry I've been unreachable all week, it's my lumbago. How did your rendezvous go on the famous park bench?"

"I didn't take him to the bench—he thinks they have long-range unidirectional mikes aimed at him. We had breakfast at a fast-food joint, the most secure location in the world."

"Progress?"

"I'll tell you when I see you. But Ace—I, uh, wanted you to know your celebrity newsgal and I didn't hit it off so well the other day."

"So I heard. She mentioned that she came on a little strong and you weren't having any of that."

"That's a fair way of putting it. She called you?"

"I called her because a couple of publishers heard I was handling her next book. The fact of my representation gave her a little extra prestige, so they expressed an interest." It was important that clients know of his direct contribution to the value of their work. "I think I can get a little auction going in hardback, maybe lock the paperback in, which should wake 'em up at the book clubs. I'll hold back electronic rights, of course—they may be an annuity for your grandchildren." He went on into the arcana of agenting, knowing Irving found this of little interest; as with most impecunious authors, to Irving the advance was all. But an analysis of the minutiae was both an opportunity to demonstrate the value of sophisticated representation and a device to give the reporter time to mull over what he might be missing without his famous collaborator.

"And she admitted our first session wasn't the greatest because she came on strong?" Ace could hear Irving working up a head of steam.

"Did she also tell you she said I was a has-been who needed her glamour to get a decent advance?"

"No, of course not. She seemed a little apologetic, but—she said that to you?"

"Did she tell you she called me a prick?"

Though that was hardly cause for any reporter to take offense, Ace let himself gasp into the tiny transmitter. "She certainly said nothing of the kind. I had no idea, Irving, first that she would use language like that—she always seemed like such a lady—and second that she would show such disrespect for the greatest reporter in the world today."

"Don't butter me up, Ace."

"As a matter of fact, Irving, those were not my words. Viveca used that very phrase when she called to share her worry with me about your reaction. Said something to the effect that all the other journalists who thought you were, quote, the greatest reporter of all time, unquote, might hold it against her if you were to take umbrage at her attitude. She's well aware of your power among your peers."

"Still, I dunno if it'll work."

"You know what? I made a mistake," the agent confessed. "And I'm the first to admit it. If she insulted you that way at the start—even though she later felt remorse about it, even a twinge of fear—that does not augur well for working closely under stress on a major book and television series. Fortunately, nothing's been signed. Let's break it off now, today."

"She really commands a big advance?"

"I know this sounds odd coming from me, Irving, but money is not everything. If you feel the personal chemistry is wrong, I can find someone else, perhaps a younger man in television, someone who could also help you with a lot of the legwork." He paused, as if thinking it over. "We'd have to settle for a lot less up front, but if the story makes world headlines, we can do well in the long run. I'm not getting any younger, but I can wait for the main commission income."

"Maybe you can, but I can't. Look, Ace—if whatshername is willing to shape up and go to work and not act like a snotnose star, I might be willing to go ahead with her."

"Think about it some more. Call me back in ten minutes."

The matchmaker signaled to his secretary to get his other client back.

"Viveca, I let him have it. I know you told me not to, but I just could not abide being the one who brought you together with someone who caused you such pain. So I told him off, and then some."

"Wish you hadn't, Matt. How did the pompous son of a bitch react?"

"He was penitent, of course. And the prospect of losing half of a huge advance, and having to find a less experienced television news-woman to be a partner, has him deeply troubled. But he deserved it. Now let's be constructive. Before I put out my feelers in the industry, tell me: can you think of someone—young, ambitious, good-looking, willing to put up with an iconoclast in pursuit of a global exclusive—someone I can recommend at your network?"

"Nobody," she said instantly. Ace suspected she knew of a few news presenters breathing down her neck who would leap at the chance. "And don't peddle the idea around yet. If he's genuinely sorry, and willing to act like a grown-up, we may be able to salvage it."

"You're sure? What if he backslides, under some tension? He may be driven by his own insecurity to assert some macho dominance. Will you be able to handle a somewhat volatile character?"

"If it means a lot to my image and my career, I can handle anybody."

The agent nodded gravely, made a date for the three of them in his office, and slapped his chest to hang up.

When Irving called again, the agent said, "You won. She says she'll behave herself. But Viveca is a nervous wreck, everybody knows that. The stress of climbing up the greasy pole of television politics to talk to thirty million people is unbelievable. Frankly, my friend, I'm worried. What if, down the line, she gets scared and starts acting like a star to cover up her vulnerability? I've done some more checking around, and her reputation is as you suggested, what we used to call high-strung."

"Borderline psychotic is what they call it now."

"That's unkind and inaccurate, and you know it. But will you be able to handle the creative tension between you?"

"For a whopping advance, I can handle anything. This story needs a big investment."

Ace told him the time and place of their meeting, with not a word to be mentioned of her apology or regret. He took the earphones and microphone off his head, wrapped them in a tidy package with the cellular unit, took off his jacket, loosened his tie, and lay down on the couch for his restorative preluncheon nap. If the world of books collapsed and there were no more role for literary agents, he could always become an arranger of high-finance hostile mergers, or a UN mediator, or a marriage counselor.

Chapter 12

NEW YORK

Irving arrived at Ace's office, with its depressing black mirrors, determined to give the knockout television announcer a second chance.

He reminded himself not to call Viveca "kid." That was what he called everybody, whatever their age, but some people took it to be a put-down, and the reporter, though content to be known as an iconoclast, did not want to insult anybody inadvertently. As Ace had explained, Viveca Farr had lived a tough life, was under debilitating strain, and had to be gentled along. She had expressed her apology to Ace for mouthing off like a goddam star—which she was not, having only the trappings of incipient stardom—and Irving was not about to be a sore winner. He resolved to keep in mind his primary interest in her was to get the big book advance, enabling him to travel and hire Mike Shu's accounting help. Any other reporting service she could perform in advancing the story would be gravy.

He would also, if she showed a hint of the proper respect, teach her a thing or two about the news business. She had spunk, Fein conceded, but it was of the lashing-out variety, sometimes useful—he used it himself on occasion—but only when intentional. He suspected her spunkiness to be brittle, not running to intellectual honesty or anywhere near moral courage. The trick, as he worked it out in his head walking down the hallway, looking in doorways, browsily snooping, was to consider her not so much a colleague but a necessary source of sustenance. And he was always prepared to do nip-ups, changing mood and approach, turning alternately sweet and sour, confiding and confidential, to milk a source. Sources deserved protection so as to earn the respect that comes from reliability.

In the doorway ahead, he could see her seated in a side chair, legs crossed, high-heeled blue shoes and a matching suit, real blond hair without one strand loose, not a long drink of water but a nice gulp. He was obliged to protect his source of funds. He hoped Ace would ignore the previous meeting and plunge directly into the business at hand: preparing enough of an outline to attract a substantial offer.

"Irving! Viveca here was telling me of your mutual interest in fine wines. I never knew you were a oenologist. To celebrate on pub date, I shall send you a case of my favorite, a Château Cheval Blanc."

Irving forced a smile at her, and she blazed a much better one back. Viveca's smile was some power smile, but warm and authoritative. Crisp. Everything about her was crisp: her demeanor, her direct gaze, the alert way she carried her head, the sound of her voice. Even her physical fragility had an element of toughness; if he were a peanut brittle sponsor, he'd snap up her show.

"I got some traction out of F Street," he told them, plunking himself down on the couch.

"What is the significance of F Street?" asked Ace.

"And what put you in traction?" she said.

Patience, he told himself; don't be a wise-ass and blow the deal. "One of the intelligence types," he explained, "who works out of the CIA house on F Street down the block from the Old EOB, gave me a few more leads to go on. My dunno sheet is longer than ever, but that's a good sign."

"Your what shit?" Ace looked offended at the language in front of a lady.

"My dunno sheet. When I'm at the beginning of a story, like everybody else, I draw up a list of what I know. Then I crack my head over it and draw up a sheet with all I do not know. That second list, the dunno sheet, is the hard part, but it's what gets you going. You have to keep adding to it, but there comes a moment in digging out a story when it begins to get shorter."

"Start with what you know," said Ace. "Like—who are the Feliks people you had me ask that attractive Russian, Davidov, about?"

"The Feliks people are the Outs of the KGB, plus a network, fairly large, of former communist big shots. Tough bunch who dream of the mean old days. They have ties to the Russian mafiya—a network of fast-buck operators and Lepke-type gangstercrats who give capitalism a bad name."

Viveca put in a question. "Who's the boss of all bosses?"

At least she didn't try to put it in Italian. "Dunno. Good question, though—I'll add it to my list. Anyway, this association of no-goodniks, the Feliks people, squirreled away a bunch of money just before the Soviet Union went under. The guy who handled the squirreling-away was a sleeper."

"A sleeper," said Viveca. Not with a rising inflection, to ask a question, but as a kind of statement, as if she knew what the hell he was talking about, which Irving was sure she did not. She didn't know what a Lepke type was, either—he remembered Louis "Lepke" Buchalter as an extortionist labor racketeer in the thirties—but at least she ran up a quick flag on this one.

"A sleeper agent," he said, spelling it out without patronization, "is a spy who was planted here a generation back. His assignment was to burrow into the American woodwork and make a respectable life for himself. He never did any spying, never took any chances, but just got himself into position for a big job when the time came."

"How do you know it's a man?" Viveca asked.

That caused him to look at her blankly. His original tipster had said "he"; Clauson had referred to the sleeper as "he," and suggested a man to handle the impersonation; Irving had just assumed it was a he. Could the sleeper be a woman? No; he left a pregnant wife behind in a marriage that had to be annulled. "It's a man, and I'll explain why later, but that was a good question. Assume nothing." Then she did something else Irving liked: she pulled a notebook out of her purse and began to take notes.

"In the early summer of 1968," Irving continued, "a very bright kid of eighteen—trained in their American Village, where they feed you apple pie and coffee and tell you Joe DiMaggio's brothers were named Vince and Dom—was selected to be planted here. The choice of the kid came right from the top of the KGB, so there may be a connection there. I'm told he left a pregnant young wife behind."

"One of those."

Irving could not envision Viveca Farr identifying with a jilted bride. "Either he was forced into marriage because he knocked her up and left because he wasn't a family man, or—more likely, given the assignment—this was a very dedicated young commie. Okay, a generation passes. Gorbachev comes on, the Soviet economy goes in the tank, the Baltics start to pull out. Just before the shit hits the fan, the KGB sends the sleeper's handler to Barbados—that's in the Caribbean somewhere—to unload all the Party holdings onto this guy. He's now an international banker here in the U.S. and knows what to do to bury big assets, or even to make a buck or two investing them."

"*The Odessa File*," Ace interrupted, for Viveca's benefit. "Frederick Forsyth. The Nazis hid the German gold after the war hoping to bring back Hitler. Helluva novel, big paperback—"

"Ace, you're starting up again," Irving warned. "This is not a novel."

"Look, a plot's a plot, this one's a proven winner. If a publisher can't sum up a book in a few words, forget it. Irving, all we have to do is tell this under a seal of secrecy to a publisher and he's going to say, 'Gee, a post–Cold War *Odessa File*,' and he'll snap it up."

Irving leaned across the agent's desk. "This is what is happening right now in the world, Ace. It could mean the overthrow of the Russian government, bloody civil war, a new arms race, God knows what-all. Nobody knows it but me and a few spooks and one underground banker who may just be a goddam financial genius." How could he impress on this man the scope and importance of the story? He took Ace's tie in his hand and pulled the little man to within three inches of his face. "It's a fucking . . . world . . . beat."

Viveca's potato-chip voice came from behind him. "What happened when the Soviet control met the sleeper agent in Barbados?"

The reporter whipped around. "That's number one on the dunno sheet. Possibility: the two of them got in cahoots, said let's steal the whole bundle and screw both the Russian government and the Feliks people. Possibility two: they're working together right now to invest the money and set up front companies and take over banks to deliver to the new Russian government and be heroes. Three: they're running up the pot until they get enough to deliver to the Feliks people to overthrow the elected government. Four: one of them killed the other."

After a long moment, Ace said, "I like possibility four."

"Actually, four makes the most sense," Irving said. "The handler would logically have stripped the files in Moscow before setting out, because the government was in a state of flux. There must be at least a couple of higher-ups in the KGB who know all about the sleeper. The handler would surely have reported back to Moscow by now—if he were alive."

"Reported back to whom?" The crisp voice, the schoolmarm's "whom."

"Makes no difference, if he's dead," said Ace.

"I'm guessing the handler is the one that's dead," Irving said, basing it on a hunch of Clauson's, whose identity he was not ready to reveal to his colleagues. "That's because only the sleeper would know how to handle the assets and be in a position to conceal them or return them."

"If the sleeper killed the control, as you suspect," reasoned Viveca, who was doing better at this than Irving had a right to expect, "he would have done it to keep the money from the Russian state. That means the sleeper wants to deliver it to the hard-liners, the Feliks people. Or keep it himself."

"Which is why," Irving led them along, "our boy Davidov in Moscow must be having fits. Somebody up top in the KGB must know who the sleeper is, but if the link of the control is broken, how does the new management of the KGB make contact with their boy?"

"You're sure that some of the KGB higher-ups must know his identity," Viveca said.

"Yeah, well, they must—but for some reason, they don't seem to. Why not? That's also on the dunno sheet."

"What's to keep the sleeper from becoming an entrepreneur?" asked Ace. "Money is a powerful motivator, as the agenting life has taught me."

"Gotta remember, this spy was indoctrinated when he was a kid, in the old days, when communism was an ideology. He sat tight for over twenty years and then did what he was told when he was activated. He's a true believer—my guess is that he's not in business for himself."

"What about the wife he left behind—would she know his current identity?"

"Tell you the truth, Viveca, I hadn't thought of her," Irving admitted. "She could be pretty pissed about being left in the lurch with a brat on her hands. More likely he has a friend or two from the training days, now in the Feliks people, who'd know him. Or maybe a mole over here. He was originally selected by some KGB big shot, remember. The KGB operates in cliques, schools of thought, even more than CIA."

"You're both missing the point of the book," said Ace. "This is a manhunt story. Who's going to find the sleeper first and kill him? How does he stay a fugitive and stay alive? Focus on the protagonist."

"Ace, think reality. Don't you know how to sell nonfiction?"

"A plot's a plot. You need a central character. Yours is in hiding."

"I have a plan to flush him out," Irving said.

"And you are going to vouchsafe that to us now."

"No." He looked out the window at Madison Avenue, pretending to think, in fact listening to the nylonic sound of Viveca uncrossing and recrossing her legs. "How we get him to come to us is a matter between me and my partner here. Not you, Ace. Can you sweat a big advance out of a publisher on the basis of an investigative book by Irving Fein and Viveca Farr, giving no other details to blow the story?"

"No outline, no sample chapter, no documents, nothing?"

"Just your word that you know what the story is, and it's big."

Ace steepled his fingers. "A challenge. I cannot think of another agent capable of rising to it." He handed each of them a manila envelope. "This contains our agreement: straight fifty-fifty partnership on all royalties, including television rights, between the two of you, after my modest commission. You can take these documents home and study them if you wish, or you can lock this up right now."

Irving took his out and scrawled his name on the last page. Viveca took a few moments to read the six pages of boilerplate, then signed her name neatly at the end.

"It's appropriate to shake hands," the Ace said.

The squeeze of her perfectly manicured fingers was cool and sure, as Irving knew it would be. He heard her saying to Ace, "The authors would like a seventy-thirty split of the paperback."

Rather than offer to buy her a drink, he suggested they walk over to the East River, where there was a bench he knew. "I call it the Irving Fein Bench of Inspiration."

She nodded and hailed a cab. That bothered him. First, the East River was maybe six blocks away, tops seven, and it was a fair November day. Furthermore, when he was with a woman, he'd hail the damn cab. He let her open the door and slide in first, the skirt of her suit riding up to show those perfect legs.

"New shoes," he noticed. "They hurt?"

She did not reply. The cab promptly got stuck in the crosstown traffic, and the bus ahead spewed its fumes their way. They sat uncomfortably and he said nothing back.

"I know what you're thinking," she said finally. "Hoity-toity broad, can't walk a few blocks, has to have a cab if her limo isn't on standby."

"You're a mind reader, all right."

"Look. If we started to walk, within thirty seconds you would see people stop and look at me. When they passed, they'd turn around and look some more. Some nice old lady would come up and say, 'Don't I know you?' Believe me, just walking down the street when you're on television regularly is an ordeal."

"Hadn't thought of that, tell you the truth."

"You're lucky to be in print. You have your famous byline and you keep your privacy."

He thought that over. Would he like walking down the street and having women snap their heads around and say, There-goes-Irving-Fein,-isn't-he-adorable? Wouldn't bother him all that much, certainly not at first. Privacy was something he had too much of. It was like the guys who complained bitterly about all the junk mail that stuffed their mailboxes. Irving liked to get junk mail; he hated to look in his mailbox and find it empty.

If his face were famous, would women he dated feel protective of him, as he now felt protective of the famous face beside him? He'd like that. Maybe if this book went over big, he'd be a part of the television special, get his face a little better known, which might lead to some speaking fees. The pundits he knew went on panel shows for peanuts to stimulate the lecture agents to book them at conventions for heavy money. He would do no promotion tours for the book, though—not that anybody wanted him to after that hoo-ha over the libel release. Let Viveca Farr, face too famous to walk across town among the Great Unwashed, do that.

"When's your birthday?"

She looked suspicious. "Next week. Thirty-three," she reminded him. "Why?"

"I was thinking of getting you a pair of those glasses with the fake nose attached," he said. Her face tightened; she opened her purse, took out a few dollars, and thrust it through the opening in the plastic barrier protecting the cabbie from passengers. He added, "They have 'em without the funny mustache, for women."

She burst out of the taxi on her side and started walking fast. He hurried to catch up, and they sped across town toward the river, her heels clicking on the cement. Nobody coming at them looked at her twice. He craned his neck back; nobody had turned around. A few particularly cutting remarks came to mind, but he bit his tongue.

If it hadn't been for the river, he thought, she would have kept going until he dropped. Breathing hard, he plopped on the bench along the riverfront with the FDR Drive traffic behind them. Time to make peace, he told himself.

"How come you know from paperback splits?"

"I do my homework before a meeting." She stared at a slow barge going upriver. "Tell me I shouldn't bother my pretty little head."

He stuck his legs out, crossing his feet near the fence. Careful, now. "On a seventy-thirty split, which of us gets the seventy?"

She looked at him for the first time since they'd left Ace's office. "You don't know?"

"I have a long dunno sheet for contracts, and I just put that on."

"After the hardcover sale," she explained, "if the book does well, or gets a big book-club sale, the hardback publisher will hold a telephone auction for the paperback rights. It used to be that half the money for those rights went to the hardback publisher, the other half to the author, to be applied against the advance on royalties. You really don't know about this?"

"Never had the problem," he said truthfully. "No book of mine ever sold enough to reach the advance. I'm glad when they don't come after me for the difference."

She put her feet out, too. "This one will sell, and reflect well on both our reputations. But this time, seventy percent of the paperback money comes to us, the authors, and thirty percent goes to the hardback publisher."

"And you and I split the seventy?"

"You've got it."

"That's pretty good. You were smart to ask for that."

She gave a small shrug and smiled. "I'm glad you have your breathing under control. The way you were puffing I thought you'd have a heart attack. You need more exercise."

Irving knew that, just as he knew all about paperback splits, of course, though Ace was never able to get him more than sixty-forty. But this little victory boosted Viveca's easily damaged amour propre at no cost to him—on the contrary, her homework and chutzpah in upping the author share would produce money in the bank for him. He gave her credit for that.

"Now tell me what you don't want Ace to know," she said, reaching for her notebook. "How we get the sleeper agent to come to us."

"Two ways to fish after you have a lead. One is to get into print in a *New York Times* or a *Washington Post* or *International Herald Trib* with what you have. Then sources come to you—packages over the transom, messages in creepy voices, spooks passing tips through all sorts of cutouts. Trouble with that way is it stirs up the competition. We got to get way out ahead on this first, so it's all ours, nobody can catch up."

She nodded, making no notes in the failing light, doodling on the page. She doodled tight little boxes.

"Any questions so far?"

"What's a transom?"

He ignored that. "The other way, our way, is to get our duck by setting out a decoy duck. We set up a parallel sleeper, our guy, a credible impostor, to attract either the Feliks people or the KGB, or both. Or"—here was where Irving hoped to get lucky—"to attract the real sleeper. Takes a banker to catch a banker."

He sketched out the plan to recruit Edward Dominick, Clauson's pick at the Memphis Merchants Bank. "I have a hunch our spooks have used him before, for minor chores, but we're not supposed to know that." He did not give her the name of his CIA source, nor did he tell her he did not know who had originally tipped him to go to Clauson. She had no need to know that, at least not yet, and if she should get cold feet he did not want her to be able to pass the source on to another reporter. He did review with her what little he had gleaned about the real sleeper: mid-forties, hard of hearing, big guy, the married name of his abandoned wife.

"Do we know his name?"

"We know his real name, the one on his Soviet birth certificate: Aleksandr Berensky. The cover name, the one he goes by here? Dunno."

"Fireflies are out. See?"

He was glad she did not want to know more; if their positions were reversed, he would be pushing, pushing to get more on the sources, more on Dominick, more on the connection—or lack of it—between the sleeper and his new handler, if there was one, or with his Feliks people contact, if that's what the sleeper preferred. There was some value to working with an amateur as a partner: she was too busy digesting what he'd told her to show a hunger for what he had not.

"There goes another one." The fireflies were out in force, early this year. It seemed to him she was not too eager to get to her television studio and other life. Irving had no place to go. "That's a female, attracting a mate," she observed.

"If it's a firefly."

She frowned, pointing at a lightning bug floating in the air with its abdomen brightly lit a greenish yellow. "You're telling me that's not a firefly?"

"Did a piece on insects once," he said. "The firefly has a natural predator, which is a good thing, because otherwise we'd be up to our ass in fireflies. The predator is called an assassination beetle. It has the same ability to glow, and it can replicate the code of flashes of a mating firefly. The firefly moves in to mate and is devoured by the beetle."

She rubbed her arms briskly. "Wish you hadn't told me that."

He had never done a piece on bugs. He knew this because Clauson had told it to him one night, along with arcana about the deceptiveness of orchids he'd picked up from his Agency hero, Jim Angleton. That famed molehunter had been fired for paranoid zealotry when the smooth new bunch took over in the seventies and later let the Russian moles penetrate the Agency. After a money-grubbing mole named Ames, operating in the eighties and nineties, all but crippled the Agency and caused the execution of its best spies in Russia, the guys at fault blamed their laxity on the reaction to Angleton's "paranoid witch-hunts." Irving was never much for insect metaphors but had filed it in his head in case he ever needed to liven up a feature lead.

"Do people still get killed in this espionage business?" she wanted to know. "I'm not afraid for myself, but I'd hate for you to get knocked off and then I'd have to finish the book all alone."

The hell she wasn't afraid. He set her mind to rest: "Cold War's over. And nobody ever kills, or even threatens, a reporter—too big a hoo-ha." He thought of Michael Shu, the accountant he'd hired on spec to go to Moscow and Riga to do some low-level digging. "That goes for people who work for reporters, too," he reassured her preemptively.

"Wonder what happened when the handler and the sleeper met in Barbados?"

He wished she hadn't brought that up. "The control was a Russian spook. They call it *mokry delo;* our boys call it 'wet work.' What those guys do to each other is their business."

"What's wet about the work?"

His heart sank; she didn't know anything about this business. What was wet was blood; he mumbled something about underwater frog-men.

She flipped her cigarette over the rail into the river. Time for the news on television. "I have to do my script. Our next step?"

A hundred words; big deal. She probably needed the time for makeup and hairdresser.

"I have a call in to Dominick in Memphis," Irving said, frowning. "He didn't call back yesterday, so I had to tell his nosy secretary who I was but not what I wanted. If he keeps ducking, I'll show up at his home Sunday. Don't like to do that—it makes 'em nervous."

"Why don't I call him?" she suggested. "He'll take my call. We want a meeting in his office, right? In the morning, so I can get back in time for the newscast."

True. Most executives, no matter how impressed with themselves, would take a call from Viveca Farr, the famous television newslady on every night at nine for forty-five snappy seconds. He gave her Dominick's number, hailed a cab, opened the door for her, said good night politely. Fame had its function. He hoped that rigmarole he'd given her about the fireflies and the assassination beetles was accurate, in case she ever checked, but that was unlikely.

Chapter 13

MOSCOW

She sensed that somebody was looking over her shoulder, even though the Shelepin file room was empty. Liana Krumins straightened, looked back, saw nobody there. She buttoned the top button of her blouse and pulled the shawl off her shoulders, placing the gauzy Latvian garment atop a file she had opened.

She had decided it was wiser to come alone this time, because the Feliks people's escort, Arkady, whom she had come to trust, said somebody else from the organization had been assigned to come with her that day; besides, male librarians tended to be more accommodating to a young woman by herself.

The archivist who sat at the desk used by the floor's chief jailer in the old Soviet days had been more than helpful this time. Liana flirted with the fellow, took his mind away from the television he was watching, explained her exasperation, beseeched his expert guidance, and sure enough, the misplaced files on the offshoot of the Shelepin clan named Berensky had been miraculously found.

She was now looking for any reference, in any of the surveillance reports, official letters, family correspondence, tombstone bills, newspaper clippings, and scrawled memoranda, to a particular member of the Shelepin family whose last name was Berensky. If she could then track him down, if he was alive, she would be the finder of a leading international spy and surely become the most respected journalist in Latvia and throughout the Baltic nations. Liana Krumins would not only have her own television program, as she already had, but as a famous journalist she would become an owner of the station. Then she would have total freedom to broadcast the truth far and wide, to

Helsinki in the north, Vilnius in the south, St. Petersburg in the east, even to Berlin in the west.

She was aware that the group most eager to find the sleeper spy called themselves "the Feliks people" because they did not view the memory of "Iron Feliks" Dzerzhinsky, Lenin's vicious chief of the Cheka, with dread. On the contrary, many of them longed for a return to the days when the manacles on the walls of some of the Lubyanka cells held dissidents for torture.

Today, the Feliks people were using her, because of her journalist's credentials, to find Berensky, just as she was using their intelligence and mafiya connections to help her; together, they were more likely to get to the sleeper. Her philosophy, gained in the ranks of the Latvian opposition to Soviet rule: use and be used. That had been driven home to her one frigid night in a prison cell when she was seventeen. Their immediate goals, though different, did not conflict: the Feliks people were after the sleeper to get their money, and she was after him for the stunning reportage, with the fame and power that would bring.

Thanks partly to Arkady, who was one of the Feliks people, she knew more than most about the sleeper's family tree.

Aleksandr Berensky's mother was Anna Berensky, a single woman who was secretary to a rising but married KGB bureaucrat whose identity was kept secret, and who probably fathered the boy. Anna and her son were sent by her married lover to live in Latvia. When the boy became seventeen, he married a Riga girl, Antonia, but after a year the marriage was annulled and its record destroyed on orders of the KGB. After abandoning his wife, who soon after gave birth to a child, Aleks Berensky volunteered for, or was sent to, the American Village operated by the First Chief Directorate's training department. Later, speaking perfect American English, he was given a "legend"—a complete background for a false identity—and slipped into a new life somewhere in the United States.

Because she was a step ahead of the Feliks people, she felt less a captive of her sources. By one of those odd happenstances, Liana knew—and was determined to keep to herself—a part of the sleeper's genealogy about which the Feliks organization was unaware. As a child, Liana's mother, Antonia Krumins, had known Anna Berensky when both were part of Stalin's Russification of Latvia. As the dictator deported hundreds of thousands of Latvians to labor camps in Siberia, he injected Russians in their place as colonists, especially around Riga; this was his plan to water down the native population and absorb the republic into Russia.

Though a generation apart, the Russian Anna Berensky and the Latvian Antonia Krumins became close friends. Liana's mother once let slip that before Anna died in 1980, she had revealed that long ago she had been the private secretary to Aleksandr Shelepin, who then rose to become the chief of the KGB through most of the sixties. That master of disinformation had worked here in this very building in Moscow. Liana could not be certain, but she had a strong hunch that Aleks Berensky not only was the sleeper, but was Shelepin's bastard son.

That must have been why, Liana reasoned, this young man had been chosen for special training in the most difficult assignment in espionage: as a "sleeper agent," implanted in another country, denied any contact with friends, relatives, or supervisors at home. He had to be young enough to build a new life with new friendships; intelligent and resourceful enough to make a success of himself in the chosen field; and ideologically reliable enough to remain loyal for decades and be ready at the moment of awakening. Who could fit those qualifications better than the son of the KGB Director?

Arkady had told her that the time to activate the sleeper had come toward the end of the eighties, in Riga, hotbed of the movement to break up the Soviet Union. The Baltic nations, unlike the other Soviet republics, had once been independent; they had been swallowed up in a deal made by Hitler and Stalin, an offense to sovereignty that was never recognized by the West. As a result, agitation for independence in Latvia, Lithuania, and Estonia had special force in America; when the deep cracks began to appear in the communist economy and the Baltics demanded freedom from the Soviet empire, that force carried over to Ukraine and tore the Soviet Union asunder.

"The KGB knew the end was coming," Arkady had told her. "The Party had billions hidden away, in gold, diamonds, foreign bearer bonds. Certain Politburo members held hundreds of millions more in secret accounts around the world. How to conserve those assets for a day when all the talk of disunion and reform would pass away, and the time of strong central authority would come again? An American banker was needed who could be trusted with it all. One of us, over there. That's when they awakened their sleeper."

Liana pushed her shawl aside and pulled out the contents of the next accordion file, but the musty air and the lateness and the complexity of the search were becoming too much for her. As she pushed the contents together, a personal letter of many pages became caught in the string around the file. She pulled it away, looked at it briefly, threw it in the file.

Then she pulled the letter out again, flipping through to the last page; her eye was caught by the signature "Anna." It was written to "Aleksandr Nikolayevich"—the patronymic of the KGB's Shelepin—from some Black Sea resort, saying it enclosed snapshots of herself and her son at the beach. But no pictures were in the envelope attached to the letter by a pin. She read: "Aleks is on the verge of tears because of the sunburn, but he reminds me he will be eight next week and is taking it like a man."

Aleks. The letter was undated, but the postmark on the envelope was June 16, 1958, about the time Shelepin made it to the top of the KGB and began his plan to oust Khrushchev and the reformers. The birth would have taken place in the third week of June in 1950 in Moscow, possibly at a hospital, surely recorded on that date in the city's bureau of birth records. Liana folded the pages quickly, took a deep breath, pulled out her blouse, stuffed the document inside her panties, tucked the blouse back in. The bulge was unmistakable; she reached in and moved it around to the small of her back.

She needed fresh air and a place to think.

After putting the files back in the cabinet, she left her shawl draped over the chair to provide an excuse for coming back if she needed it. Instead of ringing the bell for the guide, she made her way back to the main desk by herself.

The archivist was lolling back in his chair, snoring. She smiled and went to his desk to leave him a cheerful note and glanced at the television set on his desk to see what old movie had put him to sleep. The picture on the screen did not move. It showed a room with a table neatly stacked with files, her shawl draped over a chair. She felt the clutchfist of fear in her stomach: they had been looking over her shoulder. Had he seen her take the document? The snoring archivist seemed to be genuinely asleep. But was it also being taped? If so, putting the letter and envelope back would do no good. She wrote a note he could not show his superiors—"Didn't want to wake you. Back in the morning. Liana."

She walked unhurriedly down the hall to the elevator, took it down to the ground level, and walked to the checkpoint where they tested for metal objects on the way in. Two guards stood in her way, one short and balding, the other huge. She handed her visitor's pass to the smaller one and waited for them to step aside, as they had the week before. They did not.

"Are you going to let me pass?" she said, flashing a smile.

The guard motioned for her to step back and went to a telephone. He gave the number on the visitor's pass and waited. She wondered if they could hear her heart pounding. He hung up, shook his head at her, waited with his hand on the phone. After a minute it rang and he listened to the order.

He motioned her to a small room next to the entrance. Uncertain, she went in. The guard held out his hand for her attaché case, and she gave it to him. He went through it and put it aside. "Strip search."

"I will not. What do you think this is, the old days? Let me out immediately! Do you realize I am a journalist?"

The balding soldier, unsmiling, pointed at her blouse and flicked his finger.

"No. I will report you. This is a form of rape." She did not want to ask for the obvious, a woman guard, because that would mean sure discovery of the letter. The last thing she wanted was to be searched by a woman.

The huge guard tapped on the door, entered, closed it behind him. He wanted a view, too.

"Who's watching the front entrance of Lubyanka, then?" she demanded.

"We have orders to see if you have hidden any materials on your person, Miss Krumins," the bald one said. "The archivist says if you have taken nothing, you may go. If you refuse to prove that to us, we will not harm you. We will put you in a cell until further orders."

When she hesitated, the big one said, "We have seen a naked woman before." If he steps behind me, she decided, I will ask for the cell and try to brazen it through. He remained at the door; both men were in front of her. Perhaps she could get away with a visual deception, unless there was a hidden camera behind her.

She reached to her side, undid the button of her skirt, and let it fall to the floor, stepping back. They did not examine the skirt on the floor;

she took hope that they were more interested in seeing than searching. Her long legs looked best in the shoes with medium-high heels, and she left them on. She wore no stockings. She unfastened the buttons on her blouse. The guards tried to keep an official look on their faces as she opened it but did not take it off; instead, she fiddled with the catch in the front of her bra. Her object was to keep their attention focused on her breasts, which were full and firm and always had a marked effect on men.

As the catch came apart, she straightened up and shrugged her blouse back off her shoulders, reaching back with one hand to pull it back away and folding it around the letter sticking up out of her panty band. Her breasts still not fully exposed, with the guards' eyes riveted on the half-opened bra, she dropped the blouse with the enfolded document on top of her skirt on the floor.

Gaining confidence, she thumbed off her bra and took a deep breath, putting her hands on her hips and turning one way, then the other. The guards were silent, not breathing. She threw the bra at the huge man, whipped off her panties, turned around, and threw the panties at the other guard. "Now, out!" she shouted.

The big one turned to go, but the balding man was not to be fooled. "The shoes," he said. She stepped in front of the pile, hesitated as his face turned grim, then took off one shoe, handed it to him, the other to the other. The big one examined it closely and smiled; as the balding guard apologized formally, they handed back the shoes and, tossing her bra and panties toward the skirt and blouse in the pile behind her, left the room.

She reminded herself it was not over; from someplace in the room, she was still being watched. She backed close to a wall, and the letter went invisibly inside the skirt as she dressed. She left the examining room head high, winked at the guards and said, "You must enjoy your work," and marched out in Lubyanka, formerly Dzerzhinsky, Square.

Davidov shut his office door. He told Yelena, the code analyst who doubled as his secretary, that he was not to be disturbed. He picked up the clicker, sat on the ottoman in front of his television set, and played the tape again.

Not the first part of the tape showing the Latvian reporter stealing the document in the file, of course. Nothing was to be learned from that, other than what type of document it was—a letter and envelope— and where she hid it, not over her belly but in the small of her back. The part worthy of close study was the search at the front entrance.

The young woman journalist had an admirable bosom, no doubt about that. He froze frame at the crucial moment of revelation; the hidden camera eye gave him a profile view of breasts that the guards, lucky fellows, looked at directly. Davidov pressed the play button, telling himself not to be distracted. It was difficult not to be distracted; the young Latvian woman showed herself without shame, without pride, more in defiant mockery. He fast-reversed, played it again.

The security official had a legitimate purpose for studying the tape closely. She took the document from the file room—the evidence of her theft was plain—and did not have it when searched. What had she done with it? Had she stopped in some other file room unobserved by the archivist, who would not soon again fall asleep on the job? Davidov went to his easy chair, hooked his leg over the upholstered arm, played the tape again. Aside from getting a rising lump in his pants, he was getting nowhere.

Yelena knocked. He pressed the off button and told her to come in. She brought in the first report on the surveillance of the Latvian woman after she left Lubyanka late the previous afternoon.

"You are going to wear out that tape, Nikolai Andreyevich."

"In the line of duty." Yelena had a strict moral code, as did a select few of the women recruited from their service as "swallows." Trained from their teens in the arts of male satisfaction, they had skillfully prostituted themselves for their country until their age and looks no longer appealed to potential defectors; having shown themselves trustworthy, often on foreign assignments, those women with analytical skills deserved second careers.

Yelena, now in her late thirties, his own age, remained attractive, but unlike most Russian bosses, he kept their relationship on a mutually respectful level; if there was any personal encroachment, it was in her mother hen's possessiveness of a young superior. He kept in mind that he derived his power directly from the Director, who was not above indiscretions himself but who stiffly disapproved of office affairs even among his unmarried staff. Davidov was not only the first trained epistemologist ever to be appointed to this sensitive post, but the first brought in from outside the security services; he could not afford the slightest slip that would give his many bureaucratic enemies an opportunity to bring him down.

"Here, we will watch it together," he told his assistant, proving to his own satisfaction his interest in Liana was not lascivious. He clicked rapid reverse to get away from the best part, stop, then play. They watched both scenes. He shook his head in puzzlement. All Yelena said was "Humph."

"What means 'Humph'?"

His policy analyst went to his desk, picked up a blank piece of paper, and slipped it into an envelope. She stood before him, pulled out the back of her blouse, and placed it in the small of her back, held in place by her belt.

"That is where she put it," he agreed.

Yelena went to the door and closed it. She returned, turned her back to him, and started to take off her blouse. Davidov, troubled, looked at the closed door; this might be a mistake, but it might teach him something. She shrugged the blouse backward; it hooked on the envelope sticking up; she reached back, as Liana had, easily concealed the envelope in the blouse, and dropped it on the floor.

"You have not forgotten your training in the clandestine service," he said, feeling stupid. He hoped she would not turn around.

Yelena stooped, retrieved her blouse, and, after buttoning it, faced him again. "Shall I put the tape in the files, Nikolai Andreyevich?"

"Leave it right where it is. I may want to play it for my instruction on searches," Davidov replied. "But thank you. Where did she go afterward?"

"Three blocks south to the Hotel Metropole, the grand dining room, the one with the painted glass ceiling."

"Russians don't go there." In that historic room, as in the rest of the hotel, hard currency was required.

"She met an American male, and we assumed you would want him followed. No report on that yet, but our men following her to the hotel noticed another shadow."

"I hope they didn't pick him up."

"No, Director. They cellulared for backup to follow the second tail. We have a photograph of him." She produced it. "He followed her to the airport hotel and then to Riga this morning."

"And the person she met at the Metropole salon?"

"An American tourist. An accountant." She handed over a thin dossier containing nothing more than a facsimile of a passport and visa application of an American named Michael Shu.

He took the file and nodded dismissal. In what he took to be a subtle gesture of defiance, she firmly closed his door, as if to ensure his privacy. He clicked on the set and rewound the videotape, wondering about the sleeper agent.

The KGB had no written record of Aleks Berensky's current identity, at least not to Davidov's knowledge; it was possible the sleeper's background and legend was hidden in some other file. After he had taken over the dead Director's office, he had launched an exhaustive search for any slip of paper that might offer a hint of the agent's whereabouts. Nothing; apparently the late Director and his deputy had never considered the possibility of dying in the same plane accident, and had presumed the other would retain the secret.

The excuse for that lack of documentation about an important operation was its extreme sensitivity. The entire matter had been assigned to a single handler, the same assistant to Shelepin who had helped train the young agent for his implantation in the United States a generation before. Contrary to normal procedure, this handler was not required to report to a superior about the sleeper agent, because no contact at all was called for. In 1989, as the need for hiding assets became apparent to Communist Party officials, the control officer was dispatched to Barbados to resume control of Berensky. Davidov was able to infer that only from an examination of the control's expense accounts, not from any reports. After a massive initial transfer of funds and gold, years followed in which economic intelligence about Russia and from inside the United States was fed to the sleeper. Then, after the crash killed the KGB officials, not a word from the control about the operations of the sleeper or of his other field agent, the remaining mole in Washington.

The videocassette recorder beeped at him; the tape was rewound. He fingered the button that would bring back Liana Krumins but did not press it. He asked himself: was the supreme security protecting Berensky a wise precaution against exposure during the time of turmoil? Yes. But now, anxiety was rising in the Kremlin about the lack of supervision of the sleeper. The KGB, as presently constituted, did not know where its major overseas financial assets were; Davidov was certain of that. Did FI—once the KGB's foreign intelligence branch, now fiercely independent—know any more about Berensky? Davidov could not safely inquire. Did the Feliks people know? He had squeezed a few to no avail, and was offering others financial reward.

That fortune placed in the sleeper's hands to hide or to invest belonged to the Russian government, though some of the other former Soviet republics would lay claim to part of it; getting it back was Davidov's central KGB assignment. He had a fallback position, if recovery of the money proved impossible: to deny the fortune to the Feliks people.

He clicked off the power and buzzed for Yelena. "Step one is to find out more about the eighteen-year-old who had been selected for implantation in 1968," he told her. "Find me somebody in the American Village then who trained Aleks Berensky."

"Yes, Director. But that is not going to tell you where he is in America today. Or what happened to his control."

His assistant knew the KGB far better than he did, and Davidov was not above asking for advice. "How would you find him?"

"Control is dead or defected or turned by the CIA or stealing the money."

"Agreed. So?"

"Control had two agents, the sleeper and the mole. Foreign Intelligence knows who the mole is. We should establish contact with him."

Davidov shook his head. "Foreign Intelligence would have my head if I so much as asked about his identity." Definitely not a good idea for a new man, fresh from the academy; such inquiry would be used to cast suspicion on him as a bureaucratic empire-builder or a Western double agent. "Besides, we do not know if FI's Washington agent was ever in direct contact with Berensky. The mode of operation was to use the handler as the intermediary. The Washington mole was not to know Berensky's identity or vice versa." That was a guess, but he thought an informed one.

"What about our man at the Federal Reserve in New York?"

"He would be doubly cut out, twice removed from knowledge of the identity of the sleeper." And he did not want to stir bureaucratic anger by trying to communicate with that agent, either, at least for now. Yelena was trying hard, but not being helpful. And it could be she had a friend at FI; in this job, he could trust nobody. He dismissed her again, listened to the door shut, and clicked on the power.

He froze the tape at the frame that showed the deception of the stupid searchers, forcing his eyes away from the stiff nipple to her hand at her back. It reminded him how a deft magician worked his trick by distracting his audience, and he swore not to allow himself to be distracted by this deceptive young woman again.

Chapter 14

RIGA

Michael Shu, CPA, savored working on assignment for Irving Fein. The normal accounting life in New York required a suit and tie and was deskbound-dreary at times, but the interludes of research for Irving lit up his life's landscape.

Together, with Irving working the sources and Michael working the books, they had exposed wrongdoing in the government's commodity-financing schemes; had embarrassed the White House Chief of Staff in his family's ventures into Treasury-influenced businesses; had illuminated the maneuvering of a fugitive financier in the Bahamas who was running dope and guns through Panama; had made life miserable for a Federal Reserve Chairman for failing to follow up evidence of vast money movements financing illegal arms sales.

In all these prizewinning newspaper series and newsmagazine cover stories, Michael never asked for or received a byline. Media fame was for Irving to enjoy, and surely helped him open doors to other sources, but anonymity held no horrors for Michael. He took his pleasure in plumbing the lower depths of bureaucracies, where having a famous face or name would be an obstacle. His attraction was to the faceless people bearing secret grudges down below, smoldering not at abuse of power or policy misjudgments, but at short pay, lack of promotion, sexual harassment or rejection, or any of the mundane office grievances that led an unappreciated employee to take up the invitation to blow a very loud whistle.

Surely Irving was a cheapskate with his own money. Michael could charge a higher hourly rate for doing the tax returns of the clients of his four-man firm. And Irving demanded his tax returns be done gratis as a kind of commission for the borderline-profitable business he brought in. Bottom line: working with Irving didn't bring much to the bottom line.

But ah, the perks in journalism. Irving was extraordinarily generous when it came to expenses paid by a third party. Here was Michael Shu, whose father was a Vietnamese boat person and whose mother was an impoverished daughter of a Soviet diplomat who had defected to the U.S., seated in the garden of the best restaurant in Riga, Latvia, across the narrow street from the city's medieval tower. His hotel, a short stroll away, was the finest that the Baltic city had to offer, and was determinedly restoring itself after two generations of dreary Soviet occupation. The accountant took out his subnotebook computer, punched up his expense account to date, and tut-tutted at the extravagance some publisher would have to pay. Not in this city, so much—Riga was an inexpensive stop for the traveler, like nearby St. Petersburg—but Moscow cost a bundle.

The Hotel Metropole there had been worth it, though. Michael was not much at making contacts, but whenever he asked some midlevel bureaucrat at the Oil Ministry to breakfast at the great hall of the Metropole with the glass ceiling, he immediately had a date. Few of the Russians had ever been to the hard-currency palace before, or would likely be invited again. Michael offered them the opportunity to plunge into the lavish breakfast buffet—eggs, cheeses, blinis, yogurts, honey cakes—about which they could later regale envious colleagues. And Michael wasn't after contracts, which the low-level types could never deliver, or secret information, which they didn't have; all he wanted was a look at books and waybills that the bosses upstairs usually did not know existed, and the names of foreign banks and importers and shipping companies that had done business with the Soviet government in its dying days. What was wrong with telling anything about the USSR? It was another country, dead and gone.

He spoke their language. Passable Russian, yes, because his mother used it at home, but just as important was his understanding of the language of bookkeeping. He did not mind, left by himself in a roomful of records, turning page after page of accounts, sometimes looking for a specific shipment or transfer, more often just browsing, letting the records speak to him. The technology he brought along was useful, enabling him to scan lists of figures into his subnotebook, download-ing by modem to his New York office every night, but more useful was an inborn sense of what was missing, an attraction to the page or entry that was not there, like a black hole to an astronomer.

Michael was grateful that Irving had been ingenious enough to arrange a cover story that was fairly close to the truth. Deceit, even deviousness, was not Michael Shu's way. His City College chums had teased him for being a straight arrow, but he was proud of his hard-earned certification, and found himself stammering whenever he had to mislead anyone. "You could have been a master criminal," Irving once told him, "except you always get red in the face and go 'duh-duh-duh' when you try to lie. How do you manage to cheat on your wife? Only Chinaman I ever saw blush."

More recently, Irving had told him to fix the cover story in his mind: "You are an accountant working for an author writing a book about the richest man in the world. Who is it? We don't know yet. But the trail of a mysterious American billionaire leads to the old Soviet Union, because that's where communist officials were notoriously corrupt in arms and oil dealings. That will explain our interest in dealings in 1989 and the early nineties, when our boy made his first huge profits. You got it?"

Michael got it, repeated the cover story to himself, and was almost comfortable with it. Reporters did not have a license from the state of New York to protect. Certified public accountants did.

Sitting in the Baltic sunshine, Michael Shu communed with his two-pound computer, to him the most lightly pleasant of luncheon com-panions. He called it Irving.

The spreadsheet of his analysis of fund-flow charts from the Soviet central bank greeted him in infinite shades of color. The peak in the outflow of money had been in February of 1989, ostensibly in grain purchases; he would have to see if the harvest had been bad the year before, and if the Federal Reserve in New York showed funds coming from Moscow central. That could mean that the fund flow was corrupt. Then his friends in the lower echelons of Commodity Credit at Agri-culture could tell him where the hard currency came from, maybe gold transfers, and if there had been any suspicion of skimming, or "supplier commissions." The data were available, not secret, or at least not a big secret, but nobody crossed international lines to compare figures. The

East went its way in those days, the West the other way, each uninterested in preventing fraud in the other's domain. But by following the money now, he could spot the phony operators then, and discern the pattern of the sleeper's operation.

He stored that in Irving and called up his notes on a visit the day before to the *spetsfond*, the "special collection" in the library founded by Peter the Great. That trip to the Academy of Sciences in St. Petersburg had been an offbeat treat for a day off: it was where every book and publication that had been banned by the czars and the Soviets had been stored. The *spetsfond* was the world's largest collection of forbidden literature, from soft pornography to hard dissidence, a treasury of the Marxist politically incorrect.

But Shu's excursion turned out not to be a day off. When the accountant learned of the fire that had destroyed hundreds of thousands of books in late 1988, that struck him as no accident. He asked one of the librarians about catalogs of deposits to the library from the KGB dealing with money movement, or art treasure movement, or gold bullion transfers. She said she thought some items were on that subject, which she remembered because that was outside the ideology-suppressing mission of the library. Not all of those extraneous, hard-to-catalog files were destroyed in the fire; she recalled that some records had been taken to a meat-packing cold storage facility in the suburbs for safekeeping, along with fire-damaged and water-logged books. When Michael asked if he was the first to ask her about those records, the librarian—nice lady, happy to help—said no, a man from the Russian Atomic Energy Ministry had been around the week before to ask about published articles on the Cherlyabinsk-65 plutonium-processing complex in Siberia.

If I wanted to put aside a little money for a rainy day, Michael asked himself, and I had any asset in the country to choose from, what would I pick? Not diamonds; a few hundred million dollars' worth would upset the market, unless De Beers agreed to take them off your hands and off the market. Gold would be good; big enough market, asks no questions. Oil is fungible, valuable, and storable, but requires a series of fronts.

Stuff to make nuclear bombs? Hard to store, a bitch to transport, but a much-wanted asset in rogue nations. He jabbed the key on his computer to store his St. Petersburg trip, called up his dunno sheet—

an Irving Fein investigative-accounting device—and added a question about the portability of plutonium.

The subnotebook beeped and blinked a warning of low battery. Michael fished in his pocket for a couple of AA batteries, found none, but did not panic. Across the street, in the medieval tower basement, was a souvenir shop, where he was sure what he needed could be found. He was equally certain the place was infested with pickpockets preying on tourists. He put his paper across his plate to make sure nobody took his table and signaled to the waiter he'd be right back.

Clutching Irving tightly, he crossed the street and went into the ground-level shop. A customer was dickering over a long-lens camera; that struck Michael as a pretty expensive souvenir for Latvia, which specialized in knitted shawls and woodcarvings, but it turned out the man was just showing it to the proprietor. They shifted their attention to the subnotebook, admiring Irving's size, power, and ability to operate on batteries available anywhere; friendly people, spoke Russian, like most of the population of Riga. That's what bugged the Latvians, Michael knew: Stalin had Russified the country, pumping in hundreds of thousands of immigrants, while deporting Latvians to Siberia. The Latvian-Russian split in the country was now fifty-fifty, tilting heavily Russian in Riga; the newly independent Latvians were letting relatively few of the Russian-speaking residents vote. Irving—the reporter, not the computer—had told him the Feliks people were Russians who chose to operate in Latvia, unwelcome in Riga but safely out of the reach of Davidov's directorate of the KGB in Moscow.

He returned to the restaurant to find an elderly man seated at his table.

"Excuse me, but this is my table. I had to go across the street to the shop for a minute."

"I know. The photographer in that shop is taking pictures of us right now, as we are speaking." The man in the khaki jacket made a pouring motion to the waiter for a pot of tea. "He works for the Russian KGB."

Michael felt a thrill; now he was in the business. "Can he hear what we say?"

"No." The elderly man picked up the sugar bowl, emptied the packages onto the table, put them back one by one. "It is what they call a visual cover. They want to see who meets you. I want them to see me meeting you."

Irving had once instructed him never to ask questions of somebody who was trying to convey information. The way the reporter put it was "Never murder a man who's committing suicide," but that was his colleague's way of adding drama to a simple instruction.

"My name is Arkady Volkovich." He reached a hand across the table. "Let us pose shaking hands." Michael shook it cordially, wondering why this man wanted this picture together to be studied by Moscow.

"Why do I want us to be seen together?" Silence worked. "Because we have nothing to hide. You met Liana, our television news presenter, in the grand hall of the Metropole in Moscow. She suggested you come here and you would be contacted by one of us. No secrets."

"Who is 'us'?"

"We call ourselves the *organizatsiya*, a social group. You call us the Feliks people. The KGB, or Federal Security or whatever they call themselves now, suspect we may be plotting to drag the near abroad back into the old Soviet Union. That charge is a fiction, of course, but it gives the KGB what they need—an enemy and a purpose. It provides employment for many of their agents who would otherwise be out on the street."

"You mean it's all a matter of budgets?" Michael didn't believe him, but the story had a certain internal logic. The impression he had from Liana Krumins, however, was that the Feliks organization was large and strong, and that it was using her to try to get information out of the KGB files. He had been planning to pull up his notes about her and go over that fascinating Metropole dinner during dessert today; he had been saving it till last.

"Liana is not Russian," his tablemate said. "She broadcasts in Russian, her mother is Russian, but her late father was a Latvian and she is a true Latvian."

"Remarkable young woman."

"More than you know. She was the student leader in the underground campaign for independence. Because she speaks Russian, she was the liaison with the dissidents and reformers in Moscow and Pete. Because she also speaks some English, she was the movement's liaison with the Latvian émigrés in America."

So that was how Irving Fein had come to know her; all Irving had told him was that a female Latvian reporter would meet him at the hotel in Moscow and put him in touch with the Feliks people.

"None of us knew it at the time," Arkady was saying, talking freely, "but looking back, when she was nineteen years old, she was doing as much as anyone to begin the breakup of the Soviet Union. The key was here in the Baltic republics, where the Allies never recognized the Soviet annexation."

"She must have political ambitions," Michael offered, not asking a question.

His tablemate nodded, poking about in the sugar bowl for packets of artificial sweetener, which he pocketed. Maybe in his first search of the bowl he had been looking for a bugging device. "First she will become a person we all know in our homes on television every night. Then, within a decade, she will run for President of the United Baltic Republics, and lead them under the NATO umbrella." Arkady shook his head as if to admit the possibility of the unbelievable. "Did Liana tell you about her ambitions?"

"Didn't tell me anything of the sort. Nothing personal came up." Michael felt his face getting hot. Liana had been awfully frank about her future, but he hadn't sent that incidental intelligence about her grandiose political ideas on to Irving in New York. Nor was he about to confirm it to this stranger.

"Sounds crazy," his possible new ally summed up, "and I remember saying the same thing five years ago about her notions of independence for Latvia. How did your associate Fein become friendly with her?"

That, Michael knew instantly, was the question Irving had warned him not to answer. The truth was that Irving had stopped in Riga some years back doing a general piece on captive-nation dissidents and looked her up on a friend's tip. No coincidence; there weren't that many interesting young women journalists in Riga at the time who were getting into trouble with the authorities and who spoke English. Could be she was the only one in town at the time, so they met and had a few drinks and she filled him in. Journalism is a small world, like accounting. Then, when Riga became an important spot for this sleeper story, Irving had a Latvian contact in Liana Krumins.

Nobody in the intelligence world would ever believe something as simple as that. Better the KGB and the Feliks people should think Irving and Liana were in cahoots—Michael liked that term, Irving used it all the time—because it made Irving more of a player, maybe a front for the CIA or the FBI, maybe someone who had a hint about the sleeper's whereabouts. When you are a player, people come to you with information to trade, or at least with questions that give you leads. Irving always said that acting as if you knew more than you did gave you traction.

"I have no idea what started their relationship," Michael replied slowly. "It could have to do with their being in the same business. How did the Feliks people come to know her?"

"She has strong feelings against the KGB, as you know," said Arkady. "So do we." Michael knew that Irving wanted some inkling as to why the mafiya types were using this particular journalist, but the accountant got the feeling that Arkady did not know.

"Yeah, I got the impression she wasn't friendly with the KGB."

"You want to find this Russian in America who knows where are some hidden monies belonging to the former Soviet republics, including Latvia. So do we. How can we help you?"

Michael Shu was ready. "The Baltic states swapped food and manufactured goods to the central Gosplan for electricity and oil. There must have been an imbalance. How was it resolved? Where are the records of the swaps? Do you have any connections with the bank in Helsinki who can tell me of transactions from '88 to '91? Your association of young businessmen—Riga's Group of Fifty—who's their investment banker in New York? And do you know a person, low-level, I can see at your central bank tomorrow who monitors wire transfers?"

That was for starters. He watched Arkady Volkovich draw out an old-fashioned pencil and write the questions down in a pocket notebook, battered but ergonomic in its way. Michael wished the representative of the Feliks people would hurry; he wanted to go back to his hotel room and set up a videocassette recorder so he could make a tape of Liana's Riga evening newscast to send to Irving.

Chapter 15

"Do I have to read a fax intercept of an American accountant to find out about KGB records in the *spetsfond*?" Davidov was seething. "Cherlyabinsk-65 plutonium was a find you considered unimportant? Do you realize we are up against a global operation that is stealing our resources? Or have you gone over to their side?"

The public prosecutor was rattled, as Davidov intended the man to be.

"We had no idea those KGB files were at the Academy of Sciences, Nikolai Andreyevich. Neither did you. It is a huge library—nobody knows what has been filed where. Books, ledgers, are still being found in industrial refrigerators where they were put after the fire."

The new KGB official slammed his leather jacket down on the conference table, upsetting the glasses of tea.

"This is not the Kirov murder or the 'doctors' plot' or the execution of Czar Nicholas. I am not talking about ancient history. I am talking about the records of payments that a spy who was working for us made to numbered accounts in Swiss banks only a few years ago."

"Those accounts were closed. The money disappeared," the prosecutor said, blotting the tea with his napkin.

"But we owned one of the private banks through a Swiss designee," Davidov charged, unsure of his facts but dressing his guess in authority. "At least there we should know where the money went."

"We should, but there was a suicide in Bern last month." Davidov's guess had been on the mark. "The bank is out of business, and the records were not found in the suicide's home." He shrugged hopelessly.

Davidov suspected that the sleeper agent, Berensky, had arranged for the murder of the Swiss front man whose numbered accounts included more than $3 billion in gold.

"You are certain it was a suicide? When did it take place?"

The prosecutor said the Swiss authorities had closed the case. He consulted his notebook and read off a date. Davidov nodded; it was two weeks after the control officer was killed in Barbados, fifteen days after the airplane death of his predecessor as head of the Fifth Directorate. Berensky had moved quickly and ruthlessly to cut off all possibility of contact.

That murder in Bern, committed or arranged for by the sleeper, was not even suspected by the prosecutor, who had bought the Swiss police's explanation; Berensky or his accomplice was evidently skillful in faking a suicide and buying official unconcern.

Davidov was growing fearful at the extent of what he did not know about the sleeper spy or his method of operation. Worse, he was coming to doubt the ability of the organization he headed to cope with the complexity of the man's maneuvers and of his crimes. The KGB's "international sources" at the moment were not the four thousand foreign operatives in place, reporting to the Foreign Intelligence Service, no longer under KGB control. On the contrary, the source of this specific information was one American accountant of Russo-Vietnamese extraction whose daily data dumps to a journalist in New York was stretching the KGB's conception of the investigation. The list of questions apparently code-named "the Dunno excrement" was especially troubling to Davidov, because they dealt with possible assets far beyond the KGB's current understanding of how much money had originally been transferred to the sleeper.

The prosecutor, chosen by Davidov's predecessor, had no grasp of the potential danger. "We have a simple case of theft," he said. "The biggest theft in history. Rubles worth three billion dollars, transferred in bullion from the central bank depository here to the bank in Bern."

"Where are the missing gold bars?"

"We have the date of inventory that disclosed the shortfall," said the prosecutor, "and the guards are under extended interrogation."

"Leading nowhere so far."

"Maybe your missing agent was the recipient, maybe not. First we have to pick up the trail here. Police work is not as certain as in your academic world."

Davidov ignored the dig; the prosecutor would have to be replaced, but for now, circumvented. He snatched his tea-stained jacket and went to the local KGB headquarters. The handler for Arkady Volkovich, the KGB's agent within the Feliks organization, was waiting for him.

"Arkady reports he was sent by Madame Nina to meet the accountant Shu at the Tower restaurant in Riga yesterday," the handler reported. "Open café meeting."

"We gave him cover?"

"Everybody in the neighborhood saw our photographer keeping them under surveillance. Here is the transcript from the wire we had on Arkady."

Davidov assumed the Feliks people had another transcript from their own wire; there were financial efficiencies in a double agent. The questions asked by Shu were outlined by yellow marker; they corresponded to the list code-named "Dunno" sent out by the accountant last night.

The KGB chief was dismayed; his investigators, forty of them on this case, were not up to asking sophisticated questions like Shu's. Global financial manipulation requiring computer tracking was foreign to traditional KGB operations. The longtime Soviet need to control all information from the center—rooted in the Kremlin's fear of instant samizdat through personal computer networks—had limited the number of the new machines in the former Soviet Union; as a result, aptitude in what the Americans called "hacking" had not been developed in Russia in the late eighties. Today some Russian agents were placed in overseas banks to support industrial espionage payoffs, but even that was under Foreign Intelligence, beyond KGB reach. All the while that communists had prided themselves on the use of political fronts, capitalists in the West had quietly perfected financial fronts.

That made the sleeper in America all the more important; Berensky was one of the few Russians who knew the tricks of money manipulation and vast embezzlement at the moment in the recent past when such knowledge was vital to preserving the secret assets of the collapsing Soviet state. Davidov shook his head at the folly of entrusting so much money to one man and his vulnerable control. But that was not the half of it; the KGB did not have agents who knew how to police the international financial markets and stock exchanges, or who understood the methods necessary for recovering the fortune the sleeper was stealing.

"It would help me," Arkady's handler prodded, "to know the direction we are taking with our double agent." The handler was a professional just graduated from the ranks of field agent, and not one of the old crowd; Davidov almost trusted him.

"The Feliks organization is using this television presenter Liana Krumins," Davidov briefed, "as a front." Highlights of the film showing the nubile Latvian's front fast-forwarded through his mind. "They are hoping she will get information from us and our files that will help them to find the sleeper they think of as their man, because they planted him in the U.S. when they ran the KGB."

"They have lost contact with him, too?"

"He does not want to be found by any of us. Yet."

"I have a theory, sir. The sleeper and his handler decided to betray a Soviet Union that no longer exists, and to go into business for themselves."

Davidov could not bring himself to think that a child of Shelepin himself, inculcated with the visions and values of the old KGB, spending half a lifetime preparing himself for a mission, would in the end turn against his people for selfish gain. Or even worse, ally himself with an organization like the Feliks people, dedicated to snatching back power from the elected representatives of the Russian people. The likelihood, Davidov calculated, was that Berensky was at this moment weighing the alternatives, waiting to see if the government was stable or if the Feliks people would become a useful counterforce.

"Put this into your theory," he told Arkady's handler. "The Krumins woman is the contact of the American reporters Shu and Fein, whose business may be an American intelligence proprietary."

"So we are looking for the sleeper by watching the Feliks *avtoritet,*" the handler said quickly, showing he understood. "And the Feliks people are looking for their man by following the television reporter who is working with the American media, which is an arm of the CIA."

"You have it," said Davidov, admiring the symmetry. "Here, just beyond our reach in the Baltics, the old Soviet KGB crowd is tied in with mafiya thugs and is using the Latvian media to find the man with the money. Over there, the CIA is probably using the American media to find the same man."

"Does it not make us appear impotent," said the young handler, with a touch of arrogance, "to be following other organizations instead of finding the sleeper ourselves?"

The truth was as bad as it sounded. "We have been at the end of the parade," Davidov admitted. "Now we are going to lead it. We will set up a team that will find the sleeper in America on our own."

All very neat, but who in the CIA had chosen Fein, a frequent critic of the Agency whose stories had cost it budget cuts, to lead a search for the sleeper? Was Fein's a redundant or a rogue operation duplicating the CIA's own probe? And why did the Feliks organization choose to work through Liana, an independent and politically unreliable young woman who knew nothing about international fraud? And why would she so readily consent to work for the worst elements of Russian society?

In his academic field of epistemology, the study of knowledge, a central question was always "How do we know what we know?" That leads to "How do we recognize what we think we know is untrue?" He had not even approached that in this case; he was still trying to get a handle on what he did not know. And to find that out, where in Russia was he going to find a team of experts that could cope with a runaway cryptocapitalist financial brain?

Davidov rode alone in his car to the airport, uncertain of his organization's ability to counter a threat it had never faced before. If the Fein-Shu trackers found the sleeper first, Davidov could not survive the terrible embarrassment of a Russian government pleading for a return of the $3 billion plus assets in America. If the Feliks-Liana track found him first—and if the cache had grown substantially, which the Americans seemed to think—the Feliks movement would use those assets to undermine the state's economy, overthrow its government, and revive Russian despotic imperialism.

But until he could put a sophisticated financial team in place, Davidov was confined to following the followers. For his own and his President's survival, he had to identify and recover what could possibly be a vast array of stolen assets. He found it hard to believe that the KGB could not find out who its own sleeper was. Files could be expunged; records could be stolen; the keepers of secrets could die; but people remained in this vast bureaucracy with memories that no computer could erase.

Davidov boarded the train to Moscow, following that train of thought: if information about the sleeper in America was being kept from him, then the Feliks challenge went deeper than he had originally thought. The KGB would be effectively penetrated, not by a foreign service, but by disloyalists within. He could never mount a serious effort to find the worldwide assets until he crushed the clique that was protecting the sleeper.

He telephoned Yelena from the Moscow train station; he wanted the head of Section K of the Fifth Directorate to be waiting in his office when he arrived.

Chapter 16

Yasenovo was the old Soviet imitation of CIA headquarters in Langley, Virginia. A half mile outside Moscow's outer ring, equivalent to what Washington called its Beltway, twin twenty-two-story buildings rose in proud nonsecrecy in a suburban setting. For an agent far out in the field, to be "in the woods" of Yasenovo was to be at the epicenter of intelligence activity, at the source of all concerns.

"I find it inconceivable that you have been unable to find your own agent." He remained standing behind his Finnish-made desk in his wood-paneled office and did not invite his subordinate to sit down.

"The sleeper's handler made sure there were no files—"

"People here have memories. You were in the First Chief Directorate for fourteen years. You knew people there who go back to Shelepin's time, before Andropov. Somebody who worked for you knows Berensky. I want to know."

When Foreign Intelligence was separated from the KGB in Yeltsin's early days, responsibility for counterintelligence had been left in the KGB, part of the Federal Security Ministry. In the past, the combined operation had had stunning success: the Soviet mole in the CIA, Aldrich Ames, worked for KGB foreign intelligence, sending back information about American agents in Moscow. KGB counterintelligence would then pick them up, turn them, and send to the Americans whatever intelligence Moscow wanted implanted in the minds of strategic planners. The two units nicely complemented each other, resulting in the misleading of the American government about the size and health of the weak Soviet economy for a decade. Of course, the KGB's brilliant success backfired: when the Americans were misled into believing the Soviets were getting stronger, the Reagan hard-liners sped up the arms race, forcing the Kremlin to spend more until the Soviet economy buckled under the strain.

Now it was different. Internal security personnel at the KGB distrusted the independent Foreign Intelligence empire, and Davidov distrusted his own men in internal security. That made it triply difficult for Davidov, a relative newcomer, to track down the sleeper, an agent who might be defecting or absconding.

"Easy for you to say, Davidov, but this was held more closely than any other case."

"Your handler of the sleeper—who did he report to?"

"Control had only two agents. One was the mole in Washington—on him, the handler reported to FI, not to us. The other was the sleeper, investing the money. Control reported to us on the sleeper, directly to the Director or his deputy, both now dead. That's the way it always was. This particular handler had an arrangement first in the sixties with Shelepin, then with Director Andropov. Nobody else knew who his agent was."

"I cannot believe that," Davidov snapped. "Now what's all this about Barbados?"

"The handler was last seen checking into a hotel there, a bungalow on the beach. There was an explosion and fire, nothing identifiable left. We can't say for certain the few body parts that were found were the control's, but it's probable."

"How do we know he was there?"

"The day before, Moscow Central informed him of the death of the Director and his deputy in the plane crash. The control acknowledged in code. He was there, probably to meet the sleeper or his Washington penetration agent."

"Forget the mole—the deaths in the crash only have significance to the sleeper. Your man examined the hotel register?"

"Of course, Director. Apparently nobody else checked in that night or the night before. The manifests of aircraft arriving tell us nothing. One man died; no trace of another."

Davidov was sure he knew what had happened: when Berensky was told by his control of the death of the two officials in the KGB who knew his identity, the sleeper had killed the handler and the banking contact in Bern, thereby establishing total freedom of action. He

changed the subject: "You have forty-eight hours to find out everything about Aleksandr Berensky's background in Russia. His family, his
past, up to the time he left on his assignment."

"We've been trying—"

"I wonder. You know where the sleeper was trained, who were his
trainers, where they are now. You should know who prepared his new
documents, who taught him his legend. Only if you have the answer
for me day after tomorrow will you remain in the employ of Federal
Security."

"We will redouble our efforts." He spun and strode out.

Davidov went to the window facing away from the ring road, toward
the artificial lake, and contemplated the bucolic setting chosen by an
architect who, in those days, could build and landscape anything he
wanted. Unlike his counterpart at America's huge new "reconnaissance
center" in Virginia, he had not had to conceal exorbitant construction
figures in another agency's budget; when so much else was secret, no
cost overruns had to be kept secret. Those days of vodka and mushrooms were gone now, for both agencies; when the masseuse downstairs in the KGB health club turned out to be running a brothel and
had to be fired, new budgetary restraints kept her from being replaced.

To Yelena, who had listened in on his meeting with his insubordi-
nate, Davidov said: "Now we know what happened. Control was
informed of the crash and realized he was the only one who knew the
sleeper's identity. When the two met, he suggested they split the
fortune and defect. And Berensky killed him."

"Or Berensky suggested that, and the handler said no, and Berensky
killed him."

Possible. Davidov added another: "Or the handler laid out the
scheme, the sleeper objected on patriotic grounds, and the handler
killed Berensky."

"You don't believe that, Nikolai Andreyevich."

"No. The sleeper is a global financier, and a man driven by powerful
purpose. He has no restrictions whatever on carrying out his mission. I
think he learned from his control that everyone who knew his identity
had died in the crash, and he decided to take advantage of the opportunity for total isolation. He killed the handler and he is now deciding
what to do with the money." Davidov was almost certain that Berensky, as a dedicated Soviet man, his culture more communist than Rus-

sian, would lean toward enriching the Feliks people, using the fortune to destabilize the government in Moscow. He had to stop that at all costs.

"I want everything we have on the Krumins woman."

"Not the videotape again. It will wear out."

He ignored that. "Her birth certificate, passport, work papers, the surveillance reports, everything. We photocopied the Berensky file she asked to see, did we not? Beforehand?"

"Yes. And we made an inventory. I have the copy of the document she stole. I have analyzed her dossier carefully, if there is a fact you want to know immediately."

He tested her. "When was she born and where?"

"December fifteenth, 1968, in Riga, Latvian Republic of the USSR. The birth certificate of Liana Maria Krumins is a transcribed copy; I am trying to find the original."

"Find it." There were often revealing discrepancies in transcribed documents. "Parents?"

"Her mother is Antonia Krumins, a ballet instructor of Russian descent now living in Riga. Her father was Ojars Krumins, architect, Latvian, died fourteen years ago."

"Ages at the time of her birth?"

"Mother was seventeen, father was forty."

Odd, but it accounted for Liana's Russian-Latvian bilingual ability. "Where did she learn English?"

"From a man she lived with in the independence movement. At school, she was a brilliant student, declined Komsomol membership."

"Go on."

"Troublemaker, marijuana trafficker, dissident. Jailed after an illegal independence rally, but was let go the next morning; her fellow protesters were held one to three months."

"Why was she released so quickly?"

"Don't know." Yelena went on: "Expelled from university in 1988. Became spokeswoman for the independence movement, learned English to deal with Western press, broadcast on an opposition radio station. After the breakup of the Union, Krumins became a radio and then television news presenter, her current employment. Respected by her colleagues, big audience on the air."

"Lovers?"

"Lived with dissident writer for two years, threw him out, had affair with married political leader, may be still going on. Apparently attracted to older men, but treats all men like dirt. They seem to love it."

Davidov did not let himself smile. "Stick to what the files tell you. Why do you think she was chosen by the Feliks people to do their digging?"

"She's perfect for it. Journalist's credentials. Unafraid. Three languages. Striking appearance, so easy to follow or trace. And a good researcher, too."

"And why did she agree to work with them?"

"She probably had contact with the American journalist Irving Fein, when he came through here a few years ago. He could be a CIA front."

That last guess did not satisfy him. And epistemological training caused him to sense a deception in the May-December marriage on her birth certificate. Moreover, there had to be more to her selection by the Feliks people—a former lover in the inner council, perhaps. She had wide experience for a woman not yet in her late twenties. "Where is she now?"

"Here in Moscow. In Lubyanka, with the archivist in his office. This time he's awake."

Davidov was surprised to learn she was at hand. From his closed-circuit monitor in Yasenovo, he punched up the Lubyanka screen, skipped through several channels, and found her talking to the archivist.

"Yelena, where is the Krumins girl likely to go next?"

"She has asked for the Shelepin family records," the analyst said. "They're on the fourth floor, in the Chekists' Study Room."

He was familiar with that room, dominated by a heroic portrait of the founder of the Soviet secret police, "Iron Feliks" Dzerzhinsky.

"Make sure nobody is in there, and be certain no tape is made, audio or video. No surveillance at all, you understand? Tell the archivist to keep her waiting for an hour." He could be in Moscow in thirty minutes. "Tell my driver I want to go in to Lubyanka right away. Run down the original of her birth certificate—I want to see that—and hand me her file."

"The extra document is in, Nikolai Andreyevich."

There were three thick folders. "All this on a woman so young?"
"She was a troublemaker."

Liana Krumins stopped at the open doorway of the file room; a man was inside, hunched over the contents of three files spread out at the end of a long table. A low lamp lit the papers but kept his face in shadows, but he seemed youngish, with a flowing mustache in the Stalin style. An expensive black leather jacket, with the zippers and metal buttons that the fashionable set had been affecting in Moscow the last few years, hung over the chair behind him. He was wealthy or had family connections or both.

She entered, looked at the slip in her hand, went to the cabinet with the files on the Shelepin family. The numbered folder was there. An inventory sheet—done on a typewriter, which meant recently—included a cross-reference to another folder about the Berensky family, but did not give its file number. She took two Shelepin family folders out of the cabinet; they were heavy, and hit the table with a thud.

"Shhh," said the man.

"Shhh yourself," she replied. She had as much right to be here as he did.

"I'm trying to concentrate. This is important work."

She glared at him, pulled up a chair with a loud scraping noise, and went to work on her quest. She was looking for any reference to Anna Berensky, Shelepin's private secretary in his early days at the KGB, or their illegitimate son Aleks, who she suspected was the young man that some of the Feliks people sent to America when they dominated the KGB. The cryptic cross-reference in the file to a Berensky family supported her theory.

Five minutes later, the man at the end of the table looked up and said, "I apologize. I was rude to you."

She nodded her acceptance, slowly turning over another document. A handsome man, and she liked the strong black mustache, but a fool; how could he not know that these rooms were not only bugged but televised?

"I'm looking for the truth about a fascinating woman," he said, tapping the papers before him.

She rolled her eyes toward the ceiling, the universal signal of warning about surveillance.

"Oh, that." He rose, went to the mirror on the far wall, removed it from its hook, and put it on the floor. He then hung his jacket over the lens that the one-way mirror had concealed. He came toward her—moving with grace, like an athlete or a dancer—reached under the table, and pulled out a small microphone, snapping its wire with a short jerk. "Mustn't forget the audio backup. Now we're alone."

"You're going to get us in trouble. The guards will notice the blackout and be here in a minute." The man was a fool.

"Relax, I work here. I'm new, but I frighten the file clerks. Name is Nikolai." He extended his hand. She shook it firmly, as always; he had a strong hand, sensitive fingers. Instead of being a fool, he was a charmer, which put her doubly on guard. He was not wearing a pass; she asked where it was. He pulled out his wallet and showed her his ministry identification: Nikolai Andreyevich Davidov, All Floors. She interpreted that to mean he was no minor functionary. The picture showed him smiling; she had never seen a pass of any kind, even a passport, with a person smiling. She waited for his questions.

He went back to his end of the table, tapped the papers. "Fascinating, what you can learn from these. Frightening, too—in the old days, they wasted God knows how much time and money following innocent people, listening, compiling dossiers."

She pointed to his coat hanging on the lens and the ripped-out wire on the table. "Only in the old days?"

"You're right. Some of these are recent," he said, caressing the file. "But most of the reports were in the late eighties, when she was working subversively for independence."

"Where?"

"Baltics."

Probably somebody Liana knew, perhaps in Estonia; more women were trusted there by the independence movement leaders than in Latvia. "I worked for Latvian independence," she said forthrightly. It was no secret. "Maybe I know her."

He motioned her over.

On top of the file's contents was a picture of a room in what seemed like a political headquarters, a familiar sight, with a dozen or so people working on mimeograph machines in the days before photocopiers and faxes. She knew some of the faces, and looked closer. The man she had lived with at the time was in the center. It was their headquarters.

She pushed the picture aside to see the one underneath. There was her own face in the photograph, elated, the night the Americans recognized Latvian independence, holding out a bottle of champagne. A moment later, she remembered, she had poured the champagne over the head of her coworker. To the left of the pictures she saw an official document, a birth certificate in Russian, a copy of which she had at home.

"This is my file," she breathed.

"Of course, Liana Krumins. That's why we're here."

Despite the violation of her privacy, she would not let him intimidate her. "Move over," she said. "I want to look."

First, the old pictures. Her mother and father, Antonia and Ojars Krumins, on their wedding day, a brown picture in an oval mat. She had seen it before, on her mother's dressing table when she was young, but this was a slightly different pose; the photographer had given the second picture to the KGB. A high school graduation photo that the whole class bought, but another candid shot with her history teacher that she had never seen before; he was the one—gentle, malleable—she had chosen to end her virginity. A woman friend of her mother's standing at the ballet practice bar; she had come to the house often when Liana was young. A tall man she did not know standing in front of a house she did not recognize; why was that in her file?

The old documents. Application for a driver's license. A letter to her school director apologizing for leading a demonstration for better food in the cafeteria and asking not to be expelled.

Newer documents. The expulsion order from university, with backup reports from fellow students that she had not been permitted to see. Application, with DENIED stamped on top, for a visa to a media conference in Helsinki, where she had hoped to meet Western reporters. She flipped through to see who had informed on her, and her heart sank; her best girlfriend. They were still close; Liana had helped her get a job at the station. Her mind found it hard to accept such continual betrayal.

The arrest papers and booking at the prison in Riga after the rally. The memory of that building seized her: the KGB headquarters had previously been the Nazi headquarters during the war. It was the most dreaded place in Latvia.

"Just a short stay," he noted, his finger under the date of discharge. "Overnight. The others must have been greater offenders."

Not so; but she had been the only young woman among the ringleaders. A guard said, "This one needs a bath," doused her, fully dressed, with a bucket of water, and pushed her into a solitary cell with a harsh overhead light and a chair but no bed. The January night was below freezing. She had to strip off her sweater and shirt and jeans and wring them out and hope they dried before she froze to death. An hour later, exhausted from moving around the tiny room and rubbing her naked skin where it was turning blue, she looked up to see a uniformed KGB officer enter. He said she had the choice of staying in the cold cell or coming upstairs to share a warm bed with him. She accepted his kind of invitation, and even as he brutalized her, she counted herself lucky to survive. Before dawn, she was released. She did not hate him; he had kept his word, and she never forgot her unsolicited instruction on how sex could be useful.

"No," she told today's KGB representative, "it's just that I found a friend."

"Some friend." He was reading a document that had been attached to the arrest paper. "Says here you were released because you testified against the others you were arrested with, and provided a list of names to be rounded up."

She snatched the document and read it, choking with anger at the damning detail, none of it true. "This is a lie. I never gave him any of this. He never even asked for names."

"Let me see who signed that."

Reluctantly, she handed the official document back to him. It would follow her the rest of her life. The existence of it in this file was an invitation to blackmail, useful to anyone who wanted to bring her low and besmear her too-early patriotism.

"Ah, I've heard of him," Davidov said. "This was a favorite trick of his to take advantage of women prisoners. It worked, too—none of them ever complained about rape, and none of his superiors wondered why he released some prisoners early. He's no longer with the new KGB. I think he's one of the Feliks people." He set the document aside.

Liana, livid at the outrage in the past that would threaten her career in the future, continued through the file. Toward the back, where the most recent additions were placed, the handwritten papers changed to typed reports of surveillance. A night spent at the apartment of an incumbent political leader, and the next night in the rooms of the opposition leader; that evidence was true enough, and not immoral or illegal, but might be hard to explain if someone wanted to charge her with using her body to get her information. In truth, she enjoyed the interplay of the two men and never revealed any of one's political secrets to the other.

There was the last month's register of all the telephone numbers she dialed from her home. She saw one surveillance document dated only the week before—"Meeting with Michael Shu, defector's son, now U.S. citizen, accountant and possible CIA investigator"—and leaned back from the table. Now she knew why this man was in the room with her.

"Proceed with your interrogation," she said with dignity.

He signaled with upraised hands that he was not about to step into that trap. "And have you go back to Riga and go on the air to tell about how you were interrogated by the bullies of the KGB?" He shook his head. "No, thanks, Miss Krumins." He pointed to the portrait of Iron Feliks on the wall over the fireplace. "His day is over."

She picked up one of the videotapes, a white label across the back reading KRUMINS VISIT SHELEPIN FILES and the date. She put it down and picked up the next: KRUMINS VISIT BERENSKY FILES, KRUMINS SEARCH BY LUBYANKA GUARDS. The skin around her neck reddened as she looked directly at him: "You saw these?"

He nodded. She was doing the questioning, which apparently did not disturb him. She hefted the second box of tape in her hand.

"What did this show you?"

"The first part shows a commission of a minor crime, the theft of a document from the files. The second part shows you being searched by the guards, doing their duty after being told of possible theft. They properly offered to detain you until a female guard came on duty, which you declined."

"A lens like that, was it?" She pointed to his jacket hanging over the lens on the wall. "In front of me? Did you get the full view?"

"From the side. Not the full view."

"Then you saw I was innocent. I stole nothing."

"All that could be charged is that you removed a letter from one room—no doubt of that, it's right on the tape—and left it somewhere else on the premises. It's a minor infraction, as I said. Don't worry about it. They won't even take away your library card."

"Why are you letting me see my own file? That's never done. Why are you here with me now? What do you want?"

"I hate interrogations," he said. "I always confess in the end."

She smiled nervously. "Stop playing with me. Tell me what you want."

"You are conducting a legitimate search for a story you can show on television," Davidov said, his voice gentle, almost as if he were not conducting an interrogation. "The story has to do with a KGB agent you have been told is in America. I cannot say if it is true or not. We don't discuss those things." He awaited another question, which she took as an invitation to draw him out.

"What can you discuss about it?"

"What concerns me is that you are letting yourself be used by a group whose interests are not your own. We know, and you know we know"—he indicated the recent surveillance reports—"about the Feliks *organizatsiya*. These are not your people, Miss Krumins. These are the people you fought against ever since you were a schoolgirl."

"How can you be sure I am not using them?"

"Ah, that's it—you think you are. But they are manipulating you, sending you in here, arranging for you to meet the American investigator at the Metropole." He lightened. "Wonderful breakfast buffet, wasn't it, under the great glass ceiling? More European than Russian, except for the damn herring."

"You want me to break off contact with one of my sources, is that it?"

He shook his head as if it hurt. "You will do what you want. But won't you even consider the possibility that you are being used as a pawn by a group whose values you do not share?"

"Their information has been accurate so far. And Nikolai—I am onto a big story."

She thought she might use his worry about her association with the Feliks people as a lever to pry open the KGB; curiously, his half-smile seemed to say he liked that—unless it was a reaction to her artful first use of his first name, remembered from his credential.

"Perhaps I could persuade my colleagues," he suggested, "to be more helpful in finding the person you seek. But they would not want to aid the old apparatchiks—Madame Nina, Arkady Volkovich, that whole group of reactionaries. So long as you are with them, you are consorting with the enemy. The world has turned upside down, Liana—the new KGB is not your enemy."

She touched the second videotape box. "I heard the old KGB had cameras everywhere in the Hotel Berlin next door, taking pictures of foreigners in sexual acts, to compromise them. You say you have changed, then?"

"Unfair. The search of you was a reasonable precaution. And the only copy of that tape is the one you hold in your hand."

"It does not please me, knowing that these pictures of me with my clothes off may be played for the amusement of your colleagues."

"Steal it," he said. "Take a deep breath, stick it in the waistband under the back of your blouse. I understand that's the best place to hide it. Then walk past the guards. They'll never notice it."

At that, she reddened again. "No. You will take it and walk out with me." She looked hungrily at the release document on the table, set aside from the file. Its lies could ruin her. She knew how she felt about the friend she had discovered had betrayed her; she knew how all her friends in the former underground would feel if that paper were available to searchers of files. "Do you suppose that's the only copy of that?"

He inspected it closely. "It's the original. They didn't have copying machines in Riga then. A handwritten copy wouldn't be proof of anything."

She wondered if he was going to offer a warm bed in trade; that was her experience of the KGB way.

"Push over that big ashtray," Davidov said. He placed the document in it and lit it with his cigarette lighter, and they watched the sheet flare and burn to a crisp. She flicked her fingers along the top of her short hair and wondered what he wanted in return. If it was a night together, that would not be such a humiliation, except for the principle of it; he was an attractive man.

The KGB official lifted his jacket off the wall, made a face in the lens, and replaced the mirror. He beckoned to her to follow him out of the room, tossing an airy salute to the stern face of Iron Feliks. As he led her out of the building, the guards stiffened to attention. He led the way through the X-ray search, tape openly in hand.

Outside, Davidov handed the tape to her with an avuncular admonition: "Think twice about letting the Feliks people use you. If you need me, my numbers are on this card, office and home." He wrote in his fax number, she presumed for emphasis.

"This cannot be the only copy," she said, looking at the tape in her hand.

"I do not deny looking at it more than once," he replied. "It shows that you are in some ways a beautiful woman, and you have a ballerina's flair for suggestive movements that exquisitely deceive. You can believe me or not, but it is the only copy. And it does not belong in Lubyanka."

"I choose to believe you." She did not, but shook his hand firmly. Frowning afterward, she wondered what he meant by "in some ways" beautiful.

He flexed his fingers, liking the memory of the feel of her hand: on the bony side, long fingers, no-nonsense pressure and quick release. He also liked her calculated choice of words in "choosing" to believe him, which she did not, of course.

Davidov crossed his arms at the top of the steps at the front door and watched her walk past the Kazakh street merchants around the square. Hers were the long strides of the purposeful walker, rhythmic but not undulating, a woman certain she was being watched by the man she just left. Davidov knew he was not alone in the watching; he observed the Feliks shadow openly picking her up and the KGB shadow subtly picking up the Feliks shadow.

He felt noble at giving up the tape showing her fine figure in its nudity; as far as he knew, it really was the only copy. He was certain the fake release document he had burned had no copies; Yelena had created it only that morning, at his instructions, to be placed in Liana's file—a piece of disinformation worthy of Shelepin, the power-purist who had raised that form of deception to a high art before he was deposed by a General Secretary fearful of his discipline.

Davidov took the elevator back to the Cheka room's floor. Hands in his pockets, jacket over his shoulders, the economic intelligence chief looked first at the ashes in the glass ashtray and then directed his gaze at the portrait of Iron Feliks, whose Ozymandian statue no longer dominated the square outside, and whose feared name had been obliterated from street signs and maps.

In a sense, the sleeper was Dzerzhinsky's direct descendant. Willing murderer, ideologue of authority, organizational genius, visionary— the strain ran from Iron Feliks through Shelepin to the man hidden in America assembling the economic power to destabilize a nation and deliver it back to the legatees of the unbroken Cheka line.

"The Director never does any fieldwork," Yelena protested to Davidov. "Why are you doing this? If the Director makes a mistake, there can be no review."

Davidov nodded. "Some American foreign service officers do not like summit meetings. They say, if the President misses the tackle, there is no one between him and the goal line."

She was not familiar with the American football metaphor. "Remember how our dangle took in Casey himself, and the whole CIA was a laughingstock? That could happen to us, with you doing fieldwork yourself."

He shrugged. She was right, but the time spent with Liana Krumins had been the most enjoyable hour he had spent in months.

"You wanted the original birth certificate of this woman," she said. "Here it is. The facts on the replacement copy in the file are identical, down to the hour she was born."

He laid the two documents side by side, verified that, then examined the original. Davidov, trained in the more practical aspects of epistemology, was attuned to anomalies, and here was one plain to see. All the facts of name, date, hour, hospital were in one handwriting in one color ink, but the name in the space for father was in a lighter shade. The father's name—a Latvian name—was filled in by another hand, days or months later, seeking to imitate the other handwriting. There was no erasure or other alteration; the space had been left blank, presumably until a suitable father could be found, and then the name, Ojars Krumins, had been written in by the registrar of births.

"What name should have been there?"

"I am willing to bet the name is Aleks Berensky, the bastard son of Shelepin and his private secretary." He put it in a way that would strike home to his assistant. "It's as if you and I had a child, Yelena, and I send you off to Latvia to marry a respectable husband and bring up the boy. But I keep my eye on that boy, of course—he's my natural son—and when he grows up and marries unwisely and impregnates that unsuitable girl against my wishes, I am angry at him."

It fell into place in his mind as he explained it. "The son is now eighteen, a reluctant father himself, and tired of the girl he married. He realizes he has nearly wrecked his career. But I, his father, tell him that there is hope for him. He could have a new life on a most important and exciting assignment. He could be trained and sent to America under deepest cover, with no contact with any other agents, to make a career until he is called upon to serve his country."

"His wife and baby?"

"After Shelepin's son accepts the assignment, the wife becomes an inconvenience to the State, especially since she wants to bear the baby. Aleks drops out of sight, becomes a nonperson, trains at our American Village. The unwanted wife has her baby. Shelepin sends the rejected mother away from Moscow to Latvia, arranging for some Latvian to marry her, or at least to raise her daughter as his daughter. His name, Krumins, goes on the space left blank for father on the birth certificate."

Yelena nodded. "And Shelepin's son, Aleks Berensky, has no ties to anyone in Russia." She thought about that. "Possible. In the sixties, the Director of the KGB could do anything. He provided a good marriage for his secretary, Anna, when their son, Aleks, was born; he could easily have done almost the same for the son's wife when she became, as you say, inconvenient."

"I am willing to bet that the man once named Aleks Berensky is the sleeper agent now in America." He waited for the import of that guess to sink in.

"Then you are saying," said Yelena, finally catching up with him, "that Liana Krumins is the sleeper's daughter."

Davidov felt, for the first time in his brief tenure, that he was truly the chief of a directorate of the state security agency. "That is a useful piece of information for us to have. The Feliks people have connections to old hands in the KGB, and especially our retirees, who knew that the agent in America is Liana's father. That is why they chose her, of all the journalists in the country, to lead the search." That was the question that had been nagging at him: why this particular reporter?

"And here's the delicious irony, Yelena: she doesn't know it. She thinks she's onto a big story. She has no idea the man she is looking for is her father."

The analyst fell behind again. "But why doesn't somebody tell her?"

"Because we—and the Feliks people—expect her father to look for her. Liana Krumins is the bait. And the best bait does not know it is bait."

Davidov allowed himself to wallow in his insight for a while, then got to work. He called in the only supervisor he more than half trusted in the counterespionage section of the Fifth Directorate and told him to evaluate, in his new knowledge of who the sleeper was, who within the Fifth Directorate knew or should have known it. That would reveal who had been deliberately withholding that fact from the Director. Those were the new moles loyal to their old colleagues now among the Feliks people, to be exposed by what they failed to do; they would have to be arrested, removed, or turned.

And he would need a new team of investigators drawn from the central bank, the Oil Ministry, the grain traders, perhaps the new Russian entrepreneurs, to answer the questions for the KGB that the American investigators, Fein and Shu, were asking on behalf of their CIA control.

KGB surveillance of Liana would have to be obvious; the Feliks people expected it, and it established her bona fides with them as a person mistrusted by the Russian government. But a second, subtler level of surveillance would have to be in place as well, to detect any approach to her from the sleeper, her father, who had the resources that made him, in the accountant Shu's intercepted phrase, "the richest man in the world."

That was why the Feliks people had enlisted her, though she did not know it; it might also be why Shu, who worked for Fein—a possible CIA asset, but KGB and CIA had parallel interests here—had established a link with her. Sooner or later the father could be expected to reach out for the daughter he had abandoned, especially if he learned she was reaching out to him. The subtle watchers would observe the Feliks people watching the KGB following the sleeper's daughter, and would provide her a measure of protection as well.

All this might take more fieldwork on the part of the head of the Fifth Directorate, Davidov decided; but with the goal line at his back, he had better not miss the tackle. This was why he had been vaulted over more experienced, traditional operatives to be placed in this position; no other case was as vital to Russian national stability and international security, and at least he could trust himself.

PART TWO

The Impersonation

Chapter 17

MEMPHIS

Edward Dominick's reaction to Irving Fein was negative the instant the renowned reporter walked in the door. Fein lunged into the office without a modicum of deference to the lovely young woman who accompanied him.

The Memphis banker was reminded of a remark made by his late wife, looking out the window of the Plaza Hotel, where the Dominicks stayed on visits to New York City. She saw the gilded statue of Union General William Tecumseh Sherman, scourge of the South, mounted on a horse being led by the goddess of liberty; Mrs. Dominick, until her death a national board member of the Daughters of the Confederacy, observed, "Isn't that just like a Yankee to ride while the lady walks?"

Dominick reached past Fein's outstretched hand to grasp the hand of Viveca Farr. The television newsperson was shorter than he had expected. He didn't know why he was surprised at that—he had never seen her full-length before—but her onscreen carriage gave the impression of a taller woman. Fein was tallish but slumped, eyes darting, uncomfortable in his own skin, not the sort to be lent substantial funds no matter what his collateral. Dutifully, the banker shook his hand as well—the reporter's idea of a handshake was a single furtive pump, in contrast to the authoritative grip of his companion's—and motioned them to the couch against the wall in the sitting area of his spacious office.

"Great digs for a little bank," said Irving Fein.

"Memphis Merchants Bank may have only two hundred million in reserves," Dominick said cheerily, "but some of our customers find us able to meet their local needs. And on global matters, our correspondent bank in your hometown of New York is the Chemical."

"What Mr. Fein meant was," said the young woman, "that we Easterners often have a stereotype of a medium-sized Midwestern bank that's usually wrong. This is an impressive office." She looked admiringly at a bronze statue of a cowboy on a horse descending a steep slope. "That's a Remington, isn't it?"

"Yes, but a reproduction, of course. Whatever it is that brings you to Memphis, Miss Farr, I want you to know how much I enjoy your newscasts. Sometimes you're the only reason we watch your network." The flattery had the added advantage of being true. Everyone in the bank's employ had been alerted to her visit, so as to get a good look, and to point out the television star to the customers. "And your reputation, Mr. Fein, precedes you. I cannot say I've read your work, but my friends at the *Commercial-Appeal* have high regard for it."

"You checked us out, huh?"

"It's not every day I get such distinguished visitors." He was not going to ask that they get to the point; he enjoyed her presence. The nightly newsflash would never be the same.

"What I'm saying is, I hope you checked us out with a mutual friend in Washington." When Dominick maintained his most inscrutable smile, Fein stated the purpose of his visit, and as the press would say, put the story in the lead: "We're here to interest you in helping us solve the greatest theft of the century."

"Let's see, the Brink's robbery was three million—"

"No, no. That was a piddling little heist, compared to what we're after." Fein stopped fidgeting and looked directly at him. "We're talking about a major swindle, bigger than BCCI, bigger than Keating and his S&L. The figures involved are mind-boggling, because they involve a deliberate milking of a major government treasury. Interested?"

When Fein awaited some response, Dominick maintained a poker face and said only, "Tell me more."

Irving got up and began walking around the office, touching the tail on the horse of the Remington, glancing at papers on the banker's desk, checking the view from the window. He did not care if the banker considered him nosy; nosiness was the essence of the reportorial persona.

"Back in the eighties, the guys in the Kremlin began getting nervous," the reporter recounted. "Gorbachev's reforms weren't working, but they were encouraging republics like the Ukraine and the Baltic countries to pull away from the center. These guys in Moscow were no dopes; they liked their power, so they began planning for the worst."

"The worst being the breakup of the Soviet Union," added Viveca Farr quietly, "and the loss of the power and the financial assets of the Communist Party."

"Prudent," Dominick said to her. Irving assumed he was a go-go banker who had trained himself to inject the word "prudent" into the conversation whenever possible.

"You ever been over there?" Irving tossed at him.

"I was part of a trade delegation to Ukraine a few years ago," said Dominick. Irving noted that Dominick spoke of Ukraine, without the article "the," as Ukrainians preferred; that suggested a nation, separate from Moscow's domination, rather than a region, as the Soviets considered it. The reporter figured this banker must have done a few chores for the Agency in the past; Clauson would not have just picked him out of a hat because he was six foot four and the right age.

"The last people the old KGB wanted the assets to go to were the Russian reformers," Fein continued. "So the bad guys—they call themselves the Feliks organization—hatched a plan to hide the money all over the world. You follow?"

"It's not very complicated. A logical reaction, actually."

"Right. But to run the operation, they needed a banker—a helluva banker—over here. Respected. Clean. Not a big shot, not a little shot. But very smart, and completely trustworthy, loyal to the hard-liners who used to run the KGB."

Dominick looked interested. He turned to Viveca. "Who did they get?"

She looked at her partner.

"Nobody you know," Fein answered. "Years ago, a generation ago, they planted a sleeper over here."

"You mean a 'mole'? I'm a fan of John le Carré. I enjoyed *Tinker, Tailor—*"

"I do honest-to-God scandals," Fein snapped. "News stories that shake up governments and get big people canned. Jeez, why doesn't anybody want to deal with reality anymore?"

"A mole is an agent who penetrates another intelligence agency," Viveca said primly, "and sends information back home, the way Aldrich Ames did. But a sleeper is different. He's an agent who integrates himself into the enemy society. He is left to his own devices. Once his cover is established, and his legend—that's his false identity, greatly detailed—becomes a part of him, he must remain alone, unaided. He is not contacted for years, even decades, until the moment comes for him to be activated."

"That would require remarkable motivation," Dominick offered, nodding at her to go on.

"Not only loyalty, but dedication and amazing self-discipline. A free society is seductive," she said, recrossing her legs. "A new family and a career over here must exert a powerful pull. A sleeper agent faces the constant temptation to cross over, to forget his ties."

"Yeah," said Fein, wondering where she got all that.

Dominick apparently wanted to see how much she knew about intelligence tradecraft. "What did you mean by his 'legend' becoming part of him?"

"The false identity," she went on, "is constructed from childhood to resist investigation. The files of schools and motor vehicle bureaus and early employers are fixed to have a record of him, so the younger he is when he is sent over, the better. When a credit agency checks him out, for example, the legend responds consistently. And in his own mind, the sleeper almost becomes the person that the legend has built."

"That's what this guy did," Irving picked up. "He came here a generation or so ago. He got into banking. He put down roots. He blended into our landscape. So when the old KGB sent a handler to activate him, this guy was ready to direct the operation to bury all the communist assets."

"In gold?" Dominick looked skeptical. "We were all told that the Soviets, toward the end, had a dangerously low gold reserve."

"A few billion, peanuts," said Fein. He drew out a long computer printout prepared by Mike Shu and showed it to the banker. The preliminary report was mostly questions about the possibility of oil scams, grain credit fraud, overruns of paper money printings, the illicit sale of plutonium. Nothing solid; they were at the start of their investigation, and what few solid leads they had from Treasury and Fed sources were not to be shopped around until their banker-ringer had committed himself.

"And you want technical advice from me? I'm flattered, but why me? You live in New York, you've got—"

Viveca tapped a cigarette out of her pack and leaned forward. "Because we think you would be the perfect—"

"Just a second," Fein interrupted. "What do you think of that list? On the right track?"

"Kind of obvious," the banker replied. "I'm assuming what you say is true about sleepers and legends and all that. And for the sake of argument, I'll buy the whole notion of a scheme to run up a fortune using the inside information available to the KGB. But this printout approaches it from a bookkeeper's mentality."

"How would you approach it, Edward?" This from Viveca. She looked around for an ashtray. Dominick took one out of a drawer, evidently kept there for important clients, and put it in front of her. Irving figured that little byplay of hers gave him a whiff of her delicate perfume, as she had done with him in her house; Irving was glad to have her on his side, though he wished he knew who had briefed her on the tradecraft.

"The key to amassing a great fortune," Dominick said, "is not to steal money. A better way is to set up situations of guaranteed profit. If you were the government of the Soviet Union, and you wanted to channel really large sums into a secret fund, you wouldn't want to put deposits in other people's banks, especially regulated banks. Instead, you'd want to take over banks of your own, ones that could then buy their own shipping lines, which in turn would profit from hauling your oil and grain. You would construct an integrated, worldwide profit-making machine. But that's only one way, or part of one." He thought some more, willing to appear intrigued by the possibilities.

"Part of the way?" Viveca asked, from within her cloud of smoke.

"The key you have is information. Inside information. The equation is this: advance information, plus serious money—major capital to act on the data—equals big profit. A superpower like the old Soviet Union could manipulate markets on a grand scale. You could sell short on the commodity futures market and then produce a glut of that commodity, and your man on the outside would be able to make billions in a year. Or you could buy long and then create a shortage, and make more billions."

"You're going too fast for me," Viveca said. Irving was glad she'd said it.

"Miz Farr, Mr. Fein—Viveca and Irving, if I may—I really don't know if this sleeper business of yours is true or not. Maybe you're just down here pulling my leg, and this is *Candid Camera* or something. But if you knew in advance what a superpower was going to do in politics or economics, it would be like owning tomorrow's newspaper today. You'd know what to buy and sell. You'd know who won the races, where the local wars would start, what shortages would develop. You could make fortune on top of fortune."

A buzzer sounded; Irving figured Dominick had told his secretary to interrupt him with a nonexistent important call at about this point. As he spoke to his secretary on the intercom, the reporter murmured to Viveca: "He's hooked. Reel him in."

Viveca sensed it wouldn't be that easy. Dominick was apparently intrigued with the Soviet plot, but if he was anything like her banker father, he would want to protect himself against losses in any involvement. This Memphis banker reminded her of her father, Victor Farrano, when he was at the top of his profession, at the time she was away at Mount Holyoke. He was carefully easygoing, immaculately disheveled; interested in his daughter in a measuring way, requiring her to display self-confidence lest she disappoint him. Her father, who worked successfully at being outgoing, had been centered on his own being, sure of his moral moorings until he went overboard at fifty on a financial scheme and a scheming woman and lost his fortune and his home and his family. Viveca wet her lips and swallowed; whenever she thought of that benighted man, she wished she had a drink. From the heights of social prominence, so important at a top-line school, she found herself waiting on tables, her humiliation delighting the young women she had previously snubbed. Since that day she had felt as if she were standing on a trapdoor always on the verge of being sprung. At least she had been able to make the money on the air to get the Pound Ridge house back.

She was impressed with Irving's choice of a banker. Dominick exuded authority from the way he made no obvious effort to make his presence felt. A charming chuckle, but no fake heartiness; the handshake was firm, but was not followed by a too-familiar touching of the shoulder or holding of the forearm.

"Let me have lunch with him alone," she told Irving while Dominick was on the phone. "Meet me at the departure gate at three." When he hesitated, she added, "He doesn't like you."

"Nobody likes me; so what," Irving said, playing the self-mocking realist by adding, "At least he has good judgment. But you're right, he has eyes for you. Pull out all the stops."

"I'll only pull out the ones I need."

"Remember to get him to check with Clauson at Langley," Irving reminded her, "and prime him to expect 'neither confirm nor deny.' Hint that we have a source at the Fed, because I do, and that's catnip to these bankers. And don't push to close the deal."

Viveca rose as Dominick put down the phone. "Irving has to go and milk a source, as he puts it. Is there a place near here where a single woman can sit at a counter and have a lonely lunch?"

As she had expected, Dominick took her to the restaurant atop the bank building. He did not try to pour on the charm; he did not pump her for more about the reason for her interest in the world of espionage, which she hoped he would, because she preferred responding to selling. He did not come on to her, nor did he show her pictures of his late wife and away-at-school kids; the banker played it down the middle, smoothly sharing backgrounds, delighted to learn that she was the daughter of a banker, showing sincere interest in the way she presented the news. Perhaps this project would balance out; Irving the frenetic boor, Dominick the stable gentleman. Both men were daring—Dominick had to be a bit of a gambler to get ahead in the Southern banking world of the eighties—but there was a nice element of prudence to him.

Persuading him to join the enterprise became important to her, not merely to prove to Irving and Ace how valuable her participation could be, but for her own self-confidence and peace of mind. It would be good, for a change, to enjoy her work.

"And now, Miz Farr, you're about to tell me why you chose me, out of the whole world of bankers, to be your technical adviser."

"It's more than that, Edward. You know I could take Irving to any one of a dozen top bankers for good strategic advice. And Irving could take me to the best SEC enforcement people, Federal Reserve monitors, banking sources on the Hill. He has an especially good contact at the Fed." She took a step further: "Look—Irving is not our kind, but he is very good at what he does."

"I believe you. And you two make a good team. I'm glad I'm having lunch with the good cop."

"What we want is not only your technical advice, but your strategic sense. That equation of yours—about advance information plus major capital equaling big profit—was an eye-opener to me. I had no idea that the Information Age extended that far." She knew her memorization of his fairly obvious "equation" would cause him to preen, but sensed she was laying it on a little thick; she came to the point she and Irving had rehearsed. "We want your involvement, Edward. If we are going to find the sleeper agent—and I'll tell you what we know about him if you're with us—then we need somebody who can think the way he does, act the way he might act. We want you to become him, track his decision-making, get into his stream of affairs."

"I quite understand what you want of me. You set a banker to catch a banker. But I'm no detective. How's it going to work?"

"We'll have a way to make the KGB, and the other elements in Russia that are looking for the sleeper, suspect that you're him. We want them to come to you."

"Why?"

"Irving can explain this better than I can, but the idea is to become a player. Then people trade information. You find out what the investigative agencies are looking for, how much they know. He's done this before, and it works—he's won every journalistic prize that counts."

She gave him time to think it over. Then he asked the question Irving had hoped he would ask, showing he had the imagination necessary for the role. "Sooner or later, the real sleeper will get wind of this, won't he? I mean, you can't set up a parallel operation, tracking a pattern of successful trading over the past five years, without the coon gettin' wise there's a coon dog after him."

Viveca was briefed and ready for that. "There's at least a good possibility that he'll soon be aware of your impersonation, Edward. Then we have reason to believe he will approach you to act as his intermediary in some major deal."

"Why would he do that? What's the deal?"

She skipped over the why; Irving hadn't told her why. "The Russians, both the government and the antigovernment group, want their money back. That's their business. Let the sleeper work something out with either of them, I don't care. Our business, Irving's and mine, is to get the story—how the sleeper did it, who he involved, especially in our government, where the money is, and where it goes."

"If all you say is true," Dominick mused, "he's the richest man in the world. And hardly anybody knows he's alive."

"It's a fantastic story, and it will make my career."

"That's a fine deal for you, little lady, but how did you come to pick me?"

"First of all, your physical appearance. He's six-four."

"You ought to come to an American Bankers Association convention. That narrows down the field to a couple thousand."

"And you were recommended by some people in the government."
"Who?"

"Irving didn't tell me, and I don't blame him for holding his sources very tightly. I do the same. But he surely didn't get your name out of the Memphis phone book."

Dominick seemed to relax; she was telling the truth. "Viveca, if I may call you that, I can make a pretty good guess at who our mutual friend in Washington is. But I'm a businessman, right? I hate to sound crass, but this would be a lot of trouble, take a lot of time . . ."

He wanted to know what was in this for him. She had that down pat: "You would be at the center of the book, as the hero, and the star of the television series. You and I would narrate the whole story. You'd become one of the most famous bankers in the country. In the whole world."

"Fame counts, there's no denying that. But no fortune. That's not much of a return on the investment of time."

When he said that, her stomach constricted, and she took a gulp of wine. She did not want to lose him, and tried her first fallback position. "The monetary return is something we could work out with the governments that pay a fee for recovering lost assets. Or with our own government on an income-tax whistleblower reward if the sleeper evaded taxes, as he surely must have. Or if the sleeper wants to make a deal with you, to act as his agent in dealing with the Russians—" She shrugged and didn't finish that possibility. Irving had said that Michael Shu suspected that if our ringer had a little larceny in his soul, he might try to make a deal with the real sleeper to get a small cut of the fortune.

"The risk is higher than you think, Viveca. If I am to impersonate a possibly criminal figure, our investigation would have to have the color of law."

That was almost a setup; she knew precisely what to say. "We anticipated that. You are to call—do you have a pen?—a man named Walter Clauson in the counterintelligence division of the Central Intelligence Agency in Langley, Virginia. The central switchboard is in the telephone book, or the information operator will give it to you." That was so he would know he was calling a real person at a real agency, not somebody who would answer a precooked number. "You are to say you would like to discuss a matter about a man with insomnia. Remember that the call is recorded. He will make an appointment for you to come to his office in Langley, Virginia, or on F Street in the District of Columbia, all open and aboveboard."

She had memorized this perfectly, wasn't tripping over a word. A memory intruded of the mentalist reciting secrets in an ancient movie called *The 39 Steps* with Robert Donat, a reference to which would drive Irving up the wall, because this was real reality, not virtual reality. "When you get there, tell him of our visit to you and what we want you to do. He will then say these exact words: 'I cannot confirm or deny the existence of a KGB sleeper agent in the United States. You are one hundred percent on your own. Thank you and good afternoon.' Listen for that 'one hundred percent.' "

"Is that all?" He did not seem reassured.

"What that should tell you is that we are in touch with a high official in counterintelligence; that we have worked out with him who will call him and what he will say; and your recorded interview will be part of the CIA's record of the case."

She watched him assess that. As she expected, it came up short. "That's not a whole bunch of protection."

"Edward, I'm told that you're not entirely an innocent in these matters. You said it yourself—we may have a mutual friend in Washington. You can check our bona fides"—she pronounced it in proper Latin, bone-a feedays, as instructed—"by the exact way Clauson answers. He cannot give you a go-ahead, but this proves to you that he sent us to you."

Dominick remained noncommittal; she supposed he would check this out. Irving had told her not to expect an answer right away. She took out her business card, wrote on it her private numbers in New York City and Pound Ridge, and gave it to him. Personal chemistry was important here; the prospect of working with her might attract him, and she felt that she had established some rapport. "Let me know. I'd really like to work with you."

A group of men passed their table, said hello to him, looked at her, and one looked back at Dominick, eyebrows up, impressed. She was grateful for that.

"You haven't been entirely frank with me, Viveca, and I don't hold that against you, considering the business you're in. But I'm going to be very straight with you." The banker's large brown eyes were now more penetrating than mournful. "This sleeper fellow, if he exists, has to be resourceful. He isn't going to want to be found out. He's not going to want a partner. He could be dangerous, not just to the impersonator, but to you."

"I'll take that chance. Will you?"

"Don't know why I should. The monetary reward you speak of is highly problematical. The notion of being a big celebrity if we succeed is kind of attractive. I could run for office on it, but I have no political ambitions."

She put her hand on his arm. "Still, you're considering it. Tell me why." She remembered her father's advice: give a prospect a chance to sell himself on a deal.

He leaned back and looked out over Memphis and the river. "Your approach is sound. The sleeper would find out about the parallel operation soon enough, even on a small scale, because this world of big-league banking is a tight circle, and he might just reach out in one way or another. Second, working with you journalistic types would be kind of exciting, no bones about that."

He flexed his arm and she removed her hand. "Most important, though, there's the challenge. Can't ignore that. How do you take a few billion, and using the inside information of a superpower, run it up to the biggest private fortune in the world? And all the while, keep it hidden?" He all but licked his lips at that. "I bet I could figure it out, with some really good staff support backtracking market movements. Be a hell of an exercise."

He sent her to the airport in his chauffeured car.

"He sent you out alone? No riding along with you, neckin' in the backseat? That's where a lot of sexual harassment takes place, you know. In corporate cars."

She seemed so pleased with herself that Irving could not resist giving her a little zotz. But Viveca had done well, better than he could have done with the tight-assessed bank executive, and when she glared at him, the reporter hastened to say he was only kidding. She didn't have much of a sense of humor.

"Hey, where'd you get that stuff you used in his office about moles and sleepers?" he asked to make amends. "That was pretty good. Accurate, too."

"It came from *Principles and Practices of Counterespionage* by Cooper and Redlinger," she answered. "I do my homework. This espionage business is not as arcane as you think."

He shot his eyebrows up at her forty-dollar word. "I used to go to the penny arcane. You're so hot on Cooper and Redstuff, where do you come out on Golitsyn and Nosenko?"

"I haven't read their work yet."

"Lookit. Golitsyn was a Russian defector, came over here in 1960 with the whole story of the disinformation plan of Shelepin, the head of the KGB at the time. Shelepin was feeding all our spies phony stuff, in the biggest deception operation ever run. Then another defector, named Nosenko, came over after the Kennedy assassination and reassured everybody here that the Kremlin had nothing to do with Lee Harvey Oswald. The two defectors' stories collided. The question: Was Nosenko a 'dangle'?" Irving waited for her to figure out that a dangle was a false defector, not hard for a quick student.

"What was the answer?"

"Angleton at the CIA believed Golitsyn, but Hoover at the FBI believed Nosenko. For decades, that disagreement split the spook world, until a new crowd took over the CIA and decided to believe Nosenko. They fired Angleton."

"Do I have to know this?"

" 'Course not. But when you start giving me arcane, it's important for you to understand that in this business there are a lot of bodies buried you don't know about."

She said nothing. He let her brood about being caught with a superficial knowledge of the intelligence dodge, and they sat in silence waiting for the flight to be called. Finally she said, "So was Nosenko a dangle?"

He was not sorry he'd bitten her head off for being a wiseass, because a little humility was called for in this business, but at least she hung in there and asked her question again. She could get herself and a lot of other people in deep trouble with a smattering of ignorance and her inclination to fake the rest. Her knowledge was shallow, a little booklearning here and a short briefing there, no depth of experience to call up when the puzzle got complicated. Great for a forty-five-second newsbreak, but deadly in an all-day seminar or a year's sustained work on a book.

"Neither one was a dangle, I think." He wasn't sure even now. "They were both real defectors, which seems like a contradiction. The lesson is," he instructed, "students of spooks have to live with maddening contradictions. Because Angleton of the CIA was probably wrong about Nosenko, the crowd that came in during the seventies assumed he was a paranoid about penetrations. So they kicked him out—and later on, in came the moles like Ames. Jim Angleton was our counterpart to Shelepin, a scholar of deception, simultaneously right and wrong. Raised orchids."

"Why orchids?"

"Orchids fake out wasps to get pollinated."

"I can handle that," she said with her misplaced self-confidence. "It's called an anti-syzygy, and I won the spelling bee in high school on that word."

"You must have been a pisser in high school."

"You and your friend the accountant had better give me a complete briefing on the sleeper. Every detail we know. Dominick wants to deal with me, not you. This is going to take more of my time than I thought."

"You tell Dominick we think maybe the handler got his ass blown off in Barbados?"

"I didn't want to alarm him. But Dominick is sensitive to the potential danger." She fell silent. Irving hoped the banker hadn't scared her off the story.

"Lookit, some of this may be heavy-duty stuff," he warned her. "If the sleeper has a big moneymaking operation going, using inside stuff from Russia, he could get very upset at our dangle." His purpose in teaching her about the controversy over dangles was to alert her to the way they would use Dominick to stir up the KGB, the Feliks people, our CIA and Fed, and the sleeper himself. She had a lot to learn in a hurry. He, on the other hand, had no need to know how to spell "anti-syzygy."

He fed it to her gently. "I ran a Dialog search on the words 'Fifth Directorate.' " He assumed everybody in the business knew about this computerized morgue, capable of instantly searching most of the key publications in the world. "Seems that a couple of months ago, the Director and his deputy got killed in an airplane accident. Within days, there was the explosion on Barbados that wiped out a guy I think was the sleeper's handler. My guess is that the handler believed he had slipped past all central control, what with the top KGB guys who knew about the sleeper dead, and tried to put the squeeze on the sleeper and got blown to smithereens."

She had turned sickly pale. Irving sought to reassure her about her own safety; he didn't want her throwing up on his shoes. "Nobody in the spook dodge ever knocks reporters off, Viv. We're like family. But there's sometimes collateral damage, and the sleeper is the sort who can inflict it. People we use take their chances."

She took her bag, went to the john, came back composed. Irving doubted that she was a druggie; maybe she'd taken a fast belt from a pint in her bag, or maybe, to be charitable, she'd just had a sudden, frightened urge to pee. Then he thought of Ace and the sizable advance they had a real shot at, as well as the way Viveca had this banker eating out of her hand.

"There's this joke," Irving said. "Guy buys a yachtsman's cap, and goes home to his mother, and says, 'Looka-me, Ma, I'm a captain.' And the old lady says 'Son, by you, you're a captain. And by me, your mother who loves you, you're a captain. But by a captain—you're no captain.' "

"Very funny. But by a journalist, I'm no journalist."

"That's not what I meant." She missed the point, and the damn joke did damage rather than smoothed things over. "What I meant was, by a spook you're no spook. You did a pretty good job as a journalist today. Damn good job. You charmed the pants off this guy, which I might not have been able to do."

"You couldn't even get in to see him." That was a sign of life; she was up and beginning to take nourishment.

"Like I say, you have your advantages."

"Your brains and my legs, you mean?"

"Don't start with the feminism, I wrote the book."

"You know what? I didn't read that book, I just sort of flipped through it to say I did, like everybody else. And you know what else? Because they fired Angleton, counterintelligence went to hell and the Sovs penetrated the Agency with their mole Ames. And when Ames gave them the names of our agents in the Kremlin, they turned them around and fed us back misinformation for years. That's what else. And I didn't get that from a damn textbook, I got it from a network reporter who covers intelligence."

He pretended to be impressed at the ass-covering line some buddy of the Agency's had given her easily duped colleague. She used "misinformation" when she meant "disinformation"—data fed back with the strategic intent to deceive—but he bit his tongue at his urge to correct her; she needed a little victory, and he had no need to start another fight.

They listened to the flight being called. The ticket taker took the tickets, the stews now called flight attendants smiled them aboard, and the silver-haired pilot stood behind them to get a look at the celebrity passenger.

"Welcome aboard, Ms Farr," the pilot said, touching his fingertips to his flight cap.

Viveca jerked a thumb in the direction of her companion and said, "By him, you're no captain."

Irving allowed to himself he might have been wrong about her having no sense of humor.

Chapter 18

LANGLEY

"I don't like it," Director Barclay said for the record. "I don't want us to have any part of it."

The Deputy Director for Operations, briefing the DCI and the Agency's chief lawyer on the awkward request from Walter Clauson in counterintelligence, agreed. "The Agency has no official interest anymore in counterespionage within the United States. That's now the FBI's job, with oversight in the intelligence committees of Congress." He turned to the attorney. "Harry, you're the secretary of this meeting, but beyond that—do you agree that Clauson is overstepping in seeing this banker from Memphis?"

The general counsel was well aware he was in the meeting to make the notes that would cover everybody's ass. He also knew that when the DDO used the word "official" in "no official interest," that meant the Agency was interested as hell but was determined to take no steps that could get the Director at cross purposes with the FBI or in hot water with Congress. And, because he had drafted two of them, he knew that a presidential "finding," citing national security needs, could override the restriction on the CIA's counterespionage activities within the United States.

He therefore demurred, pointing out that Walter Clauson had acted by the book after receiving the call from one Edward Dominick of Memphis. "When a respectable citizen calls, especially one who has cooperated with the Agency in the past, and asks to come in for a chat about a suspicion in his mind—it's quite proper to see him."

"Then you be in Clauson's office, Harry, when this fellow walks in," Barclay told him. "And you be sure Clauson listens, and says exactly the appropriate thing, and you be there until the visitor leaves. And give me a transcript of the tape of that meeting with a cover memo from you suitable for Congressional oversight."

Why so hypersensitive? "Because I don't fully trust Clauson," she said in her bark-off style. "He's the last of the old Angleton crowd that saw moles under every bed. I'm told they ruined the lives of dozens of fine public servants with their paranoid theories."

"There are no more penetration agents in the Agency," the DDO assured her. "I'll stake my reputation on that."

"Thanks." Dorothy Barclay looked at counsel and said slowly, so he could get it down, "Though a sleeper, in certain circumstances, could do even more damage than a mole. Are we still supporting that Golitsyn, by the way?"

Yes, the lawyer informed her, the old defector was in a Southern state under a false identity, part of the Witness Protection Program, personally overseen by a retired operator. "He publishes don't-trust-the-Russians tracts under his own name. Rails at the disinformation scheme supposedly dreamed up a generation ago and still being carried on."

"Thirty years at the public trough—what a waste," she said. "And how long will it take to get rid of Clauson?"

The DDO pointed out that one member of the Senate Select Committee on Intelligence was still high on him but that member was being rotated off the committee this year.

"I'm directing you to build a firewall between us and this fellow Dominick's interest in a potential Russian agent over here," Director Barclay told her deputy, which the general counsel noted down. "Tell the Memphis banker to take whatever he has to the FBI, if he wants."

The general counsel was seated in Clauson's small office. Counterspy Clauson's job had been downgraded, as had most of that discredited division. In many ways he had been encouraged to take early retirement, but had clung to the old life protected by a veiled threat of age discrimination.

"It's good of you to take the time to protect my interests in the meeting requested by this banker," Clauson said.

"You did the right thing," the lawyer replied, which was the sentence everybody in the Agency wanted to hear. "Reputable American citizen calls, wants to discuss a matter about a fellow with insomnia, apparently a signal that you're supposed to understand. He's been told to see you, and you alert your superior. All by the book."

"And your advice as to what I should do?"

"Listen to what he has to say, Walt, but be noncommittal. No Agency involvement. If any wrongdoing to report, see the FBI. Should be a short meeting. Do you know this guy? How come he had your name?"

"Four or five years ago, he was vice-chairman of a group sponsored by the American Bankers Association to visit Kiev. He contacted us for information, and asked if he should take a course in Russian at a local university before leaving the next spring. Unfortunately, without thinking, I said he should."

"Why unfortunately?"

Clauson looked slightly embarrassed. "In Kiev, they speak Ukrainian. Well, never hurts to know a little Russian."

What the counsel would have liked to know was whether Clauson had used Dominick in any way on his Kiev trip or had debriefed him on his way back. But Clauson was not volunteering any further information, and the general counsel was not about to ask anything that would create stacks of paperwork.

Dominick's entry elevated the officials from their seats and activated the recorder. The banker from Memphis struck the lawyer as a banker from Memphis: hearty, outgoing, pleasantly rumpled mid-American conservative on the surface, probably concealing a native cunning. The printout on him that the counsel had called up beforehand revealed nothing out of the ordinary. Born in Dyersburg, Tennessee, forty-four years ago, father a textile plant worker. A student deferment kept him out of the Army during Vietnam; later, Dominick showed an aptitude for international finance and was graduated near the top of his class at Wharton. Respectable widower, best country club, appropriate mid-six-figure income, net worth nearly $7 million though mainly in unregistered stock of his own bank. Never a brush with the law, not even a speeding ticket.

Clauson introduced the general counsel as the general counsel, no name. In one of those resonant voices that big men cultivate, Dominick said, "My purpose here is to tell you about an investigative enterprise that has been brought to me, and to make certain it does not work at cross-purposes to anything being done by the U.S. government."

"Perhaps the State Department would be a better place to begin," said Clauson. "Or Commerce, if it involves overseas business."

"It has to do with a spy, so I came here. Are you aware of something called a sleeper agent, and a group in Russia called the Feliks people?"

The counsel noted Clauson's poker face. "Go on," the counterspy said.

"I have been told, by two well-known American journalists, that the KGB once placed what is called a 'sleeper' agent here. Seems he was activated a few years ago to manage and conceal the assets of the collapsing Communist Party in Russia. Does any of this ring a bell with you?"

"We're listening."

"They want me to impersonate this agent. Run a similar operation on a smaller scale, protecting myself from loss with hedges and swaps, but imitating both him and his method of operation. The idea is to attract approaches from those who are searching him out, and ultimately elicit a feeler from him." He paused, looking from one to the other. "The journalistic goal is to expose the secret activities of what may be one of the richest individuals in the world."

Clauson just looked back at him. After a longer pause, Dominick said: "What I want to know from you gentlemen is this: does this conflict with anything our government is doing to apprehend him? Will I be at any risk of interfering with any ongoing investigation?" In the ensuing silence, the banker spoke more plainly: "In a nutshell, is this an entirely legitimate venture, and if I decide to pursue it, how can I keep out of trouble with the law?"

"A banker friend of mine once gave me an enamel ashtray," said Clauson. "On it were written the words 'Everything is sweetened by risk.' "

"I understand financial risk," the banker said cheerily. "I just don't want to run the risk of getting my ass shot off or my reputation besmirched by some government agency."

"I cannot confirm or deny the existence of a KGB sleeper agent in the United States," Clauson said slowly, as if reciting from memory. "You are one hundred percent on your own." He rose and extended a hand. "Thank you and good afternoon."

"Sit down, sir. I pay a couple of hundred thousand dollars a year in federal taxes, and I think that entitles me to a moment or so more of your time."

Observing all this, the general counsel was gripped by the inescapable feeling that he was witness to another charade, this one more complex than the earlier meeting in the Director's office. For example, if Clauson had subjected this fellow to six months of unnecessary language study, some bantering reference would surely have been made at the outset. What counsel was hearing, and what was being dutifully tape-recorded, was not spontaneous conversation; the lawyer had heard enough tapings to know when he was listening to deliberate dictation on both sides. He interjected nothing and waited for the charade to play out.

"Are you telling me," asked Dominick, "in the presence of this attorney as a witness, that my impersonation of this sleeper agent will in no way conflict with any operation the Central Intelligence Agency has under way?"

"I am telling you, my heavily taxed fellow citizen, that I cannot confirm or deny the existence of the operation you mentioned."

"And if this journalistic enterprise entraps a foreign agent here in control of vast sums, which is surely in the public interest—would I become the target of an investigation?"

Clauson turned to the general counsel. "Perhaps you are in a better position to give this gentleman the legal advice he seeks."

"Mr. Dominick, you know the difference between right and wrong, especially in the financial world. If you see evidence of a crime," said the counsel, joining in the general dictation to the record, "or have reason to suspect that someone is an unregistered foreign agent, you have the obligation to report it to local law-enforcement authorities or to the FBI. The CIA is not a law-enforcement agency. If in the course of your 'journalistic enterprise,' as you call it, you are tempted to commit a crime—don't do it. Simple as that. The end, no matter how worthy, or in this case newsworthy, does not justify unlawful means."

"Good advice," said Dominick, and rose to go. He took Clauson's thin hand into his own large hands and shook it enthusiastically. "*Da svidaniya*," he said to the retirement-list counterspy. "That means 'goodbye' in Russian. I don't know how they say it in Kiev."

"Sorry about that. I hope your short course in Russian serves you in good stead someday. Goodbye."

After the banker left, the counsel said: "So what the hell was all that about?"

Clauson rose and steered him out of the office into the hallway, requiring the counsel to activate his personal recorder, which meant starting a whole new file, unless the old hand was wearing an electronic blocker.

"That was an independent individual seeking the color of law," said Clauson, "which is not ours to give. Frankly, I wish him well. How I would have liked to be able to tell him that the sleeper was planted here some twenty years ago, and was activated four or five years ago. That although the sleeper may pose no direct danger to us—hence this Agency's determined lack of interest—he does pose a danger to the stability of our Russian ally, or partner in peace, or friendly rival, or whatever we call our former adversary, which my old boss used to call our deadly enemy."

"But you're not going to file a reclama, are you, Walt?" The request for a review of a policy decision caused no end of paperwork, or whatever they called paperwork done on word processors with no printout capability.

"No, no. I just wanted you to know that the Agency is constrained from doing what I consider to be its duty in an affair of state. That I think it's scandalous that the FBI is uninformed and the Federal Reserve is asleep. And that our visitor today, if he chooses to become the impersonator of the sleeper, could easily get himself killed."

The general counsel suspected that Clauson knew more than anybody else in the Agency wanted to know about the KGB sleeper. How wise was the Director to close down official Agency interest? Perhaps they should have been more direct in telling Dominick to see the FBI. But it was not an attorney's job to intervene in evaluations or operations, unless they ran afoul of the law and required legalization through a presidential finding.

"Send me the transcript, brother Clauson, and I'll buck it upstairs. You were not in the least out of line."

Chapter 19

NEW YORK

". . . and that's tonight's update, Viveca Farr reporting."

The red light went off and she lowered her eyes from the prompter. She gathered up the blank white pages that stood for a script, tapped them together on the desk with leftover authority, and heard the director say on the floor loudspeaker, "Perfect as always, Viveca." A floor manager came to remove the mike from her lapel; when he dawdled over the simple task, she took it off and handed it to him, extricating herself from the wire in her jacket. She swiveled to watch the monitor replay. When her news spot did not readily appear, she snapped, "Let's see it."

"Rewinding." The director took his own good time, knowing it would annoy her. She had asked for a new director, but the network had turned her down, because this was the third replacement she'd asked for in a month. It was as uncomplicated a directorial job as existed; one camera started with a medium shot with Viveca on the left, the bites of film over her shoulder illustrating what she read, the last ten seconds slowly filling the screen with her face.

Those final seconds belonged to Viveca; they were the equivalent of "Walter time," the seven minutes out of twenty-three contractually guaranteed to network anchors that their faces would be on-screen. She had mastered the technique of memorizing the last ten seconds of the script so that her eyes would not appear to be reading as she looked at the prompter words scrolling up across the camera lens.

Her heart was pounding, as it always did after the light went off. She was rock-steady during the moment on the air, but beforehand she was tense and remote, and afterward she was, for no reason, frightened, and covered it by being snappish. She knew that; it was life; others who could not do what she did would have to adapt to it. And a rewind should take only a few seconds. Her impatience boiled over: "Roll it, for crissake!"

The replay began. Her delivery was near-perfect—she would prefer more modulation in her voice between a summit headline and an obituary of an actress, but that was her own high standard, nobody else's. The director, she noted, had been at least two seconds late on dollying in, and the close-up seemed hurried to her.

"Your cue was late," she said, "unless you want to blame the cameraman."

"Sor-ry, Viveca, I'll get it right one of these nights."

She threw the fake script across the set, pages fluttering, and stormed into makeup. Evelyn was quick and comforting; she closed the door—nobody was to use the other chair when Viveca Farr was being made up—tilted the chair back, and put cold, wet cotton compresses over Viveca's eyes. "You're the only one who knows what the hell she's doing around here," Viveca told the comforting aide as the heavy pancake was removed with cold cream followed by an astringent.

"You looked marvelous, if I do say so myself," the makeup technician said, dabbing and wiping. "This jacket was a good color for you, too, 'specially with the lighter hair." She stepped back, tilting her head for a good look. "It looked better on the screen, to tell the truth. You have a knack for that."

"I don't dress for myself. I dress for the fifty-year-old men who run the network and all the women at home who don't want to be threatened."

"Did you see the new writer? Cute. Young enough to be my son."

"You tell him to keep the sentences short, then. I had to rewrite the whole thing." She stretched her head back to let the woman remove the makeup from her neck. "If I was short with you before the show, Evelyn, I apologize. I sometimes go into a real funk when the director is bad and the writer is new."

"You're always impossible before a show; the word around here is 'Stay out of her way.' And right after the show, for a couple minutes, you're hell on wheels. But then you turn into a human being, like now. Maybe the makeup turns you into a monster."

Viveca turned that over in her mind. "Am I such a monster?"

"You're a pro, like me. They hate me, too, because I'm the union shop steward and I don't kowtow. Screw 'em all. You're breathing down the anchor's neck on the evening news, and he's terrified. So's his producer."

"You know for a fact, or just hear it?"

"They don't talk to me, they talk to each other like I'm not here. They say all the surveys show the viewers trust you more than anybody."

Viveca knew that was the Holy Grail of anchorhood: not smooth delivery, not familiarity with the material, not even good looks, but trust. It was why she was afraid to fix her slightly crooked nose; she would be trusted less. In the combination of news business and show business and corporate business that was the television business, trust was all.

She had come up fast—too fast, the newsies said—but she knew her strength was not in knowing the nuances of political or economic stories. She could do a human-interest interview with empathy and give a quick summary with flair, and if "paying your dues" meant sitting in the rain staking out a dodging news source, she was not prepared to pay. As Evelyn said, screw 'em.

"All finished. You want a light foundation and a little eyeshadow for going home?"

Irving Fein was picking her up here at the studio; he was probably in the Green Room now, where she had told him to go to watch her spot. She didn't need any makeup to impress him; on the contrary, he was probably more impressed by pure plain in a woman. Tonight, at her apartment, he was going to review some of the facts about the real sleeper's background and physical characteristics for her to convey to Edward. Was Dominick enough of an actor? That was an area she could help the banker with; she knew plenty about putting on a performance.

"Pretend you're not finished, Evelyn." Irving could wait.

Evelyn understood; she turned off one of the two lights in the small room and let her rest, slowly rubbing some cream around her temples. Viveca began to relax; her thoughts turned to a man she used to date and the way she had come to numb herself to the verbal abuse she had to take from him. She had needed somebody's company at the time because she hated to be friendless, as she was now. But she no longer put up with a hint of a put-down; that was why she would take none of that patronizing lip from Irving Fein, no matter how badly her reputation as a newsie needed building up.

The thought of the man she had met earlier in the week in Memphis was soothing to her mind. Edward Dominick was not like her father, who was a fraud in many ways, but more like the man she thought her father had been when she was a girl. Dominick was secure; sure of himself and his abilities; not in the least condescending, except to Irving, whose great-reporter snottiness invited a counterattack of condescension. And brave; this assignment, though Irving was flip about it, might have its risks.

Their Memphis skytop lunch had gone well. She found him to be a sexy man in his way, partly because no romantic involvement was in prospect. She would have the respect of a man she respected at work; that had not happened to her in as long as she could remember. She encouraged herself to think this sleeper story could be fun to work on; Edward might turn out to be a real hero in the post-book docudrama.

A hard two knocks on the door nearly jolted her out of the chair. "Viveca! You in there?"

The makeup woman wiped the cream off the newscaster's forehead in a single swipe and opened the door. The head of the newsroom and the director looked agitated.

"There's been a hijacking, Air Force One, for God's sake. Come into the studio quick—we're gonna have to bust into programming and go on the air."

"Has it been announced? You sure?"

"We ran the AP bulletin out of Washington. C'mon, quick."

Her first thought, twisting out of the chair, was that she had no makeup on. Then: "Air Force One? With the President on it?"

"We don't know for sure, but probably." They were all running down the hall.

"Where's Connie?"

"Out in the goddam Hamptons, two hours from here. We're sending a chopper."

"Sam—where's he?"

"He's supposed to be here in an hour, but he's out of pocket, doesn't answer the beeper. So there's nobody to anchor until then but you. You okay?" She nodded yes, but she was instantly terrified. A breaking story was not her strong suit; what the hell could she say with no copy to read and nobody to interview? This could be the end of her career.

They burst into the newsroom, where everyone's eyes were fixed on monitors displaying wire service bulletins.

"I don't want to step on anybody's story, is all. What do I have to work with? Is there any wire copy? Where's our writer?"

"There's a monitor on your anchor desk—you can read wire copy from that," the director said. "I'll be on your earphone with whatever I can get."

"The President is aboard," said a man on a telephone, "and the SecState, and the First Lady. And the press secretary and a press pool and everybody."

"Find out where the VP is!" the producer called. "Give me a feed from the White House briefing room now, quick, never mind if nobody's there." To Viveca, he said, "I'll try to find somebody to sit at the desk with you, help you fill. Terrorism expert, gotta be reachable quick. Or another reporter."

She thought of Irving. He had written a whole book about terror and the Mideast, and he was in the Green Room, twenty steps away.

"CNN's on with it," the director groaned, pointing to a monitor. "Maybe we can still beat the other nets."

Viveca started to say something, but her voice choked. She raced for the Green Room, the producer right behind her, saying no, no, the other way.

Irving Fein was lying all over the couch, eating from the lavish spread set on the coffee table out for guests, watching the network sitcom. She had never been so glad to see anyone in her life; now she had a journalist with a reputation who could share the blame.

Her fingers dug into his arm like talons.

"Somebody's hijacked Air Force One. The President is aboard, and we're going on the air right now. You have to come with me, talk about terrorism."

"Oh-shit," Irving said. "How'd he pull it off?" He made a lunge for a last handful of shrimp, realizing he had instantly identified with the daring hijacker. She dragged him up.

"Nobody knows anything yet." She was strong, he had to give her that; his arm was in a vise. They hurtled down the hallway to a big blue door, a stagehand urgently motioning them in.

"Just sit by me," she said, "and talk when I have nothing to say."

"I'm with you—leggo my arm. But if we don't know anything we're gonna look like a couple of schmucks."

"This is Irving Fein," she said to the producer. "You know him, I'm sure he's the greatest reporter ever, wrote a book about terrorism, including hijacking. Give him a lapel mike. We know anything more?"

"Thank God you're here," the producer said to Irving. To Viveca, he reported, "Whacka says they're in touch with the plane and may give everybody a feed."

Irving had a hunch Viveca did not know what Whacka was; for her sake, he asked the producer, "Who's Whacka?"

"White House Communications Agency. You sure you know about terrorism, huh?"

"Not to worry." They were at the news desk being wired up. He asked the producer if there was a telephone handy.

"You can talk to me on the earphone, here."

The red light came on the cameras pointed at her, which Irving knew from slight experience meant they were on the air. Next to his knee, below the desk, was a telephone. He hoped he could get an outside line by dialing 9. The producer would be no help, except to passively let the news flow in. To Irving, the way to report a story was to get on the hook and find somebody who would advance the story. Viveca, next to him, was speaking.

". . . now let me read you that bulletin again, exactly as we received it three—" she looked up at the clock—"four minutes ago from the Associated Press. 'Hijacker seizes Air Force One, President and First Lady and top officials aboard.' Now here's a second bulletin, this from Reuters, just coming in. 'President unharmed, press secretary reports from Air Force One. Lone hijacker in cockpit says he is loaded with explosives.' And that's all we have. With me here is Irving Fein, the Pulitzer Prize–winning expert on terrorism. Mr. Fein, what do you make of this?"

"Pretty daring maneuver," Irving observed. "The hijacker must have stowed away while the plane was parked at Andrews Air Force Base. It's been known that the President was flying tonight to a fund-raiser breakfast tomorrow in Seattle, Washington." He'd read that in the paper. "So this guy sneaks aboard—"

"How? Isn't the plane tightly guarded?"

"Good question. But somehow, he did it." He thought to add, "If it's a he. A cleaning woman might be more credible. Anyhow, as soon as the plane, Air Force One—and we don't know if it is the usual plane, it might be a backup, which then automatically becomes Air Force One when the President is on it." He had all these extraneous facts in his head to draw on to fill the time until some news came in. He kept talking, recalling a previous hijacking in Cairo that he had covered, a similar one-man job in which the hijacker was talked into giving up by his mother or his wife.

Viveca interrupted him with "Now we're going to our Washington bureau, where correspondent Mike Whelan has a report from the FBI." She must have heard something in her earpiece. The FBI interview was just horsing around, no news, but it gave Irving a chance to get on the hook. Dialing 9 didn't give him a dial tone. "You suppose you could fix this thing so I could make a call?"

"Give him an outside line, for God's sake," she said to the director. To Irving, she whispered, "Do you need to do that, Irving? Give me some questions to ask you when they come back to us. Wait, here's another bulletin." She cut abruptly into the Washington feed—"feed" was a word Irving noticed they used a lot, for people who were so diet-conscious—to read what was on her screen: " 'The press secretary aboard the hijacked Air Force One reports that the President remains unharmed and the hijacker has demanded that the plane be turned around and headed across the Atlantic.' And here's a press advisory from Whacka—that's WHCA, the White House Communications Agency," she explained knowledgeably. " 'The press secretary will be patched through to the multplug in two minutes.' That's good news, don't you think, Irving Fein?"

"It means the White House is functioning, yes," Irving said, not wanting to contradict her. "As you know better than me, Viveca, the multplug is the device that sends a single signal to all the news media plugged into it. So we'll be hearing from the horse's mouth in a couple of minutes, unless there's a delay, which there always is."

She cut back to the Washington interview in the meanwhile; Irving was glad he didn't have the producer giving him orders over the earphone. He tried the telephone again, which was okay for local calls, but went with that awful noise when he tried long distance. "How do I get the operator?" he said to Viveca. "I got a credit card."

"Make the goddam phone work anywhere in the world," Viveca hissed to the director. To Irving, she whispered, "How'm I doing?"

"You might want to powder your nose," he said. She was sweating; she looked good to him sweaty, as if she'd been making love. "Otherwise, you're better than those guys." He pointed to the monitors across the room of the competing networks, which had just begun covering the story. "They look like they're phumphing."

"Oh my God, I'm on without makeup. At the next break, send me Evelyn with whatever she can do in a hurry. Irving, what do you want me to ask you?"

"Ask me what if the guy blows himself up."

"I'm going to ask him what if the hijacker blows himself up," she said to the producer in the booth or wherever. "Right. I won't." She said, "He says that's too alarming, scare everybody. What else?"

"What might the President do right now."

Red light. "We're back at the anchor desk in New York with Irving Fein, the antiterrorism expert. Irv, at this moment, we don't have much information to work with. We're waiting for a direct report from the press secretary aboard the hijacked Air Force One. And we should reassure everyone that the President, we are told, is unharmed. Unharmed. Let me ask you directly: What options does the President have at this moment?"

"Before doing anything, he should get hold of the Vice President and tell him to go to the Sit Room in the White House and stand by." That sounded fairly stupid to him as he was saying it; what else would the VP do? "Then he could order the Secret Service to mount an assault—to shoot the terrorist in the cockpit—but that seems a little extreme. More likely, he's telling them to humor him along, and turn the plane around like he wants, maybe only halfway, and play for time and slow down and conserve fuel"—he made a note on his pad to find out how long the plane could stay in the air on fuel it had for a cross-country trip—"and get some talker-down shrink on the phone. If the hijacker speaks English. The first thing I'd find out is what languages this guy speaks, and what's his gripe, what does he want."

"In our Los Angeles studio," she said, picking up on his reference to a shrink, "I'm told we have a psychiatrist standing by with experience in dealing with hostage-takers. No—hold it—here's the plane."

"This is the President's press secretary aboard Air Force One with the President and his party." The director was ready with a still picture of the press secretary on the screen for a voice-over.

"We have a woman in the cockpit who is armed and says she has explosives on her person. The Secret Service has decided it would be prudent to believe her. She has handed us a note asking that the flight plan be altered to direct us toward the Atlantic, and we have acceded to her request. She apparently speaks no English, which makes communication difficult, but has handed us a statement in English, with a pamphlet attached, demanding the United States intercede immediately in the conflict in Nagorno-Karabakh on the side of the Armenians, who the statement says are dying by the hundreds every day. We are in a tight spot here, but there is no cause for alarm. The President has spoken to the Vice President, who will monitor events from the White House. The President has appointed his National Security Adviser to be his second-in-command here on the plane, in constant communication with the pilot. The President and the First Lady are calm and unharmed. We will continue to be in touch with the White House in Washington, and will patch through to all of you as circumstances warrant. A press pool is aboard and will be permitted to broadcast as soon as our emergency communications can be interrupted. The President has asked me to forward this message: 'Don't worry, everyone, we'll come through this fine.' "

As he listened, Irving beckoned to a stagehand and asked how to dial long distance. The man told him his phone was now programmed to let him call outside, and the code was double-zero, double-zero, then the area code and the number. He got out his address book and dialed the home number of a guy who had been a good source of his ten years before. The number still worked. "Ralph? You up and watching? Answer this lady's questions."

He put Viveca on to the retired Air Force officer who had been the pilot of Air Force One for nearly a decade. He printed a few questions on his pad for her: "How terrorist could get aboard? Fuel capacity of new AF1 and how long can stay up? Pilot prep for this? Least bad place on plane for explosion? Best altitude? Gun in cockpit?"

The screen closed in on her face and the two voices in a pretty good interview, certainly timely. The monitors of the other networks showed the anchors phumphing, recapping, adding little new. Off camera now, Irving called a source at the CIA at home, asked one question, was rebuffed, told the guy he would get him one day, and hung up. Riffling the pages of his address book—he had once tried one of those whizbang computer cards, but the book was faster—he called the duty officer at Langley, identified himself, and asked to be put through to Dorothy Barclay, the DCI, at home. In a moment, she came on.

"I'm in my car on the way back to the office, and this is an open line," she said.

"I need Davidov's home number, right now. It's on your hotline card, about tenth down on the list, in the wallet in your bag."

"It's eight in the morning in Moscow, Irving. He may already be at work."

"Not him. And it's Saturday there. You know what's going on, Dotty. We've known each other for a long time, and I really need this. I really . . . need . . . the number. I won't tell where I got it."

"I don't have Davidov's number. He's too new."

"You're lying to an old friend, Dotty. I'm surprised at you."

"I can give you Viktor Gulko's home number. He's the Russian President's right-hand man. He has a red phone on his night table to the top man. I swear he's better for your purpose than Davidov, who's down the line at the KGB."

She read off the numbers of the presidential aide's home and private line at the office, and promised the same for anybody else if this aide was not available. Irving thought it odd she did not have Davidov's number, but was glad to be given what amounted to an upgrade. He knew all along he had been smart to keep her secret years ago, at a time when her closeted lesbianism would have made her a security risk. Dorothy Barclay was a good investment. Few other reporters could call her at home at night for a piece of information, and nobody else dared call her Dotty.

He got Gulko on the line first crack, at his apartment; must have woken him up. The Russian had not yet heard about the hijacking, but he knew Irving's name from his writings on counterterrorism, and was familiar with the mess in Nagorno-Karabakh. Irving filled him in on the bare details and told him what he had in mind. Gulko, who Dotty had probably chosen because he was antibureaucratic, reacted swiftly and positively.

Irving tapped Viveca on the arm, interrupting her interview with the pilot. "I got somebody here, on the line from Moscow. He can help explain what's going on in the place where the hijacker comes from. His name is Viktor Gulko, he's the President of the Federation's right-hand man. Mr. Gulko, you're on the air to everybody in America. First tell us what's the state of the war down in Nagorno-whatever."

That was a softball to let the man wake up and gather his thoughts. Irving knew what he wanted Gulko for, and knew that what he would ask for was in the Russian Federation's best interests. The question was a setup for a yes, would advance the story, and might even help the President in his tight spot. As the Russian aide sketched the outlines of the ethnic strife between Armenians and Azeris, it occurred to Irving that he could make a reporter out of the woman seated next to him. He wrote out for Viveca: "Bust in with—would you be willing to call your contacts down in that republic and get them to find someone who will try to talk the hijacker out of her plan? We can patch whoever it is through to the plane."

One thing about Viveca—in a fluid situation, she took direction. She waited until Irving was in the middle of a question about the cause of the Armenian uprising to put her hand on his arm, on camera, and say: "Let me break in, Mr. Gulko, with this question: would you be willing, right this minute, to call your contacts down in that republic and get them to find someone who will talk the hijacker out of her plan?"

"Well, yes, of course," Gulko said after the briefest hesitation, perhaps aware he was broadcasting to millions from his bed. "I will first call my superior, who will call the Russian President. I am sure he will be eager for us to do all we can to help avert this danger to the life of the President of the United States. When I get the Armenian leader who can help, or perhaps a relative of the hijacker, I will use the hotline to the White House?"

"The switchboard may be jammed," said Irving, picking up on the Russian's rising inflection. He wanted to maintain control of the communication. "Call this number, and we'll patch you through to Whacka and onto the plane." He took off his lapel mike and gave him the number, hoping it would not go over the air to let every nut call in.

Gulko would know what Whacka was; the KGB tapped its transmissions often enough.

Viveca then started interviewing Irving about who Gulko was; the detail about the red phone on his night table to the boss added a nice touch but didn't last long, so she switched to what a successful intercession could mean to relations between the two former rivals. In time, she got a signal in her ear to do a wrap-up and switch to Washington. She stumbled through that, only slightly disoriented by all that had been going on, but still crisp and authoritative in her cue to the bureau in Washington.

"Sam's just coming in the building," said the floor manager. "He'll take over."

"That's nice," was all she said. Irving thought she was relieved but did not want to show she wanted relief. A minute into the Washington feed, however, she sat up sharply and reacted to the message in her ear. Red light. "We interrupt to bring you this transmission from Air Force One."

It was the AP reporter from the press pool. "The crisis is over," he reported. "The hijacker was shot in the head and killed instantly by the copilot, who had a concealed weapon in the cockpit. The decision to risk an explosion was taken by the National Security Adviser on the recommendation of the head of the Secret Service detail."

Other reporters on the plane came on with interviews, and finally the President himself came on with a statement of reassurance to the public and thanks to his crew. Irving figured the delay was due to a slow speechwriter, but forgave the ghost when he heard the line "I understand that the Russian government, when asked to help by an American journalist, was forthcoming, and I want to express the gratitude of the people of the United States." Now the Russians owed Irving a big one. Dotty would look good, too, when she took credit internally for making it possible.

The network coanchor came on the set, congratulated Viveca, and told her to finish the show, insisting he wasn't needed. These piranhas knew when to be gracious, Irving figured.

When it was all over, she told Irving, "You were excellent." No big hug, no you-saved-my-ass, just a prim acknowledgment of professionalism.

That was okay with Irving Fein. Television had never been his medium. He was glad to have been able to show her, as well as any real journalist who watched, how to advance a story. The grateful producer sent them home in separate limousines. Irving told the producer, who seemed overwhelmed by Viveca's ability to jump in and ask the key question of the Russian on the phone, that he would be sending in a bill for his services, maybe a grand. He never did TV just for the glory of it; he had a little stickum note on his computer with a quotation from Samuel Johnson: "No man but a blockhead ever wrote except for money."

Then he told the limo driver to drive around for an hour or so, down Fifth Avenue, around to Times Square, up to Columbus Circle. Even better than the feeling of luxury was the experience of luxury for which someone else was paying. He called everybody he could think of around the world from the car.

Chapter 20

NEW YORK

Michael Shu knew he was impressionable, but found the offices of a high-powered literary agent to be truly impressive. On top of that, he was soon to be a full participant in an impressive meeting.

Two nights before, freshly returned from a trip to Moscow, Riga, Paris, and the Bahamas, he had watched Irving Fein with his new book partner, Viveca Farr, cover the hijacking crisis. Now here he was with those media stars, invited to a meeting in the Madison Avenue offices of Matthew "Ace" McFarland, renowned as a man who made everybody rich. Shu was proud to be part of the team and grateful to Irving for dealing him in. And after lunch, he was going to meet the ringer for the sleeper, an international banker who traveled in the circles only the most senior of the Big Six accountants ever got to see. This was the big time.

He arrived early, looked at the stack of books by authors represented by McFarland ("Call him Ace, he loves it," Irving had told him), and picked up a *New York Times.* The television review of the coverage of the hijacking put Viveca's network far in the lead, not only for being the first broadcast net on the air with sustained interruption of programming, but for reaching around the world for guests that illuminated the background. "Ms. Farr, though stumbling through her wrap-ups, and quite understandably looking somewhat haggard with no makeup—she went on the air at a moment's notice—made the most significant reportorial contribution of the evening with a pointed question to a Kremlin aide. The reporter asked the Russian about reaching out to agents in the war zone to establish a phone link between the hijacker and some of her compatriots who opposed her violent demonstration."

He had to go back and read it again, but the upshot was surely favorable; Michael was sorry the reviewer did not acknowledge Irving as the first to suggest the possibility of a cleaning woman breaching security. But Irving got a plug, too: "Mr. Fein, a print media journalist well known for his dogged enterprise, scored with the timely call to his high-ranking Russian source. It pays to have a little black address book. Though clearly not comfortable before the camera, and inclined to slump in his chair and to mumble, Fein's down-home, unpolished bearing provided a nice counterpoint to Ms. Farr's crisp television professionalism."

Michael straightened in his reception-room chair. The reviewer had Irving's physical demeanor down pat; he did have a tendency to melt into whatever he was sitting on. The elevator doors opened and Irving bounded out; somewhere in the accountant's mind there was this poetic image of a great beast "slouching toward Bethlehem." He held up the paper: " '. . . scored with the timely call to his high-ranking Russian source.' You were a hit."

"I never look at reviews, waste of time. Am I late?"

"Viveca's not here yet. I didn't want to go in without you. Yeah, we're six minutes late. You should see what I got in the Bahamas."

"A tan? A dose? You really shouldn't go for those great-lookin' casino dolls, Mike—they're shills for the house."

Michael shook his head; the reporter was a kidder, almost every line ending in a rising inflection, but Irving knew what they were after: evidence of major money movements and transfers of bearer bonds through Bahamian banks to or from the Soviet Union and its satellites in 1988 and '89. These would be the clues to how and where the sleeper was operating.

One of Irving's friends, a longtime con man forced to live offshore, had led Michael to a government official who was able to allow a look at some computer records for a small fee and the promise of a journalistic favor one day. "Irv, your crooked buddy down there said to look at the barter arrangement of oil for sugar with Castro in Cuba. A lot more oil came from the Sovs than the deal called for, and was sold in Puerto Rico, and somebody made a bundle that was socked into a Bahamian bank."

"You got all that in a memo for Dominick?"

When Michael began to pull it out of his briefcase, Irving told him to save it, because Viveca was coming off the elevator.

"Lipstick and everything," was his greeting. "I liked you better the other way—'somewhat haggard.' "

So Irving had read the review; Michael Shu knew he was a kidder. She shot the reporter a mock scowl and led the way down to Ace's office without waiting to be announced.

"Viveca! Irving! And you too, young fellow. I have great news! Sit-sit."

They sat-sat. On the wall opposite was a huge painting of what seemed to Michael to be nothing. It was all white, in a slim gold frame on a white wall. Irving noticed him studying it. "Like it, kid? White cow eating celery in a snowstorm. Cost Ace a fortune. Symbol of decadence, purity, whatever you see in it." Shu assumed it was a tax-avoidance scheme he had not yet heard about.

"I have to say how proud I am to be associated with you two." Ace beamed. "Did you see the tape afterward? You were magnificent."

"I never look at myself on tape," she said.

"I never read reviews," Irving added.

"The mark of the professional. I exploited this opportunity immediately," Ace went on. "Thirty million people were coming to know the two of you, and trust the way you worked together, the other night. Viveca, you were already a household name, a familiar face, but you needed an extra boost of credibility that experience brings." He swiveled to face Irving. "And you, my old friend, were known as the greatest reporter in the world among your peers, but most people thought of you only as a byline in cold print. Now that's all changed. Today you two are fused together as a reporting team, followed and admired by millions."

"Cut the shit, Ace. How much did you get for the advance?"

"I'll do my share on this project," Viveca said, "but fusing is more than I had in mind. Did you make a sale?"

"I told the publisher that I had been negotiating with, on an exclusive basis because of the story's secrecy, that the three hundred thousand we had been talking about would no longer do. As a result of the smash hit on television the other night, I told him, I had expressions of eager interest from others, and simple fairness forced me to open it up to competitive bidding."

"Without saying what the story is," Viveca cautioned. "We don't want anyone else to get onto this, or to jeopardize the man who's to impersonate the sleeper in any way. Only the three of us—Irving, me, Michael here—know."

"Relax," Irving told her. "Ace made it all up to jack up the bid."

"I then proposed not to open the bidding to others," the agent continued, obliquely confirming Fein's analysis, "for an advance of half a million dollars. Of course, that was my asking price, to get them thinking munificently."

When neither of the coauthors wanted to ask the next question, Michael stepped in: "And what will they hold still for?"

"Three-fifty advance in two pieces, as Irving wanted, not three; plus twenty-five thousand for research, that's your fine associate here; and twenty-five more in reimbursable expenses, mainly travel." He held a triumphant finger aloft. "And—and—a seventy-thirty paperback split, as Viveca wanted. Ninety-ten on first serial, eighty-twenty on foreign sales. Of course, we retain all movie, television, and electronic rights, including CD-ROM and anything on-line."

"Grab it," said Irving.

"Take it," she agreed.

"I took it."

"I agree, too," Michael put in.

Ace seemed to ponder a moment. "I should also put in a clause retaining all dramatic rights, to give us the basis for a claim in case anybody tries to make a miniseries based on the facts you report." He held up his hand to prevent an outburst from Irving. "I still say, after this is over, there are still fictional possibilities—"

"This is not a novel," said Irving grimly, repeating it like a mantra. Michael knew of Irving's only attempt at fiction, done after a bitter experience at a magazine: a short story about a magazine editor who was murdered by a rejected author. The accountant always thought Irving's title was lively—"Kill Fee"—but publishers said the plotting was so convoluted and the background so burdened with facts that the story never got off the ground.

"I have to work out a new theory of the story," Irving declared.

Michael Shu knew what Irving was working on, but it must have been a mystery to Viveca.

"What's that supposed to mean?" she demanded.

Michael was surprised at her hostility; it was as if they had come too close in the coverage of the hijacking and she wanted to push him away. They were downstairs in a delicatessen near Ace's office, Irving helping himself to great forkfuls of the free sauerkraut, cupping his palm to catch the dripping juice.

"Like a prosecutor starts with a theory of a case," the accountant explained to her. "It's the hypothesis, what you go on. Irving starts with it, but he doesn't have to stick with it."

She seemed not to like the change of subject. "Michael here has an appointment with Edward and me tonight," she told Irving, "to go over his memo about the bank in the Bahamas. Now you want to go off in some other direction?" The accountant was glad she made that point; Irving did have a tendency to take sharp turns, sometimes wasting a lot of research time.

"An essential element has just changed, kiddo. Used to be, we were using the fake sleeper to play the KGB off the Feliks bunch. We didn't have a dog in their fight." Irving seemed to be thinking this through as he was talking. "We figured both sides would come after our boy, the fake sleeper, to get their hands on the money. That way, we'd be players, and find out from both the KGB and the Russian mafiya what they knew about what the assets were."

"Which would make it easier to find out where to find the assets," Shu put in.

"But now the Russian government tried to do the U.S. a big favor, and the President thanked them for it right in public. All very palsy-walsy. Up to now, the CIA has been antsy about this whole thing, except for my guy. But I got my Russian source's home number from Dorothy Barclay the other night, which she has surely told the President. She wants to get a little credit for the Russian gesture, too. Presidents look kindly on spooks who try to save their lives."

"So how does this change the plan?" Viveca was out of it, but Michael could see where the reporter was heading.

"Now the CIA might want to return the gesture of good faith to the KGB. They may want to line up with the good-guy Russians against the Feliks people."

The accountant stopped him there. "That gets us into Russian politics in a big way. What if Davidov and the good guys in power now get shoved out by the Feliks people?"

"We lose." Irving threw up his hands. "Story's blown, we never find the money. The real sleeper uses the fortune to finance the Feliks people, who are no better than the commie crowd that sent him over here in the first place."

The stakes in this began to dawn on Viveca. "The sleeper could use the money to foment another Russian revolution." When Michael nodded encouragingly, she added, "Upheaval. Financial panic. Maybe civil war."

"And it could spread, and there's nukes in that country," Michael noted. He believed they were embarked on a significant quest, beyond exciting journalism.

"Like I say, it's a helluva story," said Irving in his parochial way. "And there's a risk in our government betting on the losers. I think that's why Dotty wanted to keep the Agency out of it. The CIA estimate may have been that the Feliks people will win in the end."

"But now that hands-off mind-set may be changed," said Michael, picking up Irving's drift. He found this strategic stuff exciting. "The White House may want to get more involved on the side of the current regime. Help it find the money to stay afloat. Irv, you've got a good source at the CIA, and now you've got an in with the DCI herself. Maybe we should try to work a little closer to Langley?"

The heavy plates of overstuffed sandwiches, with seeded rye soaked in the juice of cole slaw and Russian dressing, were slammed down on the table. Viveca lifted off the top slice of bread and proceeded to eat the smoked turkey and corned beef with fork and knife. Irving stared at her plate as if he'd never seen that done before.

"They're very thick sandwiches," said the accountant, to avert a fight. "Hard to get your mouth around." The incredulous waiter stared, too, until Michael waved him off.

Irving was giving Michael's suggestion some thought. Shu knew the reporter hated to get in bed with spooks anywhere, even our own, because he believed the media business and the world of spies worked at cross-purposes. But the Agency's new impetus toward helping the KGB on this might open a new channel to the story.

"Our plan was to get in bed with nobody," Irving mused aloud, "not the CIA or the KGB or the Feliks people. Pick up a little here, a little there, dangle our fake sleeper out there to see what comes in."

"Doesn't Edward have anything to say about this?" Viveca seemed defensive about the banker she had helped reel in. "He's the one who's being dangled."

"Run Mike's idea about working with the CIA past Dominick at your dinner tonight," said Irving, and sank his chops deeply into his triple-decker Reuben. Michael could tell the reporter was just as glad not to be the one to recommend danglehood to the impersonator. He averted his eyes as Viveca daintily fed herself another forkful of wet sandwich.

"Irving, is that you?"

"If it sounds like me, and you dialed my number, it's very possibly me."

"I'm here at the grillroom of the Four Seasons restaurant," Shu said, shielding the phone with his hand. "Ed Dominick just went downstairs to take a leak. I'm using a cellular phone at the table."

"I always knew you'd make it big, Mike."

"This place was his suggestion. Look, I'll give you a full fill when I see you, but you ought to know right away that our boy doesn't like my new idea about the Bahamas at all. I mean, he made no bones about it. Play the field, he says, no going steady."

"He digs being dangled, then? Good for him; we stick to the plan. He like your memo?"

"He thinks like a banker and has his own ideas. I fear he may want to take the investigative bit in his teeth, if you know what I mean."

"I don't ride horses. Come on over to my hotel when you're through. See if you can draw our boy out on his own theory of the case."

"Check. And by the way, what do I do when the check comes?"

"You're only a pipsqueak bean counter and he's a big-shot banker. What do you think?"

Michael Shu hit the END button and returned the phone to the waitress, a severely attractive woman dressed like a man who gave him a nutted roll in return. It was his third delicious roll; no sooner did he finish than another appeared on the plate.

"Who's here I should know?" he ventured to ask.

She nodded toward the booths against the rosewood wall. He recognized a former National Security Adviser with a beautiful, earnest young woman who Michael presumed was his researcher. A serene television interviewer more celebrated than any celebrity booked on her show was in another booth listening to the reveries of an aging pundit whom Shu recognized from an occasional television appearance. When the accountant asked whether anyone was there from the publishing or banking worlds, the waitress smiled and said, "The rest of them."

Edward Dominick, in a dark banker's suit, trotted up the steps to the grillroom, nodded to a couple of the men at a table on the way in, but did not stop to visit; Michael assumed it was not done. As soon as he slid into the seat to Michael's left, the "power lunch" was served: a naked piece of fish, a salad of esoteric leaves, and a bottle of imported mineral water. It reminded Shu of a Mexican breakfast—a glass of water and a cigarette—but that was now an ethnic slur, and anyway, nobody in this health-conscious place drank or smoked. It would be the wrong restaurant to bring Viveca to.

"I've been thinking about your friend Fein's 'theory of the case,' " said Dominick. "I like the idea of beginning with such a hypothesis. Let me suggest one of my own that will be more useful."

Shu listened as Dominick politely dissected and dismissed much of the work he had been doing, especially in the Bahamas. "The trouble with most journalists," he said, "is that they approach the amassing of great fortunes in terms of ill-gotten gains. You want to know—where is the 'hot' money? Your mind concentrates on gambling and drugs and armaments. And that's where your sources are, right?"

The accountant nodded; that was the trail he was on.

"Here is why I would set that aside. Drug profits are laundered through gambling operations that deal in cash. The lines of power are laid, and it would be foolish for a new operator like our sleeper to try to break in."

"But dealing in armaments generates megabucks," said Michael. What was bigger than mega? "Gigabucks."

"But armaments are heavy to transport, not easy to steal without a trace. You ever try to hide a tank or an airplane?" The accountant shook his head. The banker nodded and went on: "Suppose the Communist Party leaders toward the end of the eighties said to the sleeper, here are two hundred of our latest tanks, worth ten million each. Or a hundred fighter-bombers, worth a hundred million each. Or a year's production of missiles. How does he transport them? And who will he sell them to—with nobody noticing in either the Red Army or in the CIA? It's absurd."

He had a point. "You'd have to cut in a few arms dealers, too," Mike noted, "and they take a big bite."

"Same thing with a cutout country, I think it's called. So set aside, Michael Shu, Certified Public Accountant, the obvious asset sales of military equipment. You could make a few billion that way, mind you—just as you could transfer a few billion in gold to certain banks we both know—but that's not thinking big."

"Diamonds? Russia's a big producer."

"Couple of hundred million dollars. Waste of time."

Shu liked that. He rolled his big idea forward: "Plutonium?"

That stopped the banker. "It's portable. It was surely stealable. And it's the most valuable substance in the world. Buyers like Libya and Iran could afford five billion for twenty pounds of plutonium, enough for a half-dozen bombs. You have something there. I'd invest some time in that."

Another nutted roll appeared, and Shu took it automatically. Dominick declined, sipping his fizzy water. "Commodities," Michael offered eagerly. "BCCI got away with murder, and the Banco Lavoro was worse—a hinky-dinky branch office in Atlanta ran more than five billion in grain, and it was rolled over into arms. Right under the Fed's nose."

"That's thinking bigger. The trick in making huge profits in grain is to know what the world supply will be. My guess is the Russian sleeper would be heavily into the grain business. Using U.S. Department of Agriculture guarantees for his loans, he could draw on his advance knowledge of secret Russian crop reports and Soviet satellite intelligence of Canadian and Australian production."

Shu laid down another card. "He'd use some of his original stake to buy a bank in one of the ABC islands offshore. And to buy a commodities broker in Chicago and a stockbroker in Canada. I'd also want to take over a small, classy investment bank in New York."

"Good thinking. Now what about transport?" said Dominick, urging him on.

"Yeah, ships. I would set up a front company, or better still, buy a shipping company and hollow it out, to assemble a fleet of tankers and freighters. My assets would be floating on the seas, with other commodity assets inside, every delivery a guaranteed profit."

"The trick is not to get greedy, but never to lose," Dominick said. "Keep going."

"In two years," Michael said, "I would also own a major money-exchange broker. London would be my choice. Who made a killing in the decline of the pound in 1990? Who sold the ruble short that year? And where did that profit go?"

The banker shook his head. "Now you're tempted to go into financial derivatives, swaps, butterfly straddles, all that trading on thin margin that became the craze in the early nineties. But the sleeper had to move fast in '88 and '89. Put yourself in his shoes, back then." Dominick paused, lost in a momentary reverie; Shu was just as glad not to have to dig into the world of derivatives, of which he knew little. Besides, in that market it was possible to lose big, and the trick in assembling a huge fortune quickly was never to lose. Dominick came back: "Do you know anything about transfer rubles?"

Michael did not. "I was absent the day we took transfer rubles."

"That was the currency the Comecon banks, the Soviet bloc, used for dealings between, say, the USSR and Poland. Its value was artificially set by bureaucrats, not by the market. God, the money you could steer into secret accounts by manipulating the spread between regular rubles and transfer rubles. The sleeper wouldn't speculate in ordinary currencies—only the ones he couldn't lose on."

"Stop there," the accountant said firmly. "We gotta get organized. We can't even begin to get a line on all the dealing you got in mind, and I got in mind, unless we pull the investigation together. You need a place, a setup to do this from. A war room, like they have in political campaigns. Your bank sophisticated enough?" Michael had been told by Irving to get Dominick to use his Memphis office. If the imitation sleeper was going to attract attention from the real article in the United States, it would help for the fake setup to be at an accessible address.

"We're not the hayseeds Irving Fein thinks, Michael. Memphis is the hub city of Federal Express." The accountant started to stammer an apology, but Dominick waved it off. "Do you suppose the Feliks organization, with its old KGB contacts, is ahead of everybody in this manhunt?"

"That was not the impression I got from Liana Krumins in Moscow last week. The Feliks crowd thinks he should be their man, and they're good and pissed he's disappeared."

"Tell me about her."

The accountant did not know where to begin. How could he describe what an independent force in a colorful Latvian blouse was like? As a young woman, Liana was, to Michael Shu, like no other he had ever met: serious but easily amused, sexy but aloof, a manipulative idealist. He kept telling himself to mistrust her because she was in cahoots with the sleazy Feliks outfit, but he felt a quality of authenticity about her, and thought he saw a depth of painful experience in her eyes that belied her years. None of that would he tell the banker.

"She's old for her age—twenty-six going on forty, you know? She's tied in tight to the Feliks people, and out to help them squeeze what they can learn out of the new KGB types." The accountant felt it necessary to add: "But she's a journalist. I mean, Liana's after a story, even though the wrong gang set her out after it. She's a born user, and she's using them by letting herself be used. Does that make sense?"

"Very perceptive." Then the banker threw him a fast one. "Is the CIA using Irving Fein, and Viveca Farr, and you?"

"Gee, no." Shu kicked himself for ever suggesting a close tie with the CIA; it had made Dominick suspicious. "You know, Irving zapped the Agency when everybody else was afraid to. Back when those fellas had real clout. But the reason he doesn't pop 'em much now is that they're down and out. Irving can get mean, and loves to bring down big shots, but he doesn't shoot the wounded. That doesn't mean we let the spooks manipulate us."

"I'm glad to hear that, though it would be nice to have the color of law in this enterprise."

Shu consulted an index card with the points he wanted to cover at this lunch. One to go. "Irving said to be sure you went to an ear doctor. You want to be hard of hearing in your left ear, like the sleeper."

"So Viveca told me. I have an appointment with an acoustics specialist at New York Hospital tomorrow." Dominick touched his left lobe. "And anything you can learn, from whatever source—maybe the Krumins girl—about the sleeper's first twenty years in the Soviet Union would be helpful."

The banker signaled to the captain and slid out of the booth. The accountant realized Dominick was not even going to bother signing a check; the captain would do that for him, presumably adding a prearranged tip. Shu was impressed.

"Michael, why don't you make your headquarters for the next few weeks in Memphis, Tennessee?"

Michael Shu nodded, and the banker looked relieved. "I'd feel more comfortable in this with you working closely with me."

Chapter 21

<u>RIGA</u>

Liana always had company.

Arkady or another of the Feliks people would step out of a doorway soon after she appeared in front of the station and fall into step about twenty paces behind her. She thought that when she grew old and ugly, she would stay involved with espionage in some way, so she would always be shadowed and never be lonely. And ever since her talk with Nikolai Davidov, the day he gave her the tape of her triumph over the guards at Lubyanka, a second presence could be felt, if seldom seen. Sometimes it was a man far behind the Feliks shadow; other times a woman in front of her, walking toward her home; occasionally both. Rarely the same persons; the new KGB apparently still had plenty of people to employ in subtle surveillance.

She found herself thinking about Davidov often, and not always in connection with the story. She could hear him saying, "I hate these interrogations, I always confess in the end," and it made her smile. Was he married? If so, that would not bother her. Was his a smiling new face on the same old KGB? That mattered. Did she trust him? Of course not; she had abandoned such foolishness long ago, in a cell in what had been the Nazi and Soviet headquarters. Would she use the telephone number Davidov had written on his card if the occasion arose?

She tried to come up with a way to make the occasion arise soon. His mind must be a maze of intrigue; almost equally fascinating was his mouth with that twisting grin. Why, then, the black leather jacket with all the metal zippers, like a rock star or a mafiya dealer? Not right for him; uncharacteristic; he was a serious man, an academician. She was certain he had kept a copy of the tape of her strip search. She hoped he played it every night before he went to sleep.

A babushka seated on a blanket with a baby at her breast and Russian *beriozka* dolls and surplus military hats blocked her way in the narrow street outside the station. At the outstretched hand offering a doll, Liana shook her head, but she was stopped by the voice—a man's voice—that said, "I have a message for you from America."

Liana took the doll in her hand and pretended to examine it. "Who in America?"

"From the one who sleeps. The message is: 'Do not let any of them use you to reach me. I will be in touch with you.' Do not buy the doll. Walk on."

"May I send a message back?"

"No." The hand came up and snatched back the doll, as if the bargaining for it had led to naught.

Liana started to turn to walk on, then wheeled back on the man in the babushka outfit. Who was this messenger to give her orders?

"Take this message back anyhow." The reporter Fein had taught her always to leave with a question. But she had no question of substance ready to ask. It came to her: "When and where shall we meet?"

"I'll pass it on. Walk away now."

That was better. Never remain passive. She walked away briskly; a few turnings later, she came on a man in an old Red Army hat and a boy selling similar items from Russia. To demonstrate an interest in street vendors to her followers, Liana stopped and examined a doll, dickered over the price, then bought a white marble good-luck mushroom.

She walked more slowly, wondering about the message. Who had sent it? Not the Feliks people; they could contact her at any time through Arkady, and besides, their purpose was to reach out for the sleeper, not to wait for him to come to them or the KGB. Nor was it likely the message came from the KGB; if Nikolai wanted her to know something, he would appear at her door and make himself at home. And the American accountant, Shu, representing the journalist Fein, had been open in his meeting with her.

Might the message actually have come from the sleeper agent in America? Liana did not let herself jump to that conclusion; more likely, it was a gambit of the KGB to trick the Feliks people or vice versa. Both groups liked to think of her as a pawn in their game. Most probably the sender was Davidov. His purpose was to dissuade her from letting his rivals, now centered beyond his official reach in the Baltics, use her journalist's credentials to lead them to the agent in America.

Of course, if the babushka's message was from the real sleeper, the verbal delivery by the souvenir seller would be a good way to deliver it—no way of its getting intercepted or recorded. She let herself give the contact a bit more credence; if the message was real, then it would confirm the existence of the sleeper as alive and active; up to now, he was just a distant theory of old spies.

She quickened her step. Perhaps she would be the one to get a news story that would not only shake the ministry here in Riga, like the broadcast she had done tonight about corruption in the Latvian government, but be picked up and marveled at all over the world. Liana was determined to meet Madame Nina, who apparently dominated an organization that struck fear into many hearts in Russia.

Surely Nikolai Davidov would know more about her. She debated whether to call the number on the card that the KGB operative had given her, and decided that would not be a good idea. Better that Nikolai should come after her; men usually did, for one purpose or another. She could not telephone Michael Shu in America to pass the word to Irving Fein about the sleeper's possible approach, because that transmission would be overheard by everybody.

When uncertain, press on ahead. She wanted to be the one to get this story. She decided to keep the message from the sleeper to herself. She would keep searching the files in Moscow, developing her relationship with Davidov, a high-level source in the KGB, and staying in touch with the Americans Fein and Shu. If tonight's warning message turned out to be authentic, and if her return message made the sleeper agent in America aware of her eagerness for a meeting, she could be on the verge of a coup that would make her the most famous journalist in the Baltics.

Chapter 22

CHICAGO

The sleeper, the man known to some of his searchers only by his real Russian name, Aleksandr Berensky, steepled his fingers in the darkened hotel room and considered the state of the chase.

The directors of the new KGB, who had no claim on his loyalty, were following his daughter to try to find him. Berensky found it amusing that Liana Krumins, who had never laid eyes on her real father, probably had not been told that she was the daughter of the target of her search. He believed she knew nothing of his American identity or whereabouts. She was an innocent in all this, so far; she was searching for a sleeper agent in America only for a journalistic reason, unaware that she was bait. Berensky had watched videotapes of her newscasts, provided him by his thoughtful control agent before the explosion in Barbados, and was impressed with her on-air performance. She did have what the Americans called "gumption"; the messenger he had sent to Riga had reported her refusal to take an order and her return message asking for a meeting. He would ignore it for a while.

His survival was his first priority. Did the new head of the Fifth Directorate know that the KGB's sleeper agent in America had the Soviet name of Aleksandr Berensky? Did those in Lubyanka know that the sleeper was the bastard son of Shelepin, the greatest Soviet spymaster of all?

He presumed the answer to both questions was yes. A half-dozen of his fellow students at the KGB's American Village knew of his training, and two had worked with the same handler; they surely had informed Davidov about the Russian identity of the agent sent to put down roots in the United States. But that was all they knew; the only ones who knew his American legend were the two KGB officials who had died in the air crash, plus Control, who had died trying to kill him. His legend had been exquisitely concocted and was highly resistant to background checks. The only other Russian agent with the need to know that legend was his confederate in Washington; now, Moscow did not know they worked together.

Eyes half-closed in the dark, the sleeper wondered whether Davidov's branch of the KGB knew that Anna Berensky, once Shelepin's secretary, was his mother. Did Davidov, a new man with no KGB roots, know that Shelepin's son—never given his father's last name—had married a Riga woman named Antonia, impregnated her, and then abandoned her to take on his sleeper assignment? Did Davidov know that Liana Krumins was their daughter?

He doubted it; at the very start of this great enterprise, Shelepin had told him he had erased all connections between his family in Russia and the agent who would work alone in America. Berensky believed that blackout meant not only records but any KGB staff with potentially troublesome memories. In this, he considered himself fortunate to be descended from a totally ruthless man.

The stolid wife, Antonia, was now running his late mother's ballet school in Riga, and the lively Liana was pursuing her journalism. That suggested that the KGB was in the dark, or at least Davidov's directorate was. He allowed himself to become certain of that conclusion: the sleeper deduced that Davidov and his "new" KGB operatives were unaware of Liana's true Kremlin lineage.

Seizure, torture, and swap—if he did know, what could be more natural? That is what the sleeper would do in Davidov's shoes, if the KGB knew that word of the women's arrests would get to Aleks Berensky in America. As far as he was concerned, they could do whatever they wanted with Antonia; he had always been glad to be rid of his Russian wife, and if their separation was made permanent by death, so much the better. But the daughter was of interest to him, more so as the years passed.

The agent rose and went to the hotel-room window facing Grant Park. He felt he had almost come to know Liana through videotapes of her recent Riga telecasts in Russian. In appearance, culture, and attitude, the vibrant and self-sufficient young woman seemed closer to him than his American daughters. Those two looked and acted like their late blond, all-American mother—materialistic predators roaming the shopping-mall jungle.

So much for the strangely inefficient KGB search. The pursuit of Berensky by the Feliks organization was another story. Latvia, now outside the KGB orbit, was its base; an extensive cabal of secret police old-timers was a part of its network; many of the new mafiya of entre-preneurs had become the Feliks organization's source of support. Some of those black marketers were aware of the ways Berensky offered to draw oil profits out of the country.

The dominant Madame Nina, and those in league with her, presumed—correctly—that Berensky was assembling this vast fortune for their use. He was inclined to think their trust was well placed, provided they could first bring the new Russian "reformers" to the economic brink of disaster. Yet he was aware that the clandestine orga-nization's leaders were growing impatient with him, even as they knew they could not afford to offend him.

Berensky wanted to be sure that the vast wealth he was assembling would be used for the original purpose Shelepin had drilled into his mind: to save and serve the strong Russia he was born to. His concep-tion of Russia was as a nation whose people were under the firm control of a central government in Moscow, with a leader who had a sense of Russia's imperial destiny. Communism had failed, but Russia must never be less than a superpower. The current regime in Moscow was drifting toward convergence with the West; Berensky had to be certain that the organization in Russia whose assets were entrusted to him was truly the heir of Shelepin's vision.

He wished he knew more about the leader Madame Nina. Control had failed to provide hard information about the shadowy woman.

His other pursuers were almost laughable. He viewed the American news reporters, the flamboyant Fein and the neurotic television girl Farr, as more of an inconvenient amusement than a threat. He had devised a way to monitor their amateur investigation patterned on what his father had told him about the Trust, a KGB entrapment operation started in the 1920s. Nothing they were doing was a source of concern to him.

Except for their employee, the Eurasian accountant, Michael Shu. Berensky turned away from the window and looked into the darkness of the room, irritated at a mere coincidence. Of all the offshore banks where major money could be run, why did this naive accountant have to have close connections with the Yellowbird Bank of the Bahamas? It happened to be the bank Berensky had bought five years ago and taken out of the dangerous business of laundering drug money, to be free for his far more lucrative currency trades and asset transfers. It was highly unfortunate that Shu knew most of the employees from the bank's former narcotics days.

Berensky determined to keep a close eye on Shu's poking around. If he came too close, and could not then be suborned, the accountant would have to be removed.

The sleeper found this prospect of violence neither troubling nor enjoyable; it would not be the first time he had protected his mission by creating an accident victim. Berensky recalled how, to protect his identity in the early days in America, he had arranged for the apparent suicide of a fellow agent when he discovered him doubling for the CIA. More recently, when the owner of a Swiss bank that handled the original $3 billion stake posed a threat, Berensky had been forced to direct his confederate in Helsinki to go to Bern and arrange another suicide. Now, with a $30 billion empire at stake, and the moment not yet ripe for the financing of a counter-counterrevolution, the sleeper remained ready to do whatever was necessary to protect his enterprise.

The telephone rang. He ignored it, knowing the call could not be for him.

He felt a great responsibility pressing on his chest: no less than the rejuvenation of Russia as a superpower and the regaining of an empire. He had been willing to live a lifelong lie, on his own, in enemy territory, to be ready for this moment. He presumed that his father, a Soviet man of extraordinary foresight, had envisioned as an eventuality the economic ruin of the socialist state, and had sent him into the heart of capitalism to assemble the capital needed for the recovery of national power. The sleeper agent was not about to let anything interfere with his historic mission. Especially not when it was so close to completion.

In an age when information was power, he had the information: at first from the Russian side, where advance knowledge of economic news and political acts that would affect trading had enabled him to multiply his initial stake tenfold on the anonymous and liquid currency markets.

More recently, he had been applying the same technique in the West.

A former East German Stasi cadre had offered itself for sale soon after the Berlin Wall fell, and Control had snapped it up. That was how he had gained a most valuable personnel asset, a Finnish economist, a striking and brilliant woman with ties to a source in the American Federal Reserve. Sirkka Numminen's access to inside information about moves planned at the Bundesbank and the Federal Reserve had helped Berensky build his fortune. And when called upon for wet work in Bern, she had justified the training of a lifetime.

He had positioned himself financially for one great final coup, one that would take his hoard to $100 billion. That would be enough to affect the balance of power in an impoverished Russia needful of the Shelepin vision of global dominance.

Thinking of his father, who had been hard of hearing, the sleeper pulled at the lobe of his left ear, where a small hearing aid nestled deep in the canal. One of his American daughters was complaining of not being able to hear her professors clearly. He hoped the genetic weakness had not affected Liana.

Chapter 23

"We have the first useful results of the surveillance of the sleeper's daughter, Director Davidov," Yelena said. She was irritated with herself; she was upset at the Director's unrelenting interest in the Riga television woman.

"About time."

"Our surveillance of her has been very expensive," she said. "Two people on two twelve-hour shifts. Not to mention the technical backup."

"I will retire some border guards. What results?"

"The transmitter on the clasp of her amber pendant worked this time," Yelena reported. The tiny, sensitive bug made in Taiwan had a broadcast range of nearly one hundred meters; the previous transmitter, manufactured years before in Soviet Ukraine and planted with great difficulty after a surreptitious entry of Liana's apartment, had emitted nothing but useless squeaks that were the cause of an intemperate outburst by Davidov, ordinarily a calm person. "She was accosted by a woman with a baby on a carpet selling *beriozka* dolls. Here is the transcript." She handed him the single page.

He read aloud the entire exchange between Liana Krumins and the messenger disguised as a babushka, from "I have a message for you from America" to the final "Walk away now."

Davidov held out his hand. "And now you will give me the report of the interrogation of the messenger," he said, "who we took into custody immediately."

"Unfortunately that did not happen."

The directorate chief closed his eyes and took a deep breath. "I gave specific orders to pick up anybody who made contact with this woman to pass on any information. The three men in the truck heard the exchange. The two shadows on the street saw it. The babushka messenger is the only known connection to the sleeper, if she is genuine. What happened to her?"

"Unfortunately she disappeared around the corner."

"Baby and blanket and souvenirs and all?"

"Those items were left behind. The baby turned out to be a doll. The messenger may have been a man. We can't tell from the voice."

"Fingerprints on the doll?"

"Nobody thought to check for that, Director. I'll see to it right away."

"There won't be any," Davidov said wearily. "The messenger was a professional. The sleeper agent is a professional. The only amateurs in this entire operation work for me. Unless they are extremely professional operatives who are working against me."

The intelligence analyst could not blame her boss for his touch of self-pity; a major tracing opportunity had been missed. "These are all new men and women on the case," she assured him. "So there will be no old loyalties."

He put his head in his hands, elbows on his desk. Then he looked up at her. "The sleeper is alive. He is active. He knows we are after him. He knows the Feliks people are after him. And he certainly knows we are both using his daughter to get to him. This seems to be worrying him."

"One thing he does not know," she jogged his memory, "is that we know the journalist in Riga is his daughter."

"He doesn't know whether Liana knows he is her father, either. Which she does not. An interesting epistemological situation." Yelena waited for him to come to the logical conclusion about Liana's status, and it took him longer than usual. "Which means she is a kind of hostage. And she does not realize it," he said finally.

" 'Bait' is the word you used," she reminded him. In the old days, under a different kind of Director, the sleeper's daughter would be more than "a kind of" hostage. She would be used, cruelly if necessary, to bring the father in, if the sleeper agent had any kind of paternal feelings. Perhaps he did not; a generation ago, the sleeper had willingly left his pregnant wife behind to take his American assignment. Berensky might be one of those purposeful men who treated water as thicker than blood.

"That message to Liana was like a nibble on our fishing line," he said, rising from the chair, sitting on the corner of the desk. "Not a strike, just a nibble, but we know the fish is there."

Chapter 24

"History of hearing loss in your family?"

The banker frowned. "My mother used to favor her right side, as I recall. She died thirty years ago, never wore a hearing aid. You really need to take a history?"

The hearing technician moved down her list of questions briskly; this guy was one of those executive types who wanted to waste no time. Yolanda Teeter, licensed audiologist, as the diploma on the wall attested, was the first black woman to reach the peak of her profession, and she refused to be anything less than thorough. "When did you first become aware you were having trouble in your left ear?"

"Hard to say, ma'am, been coming on a long time. Didn't want to admit it, I guess."

"But it's gotten worse recently? How can you tell?"

He moved his head to one side. "When I go like this"—he moved his head to the other side—"I can hear better than when I go like that."

"Do you have trouble distinguishing among voices when several people are speaking?"

"Yes, that too. Perhaps we can move on to the testing."

One of those. To him, the technology was more important than the technologist. "I need to know this, young man," she said with some severity. "Was there an explosion, or any loud noise trauma in the past, or any accident to the head recently, that might be connected to your loss of hearing?"

"No. It's come on slowly. I've been thinking of getting a hearing aid for years."

The audiologist noted "maternal history of presbycusis" on the chart and led him into the testing booth.

"Put these earphones on. I'll be on the other side of that window. Respond when you hear the tones." She put him through an air conduction test with the phones on to determine his sensitivity to sounds; based on his verbal responses, he had a moderate 45-decibel loss in his left ear.

She went into the booth, removed the phones, and attached a vibrator to determine the conduction of sound in his inner ear. Then, through the window again, to speech recognition; she played a tape saying: "Repeat after me—*cowboy, railroad, baseball.*" As she lowered the sound of the recorded voice, the patient said he thought *baseball* was *eraser.* He was able to discriminate *sail* from *fail* but said he heard *chew* when she said *shoe,* which suggested to the audiologist a difficulty in differentiating high-frequency sounds like the hissing of consonants.

Just to be sure, and because she was not troubled by causing the impatient client some delay and slight discomfort, she put a plug in his left ear and ran an impedance test of middle-ear function. This required no verbal response from the patient, who was subjected to pressure changes and loud, popping sounds. The machine bounced sound waves off the eardrum and analyzed the return wave, in the manner of radar; his left ear's reaction differed from his right.

"I need a hearing aid, don't I?" he asked. Without waiting, he added, "The best. Price is no problem."

She explained that she would prepare a report for his referring doctor in Atlanta, and he would then send the necessary double-negative letter—one stating there was no medical reason not to use a hearing aid. Kind of a backward prescription; she did not add her opinion that such paperwork of no disapproval was how doctors kept control of private patients and ran up fees.

"At the hearing aid evaluation next week," she said, "I'll show you what's available." She assumed he was a vain man, and would want the unnoticeable implant in the inner ear.

"Please—" he peered at the diploma—"Dr. Teeter, show me now."

Ms Teeter told him she was a technologist, not a doctor, and laid out the three systems. One was a two-inch device that hooked over the ear to rest behind it; it was easily removable but was losing popularity because of its klunkiness. Another was a smaller in-the-ear device, molded to the contour of the ear—noticeable but not obtrusive, the volume controllable directly by hand or by means of a hidden pocket unit. The third was an in-the-canal aid, all but invisible, but harder for the patient to reach and adjust. She assumed that the banker, who wore a rumpled designer suit that showed he cared about what he bought more than the way he looked, would choose the tiniest device, which was also the most expensive. He surprised her by choosing the mid-sized in-the-ear unit.

"I'm not vain, Dr. Teeter." He was obviously impressed with her specialist's degree, which she assumed required more regulation than afflicted his line of work. "I don't intend to hide the fact that I'm hard of hearing. I just want to be able to turn it on and off easily. Would you send your report to my doctor by overnight mail and tell him I want him to send his letter of authorization to you just as quick as he can? Do I get a copy of your report from you or from him?"

She said she could ethically give it to the patient directly, when he came for the fitting of the aid. "But it'll be in technical language that might upset a layman."

"I won't be upset no matter how alarming it looks, Dr. Teeter," he replied, repeating her name as bankers do when they want something. "I want the specific measurement of my hearing loss all on the record. I like to face the truth."

Chapter 25

POUND RIDGE

"It's a trap. They all want me to look bad."

"The bastards," Ace agreed. Empathizing with a client was more than a talent; it was part of his way of life.

"I'm not ready yet. I'll flop and they know it." Viveca gulped her wine, topped off his glass, and refilled her own. "Why do they hate me so, the brass at the network? I'm like a toothache they like to bite down on."

"They have no economic reason to want you to fail," the agent offered, and when he saw her glare, covered his too-rational point with a hasty "It must be envy." In her subsequent brooding silence, Ace added, "That was an excellent figure of speech, by the way. About the toothache."

"I got it from Irving Fein, and that's just the point: he's original and I'm not. He's been around forever and I'm new. He's a heavyweight newsie and I'm a—oh, I don't know what the hell I am."

You're a news presenter, Viveca, the agent said to himself, using the honest British term now making its way to America. The old term from radio days was "announcer." Nothing to be ashamed of, unless you're trying to pass yourself off as a hard-news journalist, in which case it is everything to be ashamed of.

"You're the one that the vast video audience wants to be the source of their information," he soothed. The young woman was an incipient star, and stars needed constant reassurance, providing which was another of his talents. Viveca Farr really was the perfect client for him, and her exposed-nerve vulnerability took the edge off her severe good looks, making her all the more appealing. As the elder stateman Bernard Baruch used to say to the beautiful Jinx Falkenburg, borrowing a line from Oliver Wendell Holmes, "Ah, to be seventy again."

"And you mustn't undermine your self-esteem by running down your journalistic experience," Ace cautioned, putting on a stern look. "Your performance under pressure the other day proved that."

"No, it didn't, dammit, just the opposite. Irving was carrying me, and I know it, and the network biggies know it too. That's why they want to put us together. Don't you see? He's got a lifetime of reporting to draw on, I've got nothing. It'll show."

Ace saw it quite differently. The pairing of these two wholly opposite types, which had struck a chord with television audiences that night, was originally his own idea in the literary arena. He made a mental note to remind the world of that at the proper time. He would call it "virgule matchmaking"—novice/old-timer, female/male, face/byline, crisp/sloppy—a form of casting almost as natural as Beauty/Beast, though that last was hardly fair to Irving. Juxtaposition of contrary personalities separated by a slash or virgule presented the viewer with a living oxymoron. And what worked in crisis, Ace suspected, could work as well every day when cemented by economic necessity. The network's suggestion was not all that off-the-wall, and the brass's purpose was surely not to do their property in, no matter what Viveca thought.

He could not say that, of course. Because Viveca had come too far too fast, she was in a constant state of believing the ice beneath her was thinning, and was deathly afraid of a single fissure opening up and swallowing her. With this woman, career was all. Pity about that, in a human way, but in another way—from the point of view of a skilled agent, dedicated more to the persona than the person—her fear of failing was useful and usable. Her dread of humiliation made all the more necessary the contractual protection and manipulative mothering that came so naturally to him. And the key to persuading Viveca, Ace determined from long experience with the brilliant and brittle, was in the device of reverse-selling.

"I'll tell the network you want to do exactly what you're doing," he said, "and to simultaneously deepen your journalistic background with an important book. They have to respect that."

" 'Respect' is the last thing I'll ever get from those—" Her lips formed a "p" but she stopped short of the word, he assumed out of respect for his years.

"Viveca, their reaction will be to say your collaboration with Irving on the air—with your professional ease and his likable awkwardness—would turn any book the two of you do into an automatic best-seller." He paused as if to think it over. "That's what they'll say. I'll brush that aside with the utmost scorn. How's the book coming, by the way?"

She drained her glass. The wine seemed to have no effect on her. Ace presumed she was one of the delicate-looking but hollow-legged variety of no-problem drinkers.

"The researcher, Mike Shu, is on to something in the Bahamas," she reported. "Irving is floundering, kind of—God, he's a moody one. Is this the way he usually works, a lot of rushing around and then a blue funk?"

Ace winced inwardly. He knew what that familiar behavior meant: Irving was on the outer fringes of an emotional involvement, working inward. Such attachments did not augur well for his investigative spirit now, or down the line for his timely production of pages. Irving was a sucker for a vulnerable woman, and Viveca, despite her air of mastery on the tube, fairly exuded vulnerability in person, bringing out the protective quality in men susceptible to that sort of thing.

"Fortunately," she added, "the banker we found to impersonate the sleeper is good. I'm sorry you can't know him—he insists on absolute security. But he's given a direction and a solidity to this thing. Weren't for him—" She shrugged, then looked at the thousand-day clock on the mantel. "He's coming for a dinner meeting tonight."

Ace took that to be his escape hatch and bounded to his feet. "I don't want to have to hide in the closet when he comes in the door. My French-farce days are over."

Viveca walked him out to his limo, huddling her bare arms together in the cold, and extended her cheek. Ace took that to be an improvement over the firm handshake last time; she was apparently growing more confident of his trustworthiness, which showed good judgment. He gave her an appropriate peck and waited just a brief moment, to give her a chance for some Parthian shot.

"I'm glad you didn't jump on this network offer as a way to promote the book," she said. "I suppose a regular spot on a prime-time show for the two of us would really make it a best-seller."

"Not only that, my dear. If you read the small print in your contract, you will note a clause I inserted, to wit: each appearance on the *New York Times* best-seller list triggers a bonus of twenty thousand dollars." He let that sink in before adding: "The sum doubles if the book is among the top three."

"Wow. Better not tell that to Irving."

"The only fine print he fails to read is in his own contracts." Ace caught his own pun and hastened to make it seem intentional: "*Fein Print* would be a good title for an anthology of Irving's works, wouldn't it? His next one, after this best-seller. From your point of view, of course—" He stopped. "Look at you, poor girl, goose bumps—you're practically turning blue. Go inside by the fire."

She rubbed her arms briskly and took the bait. "From my point of view, what?"

"That sort of bonus would force the publisher into a huge second printing, which would mean many more books in the stores, with posters and dumps, and a tripled advertising budget, a hot paperback auction, the whole—" He made a circular motion.

"Megillah," she concluded.

"What I had in mind was 'nine yards,' which someone once told me was the cubic content of a cement truck. Megillah? Your association with the likes of Irving Fein, my dear, is having its cultural impact." He popped into the backseat with a jaunty wave, his reverse sale well made. He would await the call sure to come with her second thoughts.

She heard the sound of a heavy car crunching the gravel. Viveca went out into the cold to greet the banker, again without a jacket, running her hands along her arms. She liked the way that her flesh, exposed to cold, made men—all men, without exception, even the media execs who perversely wanted to bring her down—plunge into a protective mode.

But the gooseflesh trick didn't work with Edward Dominick. He stood in front of the doorway for a long moment, looking back out at the view commanded from the height of the hill. "It's beautiful here," he said quietly, mournful eyes ranging along the purple ridges. "Reminds me of home."

After a while, she said, "You're right, it is beautiful, and I'm freezing my ass off." She took his arm firmly and drew him inside.

He spent the first few minutes as her father would have, examining the books lining the walls of her den. She poured the Saratoga water he asked for, grimly making another glass for herself, adding a dash of bitters to remind her of a real drink. "The books about intelligence work are on the middle shelf," she said.

"I don't read those," he said, still browsing. "And I'm not going to become a secret agent overnight, with tradecraft, dead drops, cloak-and-dagger stuff."

"If you're going to impersonate the sleeper—"

"—I have to put myself inside his mind, think the way he does."

"But he's a spy."

"No. He's a banker. He's secretly building a huge fortune. What spying has he done? None, for twenty years, as far as we know."

"Edward, the sleeper's whole life has been one long stretch of espionage."

"Strictly passive, as far as we know. Spying, for him, has always been something he would have to do, one day in the distant future. Nor is he being called on for espionage now. They want a secret financial agent, not a real spy." He ran his finger down her line of volumes about the clandestine wars. "You don't have R. V. Jones's books. He's the only one that does us any good."

She bit. "Why is that?"

"He's the Brit who teaches how to put yourself in your adversary's shoes. How to sit on both sides of the chess table."

She tried to remember what Irving had told her about that. "Angleton," she said.

That drew a blank look from Dominick; she reminded herself he was a banker, not a spook, and she would have to get some books about the history of banking—the life of J. P. Morgan, or whatever—as well as some tomes about global finance.

He took the sinkingest easy chair. She sat on the edge of the couch, giving her a few inches superiority in eye level. She had chosen a suit with a skirt, no jewelry—on the formal side for home entertaining, but she figured he would prefer an austere look, and she was eager to please.

"Where do we stand?" she asked crisply. "And how can I do more to help?"

"We've set up what Michael Shu calls a 'war room' in Memphis. I've hired a couple of computer-literate accountants from the Comptroller of the Currency, and a retired Treasury agent, as well as a customs man who moonlights. The ostensible purpose of it all is a study of global money flows from 1989 on. It's supposedly for a controversial study I'm doing to propose reforms of Fed oversight."

She could not help with that. Where did she fit in? She wanted to work closely with this man but not appear to be a novice.

He seemed to read her mind. "I don't need any help on the money angle. Shu is good, though he's off on a tangent looking into money-laundering in the Bahamas—waste of time, but you have to admire his enthusiasm. I'll get him on the commodities track in due course—grain, aluminum, oil. If I were the sleeper, that's where I'd make the big money."

"Is Irving helpful on this?"

"He keeps talking about his old CIA and KGB contacts, but that's not turning up the kind of information I need. What I need is his pattern of trading just before major events that move markets." He looked at her, expecting the natural question about what he did need, but she crossed him up by just looking back understandingly. Irving had told her she could find out more with a long look in silence than with an obvious question.

"Sooner or later, and I hope it's later, I'm going to have to impersonate the sleeper on his home ground in Russia. Meet his daughter, maybe his wife. I'll have to have ammunition for that, personal information, not just this silly thing in my ear."

Dominick cocked his head as if his new hearing aid were making a noise. "One of these days, you'll have to meet that Krumins girl, to extract everything she knows about her mother—the family details, pet names, anniversaries. That's in case I have to go there and impersonate her father. I'd sure hate to fly blind into that."

Viveca liked the notion of providing this man with information he needed to protect himself. "We're eating in the kitchen," she announced.

The caterer had left everything in pots on the stove. She had been briefed on serving the sautéed shrimps and mushrooms first, then the salad, then the tournedos of veal with rissolé potatoes. She presumed the little brown items in the pan were rissolé potatoes. The meal would be topped off with her own personal production: a pecan pie, her father's favorite, infusing the kitchen with the scent of blackstrap molasses. A man from Memphis had to like that, and when she went into detail about the recipe, he'd assume she'd made the rest of the meal, too.

She handed him a bottle of red wine and an opener to give him something to do. He popped the cork in a jiffy. Instead of admiring the wine, the details about which she was ready for, he ran his hand along the kitchen table.

"Where'd you get this French country table?"

"In France," she blurted. She had no idea where the decorator had found the table. It seemed solid enough. "Shipped it over with a whole container of stuff." She had heard somebody say that at a New York dinner party.

"You have a lovely home," he said. "Warm and authentic." He sampled the wine, nodded, poured hers. She had decided against candles as coming on too strong; the dimmable electric light in the big country kitchen was soft enough. "So your father was a banker," he said. Who had told him that? She recalled that she had, at their lunch in Memphis. What else did Edward know? Should she refer obliquely to his late wife? Better not.

She judged the meal to be a success, except for the pie, which had dried out. She blamed the caterer: "I should have baked one myself. I do a helluva pecan pie."

He went to the fridge, found a piece of Emmentaler cheese, zapped it in the microwave for ten seconds to take the chill off, and cut off slivers with a paring knife to accompany their second bottle of wine. So even the failure turned out to be a success. She felt safe with this man.

He helped her clear the table, which she would henceforward think of as her French country table—there was much to be said for previously married men—and then disappeared for a few moments, she thought to go the bathroom. He returned with a briefcase and spread the contents in neat stacks on the table.

The seminar began. He went on and on about the financial paper trail of the sleeper, about brokerage fronts and shell companies; she kept an interested look on her face. Edward was a strong man, dominant without being domineering, apparently with none of her father's weaknesses.

"You must have a lot of questions, but it's late," he finally said mercifully. Viveca was sleepily his for the taking, and she knew he knew it. She also knew that their coming together would be at some other time and place of his choosing, with mature affection, and without the need to humiliate her that drove the men who were most attracted to her. With this man, she might be neither ashamed nor rigid, the consequence of not being called upon to perform.

"I'll do my part in all this," she promised. "Tell me what you want from me, I'll do it."

"You do have a certain aura of success about you," he noted.

That drew a wry smile. "I live in dread of losing what I have. If I ever blew this career, I'd crawl in a hole and never show my face to anybody again. I mean that. A lot of people think I don't belong where I am. They're rooting for me to mess up."

"What if you did? You ever look failure in the face?"

"I saw it clearly enough in my father's face." She saw that look mixing panic and despair every time she thought of him. "If I flopped—really badly, enough to get fired, and humiliated—I'd run away and get a job slinging hash somewhere. Yucatan, maybe." Cutting off contact with everyone was the least she would do; suicide sounded too dramatic, but it was an option. She did not suppress a shudder; a career crash was her recurring, wide-awake nightmare.

Viveca was aware, and knew that he was aware, that their enterprise now had a romantic cast. With this surefooted man at the center, the sleeper seemed less menacing. She would let herself worry more for Edward's safety in this than her own.

She walked him out to the car, and this time her goose bumps worked. The impersonator kissed her tenderly and rubbed her arms warm.

Chapter 26

MEMPHIS

"Come on down to Memphis, Irv, you've got to see this." Michael Shu was all excited. "We've got a war room here at the bank. We're all organized. I'd say we're making real progress."

Irving Fein wasn't so sure. Since Edward Dominick had been recruited, a task force of financial pros had been set up that cost too much, even though the space at the Memphis bank was free. Dominick had worked out a "search strategy" to track the sleeper's moves that impressed the hell out of the accountant in Shu, but stuck Fein as being on the methodical, unimaginative side.

The second call dragged him down to Tennessee. "We have a real tiger in Edward," Viveca told him, as if she were a judge of investigative talent. "He's going to put on a briefing for me tomorrow down here. You ought to take it in, too."

She had been getting briefed by this guy all too regularly; Irving felt cut out of his own story. If the two of them were making out, that was their business, but hanky-panky within the team tended to stir up emotions that warped judgment. It gave him a small stitch in his side to think of her falling for this Southern executive smoothie, outside their world. He told his euphoric partner he had to see a money-laundering guy in the Fraud section of Justice that night but would get the first plane to Memphis in the morning.

Dominick and Shu were ready for them with a dog-and-pony show—slides, charts, the analytical works, as if to justify all the time put in so far.

"Let's assume the sleeper's first objective was to turn three billion in gold into fifty billion within three years, starting in late 1988,"

Dominick said. "The second objective has been to keep the fortune growing since then, but to conceal and tightly control the assets."

Click went the lights, clunk went the slide projector. "Advantage over Market Investors" was first on the screen, and under that, "Ability to use (a) USSR commercial power to affect markets or (b) intelligence services to obtain valuable information."

"Here are the considerations the sleeper must have had in his mind to make the most of his position," Dominick said. On the screen were five criteria:

1. ability to influence prices
2. ability to predict prices
3. liquidity
4. leverage
5. visibility

"The greatest influence on market prices," Dominick told them, "could be exerted on commodities where Moscow was the prime supplier."

"Great grain robbery," murmured Fein.

"Right, like wheat. The USSR produced a fifth of the world's wheat, and imported another tenth. Expectation of the harvest affected the price of wheat futures, along with the size of the planned purchases. You could have set up a grain-futures operation—which we've replicated in our war room down the hall—and generated enormous profits."

"Big money, plenty of liquidity," added Michael Shu. "The open interest of wheat futures in the U.S. is about eleven billion."

New slide. "Another commodity is aluminum—not as liquid as gold, but you could hide big trades, with about fifty billion traded in New York in 1989. Price is volatile, which is good for manipulation, and the USSR produced fifteen percent of the world market. You get a second play in the stocks of the three big aluminum companies."

"I dug up a story about how half the aluminum in the world went through Belgium that year," said Shu, "and Belgium doesn't manufacture aluminum. So something funny went on there in a big way. Could be the sleeper moving money through Belgium."

"Gold is more liquid?" Viveca put in, obviously wanting to be a part of the conversation. Irving had a difficult time expunging his mental picture of Dominick jumping on her bones, those slim legs trying to clasp around that big linebacker's body; that event might not have happened yet, but Irving was certain it would. "If the original stake was in gold, wouldn't that be the commodity of choice?"

"That's what everyone would expect him to do," Dominick replied. "But if I were the sleeper, I would shy away from the expected. For concealment."

"I'm looking into that, though," said Shu. "Gold production was handled by the Glavsolot, which never released official data and is still tight as a tick, but gold bullion is exported through the Vneshtorg-bank, and one of our ex-Treasury types has an in there."

Dominick shrugged and moved on to the next slide. "Oil. Now we're talking big price movements, absolute secrecy. Soviets produced a fifth of the world supply."

"Yeah, but OPEC called the shots," Irving recalled, looking for a place to doubt, "and the Sovs went along on the price." He knew something about the oil market, because several of his money-laundering contacts were active in it and kept using words like "fungibility."

"He must be heavy in oil," the banker said with certitude. "As you suggest, the Soviets were in close touch with the Arabs on pricing. And KGB agents could easily have been bugging those OPEC meetings, to make certain their information was right."

"You could hide big trading," Shu supported Dominick, "in four hundred billion a year in oil futures that year, mostly in New York and London. And you could park a lot of inventory in tankers. The first thing the sleeper would go into would be the shipping business."

"I'll grant that oil is fungible," Irving said. That drew a respectful look from Viveca; there's a word she'd be asking her banking boyfriend about over a bottle of fine red wine, not the red ink she'd served Irving Fein. Mental-picture time again: to avoid getting crushed, she would be on top. "What about currencies?" Irving knew nothing about currencies.

"Michael here and I gave a lot of thought to the currency markets." Dominick turned off the slide projector. "Excellent leverage, no problem with concealment, some ability to influence markets. But the risk is too great. One wrong move and you're set back by billions." Irving felt those mournful eyes fix on him. "The trick in amassing a great fortune quickly is not to take chances on big setbacks, to concentrate on the sure things. That's what the sleeper has been doing, I'll bet. I doubt he'd go for currency speculation."

Only because Dominick resisted, Irving hung in. "What if you had a mole in the Fed?" That thought met with silence. He went on: "We all make a big deal about a penetration agent in the CIA, but what if you had a guy sitting next to the Fed Chairman at the big meetings in New York where they decide interest rates? Or, hell, just tap the room, find out what they'll do the next day—couldn't you make a pile?"

"The place to have had such a mole," said Dominick, no longer so dismissive, "was in the Bundesbank. But no—too great a gamble. You can never be certain in currencies, even when governments try to intervene. The trick here is to limit your investments to sure things. That's the only way to build a huge fortune in a few years." He rose. "Shall we look over the war room?"

Shu led the way. In a midsized, windowless area—secure, and less valuable than space with a view—the accountant's minions were working computers and looking at teleconferencing screens.

"To parallel the other operation," the accountant said proudly, "we've set up a hedge fund in the Antilles, ostensibly run by an attorney of record in Liechtenstein. Mr. Dominick, at my suggestion, bought a little bank in the Bahamas—remember our crooked source there?—and we can put trading profits there with no questions asked."

"We've set up about thirty trading relationships with commercial and investment banks in the past three weeks," Dominick explained to Viveca, who was observing the operation with her arms crossed defensively. "Every one of the trades we've made was completely hedged, which means that what we make buying with one, we lose selling to the other."

"What's the point in that?" Good question; Irving was glad she asked.

"Makes us players, people who pay up promply, folks to trust. Here—you see this man buying and selling oil futures simultaneously? We break even, maybe costs us some small change, but we establish a relationship with both banks at the same time on millions of dollars of trading. That's surely what the sleeper did when he started."

"While we're mimicking his operation today, walking back the cat," Shu said, appropriating Irving's term.

"Mike means we're looking at past events now that we know what happened," Irving told Viveca. In tracking the first steps leading to the sleeper's overseas Soviet fortune, the idea was to find out what past events his advance knowledge would have led him to capitalize on, and what new funds and banks were set up in that time frame to contain the profits.

At each of the seven desks, an investigator researched large-scale trades in wheat, oil, aluminum, and gold. The transfers of Soviet assets to Swiss, Panamanian, and offshore banks, many of them monitored by Western financial regulators and intelligence agencies, were charted against a calendar of global news events: sharp drop in the U.S. stock market, the crackdown in Tiananmen Square, publication of surprising commodity price jumps, the teardown of the Berlin Wall.

All very well organized, but there was something in the approach that Irving did not like. He looked over some shoulders, punched in a few queries, in general looked as sour as Viveca looked impressed.

"You seem to think we're missing something," Dominick said on the way back to his office. "If it's the stock market, forget it. You have to put up a fifty percent margin, and that's not leverage. And even options are too regulated."

"No goddam imagination," Irving told him. "You're playing by the book, playing not to lose. I have a hunch the sleeper is smarter than that."

"You've got to be methodical about this," Shu said.

"You have to think like a banker, not a reporter," Viveca added.

"Bullshit."

"Come now, brother Fein," Dominick said, "don't conceal your true feelings from us. Let it all hang out."

"You talk about commodities. What the hell is the most valuable commodity in the world? What asset did the commies have that everybody in the world wanted?"

After a pause, Viveca offered: "Diamonds?"

"He's talking about plutonium, Viveca, and he's right. It's rare. It's portable. And it wasn't as tightly controlled within the Soviet Union as we were led to think."

"If I were the sleeper," said Irving, "and I got the word from Moscow to set up shop with a bunch of gold, I would want to tell my control that I needed a material more valuable than gold, so I could start off with a killing." He quickly changed that to "a financial killing.

Iran was on its ass after the war with Iraq, wanted the bomb. Iraq wanted to take over the Gulf, and Saddam was pushing for a nuke. Pakistan wanted to get even with India, and Libya with Israel, and North Korea with the rest of the world. And who can afford the kind of money we're talking about? Governments. If I were a country, and wanted to be a big power fast, I'd damn well cough up five billion or so for enough plutonium for five or six bombs."

"You have a point," Dominick conceded.

"Irving must have a line in somewhere," Michael Shu told the others. "You got a source on this, Irv? It would speed things up."

Irving did not; all he had was a theory of the story, and he did not want it flushed out as yet; he hadn't worked it over in his mind. "A friend of mine in the Bureau of Mines told me about a radioactive material called red mercury." It was a vague lead; he didn't want to say more about it until he spoke to a reporter friend in Rome. "The Russians got a real mafiya working over there on selling this sort of stuff."

"More financial assets were sent out of Russia in the past year," Viveca declared, "than were generated in their GNP. I just did a line on that Russian underworld, maybe ten seconds, but it struck me."

"The more you can get on that," Irving told her, "the better. See what the Dialog databank says about the underground network." Her network had access to that electronic morgue; he didn't want to run up a big bill on the competing Nexis. "The KGB is after our boy's money, and the Russian mafiya must be after it too. There's got to be a competition here, and the sleeper's got to know about it, and worry about it."

"Not just a banking line inquiry," Shu said to Dominick. "Irving thinks there should be international underworld links. That should fit into the money-laundering end of our banking line. All these guys like to know where the money is." He thought about it a bit. "Could mean that organized crime types here in the U.S. are probably after the sleeper, too, in cahoots with the Feliks people, the Russian mafiya. Jeez."

"More the merrier."

That comment of Dominick's raised him in Irving's eyes: either the man was gutsy or crazy. It was the impostor's ass that was sticking up over the parapet.

"I gotta get over there to work my end of this," Irving said. The opening to be exploited was the division between official and unofficial Russian interests. He also wanted to meet Davidov, who had probably been placed in his new job by the Kremlin specifically to find the fortune before the Feliks people did. Then there was the girl in Riga that he had met the year before and sent Shu to see. He suspected Liana Krumins knew more than she knew she knew and wondered how he could dig it out.

Could he make the mountain come to Mohammed? That was a thought; if he could bring Liana over to the United States, then the KGB types, maybe Davidov himself, might follow. Both the KGB and the Feliks people seemed to be using her. What's more, by inducing her to come over here, with her KGB follower, Irving could save a bundle on expenses. He hated having a fixed amount to draw down for expenses, because it seemed like spending his own money. Besides, it would do Viveca good to see what a hungry Eastern European TV newswoman, somebody who had suffered under communism, looked and acted like. And was twentysomething, not thirtysomething.

Liana's curious centrality in this, despite her age, stopped him. "Why is a young broad in some hinky-dink Baltic city," he wondered aloud, "the only other reporter on this story? She's got no credentials."

That got a rise out of Viveca. "You are one sexist bastard, Irving Fein."

He rolled his eyes to say he knew how all of them stuck together. But something was out of whack in this. He tapped his palm against the side of his head, gently, time and again; it was his way of jarring loose an idea. In less than a dozen taps, he had it and fished his address book out of his wallet.

Chapter 27

RIGA

"It came in routinely, so I looked at it," said Nikolai Davidov, not in the least uncomfortable in the cramped space of a television control room in what was now the capital of a foreign country. "Nothing personal."

"You have no right to read my mail. You are a foreigner in Latvia. You have no authority here." Liana Krumins kept hammering at him with short, declarative sentences, strong as her opinions. "Latvia is no longer enslaved by the Soviet Union. I ought to have you arrested."

"I have taken an interest in your safety," observed the man recently placed atop the Fifth Directorate. He was feeling good, not merely because he was again in the company of this remarkable young woman, but because his bureaucratic scope had been expanded in the last week to include all economic counterintelligence.

There was a growing interest up top in the possibility of finding the sleeper and laying hands on more money than had originally been thought of. Under personal pressure from Davidov, a Swiss investigator had found that the banker in Bern who supposedly had committed suicide soon after Berensky's control was blown up in Barbados had converted the $3 billion in gold to marketable securities years ago. That suggested the money had been invested for profit rather than held in gold at no interest. There could be much more to the fortune.

He was seated in her tiny office in the television station, his jacket slung over the back of a rickety Latvian-made chair. His central purpose in Riga was to look into the activities of a woman with the pseudonym Madame Nina, who was apparently the leader of the Feliks organization. His secondary purpose was to dissuade Liana Krumins from going to America.

The United States Information Agency, acting on what it announced was "the recommendation of a panel of distinguished American journalists," had extended a one-month, all-expense-paid visiting fellowship to the young Riga newscaster. Davidov knew she had never applied, nor had such an invitation ever been issued to a Latvian broadcaster. The CIA must want her presence in America quickly, and had used USIA as its magnet. Perhaps the CIA had learned of the relationship of Liana Krumins to the sleeper.

The cover story was a logical one: she had just shaken up the local power structure with a report on government corruption, and favorable public comment quoted in emboldened newspapers made it impossible for Latvian authorities to discipline her. This young pioneer in post-communist television journalism would visit the studios of U.S. networks to learn the latest techniques, and would participate in a seminar on investigative reporting at the prestigious Newhouse School of Journalism at Syracuse University in the state of New York.

"It's the doing of Fein," Davidov told her, "who, as you must know, is a tool of American intelligence."

"I don't know that at all. And how do you know it's his doing? You still have a mole in the CIA?"

He closed his eyes; that was a question he never dared ask any of his colleagues. As a matter of compartmented fact, Davidov did not know if the Foreign Intelligence Service, now independent of the KGB, had made further penetrations of its American counterpart. However, because of the enlargement of his directorate to include protection of economic secrets, Davidov did know of a longtime Soviet penetration agent in the United States who might provide a lead to Berensky: the KGB had for decades had an active agent in the Federal Reserve in New York.

Did Berensky know about this agent at the Fed, code-named Mariner, or vice versa? Certainly access to his inside knowledge of coming interest-rate changes could do wonders for Berensky's money-making mission, now that the death of the control agent had broken off his access to Russian data. Davidov's new scope now entitled him to know about Mariner, which was why he had pressed for the additional responsibility—certainly it was not to protect economic secrets, of which Russia had so few.

"Liana, you are already caught up in the web of the Feliks people and Madame Nina, who are enemies of freedom. Are you also planning to become a pawn of the American spy service?"

"Of course not. I am thinking of visiting America to become a better journalist."

"You haven't decided yet."

"If you tell me not to go, you will see me decide in one second."

He was aware of that. "How can I persuade you not to go?"

She rose, threw some papers, books, and videotapes in a large cloth sack, slung it over her shoulder. "You can try offering me the one thing you have that I want." She smiled. "Information."

He followed her down the stone steps into the darkening street. The television station was in the maze of streets in the Old Town, near St. Peter's Church. He gambled on asking a question he had carefully prepared: "What is your relationship to this sleeper, that makes you want to compromise your journalistic integrity to go to work for the Americans to find him?"

"That's your idea of giving me information—asking questions?"

That told him she did not know. If she knew, this woman with a flair for the dramatic could never have resisted giving the direct and stunning answer: I am his daughter. Liana would have blurted it out to see him turn white. But everybody was keeping her in the dark—the Feliks people, the KGB, perhaps CIA-Fein if they knew, even the sleeper himself in that do-nothing message through the slippery babushka.

He started to take her arm, and she gave him the heavy bag of tapes and books to carry instead. He fed her a fact: "Syracuse in the winter is almost like Moscow." Riga was relatively temperate.

"Wait here." She darted into a food store, picked up an order waiting for her in a string sack, came out, and took his free arm. "You are coming home with me and I will feed you, and give you wine, and you will tell me everything."

Her room was just that, one room looking out on 13 Janvara Iela and across the narrow river. A few revolutionary posters hung on the wall, some askew; dreary furniture from pre-independence times; a picture of a couple he presumed were her parents; a narrow couch to sleep on. Evidently Liana had little interest in her surroundings. She put the food in the half-kitchen and handed him the wine to open as she lit two half-consumed candles.

"First tell me why it is so important to the chief of the Sixth Directorate of the KGB that I not accept the American offer."

"You are being manipulated, used as bait. And who told you about my directorate?"

She smiled mysteriously, as if she knew. He knew she was just guessing. The Sixth Directorate, formerly the home of the antidissident ideologues, was now in charge of "constitutional protection" and was a parking place for the President's hacks who could not find honest work. Davidov's directorate, the Fifth, was now the center of economic intelligence and counterespionage. When it came to the real world of intelligence, Liana was naive. But he wanted to give her the benefit of the doubt; perhaps she was using a reporter's trick, throwing out a number so that he would correct her by saying his was the Fifth, which was why he did not.

"I asked Michael Shu to tell me more about Irving Fein, because our meeting last year was too brief," she said. "He told me that even in ordinary conversation, Fein would always finish what he said with a question. You do the same."

Davidov wanted to ask more, but now she had intimidated him; he kicked himself for being less than masterful in this situation. He was hungry, too. To assert himself, he went to the bag of food and tore a chunk off a loaf of bread.

"I admire Fein greatly," she said. "Everybody agrees he is a wonderful reporter. I don't believe what you say about his being a tool of the government. You're a Russian, you must be nearly forty years old— what do you know about a free press? We're just beginning to get one here. If Irving Fein was the one who persuaded the USIA to offer me a university fellowship, that only shows his generous nature. That doesn't mean the government controls him."

"I'm thirty-eight." He added another fact: "Fein is forty-eight."

"Did you see him on the Skytel that night of the hijacking? Wasn't he enterprising?" He knew she knew this was getting to him. "He knew just who to reach, and even had the home telephone number of the chief aide to the President of the Russian Federation, in his little book.

That was a lesson in journalism." She gave an elaborate sigh. "You are an attractive man in some ways, Nikolai Andreyevich, but no man is so attractive to me as a man of integrity. Because of the business you are in, corrupting people for some reason of state, you cannot understand the purity of motive of a journalist like Irving Fein."

"He sent you a message the other day. Did you get it?"

"No."

"One of my men in New York says he arranged for a message to be given to you by a CIA agent disguised as a babushka selling dolls," he said. He took a large bite of the bread and chewed for a while; not the brown bread he liked, but not bad for Latvia. He did not elaborate his lie; let her ask him about it, which he was certain she would. In the interim, as if idly, he peered at the photograph on the wall. "This picture wasn't in your file. Your parents?"

"My papa has been dead since I was a little girl. Mama does not approve of the way I live." Looking at the picture of the grim-faced woman, he waited for more. "Five years ago she threw me out of the house. Called me a counterrevolutionary whore."

"And now that your counterrevolution won?"

"An ordinary slut. An improvement, no? She lives in the past. We had a terrible fight and we don't see each other anymore. I told her I will not attend her funeral and I hope it comes soon." She shook off that memory and came around to the point: "What did you mean about a message from Fein?"

"We've been listening to his telephone in New York, as you can imagine. He told your friend Shu in the Antilles that he had a plan to send you a message, supposedly from the sleeper, telling you not to look for him, but to wait for word from him."

She froze. As if to keep the conversation going, the KGB man added: "I guess they never made contact with you. We would have known. I'm not criticizing Fein, or his CIA control—we also have difficulty getting messages through in the U.S. Tradecraft is difficult, operating in another country."

Liana thought about that for a long while, twisting the glass in her hand. "If Fein wanted me to stay here last week, why did he send for me through the USIA today?"

Davidov did not have a good answer to that good question. He took the honesty escape: "I don't know. The Americans are not being consistent. That's why I wish you would put them off, at least for a while."

His purpose in this simple deception was to induce Berensky to come to Riga to find his daughter rather than have Liana go to the United States. If the sleeper came here, he could be kidnapped easily, taken to Moscow, and interrogated. Or put together with Liana, with their classic recognition scene eavesdropped on. One way or another, through psychological coercion, truth drugs, or more old-fashioned methods, the sleeper could be made willing to reveal the extent and disposition of the fortune he held in trust for Russia. Not for the detritus of the Communist Party; not for corrupt apparatchiks nimble enough to survive in the new atmosphere. Davidov's mission was unequivocal: to recapture that money for the democratically elected, legitimate government of Russia. If he failed in that, his fast rise would be followed by a faster fall.

Davidov could not tell Liana why he wished her to stay in Eastern Europe, of course, but his job obliged him to dissuade her from trusting Fein. The quickest way to do that was to impugn the American journalist's independence. Though it troubled him to mislead her on the babushka messenger—whom the idiots or subversives who worked for him had failed to detain—Davidov suspected that his concoction was not wholly false. Fein might well be working for or with some faction of the American intelligence agency, perhaps in a rogue or tightly compartmented operation. Therefore, the blatant lie to Liana could be construed as a subterfuge within a larger truth.

Subdued by his deception, she said, "I brought you here with the promise of food, Nikolai Andreyevich." She brought out the sausage and cheese, heated some bean soup on a one-burner electric grill, dished it out, and watched him eat. She nibbled as if she had lost her appetite, leaned back, and brushed her stubbly hair with her fingertips. No more questions. He tried to envision her with long hair and could not.

When he finished, she poured the last of the wine and looked at him in her direct way. "I said I would take you home and feed you, and you would give me information."

"That was the arrangement," he agreed.

"We both did our part. Now I will be the one to give you information. That message you spoke about? I received it."

He raised his eyebrows.

"Yes, a babushka selling dolls whispered to me around the corner from the Tower café that she had a message from 'the one who sleeps.' I thought it was truly from him—how was I to know it was from Fein and the CIA?"

"You couldn't know." Davidov began to feel a little guilty about taking advantage of her intelligence inexperience, but it was for a greater good. He added a touch of authenticity, knowing she knew of her own surveillance: "I'm surprised that our man following you didn't see the contact."

She looked at the red wine in her glass for what seemed like a long time. "There is something I want to show you, Nikolai." She undid the two top buttons of her blouse, reached inside, and took out an amber pendant on a long silver chain. "I was given this by a man who loved me before the day of freedom."

"You were very young then." He was reminded of her file, and the deal she had made for her early release; she had matured early. "Brave, too, they say—this is where the breakup of the Soviet Union began."

She nodded yes. "It is a memento of some sentiment. The other day, I was wearing it outside my blouse. The engineer in the control room asked if he could look closely at it. I let him."

Davidov did not know where this uncharacteristic story was leading, but he felt uneasy.

"The sound engineer looked very closely at my pendant. And then he used a little screwdriver to pick at the clasp here. Right here, you see? And what do you suppose he found? He found a tiny transmitter." She rose from the table, went to a chest of drawers, and came back with a KGB bug held between her thumb and forefinger. Davidov noted it was one of the ones that worked, made in Taiwan. "The technology is amazing. Every word I said was overheard."

The KGB official awaited the rest.

"Of course, I was wearing it when the babushka offered me the *beriozka* doll. The message from the sleeper was transmitted to the KGB surveillance unit in the area. And you heard it all."

Denial was not an option. "True. Your engineer friend deactivated the damn thing last Tuesday."

"And this information you have given me, in return for my food and wine, is all a lie."

All he could do was nod yes.

"That babushka's message," she continued in a steady, cold voice, "did not come from Fein or the CIA, as you pretend, but from Aleksandr Berensky, the sleeper."

"There's a lesson in this," he said. "You should never trust anybody from the KGB."

"I won't. Get out."

He stood up and looked around for his jacket. He was disappointed with himself in the way he had overplayed his hand; overconfidence, or the need to manipulate her, had gotten the better of him.

She had the leather jacket in her hands, held in front of her, concealing her unbuttoned blouse and the amber pendant. In the now-unromantic candlelight, he could see her eyes moist with hot tears. "I hate this jacket," she growled, throwing it on the floor and kicking it out of her way. She stepped up to him, placed five hard fingers of her hand on his chest, and surprised him by pushing sharply. The backs of his knees were against the couch and he fell backward onto it.

Next he knew she was pulling at his belt and then dragging his pants down. She straddled him before he was ready—he even had his shoes on—and she reached inside her skirt, pulled her blouse over her head, and freed her breasts from her bra. "Live, in color," she hissed. "Better than videotape." That made him ready instantly, and she forced herself down on him, pale horse on impaled rider.

The sex act must have lasted forty minutes, because every time he came close to climax he realized he was trapped with his pants around his shoes; that absurd thought would pull him back from the brink long enough to permit a fresh bout. After a time, her attack softened, his strokes lengthened, they cried out together as she rode him to their consummation. After a few moments, she gave a moaning laugh, but he was too exhausted to do anything other than let his heartbeat slow down. He became acutely aware of his shoes held immobile by his pants.

"You need a younger man." He watched her slender back twist and stoop as she took off his shoes. Freed at last, he stretched his legs alongside hers on the couch and contemplated the consequences of lying to an underestimated member of the near abroad.

"Something I've wanted to do ever since that afternoon in Lubyanka," he told her in a restrained form of tenderness, "is this." He passed his fingers along the top of her chopped-off hair. It felt like rubbing an army shoebrush.

She pulled her head back. "Don't do that. I'm not your possession." Davidov, rudely reminded of who he was and where he was, went into full emotional withdrawal.

Liana must have sensed his retreat, because she got up and, still naked, brought back a washcloth, presenting it to him with what he thought might be a trace of affection. "I'm going to the seminar at Syracuse, you know."

"I'll be in America at the same time, whenever it is," he told her. "I don't trust you alone with Fein."

"Possessive again, with no right to be." She sat alongside him on the couch and dragged her fingertips across his chest down to his navel. "Won't they miss you at the Fifth Directorate?"

Her previous guess was a deception; someone had told her exactly where he worked and what he did. At thirty-eight, an age that no longer required him to participate in the KGB's exercise program, he amazed himself with his response.

Chapter 28

NEW YORK

Camel's-hair topcoat draped over his shoulders, Aleksandr Berensky, who had not been known by his real name for more than twenty years, walked down the steps to the Sutton Place park a few minutes after 10:00 A.M.

Like a man with nothing to do, he sat on a bench in the fenced triangle of asphalt and azaleas and looked across the traffic of the East River Drive. Or perhaps it was the Franklin D. Roosevelt Drive; he never could figure out where one ended and the other began. Across the water, the New York Fire Department, to train its recruits, regularly set the same building ablaze. That incendiary facility was on Roosevelt Island, which he had read was formerly Welfare Island, and before that word gained a pejorative connotation, Blackwell Island; it changed its name as often as the Cheka, OGPU, NKVD—and the Federal Security Ministry, as the KGB was currently called. The traffic on the riverside highway made his urban oasis serenely noisy, as restful as a spot beside a waterfall. In audio contrast, a coal barge crept noiselessly upriver.

At exactly ten-fifteen, Berensky walked to the public telephone at the corner of the park. When it rang, he snapped an encryption device over the mouthpiece and a decoder over the earpiece. The transmission would be scrambled in a way that caused the FBI to oppose sale of the devices to the public. Not only did they disguise the voices; the scramblers made the mouthpiece of a public phone more sanitary.

The person on the other end of the line was similarly equipped; his voice was unnaturally tinny. He was not Berensky's handler; the sleeper no longer had any control, nor did he plan to have one. He would operate on his own.

The caller was a fellow Russian agent, officially reporting to Foreign Intelligence rather than the KGB, but who was now working with Berensky in their own private and unauthorized channel. With Control cut off, this unofficial contact was the sleeper's source of inside data on future American government actions.

Berensky now thought of himself as a patriot without a country, and he wasted no time. "The word from Mariner?"

"At the meeting of the Open Market Committee up in New York next Tuesday," said the tinny voice, "the federal funds rate will be raised a full percent. That's one hundred basis points. Three votes for this, and the Chairman will go along."

"The Chairman still relies primarily on the price of gold? Not a basket of commodities?"

That intelligence, first relayed to him by Control as he moved his sources westward after the Soviet Union's dissolution, was probably the most useful piece of information elicited from their agent in the Federal Reserve System. Economists' forecasts were influenced by a variety of indicators; to know the single most important factor in the decisions of the Chairman of the Fed gave the speculator not merely a tip but a strategic advantage. His out-of-channel contact now on the telephone knew the Fed mole as well as that agent's control in Bonn, Sirkka Numminen, but he kept the mole's identity to himself. Berensky accepted that compartmentalism as standard practice; he knew FI's man at the Fed only by his code name: Mariner.

"Less so, Mariner says. Soybeans are the indicator of choice now. Something about the Humboldt Current."

Berensky understood, as his caller did not, what Mariner was signaling. Fishermen along the east coast of South America called that cold Humboldt ocean current El Niño, the Christ Child; when the current warmed, or was overfished, the supply of anchovies dropped disastrously, and fish meal became scarce. That scarcity drove up the world price of soybeans, the alternative protein on world markets. El Niño also influenced world climate, and was blamed for hurricanes in the Western Hemisphere.

"Does Rowboat confirm this?" Rowboat was a climatologist who worked for the CIA, under cover of the Bureau of Wildlife and Fisheries, measuring winds and currents from a small craft off the coast of Peru.

"He was riffed in the last budget cut," said the voice. "I may be the next to go."

"What will you do?"

"Going home is not an option. Run a think tank or a foundation, maybe. I know a generous philanthropist."

Berensky did not disabuse his lone source of the possibility. "One day you must let me meet Mariner."

"Why expose yourself? Besides, Mariner doesn't want to meet anybody but me. And those who run him in another channel wouldn't like that. Never intermingle operations." That was a reference to FI. "Besides, if you met him, you might be tempted to eliminate the middleman. Me."

"Don't make bad jokes. You know how I feel about violence—it's bad for banking." If this agent was dismissed in a government-wide reduction in force, and if he then retired from the KGB and stayed in the United States, he could still be useful as Berensky's unofficial contact with the source at the Fed. The continuance of an intermediary offered an additional advantage: it would be safer to keep the Fed source in the dark about the identity of the sleeper, in case the Fed awoke to its breached security. Sooner or later somebody was bound to discover hugely profitable currency activity based on insider knowledge of Fed interest-rate actions. "Simple enough to steer a respectable bundle into a charitable foundation," Berensky told him, "and put you in charge. Think seriously about double retirement. You have nothing to go back to in the old country."

"We're in the same boat on that, you and I. You're not concerned about what that accountant calls his war room?"

"Spinning its wheels. And the reporter is off after 'red mercury' and could waste months on that. You're monitoring all his calls?"

"Unofficially. The only troublesome thing is what he keeps calling 'a mole in the Fed.' Nobody else on this side has ever mentioned that, ever."

"Stab in the dark on his part," Berensky assured him. "It's a reporter's profession to conjure up conspiracy theories. Lucky thing the FBI doesn't operate on hunches."

"Fein calls it his sniffer, but there is no bloodhound quality to his work. He seems to work intuitively—on hunches, as you say. And yet the best intelligence analyst is a lucky guesser."

"Forget the reporter," said Berensky. "This whole group is off after commodity trading and plutonium sales. 'Wild goose chase' is the local expression. What about High Five?" That was what the two of them labeled Davidov of the Fifth Directorate. Berensky knew he did not have to make up half-coded allusions like "High Five"—either the encryption chips worked or they did not—but the habit of a lifetime under cover made him feel safer avoiding the verbalization of names and incriminating words. To a sleeper, guardedness was next to godliness.

"I'm told High Five has put in a request to visit the U.S.," the voice reported, sounding as worried as the garbling would allow. "Mainly the state of New York. Now that the FBI has an office in Moscow, CIA can't very well object. And the DCI wants to meet him, I think."

"High Five worries me less than the independent operators with their headquarters in Riga. Find out what you can about the woman who runs it." He knew her as Madame Nina, but the Washington double agent might have access to a CIA file on her. "Somebody's pulling together the family authorities and our old friends. She may be the one."

"I don't believe in a world underworld," said his colleague.

"All I know is, somebody's competing with me." Competition for money-laundering channels had become keen; legitimate fronts were harder and harder to find. Berensky consulted his watch. "I'm going to short the yen heavily on the basis of what Mariner says, and plunge in soybean future derivatives."

"A butterfly straddle?"

"You don't even know what that means. You must have read about them somewhere."

"You're right. I sure hope you know all about them."

"It's a very shapely swap, but it's playing it safe. What I have in mind, if Mariner is correct, should take us up to fifty biggest ones."

"Getting over half the magic number."

"By then, I'll know what to do." He either would have a country to return to as a hero, or would have a big player's place at the table of the "world underworld," as his contact rather creatively put it. A third possibility would be to go into business for himself, a patriot without a country, reviled as a traitor by all—but very, very rich. That was what Control had had in mind in Barbados, and the would-be defector to greed's lust had rightfully paid with his life. "It's getting harder to hide the profits than to make them. Your messenger delivered the message to—" He stopped himself from saying "my daughter" and substituted "—the younger woman in Riga?"

"She got it and sent a return message."

Berensky frowned. "She was not supposed to. I specifically said this was to be a one-way channel."

"She told the messenger to go to hell with his orders and to deliver her reply. She wants to set a time and place for you two to meet. Pushed hard for it."

Her aggressive attitude could get them both in trouble, but the spiritedness of the girl's response did not displease him. "Let her learn the value of patience."

"She wasn't the only one to get your message," said the Washington contact. "As you expected, everyone did. They're all looking for you. You're in play."

Chapter 29

NEW YORK

"You're eating up your advance on these expenses down in Memphis," Ace told Irving sternly, "and I don't see a line on paper."

"Yeah-yeah. Big story takes time."

"It's been three months, and the world's greatest reporter doesn't seem to have much to show for it."

"Goddam red mercury threw me off. Turns out there ain't no such thing, it's just a cover for piddling little sales of plutonium and enriched uranium. Four hundred grams of enriched Russian uranium went to Iran last month for eighty million bucks. Chicken feed. Wild goose chase."

"And what of your secret endeavor in Memphis?"

"Mike Shu thinks he's on the edge of something, but he's been saying that from the start."

"Viveca?" Ace had not heard from her, which was uncharacteristic.

"She's banging some guy down there who works with us. Practically commutes between here and there."

Ace nodded; the green-eyed monster was probably the main reason Irving was distracted. "Is there any way of dispensing with her—" the agent rejected "boyfriend" as puerile and "companion" as euphemistic—"inamorata, so the two of you can work without emotional distraction?"

"Nah. I got somebody coming over next week from Latvia, maybe flush out some action from the sleeper. She says she's bringing along an even bigger fish, your friend Davidov from Moscow. That should stir the pot."

Too many metaphors, from flushing to fishing to stirring; Irving was not a classy writer, nor was his partner in this endeavor. The expectation of the visit to New York of a high KGB official, however, triggered a creative synapse in the agent's mind.

"I should be pleased to give one of my legendary little dinner parties for Director Davidov, Irving. Perhaps he has a few properties now that he was reluctant to part with before."

Fein was not a social being, but the agent's notion of using an elegant Park Avenue dinner party to commingle disparate sources intrigued him. "Let me check around before you invite anybody. A friend of mine may have an idea for a guest or two."

Ace presumed Irving would seek a suggestion from his sources within the cloak-and-dagger world. "Be highly selective," the experienced host cautioned. "My parties are for twelve—never more, never less."

Chapter 30

MEMPHIS

Viveca was astonished at the virulence of the attack Irving launched at Michael Shu.

"You've been screwing around down here for three months, with all these fancy maps and charts"—he grabbed a handful and threw them up in the air—"and what the hell do you have to show for it? Zilch!"

"We have a line on a bank in the Antilles," Shu offered. "Could be the sleeper owns it."

"Five guys on computers, a chronology of every big trade that ever happened for the past five years, and all you've come up with is one lousy clue about a bank that every drug runner uses to launder his money? You call that progress?"

Shu took it in silence.

"We should have a pattern by now," Irving went on, "of where and how the sleeper operates and what he's doing to hide his assets. That would be progress."

Edward Dominick, in whose office this explosion was taking place, was staring determinedly out the window at the damn Mississippi River.

Viveca was not one to let such bullying continue. "Five hundred million dollars in oil future profits to one trading company is not 'zilch,' Irving. Michael tracked that down, and the war room is following it up. Might lead to more leads."

Fein turned that around and threw it at Shu. "Maybe fifty billion bucks socked away, and you find one percent? Chicken feed! After two months of digging with all this hotshot machinery? You satisfied with that, Shu-fly? Tell her."

Michael said, "What can I say? We're not getting as much traction as we hoped."

Then Irving wheeled on Viveca. "And have we had so much as one goddam useful fact out of you? You've been commuting to Memphis every weekend. What the hell for?"

"What about your 'red mercury'?" she shot back. "I checked with our network man in Rome and he said it was the biggest journalistic hoax of the year. There's no such thing as red mercury—it was a fence for two or three sales of uranium to Germany worth a few million dollars. You were spinning your wheels on that for a month."

"Not every lead works out," Irving muttered.

Viveca had him on the defensive and knew better than to let up: "What did you come up with? Zilch! That great dunno sheet of yours is longer than ever."

"I was sure wheat futures would pay off for us," Michael Shu said, still shaking his head at Irving's attack. "We know all there is to know about that particular commodity now. One thing we know: Berensky sure didn't make his money on wheat."

Irving returned to the offensive. "You gonna find him by the process of elimination? By what he's not doing? That'll take forever, and we don't have the budget for forever."

Viveca looked again at Dominick, who at last swiveled in his chair and interceded.

"Haven't heard a word you said, brother Fein." He tapped the new hearing device in his ear. "Hard of hearing, you know. Our colleague Shu, here, has done a superb job in a process more infinitely complex than you can imagine. He is thorough, careful. My hat's off to him."

Irving leaned forward and knocked on the table. "Hello? Hello? It's all been a flop, Eddie. Wake up to reality." He turned to Viveca. "I got a buddy at USIA to bring Liana Krumins over here from Latvia on a cockamamie fellowship. That suckered Davidov into following her, which tells me he's using her as bait for something. So we'll have a chance to work them over right here on our turf. I'm pulling my weight, which is more than I can say for you guys."

"Let's have a private cup of coffee, Irving," Shu said. To Viveca, as if the great reporter were not in the room, the accountant said, "He gets this way when a story doesn't come together. But sometimes Irving's at his best when he's at his worst."

As the two of them left, Viveca called out to Irving, "You're lucky to have such an understanding associate."

He shot a look at Dominick. "You, too."

"What do you suppose that last crack meant?"

Dominick chuckled. "He's jealous, is all. He thinks I moved in on his woman."

She could hear herself sputtering, but she couldn't stop. "I'm not his woman. I never was his woman. I found him repugnant from the start, and he knows it. He has no right to be jealous. He never had any claim on me of any kind—"

"Not a question of legal standing." Dominick was still chuckling—a warm, low laugh that usually charmed her but was a source of irritation now. "It's how he feels. He looks at you, and then at me, and he sees a real affection there that he's been denied. Plain as day."

That stopped her. She was convinced he was wrong about Irving—professional frustration at being denied a story, not personal jealousy, was at the core of his blowup—but Dominick had at last alluded to their own relationship. "The real affection Irving sees—is it there?"

"Of course, Viveca. You know that."

"Oh. The Process." She bit her knuckle to keep quiet. He must have known from the start that she was his for the taking, but she had not thrown herself at him. He kept talking about "the Process," as if a love affair were like making peace in the Mideast or arriving at courtroom justice, and aside from some affectionate holdings and fraternal kisses, nothing had happened to complicate her life. Usually this was because of her icebox reputation, or the way she intimidated the men she worked with; but when she liked somebody, she thought she sent out unmistakable signals of availability. Edward Dominick surely received them—he was, if anything, sensitive—but he kept saying he didn't want to hurry the Process.

She veered back to the subject. "Is Irving right? Are we spinning our wheels? You know, finding Berensky could make all the difference in my career." Failure in this project would hurt her at the network. The remote possibility of losing her job always gave her the feeling she was standing at the edge of an abyss.

"We're on the right track, don't worry. Remember the story of the turtle and the rabbit? I'm the turtle, slow and steady, and we'll win in the end."

It's the tortoise and the hare, she felt like telling him, but restrained herself; Southerners had their own slant on the folklore. "I'm not being much help to you," she admitted.

"Maybe you can find out what Irving was hinting at," he suggested, "when he spoke of a mole at the Federal Reserve. That's a fascinating thought. And it would help if we had some sources at the Fed's enforcement branch."

"Why not ask him yourself? We're all in this together."

"He may be reluctant to share his source with me, but perhaps he'd be more forthcoming with a fellow journalist."

She promised to try to find out. It wasn't being disloyal to Irving to pass on a lead to Edward; as she said, they were all on the same team. But she allowed herself to admit that there might be an edge of jealousy involved.

"And I'd like to be exposed to Liana Krumins," he went on. "It would be great if you could establish some rapport with her. Shu says she knows about Berensky's early years in Russia from the KGB files, his family life especially. Little things—nicknames, birthdays, schools, whatever. Somebody's going to ask me about his early past," he explained, "and I'd better be familiar with it."

She took on that assignment, too. If Dominick was going to play the sleeper, especially to Russians who might have known the young Berensky, he would have to be supplied with the kind of detail that actors needed for their roles. Twenty-odd years of aging would explain away the change in features, but an impersonator could be trapped by not knowing some silly detail a family member would know.

"I'm surprised you can get a bagel in Memphis."

Michael Shu tidily placed a napkin in the saucer under his coffee cup to absorb the spillage. "Don't be ethnocentric, Irving. More bagels are consumed in America today than doughnuts."

"How the hell can you be so sure of that?"

"One of the Big Six firms did a study for a doughnut bakery chain. They tried to keep the results from the bagel people, but it leaked." He watched Irving smear cream cheese on half his toasted poppy-seed bagel. "You think we rattled Dominick?"

"You could have whimpered a little more, for crissake. The day of the stoic Oriental is long gone."

"I like the way Viveca came to my defense."

"Wasn't you she was protecting, it was the guy who's been shtupping her."

"I don't think they're having an affair, Irving. Nothing wrong if they are, but I doubt it."

Irving and he had worked out a charade to jar Dominick off his careful, methodical course of investigation without offending and losing him. The solution was for Fein to blast Shu; the banker would get the message. Viveca's intercession was unexpected; Shu liked to think it was rooted in a respect she had for him, but he suspected it had more to do with defending Dominick, as Irving suggested. "Could it be he's in business for himself on this?"

"Sure he is. We all are." Irving gave his foxy grin. "This guy wants to contact the sleeper in his own way, in his own time, on his own terms, and cut himself in on the biggest fortune in the world. He'll sell us out in a minute."

"If you say so." Shu did not want to believe it. Dominick operated in a sensible, businesslike way, even if his strategy had not turned up really major movements of money into the likeliest banks and mutual funds. "You do tend to be impatient, Irv."

"I get heat, I pass it along. And if you come across a real lead to Berensky, tell me first—we can't trust Dominick completely, and he's got Little Miss Icebox in his pocket, no matter what you say. So don't confide in her, either."

"Helluva team."

"It'll work. We're only striking out on the tracking-down of Berensky through the money end. We're not doing so bad, I bet, on—" He took a large bite of the bagel, and his conclusion was difficult to hear through the chewing.

"On making him come to us?" the accountant guessed.

"That's what I said. I got a guy in the enforcement branch of the Fed, and he's grateful to me. I gave him a tip last week about a Chinese mole in his agency."

"How'd you find out about a Chinese mole, Irving?" The reporter's sources were the best.

"Lookit—I don't have the foggiest notion if there is or ever was a mole in the Fed, Chinese or Martian. But it's logical, isn't it? If you're gonna penetrate the CIA, or the Defense Department, why not the Fed? So I dress it up as a tip and give it to my guy in the enforcement branch. It's catnip to him. He can then go to his boss, say he heard about it from the great reporter Fein, and get all sorts of money and staff to go after him. Big bureaucratic power play; nobody at the Fed can stop it, because nobody wants to be the one on record for blocking an investigation that, who knows, may turn up something. Bulgarian mole, whatever. And in a year, maybe the horse will fly."

Shu assumed that last was the punchline of a joke but did not want to take Irving off the point. He marveled at his associate's approach; Irving was able to create an indebtedness in a source out of nothing but an idea. "So then what does your guy at the Fed do for you? Give you the story if the nontip leads to something?"

"That's not to hold your breath waiting for. You just don't have the feel for this, Mike." He held up a finger smeared with cream cheese. "One—I can get an answer from him right away on all whopping transfers he looked into since late '89."

"That saves us a lot of time."

"Two." Up went a thumb of the other hand. "He runs the traps for me."

Michael knew that was one of Irving's metaphors that he was expected to understand. To "run the traps" was a hunting-trapping expression, he supposed; in early morning, the trapper ran around to all the traps he had set out the night before, to see if any animal had been caught. So the Fed source was checking for Irving on all other current investigations of major money transfers. Shu nodded for Irving to go on.

"Three." Fein licked the cream cheese off another finger and added it to the display. "In his investigation of the mole, he looks into the recent surreptitious banking activities of one Edward Dominick of Memphis, Tennessee."

Shu's heart sank. "And me."

"Don't worry, I'll cover your ass. Part of my theory of the story is this: the sleeper, once activated, had to have developed some of the

Soviet assets here. Obvious places to get advanced information to make money: Treasury, maybe the Bureau of Labor Statistics, the FTC, but especially the Fed."

Which meant currency trading. Which Dominick thought that the sleeper would have thought was too risky. "So why do you want the Fed looking into our fake sleeper operation?"

Irving made a beckoning gesture. "You tell me, Mike."

The landscape was suddenly illuminated. "Because whatever contact Berensky has at the Fed will sure as hell tell him all about the trading we're doing to parallel his. And about the banks we're dealing with. And then the sleeper will think we're hot on his trail and will come to us to buy us off."

"Neat, huh?"

"Jesus, Irving, I hope you know what the hell you're doing."

Chapter 31

WASHINGTON

"This is your archfriend."

Irving recognized the voice of Walter Clauson of the CIA; a split second later, he caught the allusion to the arches of McDonald's, impenetrably innocent scene of their last rendezvous.

"The bagels are better in Memphis," the reporter replied.

"My God, that sounds like a recognition code in the Mossad."

"My agent says that's my problem," Irving confessed. "Nobody can understand what I write. You got something for me?"

"I just thought you might enjoy a day's fishing."

The only fishing Irving had done was as a kid over the fence at Riverside Park, and the gang had made a big deal out of fishing condoms out of the polluted waters of the Hudson River. But Clauson was his best source at the Agency, and the reporter told his caller he was ready to fish, metaphorically and otherwise.

"Friends' Creek is the best place this time of year," Clauson noted. "Up in the Catoctins, not all that far from Camp David. Ever been there? Beautiful country."

"Isn't this the hunting season? Guys in red hats going after Bambi?"

"On the chilly side for fishing," Clauson admitted, "but it is a more contemplative activity. Your current endeavor has become like an albatross around my neck, and I want to regale you as if you were a wedding guest."

That was probably some arcane literary allusion outside Irving's ken. "You're slipping into your Angleton mode, Clauson. Talk plain English. I'm bothering somebody?"

"More than you know. You and your companions have made me a sadder and a wiser man."

"That's my job, right? If I'm the guest, where's the wedding?"

"We will meet at the Mountaingate Family Inn in Thurmont, Maryland. Take the Beltway to 270 North, past Frederick to Route 15. Sixty miles from D.C., hardly more than an hour's drive. My cabin in Harbaugh Valley, near the best fishing creek, is fifteen minutes from there."

"Wait, I'm writing it down." Irving hated these long schleps for stories, but sources had to be indulged. He went into his looking-for-paper, fumbling-for-a-pencil routine, stalling for time to frame the right question. "Which one of my queries touched a nerve?"

"Sure wasn't red mercury."

"Get off my back. That bank in the Antilles, wasn't it? Stepped on the Agency's toes there, hunh?"

"Wear boots, and a slicker in case it rains. I once caught some marvelous trout in a light snow."

"Lookit, if I'm risking pneumonia, I deserve a hint. Gimme one so I can do some homework."

"Already have." Clauson set the date and hour and hung up. Irving made careful notes of the cryptic conversation; within a couple of minutes of hearing something, he could set it down verbatim. If he delayed writing it down a couple of hours, he had to fake it.

He sat wriggling for two hours at the Mountaingate, in his heavy boots and old clothes, waiting for Clauson. Every fifteen minutes, Irving would go back to the buffet table, heap on a mountaineer breakfast, come back and eat it, look at his watch, and wonder if he got the day wrong. He tried his answering machine: Ace wanted him, and Mike Shu had a question, and the lawyer for his ex-wife was dunning him again, and a journalism student wanted a statement from him about the ethics of investigative reporting. He punched star-D for delete and obliterated the last two.

Where was his source? He couldn't call Clauson's office. He tried the spook's home number; no luck; he did not leave a message on the machine.

Irving had eaten too much and felt sick, but all-you-can-eat buffets were a challenge. He was going up again for more sausages when the troopers came in.

Four of them, burly as usual, two carloads' worth, piled into the booth behind him.

"Couldn't be an ordinary government employee, like his ID said," one of them said. "Two minutes after I reported it, the FBI was on the phone, and then CIA security."

"Lieutenant said there's somebody coming from Annapolis," another voice said. "Gotta be a big shot."

"How come no reporters, then? Been ten-twelve hours since the drowning, four since we got called, nearly three since we told the feds."

"Maybe we ought to tip the *Frederick News-Post*."

"No foul play. They only like foul play. Accidents are no big deal."

The chubby waitress poured their coffee and recommended the strawberry shortcake. The troopers got up as one and made for the dessert buffet. Irving followed as far as the breakfast spread and got two sausages and another waffle, listening.

White male, sixty-two, found facedown in Friends' Creek, drowned at about 10:00 P.M. No fishing tackle nearby. Bottle of gin on bank. Apparently staggered out for a walk behind his cabin, fell in the creek, and drowned. No marks of blows or strangulation. Wallet in back pocket containing U.S. government identification as Walter Clauson, credit cards, and $80. Unlikely a homicide; robbery was no motive. Lights left on in cabin, large black Newfoundland dog barking awakened neighbor in cabin four hundred feet away, who found body at first light and called police. No suspicious circumstances, but feds probably would do blood test, maybe autopsy.

Irving Fein paid his bill, noting he had not eaten so much for so little in a long time. He went outside to the gas station and asked the attendant for directions to Friends' Creek. The name, he was told, had to do with Quakers who settled the area. He drove his rented utility vehicle to Sabillasville, observed the signs for Fort Ritchie, where the President and everybody who counted would go to run the country from underground in case of a nuclear attack, and then followed the Sunshine Trail to the scene.

The body had already been put in a bag, he was told by one of the three troopers on the porch of Clauson's cabin, and had been taken to the Frederick morgue. The troopers were awaiting a visit from "other authorities," presumably from Washington, before leaving the cabin.

Irving identified himself as a neighbor and on a quick inspiration offered to take care of the dog. The troopers waiting on the porch saw that as a blessing and let him into the house. The reporter befriended the large animal, who seemed appropriately lost with the body of his master gone. Irving got him some Milk-Bones, the biggest they made, from the kitchen cabinet. Then he looked around the house, touching nothing.

Clauson's portable computer, connected to the wall and taking an unnecessary charge, was on a rustic desk. Heavy laptop, maybe five years old. Irving presumed the government worked on WordPerfect, which he knew, and turned it on. Talking nonsense to the dog, whom he called Blackie for the benefit of the troopers lounging on the porch, Irving looked through the dead man's directories. He word-searched using "sleeper" and "Berensky" and "Feliks" and came up with nothing. He looked at the root directory to find out if any files were encrypted; no luck, none were. The batch files yielded nothing unusual. He called up the modem menu and saw a dozen frequently called numbers. He copied those down and with his handkerchief wiped his fingerprints from the keys.

On the arm of Clauson's easy chair, under a reading lamp, a book was open. The reporter picked it up. It was *The Classic Hundred: All-Time Favorite Poems,* and the binding was cracked where the book was open, at a long poem by Samuel Taylor Coleridge. He looked for underlining or any notes anywhere in the book; nothing. He wiped again and put the book back on the arm, open as he had found it. Another book was on the seat of the chair, titled *FDR's Moneybags.* He thumbed the tattered volume quickly, noted it was about economic policy in the Roosevelt administration, shook it for a note, came up with nothing, and chucked it back in the seat. The dog whimpered, a small white sound from a big black animal; the reporter talked reassuringly to it and dangled his hand in a nonthreatening manner to be licked. The dog didn't lick but sniffed and at least shut up.

Irving looked back at the computer, nagged by the thought that he had missed some message on it from the dead man. A chair on the porch creaked as a trooper came out of it; no time.

The masterless dog followed him to the car. Irving looked at him;

the troopers expected him to do something about the dog, which had been his excuse for poking around. He went back into the house, gave the massive animal a couple more Milk-Bones, and set out a bowl of water on the porch. To the sound of heavy lapping, Irving put on his best rustic demeanor. "I heard down in Thurmont ol' Walt was drinkin'."

"Looks like it." A trooper indicated a gin bottle with a label attached, presumably for their report. "Was he a gin drinker?"

"I dunno," Irving replied. "Actually, he wasn't much of a drinker at all. Guess maybe you should give him a blood test, if that's what you do."

"Been twelve hours; hard to tell now."

The dog followed him out to the car again. One of the troopers called, "Give him a good home, mister," and Irving called back, "I think I'll have to take him to the shelter in Thurmont." The cops seemed disappointed. The dog climbed into the front seat next to the driver, as he must have done with Clauson, and waited for his ride, panting out the window. Irving started the vehicle and made the rounds of three neighbors' cabins, asking if anybody wanted Clauson's dog. Two of the kids warmly greeted him by name, Spook—Clauson had given an appropriate name to a spy's pet—but no adult would take on the expense of a dog that looked to weigh about 130 pounds.

No time to look up the Humane Society. With the panting animal as company, the reporter drove south to Virginia. He was unfamiliar with dogs, had never owned one; often they growled at him, even dogs friendly to most other people, presumably because he was tense and moved in lurches. Dogs liked calm people, which Irving Fein was not. This one did not seem to treat him with distrust, though. Then it clicked; Spook was accustomed to a stress-ridden master pretending to be calm.

"You think Clauson got drunk and fell on his face in the water, Spook?" The animal, trained by a master skilled at resisting interrogation and fooling a polygraph, maintained a discreet silence. "Of course not. Nothing happens by accident in this dodge. So what I am going to do now is to go see his boss, who is an old buddy of mine, and tell her not to jump to easy conclusions the way state troopers do. You're going to have to wait in the car until I can take you to the pound. You helped me out, but you're not my goddam responsibility."

He consulted a road map that told him he was near Fort Ritchie; good place to be near if you're an intelligence analyst calculating the likelihood of war. Irving made a mental note to remember how to get back here in case of nuclear attack, which nobody worried about anymore. He found his way back down to Frederick, continued down I-270, and turned off at the sign that said CIA on the George Washington Parkway. He drove up to the fence at the complex and said to a guard at the gate, "I don't have an appointment but I need to see the Director." Before the guard could press the I've-got-a-nut-at-the-gate button, he said, "Ring the secretary to Dorothy Barclay and say Irving Fein is here and wants to see her. You'll see, they know me."

The guard made the call, was surprised at the quick okay, but said, "You can't bring a dog in here. Nobody can, not even if you work here."

"Not even a seeing-eye dog?"

"How can you be blind and drive?"

"I'll lock him in the car in the visitors' parking. It'll be okay, I'll get a pass from the Director, we're very close." He sped ahead before the guard could make a decision or a call.

"One of your boys was knocked off in a very skillful way."

"Walter Clauson had a drinking problem," Dorothy Barclay said, tapping the dossier on her desk. "He was a respected analyst, with the Agency for over thirty years, and so we made allowances. But he was going to be retired, or else riffed, this year. And his history of alcohol abuse was not inconsistent with the accident the Maryland authorities say took place at his cabin."

"I'm telling you it was no accident."

"Were you there, Irving? The troopers on the scene filed a preliminary report, I have the fax here—"

"The troopers never got off the porch when I was inside Clauson's cabin this morning searching through his stuff."

Less certainly, she looked at her fax. "It doesn't say anything about any press interest, much less a reporter being there—"

"I was there an hour ago. I've got the dead man's big black dog in my car outside—you want me to bring him in?"

"I believe you, Irving. And your hunches are legendary. But it would be wrong for me to launch an investigation on the basis of your hunch. The FBI is looking into it, I understand. I spoke to the Director as you were on your way up here from the gate, and he says it's unlikely there was any foul play."

"You stick to that story, Director Barclay. Don't budge an inch. Don't investigate. And when it comes out that you covered up the murder of one of your own veteran employees, you'll be ridden out of this place on a rail, and the President will say he doesn't even know you, and that's the last time they'll appoint a woman to this job, much less a lesbian, until they turn this place into a funny farm."

"Irving, what do you want from my life? I'm trying to keep this agency's nose clean for the first time in its life. An old dirty-tricks operative who's a known drunk is found facedown in the creek. And I'm supposed to turn this place upside down looking into every operation he's ever been a part of, because you had an appointment with him to go fishing? Give me a break."

He'd never told Dorothy about any fishing plans. "How do you know I had an appointment with Clauson?"

The reply was slow coming. "There was no tap on your phone, only on his." She was immediately on the defensive. "Don't get me wrong, Irving—there was nothing improper about him being a source for you, or for you two to plan to go fishing or whatever. I'm all for male bonding."

"Clauson was on to a sleeper agent, and so am I, and so is the KGB, and it offends my sniffer that your agency wants no part of it."

"Counterintelligence belongs to the FBI, not to us. Go talk to them."

"Dotty, this is Irving Fein you're talking to, remember?"

"You knew me when the world was young," she said, sighing elaborately. "You suppressed a story that could have hurt me as a lawyer. You made me a hero in the President's eyes only last month, and I love you dearly, and I'll treat you like no other journalist in the world. Nobody else can walk in here off the street and see the Director of Central Intelligence on demand."

Only slightly mollified, Irving muttered, "Had a hard time getting the dog past the gate."

"We'll have a special pass made with his picture on it. Forgive me, Irving, but the story about the sleeper agent with the huge fortune is another red mercury hoax, and any involvement with CIA personnel would be a great embarrassment. Deal us out. And on Clauson, let the law take its course. I'll attend his funeral if you like, give him a posthumous medal."

Huge fortune? That was the second time she'd let something slip, and it occurred to him that this very smart lady was not letting anything slip. He figured she was telling him her agency had an interest in all this, and it didn't bother her that he and his friends were poking around, but she had to keep her official hands off. Did she know about the sleeper and the huge fortune from Clauson, or had Clauson gotten it from the Agency and leaked it to a reporter for reasons of his own? Was she making a record of this conversation for Congress to cover her ass?

It was Irving's turn for an elaborate sigh. "I'll do what I can for you, kiddo, when the story breaks about an Agency man murdered and an FBI-CIA cover-up, and all the homophobe senators and bleeding-heart editorial writers come after your scalp." He rose to go. "You live in an apartment here, or a house?"

"An apartment in McLean."

"Big and roomy?"

"Not especially, you know me. Why?"

"No backyard?"

"It's on the sixth floor. Irving, what are you getting at?"

"Can you use a big black dog? Better security than any of your goons."

"No. You keep the dog. What's its name?"

"I'm thinking of renaming him Feliks."

Dorothy Barclay shook her head, ushering him out. "Felix is a cat."

Chapter 32

POUND RIDGE

"You're not going to wish that mutt on me. This house is not a kennel."

"It's a nice big place, acres and acres, even a pond, and besides, you need protection." Irving had left the dog outside, sniffing around, while he tried to wish him on Viveca in the library of her Westchester mansion.

"You drove him all the way up here from Langley, Virginia?"

"Seven hours. Couldn't put a dog in a box on a plane. And don't call him a mutt, he's a purebred Newfoundland." He pointed out the window. "Look at that coat, look at those lines. He could be a champ. And watch out, he inhales people who call him a mutt."

She could not understand Fein. One day he was savaging his closest associate; next day he was Dog's Best Friend, trying to find a home for the pet of a source who had died.

"Sorry. I once had a Yorkie, about three pounds," she said, "but she was too much trouble. That shaggy black monster outside must be forty times bigger. Big dogs scare me, especially males." And they reminded her of her father in his heyday, who was so proud of his pair of Great Danes.

"His name is Spook." At her sad and final shake of the head, Irving shrugged. "I'll drop him off at the pound. They'll dispose of him in a humane way, with an injection." That was to make her feel like a murderess, and was more like the Irving Fein she knew.

"The guy who died was the one who steered me to Dominick," he said, down to business. "They must have done some work together. The CIA man wouldn't pull the name out of a hat."

"He's the same one that we sent Edward back to see?"

"Yeah. See what your pal in Memphis can tell you about Walter Clauson."

She let "your pal in Memphis" go by; if Irving was afflicted with unfounded jealousy, as Edward suspected, she would treat it as a compliment. "How did he die?"

"Some dumb fishing accident. No foul play, the cops say. He drank a lot, like most of the old spooks."

"You look like you could use one." She poured them both a glass of wine.

He took out his notebook, riffled through till he came to notes he wanted, and said, "I'm breaking my head over something Clauson told me the night before he died. Let me run it past you, see if it rings a bell. He wanted to fish at Friends' Creek."

"Quaker," she said. No bell there.

" 'Your current endeavor has become like an albatross around my neck,' " he read from his notes. "Mean anything to you?"

"Just that it's something weighing him down. It's an old expression about bad luck. That's what an albatross is supposed to be, I think."

"Um. 'I want to regale you as if you were a wedding guest.' "

She focused on "regale": "That means tell a joke, doesn't it? Cause gales of laughter."

"Could be." No progress; she wished she could be more helpful, because this was evidently important to him. So far, her contribution to this story had been minimal. Lucky thing she had a contract.

" 'As if' what?" she asked.

" 'As if you were a wedding guest.' What goes on at weddings that—"

"The Wedding Guest. That's from a famous poem, and it has to be right here." She went to her father's books on the wall.

He looked at his notes. "By Samuel Taylor Coleridge?"

"That's it—'The Rime of the Ancient Mariner.' "

Irving did not know that one. She knew him to have had an eclectic education, reaching wide and deep but leaving great gaps; poetry was apparently one. "So who is the Wedding Guest?"

"He's the person who gets told the tale of horrible sufferings by the Ancient Mariner." Viveca, hefting a leather-bound volume of Coleridge's poems, turned to the table of contents, then to the poem.

"And here's the albatross. I forgot, it was a bird that symbolized heaven, and the Mariner killed it with an arrow, and all the terrible things flowed from that." She closed the book. "I know the end by heart. 'He went like one that hath been stunned / And is of sense forlorn: / A sadder and a wiser man, / He rose the morrow morn.' "

Irving winced. "Clauson said that something I did made him a sadder and a wiser man."

"Then Clauson was the Ancient Mariner, with the albatross from heaven that he killed hanging around his neck, telling his awful tale to you, the Wedding Guest."

"I'm not good at this. I wish to hell these Agency types wouldn't show off, playing literary games, when there's important stuff at stake."

"Maybe they're influenced by spy novels," she said.

"Nah. It all started with Angleton, who published a poetry magazine in the thirties and never let anybody forget it."

She broached the delicate subject. "What was it you did, Irving, or failed to do, that made your source sadder and wiser?"

That seemed to trouble him. "I stirred up some trouble at the Fed, I guess. It was just an idea, to stir the pot. Never figured it might lead to this." He stopped looking guilty and snapped his fingers in frustration. "He was on to something about the sleeper, and the DCI wouldn't listen, and he was about to spill to me."

He was holding back; Edward, who also knew the dead man, would know more about it. She reluctantly agreed to board the dog for a few days while Irving made other arrangements. That cheered him up some. He opened the back gate of his four-wheel-drive vehicle and left her two twenty-five-pound sacks of dog meal, a new leather leash, a stainless-steel feeding dish, a yard-long knotted rawhide bone, and a red rubber chew-toy that squeaked.

The dog trotted a few steps after the car, stopped when catching up became impossible, turned, looked at her, sniffed, and squatted to pee on the front lawn.

"That's all you know about dogs," she said to the disappearing car. "This one's a bitch."

Chapter 33

NEW YORK

In a lifetime of giving the most elegant power-dinner parties in Manhattan—orchestrated, themed soirées to which invitations were more coveted than the highest-society functions—Ace McFarland had never before been faced with this particular invitation and seating problem.

He had always been scrupulous about boy-girl-boy-girl seating and was determined to remain so. In the aerie of a Park Avenue triplex that was his dining room, an odd number of people at a table could never be permitted. Having people of the same sex seated alongside each other was inelegant. If, at the last minute, some guest called in sick or was unable to land at any of the city's socked-in airports, Ace had a substitute single male or female standing by.

A social conundrum: what did the thoughtful host do when the Director of Central Intelligence was a famously avowed lesbian? To invite another female homosexual would be to throw off the boy-girl seating; to invite a straight single man, or even a gay single man, might be seen as inappropriate by the lesbian invitee. Ace wished he were the agent for "Miss Manners," whose modern etiquette books probably had a CD-ROM dimension that her agent had overlooked.

After much deliberation, the full-disclosure solution for his modern seating problem came to him: he notified the Director's secretary by telephone that the Director would soon receive a formal invitation to a dinner party at which her partner would be one of the two guests of honor, the Director of the Russian Federation's Security Ministry economic section, Nikolai Andreyevich Davidov. She would be the other guest of honor.

Fortunately, Davidov was single. The young Latvian woman that Irving Fein asked be put on the guest list was—as Irving mysteriously put it—"on a parallel visit" with the KGB executive, and could therefore be balanced off by another single male, namely Irving. Viveca Farr, invited with "and guest," nominated a Memphis banker named Edward Dominick, who Ace presumed was presentable. The Republican co-chairman of the Senate Select Committee on Intelligence, Harry Evashevsky, would come with his wife, and that couple could ethically hitch a ride from Washington to New York on the government plane required for Director Barclay, who was not permitted to fly commercial. That travel arrangement would both save the government money and provide mutual cover in case the United States and Russia again came into confrontation and fraternizers during the thaw became suspect.

As a widower for many years, and as the arts-social-business icon who could respectably escort a woman fifty years his junior, Ace would enliven the table with his traditional choice of the season's most celebrated actress. For this occasion, he chose Ari Covair, the sensually emaciated French import who had starred as the heroine of the heavy-grossing movie based on Jim Lehrer's espionage novel *Blue Hearts*. She could legitimately say she wasn't a spy but she played one in the movies.

For the publisher to bear the cost of this admirable admixture, Ace went a level higher than the fellow in the publishing house who had signed the contract for the Farr-Fein book about the sleeper. A source of Irving's had tipped the reporter to the useful tidbit that the chairman of the publisher's parent corporation, Unimedia, was in town from Frankfurt. This piquant bit of business-social data, when passed along casually by Irving, had been seized on by Ace. Karl von Schwebel was also a director of the Bundesbank and conversant with Russia's economic difficulties, of interest to the Russian guest of honor.

Von Schwebel's wife, whose family fortune was the base of his empire, was probably a frump. But Ace already had glamorous celebrities in Viveca and Ari, with a possible third interesting woman in the Latvian reporter. Evangeline Evashevsky was a notoriously good listener. One frump could stand as contrast to all of them.

The rectangular table was set for twelve. That was the perfect number, in Ace's mind, for three separate dinner-table conversations running simultaneously, followed by some charming speeches unifying the dozen diverse people present. He looked over the menu card to make certain the passion-fruit sorbet had been substituted for the mango sorbet of the last party, which he thought lacked the necessary subtle tang. The superagent nodded, satisfied, at the passion-fruit listing on the engraved menu and proceeded to lay out the place cards. The order of battle was crucial to a dinner party's success.

Clockwise from Ace at the head of the table: the actress Ari was to his immediate left, next to her Davidov, then the expected von Schwebel frump, then the man from Memphis Viveca was bringing, and the senator's nice wife. Irving was at the far other end of the table. Then coming up toward Ace was the girl from Latvia, Karl von Schwebel, Viveca, the senator, and Dorothy Barclay in the place of honor on the host's right.

That way Viveca would get Senator Evashevsky on one side and the global media baron on the other; Davidov, though stuck with the frump on his left, would be more than compensated by having the delectable French morsel on his right, and would be directly across from the senator; and Irving would have the senator's wife and the girl from Latvia he wanted to be next to on his left. Ace would be able to share his attention with the piquant Ari on his left and the substantive Dorothy Barclay on his right. A good group, nicely mixed. The least desirable seat—between the frump and the senator's nice wife—was to be occupied by the Memphis fellow, but that was the price one paid for being a nobody.

Ace chose a Piesporter Goldtröpfchen for the first course, to please the German with "tiny little drops of gold," and a Château Margaux to go with the lamb, to please himself. This would not be a drinking crowd, however, as most of the diners would be fearful of letting something slip or missing somebody else's hint; the waiters were ready with bottles of Pellegrino for the sparkling water fanciers, Evian for those who preferred still water to run deep. Taittinger would do for the champagne toast; absent a major anniversary, Dom Pérignon would be ostentatious.

The orchestration was complete. Ace, the maestro, was ready to conduct. Legs crossed, holding an unlit cigarette in a silver holder as his baton, the host awaited the sound of the chimes.

As a butler lifted her Halston-era cashmere cape off her naked shoulders, Viveca checked out the competition. The French actress was delicious and momentarily captivating, with a figure that made feminists attach strips to her posters that read FEED THIS WOMAN, but her mind was probably stuffed with fluff. Dorothy Barclay, on the contrary, was a heavy hitter: the DCI looked serious, purposeful, attractively forbidding, and her presence was freighted with being the first woman in that position of power; Viveca resolved to work on getting to know her. Evangeline Evashevsky seemed to her almost every senator's first wife: dutiful, homespun, wary of attention paid her man by good-looking women. Let Irving cultivate her.

Ace had told her the German publisher's wife would be a plain dumpling, but the agent was wholly misinformed; he must have been briefed on an earlier wife of the media baron. The fluidly gowned woman with him turned out to be a Finnish economist, articulate in several languages, who drew every man's attention because her reputed brainpower came atop a statuesque figure and a classic Nordic face. She was the object of Director Barclay's economic questioning early in the cocktail hour, and Viveca was sure Edward would be all over Sirkka von Schwebel in the forty-five minutes that Viveca required to slip out and do her newscast.

No competition at all was Liana Krumins. The Latvian's long, dowdy Eastern European dress, inadequate makeup, and weird hairdo made her out of place in this sophisticated setting. Viveca noted how Davidov kept his distance from her; Ace tried to draw her out, failed, moved on; Edward observed her from afar, but made no effort to strike up a conversation; Irving, busy working over Davidov, had no time for her. Only the senator, a kindly soul, stayed by her side to put the girl at ease in a strange country, and she listened raptly to long anecdotes about his days as a cold warrior.

At Edward's urgent glance, Viveca peeled the Latvian away from Evashevsky and invited her to watch a nightly newscast from the set later in the week. She would bring Edward along to pick up any revelations from the very young television reporter about the early life of the sleeper in the Berensky file. Viveca categorized the Latvian presenter as an uptight bumpkin out of her element and in dire need of a hairdresser; what had Irving and Michael Shu been so impressed about? The girl did perk up at the prospect of watching American television news in production.

Viveca noticed Davidov, cornered by Irving, looking uncomfortable and glancing her way. She knew the Russian was sizing her up: a short, thirtyish, intelligent-looking woman in a loose Donna Karan outfit with a long gold chain. Not especially threatening to his ego, as the brainy Finnish stunner probably was; the KGB man would probably trust the cool American newswoman more than the high-powered Irving Fein. She was sorry there was no time to get Irving to suggest some leading questions. Viveca picked up a plate of crudités, offered them to the two men, then handed the plate to Irving and left him standing with it as she took Davidov over to the couch and sat next to him.

"You mustn't mind reporters," she said, "they're always working. I promise not to ask what brings you to America."

The Russian official had never been in such an apartment before. Three stories tall in an old building on an avenue with long islands of shrubbery in the center, with the cathedral ceiling reminding him of St. Vladimir's Hall in the Kremlin, and a garden of evergreens and crabapple trees on the roof terrace; and this man McFarland was only a literary agent. Was all this possible, Davidov wondered, on a small percentage of other people's earnings?

If Ace, as he knew not to call him, could live this well, he must be tightly associated with success. Doing business with him, the KGB man allowed himself to think, might not be a bad idea. The promotion of book business was surely the purpose of this dinner party, and it was suitable, in the all-capitalist world, that a social gathering serve a purpose. Davidov had discussed this invitation with his superiors and recommended to them he turn it down because of Director Barclay's presence; they had overruled him, directed him to attend, and even cautioned him against wearing a wire. He was pleased at their expression of confidence in his ability to work in the field.

Every good party should have a surprise, which this one did before dinner was served. The Russian had not expected to be confronted with Sirkka von Schwebel. The striking Finnish economist was known to him: files recovered by the KGB from Stasi before they fell into the hands of the West included long reports from her about the operation of the Bundesbank. Rather than allow her to be exposed as an East German police informant, as tens of thousands were, Russian Foreign

Intelligence had taken her under its wing and made her a productive agent, though not entirely trusted, because there was always the danger of public exposure as the flat rock of East German espionage was flipped over. She must live with that concern every day. FI had told him nothing about her, as usual, and he was reluctant to ask, but he was sure her service would be to exploit her Bundesbank links; he recalled she was reported to have access to a Federal Reserve asset in New York as well. She and Davidov had crossed paths once, before any of this, at a Helsinki academic conference, but his unprofessional interest in her had not been reciprocated.

Why was Sirkka here tonight? Her husband owned Fein's publisher, and the couple's presence at Ace's party was logical enough. But Davidov wondered if she might be the sleeper's Bundesbank source. If so, surely the two were separated by a cutout, but might she have any idea of the identity of Berensky in America? It was inconceivable to him that Fein and the CIA Director were not aware of her Stasi background, if not her present Russian FI employment.

Davidov reminded himself of the danger of his own bureaucratic overstepping: FI would hotly resent any contact initiated by KGB counterintelligence. Still, Sirkka and he were thrown together in the same room, possibly, though not likely, by coincidence.

He made a mental note to have his men currently trying to surveil the Memphis Merchants Bank, an effort which had grown out of a wiretap on Fein, run a check on Edward Dominick. To overcome the extraordinary security procedures in the Tennessee bank's communications, they had aimed a long-range vibration sensor at the bank's windows. One corner suite, probably the bank president's, was equipped with a blocking device to vibrate the windows and make the pickup of conversations from a distance impossible. That was sophisticated enough a countermeasure to arouse suspicion. Was Dominick that Memphis banker? Unlikely, but easy enough to check. Was the well-protected banker the sleeper himself? Even more unlikely again, but no lead could go unfollowed.

In a nation of 250 million, the likelihood of a visiting KGB official running across the sleeper at the first American dinner party he attended was remote, to say the least, but why was he being led to suspect that? Answer: a deception was under way. An overhear pointing to a Memphis bank, followed quickly by a party with a Memphis banker: Davidov instantly sensed a dangle. He focused on its perpetrator; someone had drawn up the guest list for this party with infinite care, and that someone—Fein and the striking television newswoman?—also wanted to plant a seed in his mind that Edward Dominick might possibly be the sleeper.

Harry Evashevsky noticed Irving Fein, his back to the party, looking across Park Avenue through the cathedral window. He excused himself from his group to get at the platter of shrimps wrapped in snow peas, and took up a viewing position next to Fein.

"Dorothy told me on the plane up here," he said to the reporter, "that you were up at Walt Clauson's cabin this morning."

"Your committee gonna look into that?"

"She says she thinks it was an accident. FBI does, too."

"So?"

"You don't buy that, I take it."

"You knew Clauson, Harry. He belted 'em down like the rest of the old boys, but he was no big boozer. And do you suppose Walt would tie on a load if he had a date next morning with a reporter? No way."

"If you were to write a letter to the committee—"

"Never happen. I write in the paper, or in a book. Whyncha wake up the IG?"

"I remember when Clauson testified alongside a DCI, when we were being misled." The old-timer had a way of rubbing the side of his nose with his thumb, a visual allusion to Pinocchio, whenever that former Director shaved the truth. "Might be a good idea to ask the Inspector General at Langley for a report about what Clauson was working on, just for old times' sake." He turned, and his gaze fell on the French actress. "My bride, Evangeline, was just asking me—how can a woman be so skinny and so sexy at the same time?"

Ari Covair took a long drink of sparkling water to assuage her hunger. She would have to pretend to be not hungry all through another delicious dinner.

Of the men at the party, Ace, harmlessly attentive, could probably do her the most immediate good; he was connected in Hollywood as well as New York. The Russian was the most attractive, face starkly planed, a mustache with authority, tightly coiled body; he could play the romantic espionage role he lived. The senator was cuddly, the famous print reporter a slob. The German multimedia magnate exuded the aura of power and would probably be dominant in bed, with the most profitable long-term possibilities for her career, but would be reachable on his cellular phone during an orgasm. Their eyes met and she looked down demurely; he would surely be on the phone to her the next morning.

The one Ari wished would offer her a ride home was the tall, easy-sounding banker with the knocked-about face and the soulful eyes. She sensed deep currents in him. But he had come to the party with the hard, bitchy-looking television news presenter, tough American to the core; poor fellow was the sort who needed the restorative of genuine femininity.

Edward Dominick found a spot in the elegant living room where he could observe Liana Krumins through a mirror, thereby seeming not to stare. Why was she so determined to make herself appear unattractive? Through dress, makeup, and hair, her self-effacement took an effort; moreover, she was hunching her shoulders, as if to protect herself in a cageful of predators.

The banker's glance flicked to Irving Fein, who had given up on Davidov for the moment and had turned his attention to von Schwebel. Dominick was curious to see how his new associate worked in this situation, and how a director of the Bundesbank would react. He joined their conversation.

"I'm one of your authors."

Von Schwebel nodded graciously. "I know, and we are honored." The book publishing house was a relatively tiny part of the multimedia empire, but not insignificant: his recent acquisition of a prestigious house, with a history and a backlist, added intellectual weight to the commercial enterprise. He had been criticized for paying too much for prestige, but a publishing house had value beyond the accountant's figures, bringing the firm's executives into contact with such people as

Ace McFarland had put together tonight. The German found this gathering most impressive.

"Took a lot of guts for you to buy a pig in a poke," Irving observed.

Von Schwebel did not catch the American allusion, and was grateful when the tall banker explained. "Mr. Fein was complimenting you for the courage to believe in him and Ms Farr, without knowing much more about their project."

"Ah, yes."

"But I think you made a wise investment," Dominick went on. "Fein here is a world-class investigative reporter, and Viveca gives a dimension to the story that you can exploit through all your media."

Von Schwebel presumed this buttering-up was to cover a late delivery of manuscript, but he did not get involved in such detail. He saw the television newscaster putting on her long black wrap and slipping out. "Ms Farr is leaving so soon?"

"Just to do the nine-o'clock news," Dominick said. "She'll be back before the main course."

Fein threw in a question abruptly: "What do you hear from the old Mariner?"

The German did not catch the meaning of what he assumed was another American idiom. He looked to Dominick for an explanation, but his face was impassive.

"Never mind. What was the biggest event in Germany in 1989?" Fein was a man with an inexhaustible supply of questions.

"That's easy," von Schwebel answered. "The fall of the Berlin Wall in November."

"How could you have made a lot of money if you knew it was going to happen?"

"Nobody knew." That was the truth. "Gorbachev's announcement that the Red Army would no longer keep communist parties in power in Eastern Europe caught us all with flat feet, as you say."

"But just suppose you did know beforehand? How could you make a bundle?"

"I am a director of the Bundesbank," he said. "I could not ethically have done a thing."

"But Dominick here doesn't have that problem," the reporter persisted. "How could he have cashed in on that news?"

"He is speaking hypothetically," said Dominick, a little embarrassed. "I was as astounded as anybody at the Soviet move."

"You would have bought the mark and shorted the yen and the dollar," von Schwebel said. "In the last quarter of that year—I remember it well—the deutsche mark jumped twenty percent against the major currencies. With the sort of leverage that currency trading provides, any trader would have made ten thousand percent on his money before the year was out. Much more, even, if he was sophisticated in derivatives."

Fein whistled. "Then right after the news broke, the smart money would go in the opposite direction, right? Sell on the news?"

"Wrong." The German smiled, remembering. "The Bundesbank was talking down the dollar, because our perception was that the opening of Eastern Europe would stimulate Germany's economy, ultimately raising our interest rates. Nobody realized—except the Soviets—what a drain East Germany would be on West Germany for years."

"But sitting in the Kremlin, you'd know what a basket case East Germany was," said Fein. "And you'd sell more dollars and buy marks. But I have a friend who tells me currency trading is awful risky—is he right?"

"Of course. But not if you had a crystal ball, which nobody does."

"I read a translation of your wife's article on the threat of disintermediation on banks in Sweden," Dominick said, changing the subject. "Brilliant."

"She will be pleased to hear that," von Schwebel said. "Can't say I read it myself." He excused himself to get a drink; the conversation about the recent past depressed him. That was the time he divorced his wife and faced down her relatives on the board, and after a decent interval married Sirkka, only to discover her Stasi connection. How long had she been passing secrets of the Bundesbank on to Leipzig and then to Moscow? To this day, she did not know he knew of her espionage past, or how he had moved heaven and earth to prevent the Stasi file on her from being revealed.

He looked across the room at the KGB's Nikolai Davidov politely chatting with the senator and the CIA's Dorothy Barclay. It was the job of Davidov's Fifth Directorate to help catch and kill the spies Barclay ran into the Kremlin, but this anomaly was to be expected in an age when the Russians allowed the FBI to open a Moscow field office, ostensibly for cooperative drug investigations.

Von Schwebel had little concern about the CIA's knowing of Sirkka's activities, but the KGB had taken her file out of Germany just in time; did Davidov know about her? He was in Federal Security, separate from Foreign Intelligence, but sometimes the top people shared information. Von Schwebel's stomach constricted as the CIA woman was called aside by the host and the KGB man walked up to Sirkka; Davidov admired a pin she was wearing, and said something to her, it seemed in German; he couldn't hear the words but she sighed and smiled a response. She had a heart too soon made glad.

Why, the German publisher asked himself, had the American reporter been asking about advance information from the Bundesbank? These things were never coincidences. Could Fein be after Sirkka, despite the fact that an advance from one of von Schwebel's companies was financing his investigation? That would be an awful irony, but American reporters were known to take a perverse delight in biting the hand that fed them. The media baron would have to tell the publishing subsidiary to get one of the editors in the trade book division to press Ace for more information about the Fein-Farr project.

"I take your point about currency trading," Dominick said to Irving Fein.

"You got Mike Shu up to his ass in aluminum."

"That's going to be productive," the banker insisted. "Dropped by more than thirty-five percent in 1989, with the Russians big players. But you may be right about currencies. We'll get started on who speculated most successfully in the mark in '89."

"Explain it all to Mike. I'm just a country boy."

Dominick smiled. "Who's your next target tonight? Von Schwebel's wife?"

"More your type, if you like to waste time." Fein looked past the tall Finn, around the room.

"I have to hand it to you. Not many people would consider that woman a waste of time."

Fein tapped the side of his nose. "I have a sniffer for news. I can spot a good source—von Schwebel is—and I can tell a trophy wife who's not. But feel free to go after her, break poor Viveca's heart. Do her good."

Dominick, having established some rapport with his mercurial co-venturer, did not bring up the time wasted on the red mercury blind alley. "I'll work on our German friend over a cigar after dinner. How did Ace know to invite him?"

"I passed along a tip from an old pal."

"You know what? You and I underestimated each other." The banker put out a feeler: "What do you say I stop calling you 'brother Fein' and you stop calling me 'Slow Eddie'?"

"Tsadeal. But time's a-wastin'."

Liana, ignored by Nikolai Davidov, resolved to retaliate by fixing her attention on Irving Fein and the way he was working his way around the room. Watching him at work would be a journalism lesson. Why had he not approached the American Director of Central Intelligence? Perhaps because they were working closely together and did not want others to know. Although Nikolai wanted her to believe that Fein was a CIA agent in the search for the sleeper, Liana was not so sure; she decided on the direct approach and went directly to the source Fein was avoiding.

"Your appointment gave heart to many women around the world," she said to Dorothy Barclay, and then asserted her anticommunist credentials. She awaited the what-brings-you-to-America reply. When it came, Liana said: "The surface reason is to speak at a seminar for journalists in Syracuse. The real reason is to make contact with a Russian agent who has disappeared."

"It's wonderful that your country now has a free press," said Barclay, veering to another subject, "after so many decades of occupation by the Nazis and the communists."

Liana would not be so easily parried. "I would be interested in talking to somebody here who might know about such a deep-cover agent."

"The FBI, but don't tell them I sent you. Or better still, try Irving Fein over there. God knows what you could learn from him. And you'll find he's not only a great journalist, but a wonderful man." The DCI beckoned across the room, and the reporter came over. "Irving, this young woman and you share an abiding interest in the same subject. Help each other." She slipped away.

"When you and I had that great lunch a year ago," he said, "you were a knockout. Why do you make yourself look like such a schlump?"

"What means 'schlump'?"

He ignored the counterquestion and came at her with another. "You're after the sleeper, same as me, and you're important enough to have Davidov follow you all the way over here. Why? What makes you such a big deal to the Russians?"

She admired such directness. "My program is not limited to Riga. The signal carries to Petersburg and is talked about in Moscow."

"So who's Madame Nina?"

She blinked; he was so direct so quickly, here at a dinner party. Was this how journalism was done here? "I don't know. Yet."

"You got a line on this guy Berensky over here?"

"No. Do you?"

"Yes. Where are you staying?"

She told him the name of her inexpensive hotel; he described it as a "fleabag," another word to look up. Then he said, "Lookit"—yet another word she did not know—"I like you. You can trust me. We'll leave here together tonight. We'll take a long walk down Fifth Avenue, which is safe enough, and we'll compare notes, and then we'll find a bar and talk some more. It'll drive your friend Davidov up the wall."

"Yes to everything."

"Good. I'll leave you alone till it's time to go. I checked the place cards and you're sitting between me and the German. Talk to von Schwebel about television stuff—it couldn't hurt your career—and he may be worth cultivating about Berensky. This is not a social occasion. Use every minute. Remember why you're here."

She nodded vigorously, feeling much better. She had told him, through Mike Shu, that the sleeper was named Berensky; Fein owed her that. She went to the bathroom—an amazing, spacious room, all marble and mirrors and a tub with marvelous nozzles inside—and made the concession to vanity of applying a small amount of eyeshadow.

At the dinner table, flanked by Liana and the senator's shrewd wife, Evangeline, who worked a motherly shtick, Irving treated himself to his favorite mental party game: who was going to wind up in the sack with whom—not necessarily that night, but soon.

Ace, pushing eighty, was out of it; all cattle and no hat, or whatever the Texans said. His dinner partner, the sexy French actress, was probably too weak from hunger to make it with anybody, but the likeliest to bed her down was von Schwebel. He was working at it right now, stealing glances at her; guys with clout in showbiz like him didn't miss.

Viveca and Edward—Slow Eddie wasn't so slow—either were already having what used to be called a torrid affair or, if Mike Shu was right, were about to make it, maybe that very night for the first damn time. Viveca was watching her boy watch the others: seeing a person you are about to get involved with interacting with others at a dinner party was not a deliberate tease but nevertheless a turn-on. The odious mental picture drew a sigh from Irving; Dominick was too big for her, a bit too detached, and she'd wind up hurt, which she couldn't complain about, because she would have brought it on herself. That was some consolation to Irving.

Davidov of the KGB was going to jump on the bones of Sirkka von Schwebel. The way the two of them avoided each other—maybe one brief conversational pass—was a dead giveaway, considering all they had to say to each other about economic intelligence. Moreover, Irving could sense the tension. Next to his corruption sniffer, his sexual-tension sensor was his major reporting asset. Hard to put a finger on how he could tell, but Irving was certain the KGB man was going to waste a lot of time in America in the sack with the Finnish financial whiz. That was fine; it would cut down his snooping around after Liana Krumins.

He put down one of his three forks—Ace was big on silverware and glassware—closed his eyes, and gently banged his palm on the side of his head five, six times. The answer did not come as to what made this Latvian kid valuable to both the KGB and the Feliks organization. He looked to his left at her, as she was getting her second wind, talking animatedly to Karl von Schwebel, as Irving had instructed, about the radar base the Russians still held a lease on in Latvia.

He couldn't tell in that outfit if Liana had much of a figure, but she was fresh and eager, and maybe Irving would get lucky. No; he put that thought out of his mind; worse than dishonorable with a source, it would be a mistake for him to knock over a girl half his age. Certainly not tonight. Something could happen with her in Syracuse, where he would call a buddy on the faculty of the journalism school to arrange for him to give a lecture during her seminar.

Even then, he promised himself he would make a move on her only if it moved the story along and she expressed an interest: maybe she'd open up to him when she was opening up to him. The Latvian girl was one of the good guys in all this, he was sure; something about her reverberated with journalistic integrity, a value akin to virginity, and it was not his way to violate either. He noted that even Dominick, as he was getting ready to have his way with Viveca's body, kept stealing observations of Liana in the mirror, not so much attracted as fascinated.

Dorothy Barclay? She would sleep with her lifelong companion in Washington that night, a relationship Irving had not exposed when it might have been a story long ago; he liked both women, and personal loyalty sometimes got in the way of printing gossip. He justified that lapse by thinking how it had ultimately paid off with a bigger story.

The senator would sleep with his wife. Harry and Evangeline Evashevsky had enjoyed each other's company for forty years, complaining but not meaning it all the way, and each was the repository of a different set of the nation's secrets. Irving had to smile. If those two ever disgorged what they knew about who was doing what to whom in Washington and Moscow, the intelligence establishment in the United States would be in the same leakage mess as its counterpart in Russia.

Ace raised a champagne flute. "This evening is symbolic of the new era, which some call 'post–Cold War,' and which someone will soon find a really good name for in the title of a book.

"Here, at one table, are the top intelligence brains of the twentieth century's great powers. In some matters, and I shall not elaborate, they still compete, although now as peaceful rivals and not as angry adversaries. In other fields, such as antiterrorism and international crime, these intelligence professionals are joined as Globocops. But who am I, a mere literary man, to toast this unique new relationship? I yield to the senator from Nebraska, who was overseeing espionage when Dorothy

Barclay and Nikolai Davidov were teenagers dreaming of being lawyers and epistemologists."

The senator rose to give the toast to the two spymasters, recalling the duplicities of the past, noting the tentative and limited working-together of the present, looking toward the cooperation of the future. Nice toast, spiced with a couple of anecdotes Ace had heard before, and so carefully couched that it would not get him into trouble if the two nations found themselves at loggerheads overnight. Davidov responded informally and briefly; Barclay rose and at some length recalled the Russian help at a time of danger for the U.S. President, a message of appreciation that Ace presumed Davidov would carry back to his superiors in Lubyanka, if he wasn't already wired and transmitting. He wondered how many recorders were going in vans on the street outside.

Later, seeing Irving and Liana to the door, Ace said: "Enjoy the party?"

"It was an honor to be included," the Latvian reporter said.

"Advanced the story," said Irving.

Chapter 34

NEW YORK

"These are not exactly the secrets of the Republic," the Federal Reserve's enforcement chief told Irving, pushing the printouts across the coffee-shop table, "but you don't want to get the butter from your bialy all over them."

The reporter stuffed the sheaf into the pocket of his overcoat, hanging within reach on a wall hook. "What do they tell me?"

"There were two hedge funds and one bank that led the parade in buying marks and selling dollars in the last quarter of '89," the Fed official, Hanrahan, said. "Really heavy plunge by the Vasco da Gama Fund, maybe came out ahead by two billion bucks, if they were leveraged out to ninety-five percent. Not that big a fund, either, and they were new back then."

"What do we know about them?"

"Not a hell of a lot. This isn't securities, with the SEC and registrations and stock exchange rules—this is the currency market, Irving, does a trillion dollars a day, and more on busy days. We miss a lot."

"You missed the whole Lavoro swindle. Billions to build Iraqi nukes through a hinky-dinky branch bank in Atlanta. Remember?"

Hanrahan nodded grimly and stirred his coffee. "My belief that you are operating in the public interest is the only reason I'm stretching the rules a little to give you a look at the old trading."

"You were telling me what we know about Vasco da Gama. Italian outfit?"

"No, a lot of the funds like the names of explorers. Like they're going to find something. This one is headquartered in Liechtenstein, represented by a front-man lawyer there, with the ownership of the mutual fund in the Antilles. But the names listed there will just be nominees."

"So they made two billion dollars. Where did the money go?"

"We spotted some big transfers late that year to U.S. banks—maybe half of it—and the biggest bite of that to Chicago National. Another to a multinational controlled by a shipping magnate. It's all there in the printouts. For the overseas transfers, you'll have to talk to the big ears."

"No Such Agency?" That was what the ever-eavesdropping NSA, or National Security Agency, was called. Irving didn't like those high-budget snoops and had few contacts at their Fort Meade headquarters.

Hanrahan nodded. "The other things I flagged in that stuff are, one, the Privet Fund had nearly four hundred million in currency profits the week the Berlin Wall fell, and two, that's the outfit that's been killing the competition in gold futures ever since. I have my eye on the Privet Fund managers, who mainly live in Coral Gables, because they're so good at guessing Fed actions. I put the key transactions in there even though you didn't ask for it."

"And now it's payback time, hunh?"

"Exactly," said the official. "You got us all steamed up about a mole in the Fed and now I got to show progress. The Chairman nearly peed in his pants, never saw him so excited. What do you have in the way of specifics?"

"Has to be somebody who started making real money in '89," Irving said. "You got a Fed governor, or a staffer in close, had his net worth increase then, or was doing a lot of traveling to the Bahamas or Switzerland?"

"We're working on that. I need a name, Irving, or a few names."

"I don't have it. But I got a lead. Check to see if you have any old sea dogs in sensitive spots, maybe Navy veterans, or yachtsmen. Or a retired Marine."

"What's the basis of your lead?"

Irving shook his head; he couldn't very well quote a poem. "Another word you want to run through your computers is 'albatross.' "

"That's what you'll be to me—hung around my neck—if none of this pans out."

"Baloney. Who's gonna prove a negative, that there's no mole? You get a safe run on this clear through to retirement."

"Yeah, but I got this conscience. Irving, what does your sniffer say?"

The reporter wiped his nose. "You got a mole, all right. Oceangoing. Look into that."

"We're getting some traction," said Michael Shu on one of his trips to New York. "The Privet Fund? Same outfit that cashed in on the drop in aluminum when the sleeper went into business. And the banking relationships of the two funds are almost parallel."

"Which means?"

"Irv, it's as if somebody said not to put all the action in one fund, to split it between two."

"Why not three?"

"I'm way ahead of you. We're running a computer check of the transfer patterns of these two funds against similar-sized funds, or against funds and banks that changed hands during Berensky's launch. The two funds, plus the Antilles bank—it's like a Rosetta stone. We have all sorts of leads to real places that made real money."

"You got a list of every political event in '89 and '90 that affected the markets? Ones that Berensky would know about in advance?"

"Right out of the almanac," Mike said, "and we're cross-checking the activity on each by the suspect funds and bank."

"Now fast-forward ahead a few years. He kills his KGB handler in Barbados, and kills the banker in Bern, and that costs him his stream of inside poop from Russia." Irving had the feeling they were indeed getting what Shu called traction. "He begins using his KGB connections in the West. You got anything on somebody making big bucks anticipating the Fed's changes in interest rates?"

"We're working on that. Just a matter of time."

"Same with the Bundesbank?"

"Haven't started on that yet, but it won't be a big deal to get."

Irving looked at his telephone. "That phone, as you know, is tapped." His counterspy equipment, an electronic toy that had cost a bundle, indicated at least two taps on the same number.

"I never say anything on it, Irv, or fax you here. Everything by snail mail, like you said, or if it's urgent, FedEx."

"I want you to call me on it from Memphis," Irving told him, "and say you got a lead on the Memphis Merchants Bank as a possible sleeper front. Don't use the word 'sleeper.' Instead, get cute—'the one who snores,' which should make it seem like you're worried about being overheard. And then ask me if I have a lead on the old Mariner."

Shu made a note. "That'll get somebody suspecting Dominick is Berensky, maybe, if the guy doing the tap doesn't screw up. Who's the old Mariner?"

"That's right near the top of the dunno sheet. It may be the code name of somebody in contact with the sleeper."

Irving hoped that by now Berensky, and perhaps the KGB, and maybe the Feliks people out of Riga—and maybe even the FBI at Dorothy's request—would be attempting to tap the Memphis operation's phones. The countertap activity, including bug sweeps twice daily and a Taiwanese encryption chip to block the FBI's access to a clipper chip, was to mimic the security at the real sleeper's home base. Any business office so secure would be suspect to all interested parties, especially when it became known to the parties listening to Irving's home phone that Shu was staking it out. Only Berensky himself could then be sure the Memphis bank was not the sleeper's front.

His purpose in the whole impersonation business was to force Berensky into initiating contact with Dominick. The trick was in deceiving all the others tracking Berensky into the belief that Dominick was their man. Irving was not competing with other news organizations, which would require him to hoard what little he knew, but was competing with world spookery, drawn up in vast, cumbrous array; that's what made this enterprise so different and required such an elaborate trap. As long as the others did not suspect Irving suspected his conversations were overheard, his home telephone would be his double-agent conduit, feeding disinformation back to his adversaries. By transmitting back to the surveillers the pretense that he knew who Mariner was—the mole at the Fed—he might flush out the real Berensky himself.

Irving asked himself what he would do if he were the sleeper and found out that the investigators were closing in on Mariner at the Fed. Though a protective cutout was a possibility, the reporter presumed that Berensky and Mariner knew each other's real identities. With the fate of Clauson in mind, he said aloud, "I'd rub him out."

"You'd what? You're mumbling, Irving."

"Need a rubdown. Gonna go to the gym." He caught himself asking himself: What was the number for disinformation?

Chapter 35

NEW YORK

Davidov told the statuesque Finn he hoped she had not found it too difficult getting away from her husband for a few hours.

"My husband," the former Sirkka Numminen coolly informed him, "is probably with the young actress who was at the party last night, indulging in what the Americans call a 'matinee.' I wonder what the French word is for matinee."

Nicely embittered, Davidov judged, and she was adept at the nuances of multilingual slang. "Is he aware of your service for Stasi?"

"No. And I would do anything to keep it from him."

But that showed the Finnish economist was not very well informed. The KGB man could recall documents demonstrating beyond doubt that Karl von Schwebel was fully aware of his second wife's work for Stasi, the East German secret service, and suggesting he was at least partially aware of her subsequent service to Russian FI. Obtaining that information about Sirkka and suppressing it at the source had cost the publisher a great deal of money. Von Schwebel was either very much in love with his second wife or eager to protect his reputation for sound judgment at the Bundesbank. Probably the latter; if he were motivated by love, the media magnate would have told her what steps he had taken to protect the both of them. As matters stood, he could take advantage of her guilty conscience about what she thought she was withholding from him.

The Fifth Directorate chief held up his hand lightly, indicating he would not take advantage of his position or hers. The woman in his thoughts along those lines at the moment was Liana, who he considered had comported herself with more dignity than the other women at the party. Her departure with Fein disturbed him more than he wanted to admit; the KGB tail had lost them in a noisy bar in Greenwich Village. Davidov presumed the other shadow, reporting to the Feliks people, had not been so easily shaken. Those followers were longtime professionals.

He had to work his way around to the "Who is Mariner?" question lest she refer him to her Foreign Intelligence handler. "I have seen some of your economic reports," he lied, "and congratulate you on their value." He assumed she had passed on the early realization by the Bundesbank directors that the incorporation of East Germany would depress the Federal Republic's economy. "Your assessment of the likelihood of Kohl's raising taxes to avert a huge deficit was on the mark."

"You are the first to say that. My work is rarely appreciated." She corrected herself: "The Memphis banker told my husband last night my piece on disintermediation was brilliant. That was extra nice of him, to say it behind my back that way."

When he asked what were some of her other achievements, she inundated him with useful data about transmissions to Moscow of the German central bank's deliberations in the early nineties. He wished he had his own Michael Shu to follow them up instead of his bumbling crew at Yasenovo; to remember the specifics, he used his epistemologist's trick of placing key words and names in three-dimensional mental space.

"And more recently, were you able to coordinate with your counterpart at the American Fed?"

She hesitated. "These are matters for you to discuss with my handler, or his superior in Moscow."

That door back home would surely be slammed in his face. "The correct answer. But I must move quickly on a matter while I am here, and will straighten out the channels when I return." He used the code word picked up from a Memphis wiretap: "Have you dealt directly with the old Mariner?"

Reluctantly, Sirkka answered, "Usually not. Someone in the U.S. coordinates our data. I should not be discussing this with anyone, even you, with no disrespect."

"Usually not, but sometimes you deal directly with him." He hardened his voice. "Madame von Schwebel, I am a KGB counterintelligence officer. I have reason to suspect the Mariner may have been turned by the Americans. I expect you to help my investigation."

"Of course, Director Davidov."

He could not reveal he did not know the Fed mole's identity. "When did you see him last?"

"At the World Economic Forum in Davos, Switzerland, in January."

"What was he doing there?"

"Acting as spinmeister to the press on behalf of the Americans. He has credibility, assisting the Chairman of the Federal Reserve on international negotiations, as always."

"As always."

"Yes. Mort has had that job with Fed Chairmen going back to Arthur Burns. It's as close as the Americans come to a British civil service."

First name Morton or Mortimer; that was all he needed, but Davidov continued questioning as a cover. "Careful, now. Has he given you any reason to think he is under suspicion by American counterintelligence? Or has already been turned? Any sign at all?"

She leaned back in the armchair of the cocktail lounge and drew her tawny hair back. Scandinavian women bloomed in their forties; Davidov enjoyed playing with her this way. "Recently we had occasion to speak on the telephone—openly, as sherpas for our countries, preparing for next year's Davos meeting. He seemed worried, not his usual smooth self, and cut me off in the middle of a sentence. Said he was under great stress."

That was a bonus. He gambled: "Was he worried about a sleeper?"

"About what?"

"Worried about his sleep, loss of sleep, from feelings of guilt, now that capitalism has triumphed over communism?"

"Maybe. I couldn't read his mind."

"Okay, end of interrogation. I must warn you not to report this meeting to your handler or anyone else in FI. This is a Federal Security Ministry counterintelligence matter. Do you understand?"

"Yes, sir."

He picked up his ginger ale. "I am always interested in the origin of code names. Was the Mariner a Marine, or some sort of sailor? Did Mort reach into some poetry?"

"Nothing to do with that." Sirkka recrossed long legs in raw silk trousers. "The first Chairman of the Federal Reserve was a man named Marriner Eccles. Mort wrote his biography long ago."

Davidov had to laugh; there was such a thing as overanalysis. "You've been helpful to me. How can I be helpful to you?"

"Keep the secret of my Stasi work from my husband."

"Why is that so important to you?"

"He would be ashamed of me. He would be ashamed of himself. And Karl is a vengeful man—he would cut me loose, and make sure I never worked again."

The KGB man pondered that a moment. Sirkka Numminen von Schwebel had been more helpful to him than she knew; he now had learned of a person who might know the American identity of Berensky, or at least know a cutout who did.

"Your husband knows all about you," Davidov said at last. "He bought your file from the Stasi keeper of archives in 1989 for five hundred thousand marks. The only copy of your file, and only a small part of it, is under the Foreign Intelligence chief's personal control in Moscow. Those files are state secrets, never to be revealed, not to the Foreign Ministry, not even to our Ministry. I know of your file's existence, but I have not seen it, probably never will."

She sat stunned. Finally: "That bastard. He knew all along."

"Yes, but on the other hand, he never betrayed you." He gave her husband the benefit of the doubt. "Possibly he didn't want you to know that he knew because he loves you."

"I have no reason to believe that. Karl just wants total control of me."

"Well, now you won't tell him that you know—that he won't tell you that he knows. Puts you in control, although you're the only one who knows it."

She smiled faintly at the prospect of a walk down that silvered corridor.

Davidov, interested in the triple cross as epistemological sport, took her one reflection further. "Or you could confess to him, never letting on you know he already knows. That would establish your bona fides with him, and he could never reveal he knew all along, putting him on the defensive with you." When she blinked, he added, "We do this all the time. Consider it part of your training as an agent, an occupation from which nobody can ever resign."

"I'm grateful to you, Nikolai Andreyevich. Tell me—if one copy of my file exists in Moscow, and it's not in your agency, how did you come to see all my economic reports?"

"I never saw them."

Her look was blank, not understanding.

"I tricked you just now, playing on your professional vanity. I needed your secret."

Her expression changed from puzzlement to profound shame. Davidov added in his kindest voice: "No, do not be angry with yourself: learn. Never trust anybody in this business. Never assume the obvious truth is true."

Chapter 36

CHICAGO

A chime sounded and the green light on the telephone went on, signaling a call from Leo Bellow's highest-activity account. The broker put earphones on so he could use the computer with his hands unimpeded.

"Bellow here."

"Leo," the familiar voice said, "I have an order for you that may take up most of your morning."

"I have the summary of your account on my screen, sir."

"Will you call me from the candy store?"

The broker switched to an encrypted line for both the talkphone and the modem. Use of the antitapping device would one day call suspicion on his actions from the regulators, but the account insisted on impenetrable secrecy, and what this account wanted, it got.

"I want to liquidate my long position in yen options and use it all to buy dollar options before noon. Full leverage."

He took a deep breath—this was a $400 million switch in position—and typed the order, hitting the modem switch for visual confirmation by the client, wherever he was. He always reached his client with a local call, but it could be automatically switched to London or Hong Kong. Or maybe the man placing the order was in Chicago today, down the hall in the Merc.

"Accurate. Execute the order."

Bellow typed the command that started the huge switch in position. The computer automatically asked, "Are you sure?" and he felt like passing that question along to the client, but did not. He typed "Y" and hit the enter key.

"I should tell you, sir, that I got a query from VDG Investment Advisers about a visit they got in Miami from a man who said he was a financial reporter. Asking about ownership, clients, all the things he couldn't find from a D&B."

"What sort of reporter?"

"They think he was more of an accountant. An Asian-American. I wouldn't bother you with this, but the same fellow showed up next day in the Antilles doing a story about offshore banks."

"Anything else along that line?"

He didn't want to unduly worry the client, nor did he want to hold back any relevant data. "Maybe a coincidence—probably is—but the Federal Reserve notified all national banks it is doing a detailed survey of all major incoming transfers, using the first week of this month. The questionnaire concentrates on the Antilles and Liechtenstein. You'll recall how busy a time that was for us."

"Nice to know. Keep me informed and notify me of the completion of the order before noon Chicago time."

"It will be done."

"This afternoon, I will want to know how many swaptions are available on corporate bonds with calls attached."

"They would go through the roof if interest rates drop," the broker said. The Open Market Committee of the Federal Reserve was scheduled to meet in New York later in the week, and was not expected to take any action on rates. But this client was remarkably intuitive about the Fed's decisions, guessing right nine out of ten times, if guessing was what he was doing. Bellow had an agreement with his other funds not to follow VDG judgment with his own trades until the client's trades were concluded, which gave him an added incentive to conclude them quickly. The last broker to try to jump the gun on this client lost all the business and had to close up shop; Bellow would do what he was told.

He could get fifty-to-one leverage on these bonds: for $400 million of the client's investment, he could buy options on $20 billion worth of bonds. If the Fed surprised the market and lowered interest rates, the bonds would jump, but the bonds with calls would add a substantial kicker. The gamble was on the grand scale: if the Fed went one way, the client would lose his whole $400 million; but if the Fed went the way the plunging investor anticipated, the client would stand to make double-digit billions.

By asking no questions, Leo Bellow learned no guilty knowledge. If he ever had to testify, he would say that some Fed-watchers were just more adept than others.

Chapter 37

MEMPHIS

"Can I be absolutely honest with you?"

The banker looked at her quizically. "Are you sure you want to be?"

Viveca said yes. Having finally consummated her relationship with Edward Dominick after Ace's party, she felt safe in revealing her economic ignorance.

"I'm an intelligent woman. I was graduated *magna cum laude* and I went to night school to earn a master's degree in politics. I can grasp complexities and am willing to do my homework."

"I'll attest to that. You got out of bed afterward to read the on-line news."

"Then why is all this financial derivatives stuff such a mystery to me? I walk through your war room, and listen to Mike Shu and the others talk about swaps and forwards and butterfly straddles, and I can't put it together. Frankly, I've been faking it, Edward." It was such a relief to let her guard down. "Would you explain to me what the hell you're doing with all these numbers? Is it real money?"

His large hand reached out for her shoulder, and then slid down the back of her suit and caressed her intimately. She found it a pleasure not to have to draw back, even in an office; the door was closed and no building nearby was tall enough to provide a look into these windows. If he wanted to act possessive about her now, he had a right, as she hoped she did about him.

"With your master's degree, you surely read Aristotle's *Politics*," he began, obviously delighted to turn teacher. "Do you recall his account of Thales the Milesian?"

"I could have been absent that night."

"Thales was a philosopher, like Aristotle, but with a practical bent. He anticipated a big olive crop that year, and used what little money he had to rent in advance all the local olive presses. In a few months, when the bumper crop of olives came in as Thales the Milesian foresaw, he had the only equipment to squeeze out the olive oil. He made more money on that than Aristotle ever did in his life."

"Got it."

"Then you understand the basis of the theory of financial derivatives," Dominick said. "Thales was buying an option—the ability to squeeze the olives at a rate agreed in advance. Underlying that option was the rental rate of the presses, which became much more valuable when the olives rolled in—but our Greek friend had his low rate locked in."

"He gained what those who rented him the presses lost."

"That's the game. When the value of the 'underlying' changes, one party wins what the other party loses."

"But what benefit is that to society?" That sounded pretentious. "I mean, if it's just a crapshoot, what economic good does it do?"

"It transfers risk. When you want to limit your risk, you sell it to somebody willing to assume it. That's what the owners of the olive presses did. Derivatives serve a business purpose, which is why they're running at a rate of twelve trillion a year. And they were just beginning to boom when Berensky entered the markets."

"Now show me what it did for him."

Dominick reached over and lifted a long gold chain from her neck. He hefted it in his hand. "Three or four ounces."

"I never weighed it. It was a gift." From her first producer, who had dominated her life before she broke free of his malign influence. She wore it as a kind of vengeance; she would not see him again, but he did have good taste.

"If you want to sell this to me, I'm ready to pay the going price for four ounces of gold. Fifteen hundred dollars. Now come into the war room, and watch what I do." Still carrying her necklace, hefting its weight in his hand, he led her to the "gold desk," a trader sitting at a computer and wearing telephone earphones. "You feeling good or bad about this necklace today?"

"Good," she said. She felt upbeat about a lot of things: man, career, the sleeper story, life in general.

"Buy a hundred ounces of gold," he told the trader. The screen showed the current cost, about $38,000.

"Don't do it on my say-so," she cautioned.

"Worried? Okay—sell a hundred ounces with a different broker. See? We didn't make or lose anything, though we did establish a reputation for prompt payment with two brokers. Now let's do what the sleeper does." He ordered the trader to prepare to buy gold futures options. "Now, let's say Berensky knows from somebody in our government that the economic indicators index is going to go up tomorrow."

"Threat of inflation," she responded. "Seek safety in gold."

"Or he learns, before anyone else, that the German central bank will raise interest rates."

"That stops inflation. Sell gold."

"Or that Russia is unable to meet its gold production quota."

"Shortage drives up prices," she responded. "Buy gold."

"Here we go." He told the trader to buy the designated block of gold options.

Viveca worried about what they had just done. "Have we actually invested all that money? Just on a test?"

"If you're worried about your information, let's hedge." With other traders, he put in orders to sell gold option futures. "Now it's a wash. We're about even no matter which way gold goes today."

"So how will all this help us find the sleeper?"

"He's doing the same thing," Dominick said, "only without the hedging. We're finding out who's been incredibly right about gold futures in the past few years, and we've begun to mimic him. We have some of the same brokers, and not all of them are completely discreet. In time, we'll have an almost parallel operation, though not with his resources. We'll be capable of a financial impersonation." He seemed very proud of that.

"And then an actual impersonation?"

"If he hasn't come to us, and if I can get more about his personal background, it would come to that."

"Irving says he'll try to pump some KGB file information out of Liana," she assured him. Dominick walked her to the elevator; his chauffeur awaited her downstairs. Viveca hoped he would suggest a specific date for getting together again, but his mind was apparently on his job.

"I may have to poke around in Moscow and Riga, looking for places to invest big money. That's something Berensky might do. Take care."

The elevator door parted them. Viveca jabbed at the lobby button. Coming on top of Irving's agitation about the death of his CIA friend, the prospect of Edward's visiting the centers of the search for Berensky worried her. She told the chauffeur to stop at a gourmet food shop on the way to the airport and sent Edward a liter of extra-virgin olive oil wrapped in a big red ribbon.

Chapter 38

Liana, elated, sat with Irving Fein on the steps leading to the Hall of Languages at Syracuse University. Behind them, a semicircular wall listed in granite the names of all the students lost in the Libyan terrorist sabotage of Pan Am flight 103. She had just participated in the first session of the first day of her two-week academic seminar. Thanks to his coaching, she had not done badly, considering she had dropped out of university to become a full-time anticommunist activist in the late eighties.

"The students looked up to me, the way I look up to you," the Latvian told him. She pulled her mackinaw close, smiling through her shivering; Syracuse was as cold as they said it would be, but her welcome as warm.

The trip to America and her reception at the university were Fein's doing, Liana knew. The famous reporter was behind her invitation by USIA. The seminar—Media Techniques Around the World, televised by the university station WAER—followed a short speech and long question-and-answer session by Fein to many of the Newhouse School of Journalism students.

In her much smaller seminar about reporting in newly independent states, he was a "facilitator," shaping the discussion to play to her strengths. And the Latvian had plenty to say—more than she had thought—about television reporting in Eastern Europe, especially in a country riven by language; whenever others in the discussion group went off on tangents, Irving Fein sternly centered the students on the points she had raised. The notion of the media as participant as well as observer in the making of news was exhilarating; she would have to teach a course at Riga University on this exciting subject, based on this experience and her new academic credentials as a two-day lecturer at a great American university.

"You did all right," he said. "English was a little weak at the start, but there's a ferocity about you that takes over and then you forget to be worried about words. Have a glass of wine, like Viveca does, before you go on—it'll loosen you up on your English."

She grinned at him; a good man, getting older in an intriguing way. One of the student editors had asked her about "mentors" in Eastern European media, and Liana had asked right back—what was a mentor? To her, it was as foreign a word as "facilitator." From the answer, she hoped this famous journalist would be her mentor and facilitator. She was honored to be working on the same story in tandem with him. She asked about his partner in New York City, Viveca Farr. From his shrugs and the ducking of his head, though never from anything he said, Liana Krumins gathered that Fein considered Farr to be more presenter than reporter; necessary in her way, but without the hunger and passion of a real journalist.

"The passion of the eighties was political revolution," she offered, "and the passion of the nineties is the information revolution." That was to be the theme of her second day's seminar.

"That's banal," he said, waving it aside. "Think-tank thinking." She was immediately glad she had not announced the theme in class.

"What I mean," she amended, "is that the movement in the world is no longer dominated by political activists, as I was, but by journalists with opinions, as I am beginning to be now. We not only report the news, we help to make the news. Because we journalists focus attention on the forces of change, we become agents of change." That was surely not banal.

"Yeah-yeah. When you get home, look up Heisenberg's Uncertainty Principle in physics." When she gave him her most helpless look, which rarely failed her, he explained: "The energy involved in the measurement of a particle knocks the particle around and makes it impossible to get a precise measurement. That's why you can never get a true fix on both position and momentum."

That was an insight about the news business, Liana recognized, in contrast to her feeble attempts at profundity. She took out her notepad and got the spelling of the German physicist's name, noting next to it, "The reporting of news changes the news."

He looked at her notes. "If you're going to boil something down, boil it all the way down," he instructed. "Make it 'The reporting changes the report.' Save words."

She crossed out the excess verbiage, nodding yes, less was stronger. "I have so much to learn, and you have so much to teach."

He did not deny that, but took the edge off the praise: "At least you don't have to be taught to be straight. You either have that internal balance wheel or you don't. It isn't hard to get a story, but it's a bitch to hold it straight when you got it."

She wrote that down too, not to flatter him, but because she could use it—though she was aware it flattered him, too.

"There's a corollary to that, which is called Fein's Underestimation Principle." He spelled "underestimation" for her. "For example, here we are, working on a heavy, world-class beat about the sleeper agent. There is a time in a big story when you don't know how much you know. You make the mistake of concentrating on how little you know, and you miss the useful details already inside your head."

She nodded, writing.

"First thing to ask yourself, Liana," he continued, "is—why you? Here you are, still in your twenties, not much experience, not a knockout, but you have one of the KGB's top guys eating out of your hand. You have this Madame Nina dame and her Feliks outfit, with half the crooks in the old Soviet Union, following you around. And you have Berensky himself making contact with you—something I'd give my eyeteeth for. That's the first real evidence any of us have that the sleeper is not some sort of dream. Now ask yourself: of all the reporters in the world—why you?"

"I have the news program in Riga that everybody listens to," she declared. "And it reaches Petersburg, too, and because it is in Russian, its rating is high." She was not yet in a position to boast, but that was not nothing.

"Gotta be more. So keep asking yourself: 'Why me?' Got it?"

" 'Why me?' " She said it again to please him, writing it in capitals and underlining the words. "Why me? I will try it on Nikolai Davidov."

"You and he—close?"

"We have had sex, but we are not close."

The American reporter shook his head as if slapped, then pressed on: "That was when you told him you knew about the bug in your pendant, huh? Dumb of you. Never give 'em anything for nothing. Always trade."

She would remember that, but his advice struck her as contradictory. "You mean Davidov does not know," she wondered, "that you are aware of his listening to your calls at home?"

"Nope. He thinks we're stupid. That's okay with me."

"Davidov thinks you are a tool of the CIA."

"Then he's the one who's not only stupid, but paranoid."

Liana was glad to hear the journalist verify that. She remembered she was at a university, and asked a professional question in a stiffly academic way: "What should be the relationship between the media and the intelligence services?"

"You gave me the answer to that a minute ago about you and Nikolai Davidov. Okay to fuck around, but don't get too close."

The great reporter gave her a smile, more lopsided than leering, that warmed her heart. "The spooks and the reporters, we're both in the meaning-of-information dodge. We both gather up all the facts we can and then we noodle them around in our heads to see what it all means. Then the spooks tell the government secretly what a little of it means, while the press tells the people publicly what it all means."

"Then the spies and the reporters are very much alike in what we do."

He shook his head vigorously. "Big difference. It's fashionable to be cynical in this dodge, but you mustn't be afraid to get cornball now and then. Get this: At the heart of secrecy is mass manipulation, but at the heart of publicity is democratic dealing. That's why reporters and spooks can be occasional bedfellows, but never permanent allies. We use each other for our different ends, and whoever gets the most use out of the other wins."

He stood up, pulled her to her feet, and set off across the campus. "Here's the deal. Up to last month, I've been letting Davidov in on a lot of what Mike Shu and I learned about Berensky. That stirred the pot and used the KGB to put the heat on the sleeper. But as soon as Davidov got hooked on our data, we crossed him up."

"How did we do that?" Her "we" was intentional; she considered herself more on his side than on the side of the Feliks people or the KGB.

"We encrypted. Whammo, like that, everything in code. All he gets on his earphones out of our Memphis operation is static. His fax tap is a garble. He knows that Dominick is right on the edge of closing in on the key bank Berensky owns, way ahead of the KGB accountants, who can't count beans." He licked his lips. "We have Davidov's mouth watering. By the way, you got a dog? Could you use a dog?"

"No, I live in a tiny apartment in Riga, and I'm not home every night."

"Never mind. You like him? Davidov?"

"I hate the KGB. Nikolai is personally attractive."

"He's a smoothie, but he's KGB. He's not on our side. We're after the truth and he's after the money. You won't turn into a lovesick puppy and forget that?"

"I will be careful." She had never been happy enough to be a lovesick puppy, but was pleased that he thought she had had a normal girlhood.

"Can I trust you to plant three lies on him? See how he reacts? You'd better write these down." They sat on a bench. "First, you're telling him I know 'why you.' Here: you said to me, 'Why me?' And then I said to you: 'I know all about why you, Liana Krumins, of all people, were selected as the stalking horse.' "

"The horse?" Fein was going too fast.

"Tell your playmate Nikolai that I know why you're in this right up to your sweet little keister." He shook his head in irritation at language gaps and started again. "Tell him—this is important—tell him I told you that I know why you personally are so central to the search for the sleeper."

"You do?"

"No, I don't." She could see he was trying to be patient. "But I want you to lie to him—tell him I told you I do know. Okay? Then tell him another lie—you don't know why you were chosen, and the fact I won't tell you why makes you irritated with me. Got it? It'll shake him up. Maybe he'll give you a hint. At any rate, he'll have to operate as if I do know, and wonder why I'm not acting on it."

"I understand." Almost; she would work it out later. It did not bother her at all to help play a trick on the KGB. "And what is the third lie you want me to plant on him?" She kept count, even when he did not, and liked the mental picture of "planting" lies.

"The third lie. Duh. It'll come to me in a minute—this four-wall-squash-court deception stuff is tricky, and I got a lot going on in my head. Yeah, here it is: you want him to believe that you believe that the sleeper may be Edward Dominick."

"The man who brought Viveca to the party in New York? The banker from Memphis, Tennessee?"

"The same. You're not sure, but you suspect. No reason, just intuition. A hunch. They can never argue with that."

"Is it true? Is Dominick really Berensky?"

He reached out as if to pat her on the head, then drew his hand back. "No, kid, that's why I called it a lie. But we want the KGB and the Riga crowd to think it's true. Then it'll get back to Berensky and he may see how we could be helpful to him. It could draw him into doing business with us. See? Worth trying, and you can help. Give it a shot."

He turned to the information she had gathered from the Berensky file. Irving asked a lot about Arkady Volkovich, what he knew about Madame Nina and the Feliks people, and if she thought Arkady was a double agent, working for the KGB as well. She had not considered that before; she thought not. "And I certainly don't think he's a double agent for the CIA."

"Hadn't thought of that myself. But I think the CIA interest died with Clauson." He looked at her proudly. "Good for you, kid, you're getting the hang of it. Nothing is certain in the who-uses-who-dodge." He frowned. "Who-uses-whom, it may be."

Liana expressed her interest in his examination of the dead CIA man's cabin. To her surprise, Fein filled her in eagerly: the room, the dog, the trooprs, the computer, the books on the chair, how the poem in the open book might be a clue.

"What was the other book?" The question was so obvious she was afraid she looked foolish in asking.

"I dunno. Why?"

"If you think he was sending you a message with the poetry book," she said with what seemed to her logic, "why not the other as well?"

Irving Fein did a strange thing. He stopped and closed his eyes, gently tapping the butt of his palm against his temple. After a bit, he said, "*Moneybags. FDR's Moneybags.* Wasn't open, no pages turned down, nothing written in it, nothing fell out when I shook it."

"What was it about? Who wrote it?"

"Economic history, President Roosevelt, the New Deal. I forget the author."

"I guess it's not important." They walked for a while, briskly, passing clumps of students sauntering across the quadrangle at the heart of the school. She stopped him to look at a statue in a sculpture garden of the biblical figure Job, the innocent sufferer who questioned God's injustice, by the Serb sculptor Městrovíc. The reporter took a deep breath of the late November air, exhaled, and set off on a march back to where they had been sitting, farther down the hill to a large new building marked BIRD MEMORIAL LIBRARY.

"The lesson here," he said, pushing her in the door ahead of him, "is to follow up every lead even when they're blind alleys. After ten blind alleys you're entitled to a hit, like an oil wildcatter deserves a gusher after a string of dry holes. The commodity-of-wheat theory was a blind alley. This'll be blind alley number six."

He said to the woman at the desk, "You got a gizmo that will see if you got a book, like a card catalog? I got a title, not an author."

The librarian said the card catalog had been computerized and showed them to a workstation. Irving Fein entered "FDR's Moneybags" in the title slot and the screen instantly showed author, publisher, date of publication—1951—and the fact that the book was in the Bird Library stacks, gift of an economic foundation.

"I don't have a library card, but I'm a friend of this foreign scholar who just ran a seminar here," he explained. The librarian said he could not take the book out, but he was free to examine it in the reading room behind her. In a few moments, she produced the book, rebound in buckram without the jacket.

Fein turned to the title page and read aloud, " '*FDR's Moneybags: A Biography of Marriner Eccles.*' Oh-shit."

Liana asked what that last stood for.

"That's the Mariner I've been looking for. 'By Mortimer Speigal.' Oh-shit. I know him. He still works at the Fed."

Liana flipped back through her pages of notes. " 'There is a time in a big story,' " she read aloud, " 'when you don't know how much you know.' "

He took the notebook out of her hand, enfolded her in his arms for a long hug, lifted her a couple of inches off the ground and swung her slowly from side to side, and—on less of an impulse, she thought— kissed her hard on the mouth before going back to the avuncular hug. Over his shoulder, she could see the librarian shoot them a mock-frown.

Chapter 39

RIGA

A driver in a worn army uniform met him at the airport gate in Riga carrying a hand-lettered sign that read UNIMEDIA. Karl von Schwebel handed the veteran his rolling overnight case and followed him to the car. Though most of the limousines were German or Swedish, a few British, this car was an old Russian Zis. In the airport lounges all the signs were in Latvian, not, as he recalled, in Russian; these Balts were eager to turn westward and throw off the detritus of a half century of hated Russification.

The publisher remembered the Feliks organization driver, Arkady, from his last visit to his corporate benefactors. Arkady would be discreet, trustworthy, uninformative, a good soldier in their clandestine army. Von Schwebel had read his reports about accompanying Liana Krumins to Lubyanka to inspect the Berensky and Shelepin files.

"Is Madame Nina well, Arkady?"

"As well as can be expected, Herr von Schwebel," Arkady said over his shoulder in German. "She is under great pressure."

That invited communication; though their roles in the organization were wholly different, they were under the same command. "And what is the source of the stress?" A generation ago, the word used was simple "pressure"; these days, it was psychologically dressed up as "stress," from "distress," in Old French *estrece*, drawing tight, like a noose. Von Schwebel, whose media communicated words in many languages all over the world, dabbled in the roots of words.

"That is the subject of the meeting of the committee. The search for the agent who disappeared in America. Our concern is that the KGB and the CIA are ahead of us."

The committee would have to be disabused of that. He half-changed the subject: "Your friend the television reporter I met the other night in New York. She was charming, in a shy way." In fact, he thought of the Krumins girl as ill at ease and withdrawn, with no future in the media world, in contrast to the self-assured Viveca Farr, who was obviously an incipient star.

"The committee wants a full report on that gathering. Madame Nina will ask why you were invited."

Arkady's unexpected communicativeness was good news. Evidently Madame Nina—he knew the woman only as that, and accepted the secrecy around her as part of the mystique of the organization—wanted him to be prepared for the questioning. That meant she had an interest in his success. Following up on Arkady's opening, he asked: "Who will be at the meeting?"

"Kudishkin from the old KGB. Then our Agrarian Party man, close to the former communists. One of the bankers in the Group of Fifty capitalists. The leader of the Chechen gangs, a killer, becoming more important now that enforcement is needed."

The only one von Schwebel did not know was the Chechen. Oleg Kudishkin had been head of the KGB's Second Chief Directorate, in charge of internal security and counterintelligence, and had been fired when Yeltsin first took over. The long-feared counterspy was able to maintain a network of unreconstructed agents still inside, as well as an allied network of apparatchiks who had left to become strategically placed in major industries. The Agrarian Party politician was a man von Schwebel knew to be at the center of political payoffs by the new capitalists, because he had employed his fixing services himself.

Whichever banker came from the Group of Fifty was unimportant, because its members were interchangeable; that group was the Baltic window on the West for the mafiya fiefdoms channeling untaxed money out of the republics of the former Soviet Union, and the source of funds that made possible the creation of von Schwebel's empire in television news, books, feature films, broadcast stations; it was also the source of $2 billion in seed money for his newest venture in computer hardware and software. He presumed that the Chechen gangs, from the rebellious area of corruption and violence in the midst of Russia, dispersed after the uprising in Chechnya had been crushed, provided extortion and enforcement muscle to the other parts of the Feliks organization.

He flipped open his subnotebook and called up the directory of files. Before the meeting, he would have to print out hard copies for the committee, whose members still liked the feel of paper reports in their hands. He was especially proud of the report on his penetration of what he was sure was the Fein-CIA proprietary in Memphis; that would prove he was ahead of both the KGB and the CIA in the hunt for the sleeper, not behind them.

He closed the lid and looked out at the bleak Baltic countryside and the cheap housing built on it by the Russian colonizers. Madame Nina had just let him know that she would be asking why he had been invited to the New York party of Matthew McFarland; Kudishkin would probably follow up by asking who had suggested he and his wife, Sirkka, be included. It was known that the literary agent called Ace had visited Nikolai Davidov in Moscow; did the new head of the KGB's Fifth Directorate know of Unimedia's control by the Feliks organization?

Why me? he had to ask himself. Who wanted Sirkka and me there? And he had to have an acceptable answer.

The former KGB chief, Kudishkin, asked the first question: "On your advice, we permitted the Krumins woman to accept the CIA trip to New York. Has the sleeper tried to contact her there, as you said was likely? And was the contact made and observed?"

Von Schwebel hated the atmosphere of these meetings. Instead of being conducted in a conference room with decent lighting and audiovisual capabilities, the *organizatsiya* insisted on the melodramatic venue of a basement room in an old café. The murky lighting made it difficult to catch expressions on faces, much less refer to documents. It was as if organized crime in the East refused to accept the need for modern organization, as had its counterpart in the West; instead, the Russians preferred the dank atmosphere of forgotten penny mysteries. The cultural gap was troubling, but he could not argue with success; in their own archaic way, the disgruntled and corrupt Feliks people had created a syndicate in a few years with a savage esprit that had taken the Italian mafiosi centuries and the Americans generations to attain.

"I call your attention to section three of my report, in your blue folder, on the simultaneous Davidov and Krumins visits." There was some shuffling of papers around the table, but in this light he would have to summarize orally.

"American intelligence, through its front of Irving Fein and his so-called literary agent McFarland, arranged the Krumins visit and her surveillance. Fein established close rapport with her and traveled with her to Syracuse, a city in New York State about a fourth the size of Riga. They have separate rooms on the eighth floor of the Hotel Syracuse; our man is in the room adjacent to hers with through-the-wall surveillance. No contact has been made so far by Berensky."

"Does Krumins know that she was selected because the sleeper is her father?" Kudishkin was following section three of the report the most closely.

"No."

"Does the CIA know?"

"Evidently not." Von Schwebel was not certain. "Their agents Fein and Farr have given no indication that they know."

"The Fifth Directorate knows."

"Of course. Davidov saw the files that the Krumins girl led us all to, and has access to the Shelepin file. He is fully aware of Shelepin's selection of his bastard son, Berensky, as the sleeper, and of the pregnant wife the young man left behind."

"I believe the KGB is working with the CIA on this," said Kudishkin. "They are in direct contact. They have a mutual interest in keeping the Feliks fortune out of our hands."

"All I can report," von Schwebel said carefully, "is that we have picked up no evidence that Davidov has informed the CIA or the Krumins girl of her relationship with Berensky."

Madame Nina, arms folded and sitting back in her chair, said nothing. Her round, lined faced impassive, she looked to the representative of the Group of Fifty, who changed the subject.

"What did you observe at the remarkable party hosted for Davidov by American intelligence? Forget the French actress—focus on the search for Berensky."

"Section two, green folder." Did they know about his rendezvous the afternoon afterward with Ari Covair? Unlikely; his Globocop security subsidiary was on the lookout for a second surveillance, and reported none, not even KGB. Unimportant in any event, except it might show a lack of seriousness on his part.

"As we expected, the front man Fein used the occasion to cement his relationship with Krumins. Davidov's contact with the Director of Central Intelligence and the senator was minimal; everyone was being careful not to be alone with anyone for more than a few moments."

"What about Davidov and your wife, Sirkka?"

"Casual contact. Believe me, I had my eye on that."

"Does she know we are aware of her work for Stasi and later for the KGB?"

"No. I have never told her I know."

"Are you aware that Sirkka von Schwebel met the following afternoon with Davidov for forty-five minutes at the Oak Room of the Plaza Hotel, while you were entertaining the French actress?"

He swallowed; they had been watching him. And Sirkka had betrayed him.

Madame Nina leaned forward. "You must assume from now on that your wife is an active asset of the KGB. She will tell them whatever you tell her about our search for the sleeper. She is the enemy."

"But do nothing to let her know of your knowledge," Kudishkin instructed. "We may want to use her to send back disinformation."

"That was a serious failure on your part, von Schwebel," said Madame Nina. "We are disappointed."

"Come back to the dinner party," said the banker from the Group of Fifty. "Tell us what you observed about the banker from Memphis, Dominick."

"The import of your question," von Schwebel said, setting up his comeback, "is whether we have fallen behind the CIA and KGB in our search for the sleeper. I direct you to section one of my report, the red folder."

Nobody touched any papers; they were looking at him for the explanation.

"Edward Dominick is a banker, born in Dyersburg, Tennessee, parents dead, no siblings, a widower, two teenage daughters. He is forty-eight years old and was educated at Emory University in Atlanta and Wharton. He has been working for Memphis Merchants for fifteen years and has built it into the third-largest bank in the area. His net worth is about seven million dollars, though more than half of that is in restricted bank stock."

He turned to a new page in the red folder. "Dominick's office, and telecommunications serving it, is extremely—suspiciously—secure. Windows vibrated to block long-range surveillance, for example. Also sophisticated encryption of data." He paused for effect. "Davidov's KGB team has been unable to penetrate this, which I believe has led them to suspect Dominick may be a front for Berensky, if not the sleeper himself."

"You think this is an elaborate deception," said his questioner. "An American version of the Trust."

"It is," said von Schwebel with finality. "I am certain of this because the firm that the Memphis Merchants Bank hired to set up the computer security is Globocop, a subsidiary of our Unimedia. Our supervisor there recommended an affiliate to handle the telephonic encryption and daily sweeps. We track everything. The Committee was wise to finance my purchase and expansion of these companies."

"I supported that," Kudishkin reminded everybody.

"The key operative in these offices is Michael Shu," von Schwebel continued, "an accountant connected to Irving Fein, the CIA contract agent. Shu's transmissions show he is using Federal Reserve and U.S. Treasury data to discover the mutual funds and banks used by the sleeper agent. Dominick's transmissions show he is running a parallel operation to the Berensky trading, though heavily hedged because he does not have the huge capital of Berensky."

"You are convinced this Dominick operation in Memphis is a CIA proprietary."

"Yes. The alternate possibility is that this is a purely journalistic enterprise, run by one reporter and a television newscaster, with incredible access to U.S. government data, with a large bank's active cooperation, and financed by a book advance from a division of Unimedia."

That far-fetched notion drew the first smile from those around the table, except for the Chechen, a criminal who apparently did not appreciate the fine points of intelligence work.

"Back to the McFarland party," von Schwebel said to the Group of Fifty banker. "Dominick was obviously allied with Viveca Farr, the newscaster, whose home in the suburb Westchester he slept in that night. The following week, we have an audio pickup of their lovemaking on his office couch and videotape of some groping in the building elevator. Dominick was also a visitor to the CIA in Langley two months ago. There is no doubt in my mind that that Memphis operation is masterminded by Dorothy Barclay of the CIA, and that Davidov does not know what to make of it."

"Where is the money?" said the Chechen. He did not deal in subtleties.

"You mean the real Berensky assets?"

"The money. The tens of billions. Where we can get our hands on it?"

"It's not in gold or in cash," von Schwebel explained. "You cannot just walk in someplace and take it." He took a deep breath. "Often it is in an option, an agreement, to buy a commodity or currency, held by a mutual fund, which is owned by a shell company, which is controlled by a secret group of investors, who are designees of Berensky. That's putting it simply. It's much more complicated than that."

"For example?" said the banker.

"Two days ago, Shu informed Fein in New York that an affiliate of a bank in the Antilles controlled by the sleeper owned a shipping company headquartered in Athens."

This transmission, he did not bother to say, went by the most secure method of all: "snail mail," requiring the opening of an apartment mailbox at night, removing and steaming open and copying the contents in the most old-fashioned and nonelectronic way, and replacing the originals in pristine condition. The team leader surveilling Fein was certain that as soon as he dropped his guard, Shu would start transmitting through this technique. Von Schwebel was doubtful: Fein was obviously being careful about his home telephone and fax modem, on which there were three separate taps, and would not be wholly confident about his snail mail.

"Thus, we can put on the Feliks asset list seven of the largest supertankers, worth one hundred million dollars each. The capacity of each of those tankers is two million barrels of oil; at seventeen dollars a barrel, that's thirty-four million times seven tankers, or two hundred and thirty-eight million dollars in oil being carried by the tankers." Von Schwebel added it up in his head. "To round it off, that's just short of a billion dollars in tankers and oil. Then add the contracts the shipping company owns to buy oil in the future at a fixed price, which may be worth a few hundred million more."

Even Madame Nina looked impressed at his grasp of the scope of the sleeper's assets.

"Dominick, in his Memphis operation mimicking the Berensky trading, but on a small scale," said von Schwebel, "just used a shipping company to buy a few oil wells in Qatar. Now, if Berensky has been doing this for five years, God knows how much he controls in oil reserves."

Kudishkin turned to the Chechen. "He means we must have Berensky himself. Only he can turn his assets into gold and deliver it to us. We need the sleeper's willing body and brain."

"When I get my hands on him," said the Chechen, "he will be willing."

"First we must identify him, ahead of the Memphis CIA operation," said Madame Nina hoarsely, "and then bring him here to cooperate with us, the only legitimate successors to those who sent him to America in the first place." She looked at von Schwebel. "He will make another attempt to reach his daugher."

"Not without our knowledge."

"Why do you suppose you and your wife were invited to the McFarland party?" she asked, as Arkady had forewarned she would. "The literary agent did not know you or she were intelligence assets."

"The simple and logical answer is that I am the head of the parent company of Fein's publisher. My visitation to the subsidiary was long planned, and a well-connected literary agent would make it his business to know about it and cultivate me."

"And what is the real answer?" asked the woman dominating the table.

"My guess is that Director Barclay made up the guest list. She must know of my wife's connection to the KGB, or knew of my connection to the Feliks organization."

"You are saying that we may be penetrated," said Kudishkin.

"The presence of a KGB or CIA mole within the Feliks organization is something for you to consider," said von Schwebel, hoping it would turn suspicion inward instead of toward him.

After a long look around the table, Madame Nina rose, which ended the meeting.

Chapter 40

NEW YORK

Viveca indulged Irving's fixation on secrecy by calling his answering services, identifying herself as Ava Gardner—evidently his beau ideal of womanhood—and telling him to meet her on the set of *The Barefoot Contessa* in Portofino for dinner. That meant the coffee shop on the ground floor of her studio on the West Side for breakfast. The silly intrigue had a practical purpose, she knew: it would add to the drama of the retelling of the story on television.

"You look a little hung over, kiddo."

"I have never been happier or better-looking in my life," she replied. Half of that was true; Edward was the first man she had become involved with who was secure enough not to resent her success. In long talks at little restaurants, they compared and consulted rather than competed; he absorbed the details of her harassment by envious brass and other network talent, and advised her with the intense interest of a long-term lover. She, in turn, was picking up the elements of financial derivatives, the delicious complexities of which he delighted in explaining. She was sorry she could not help him with the intimate details of Liana Krumins's life, as they had hoped; the uptight Latvian girl was obviously envious of her and froze a rival newswoman out. Let Irving work on her.

The other half of her rebuttal to Irving's crack, Viveca was aware, was false: she was looking drawn from commuting to Memphis almost like a FedEx package. And at thirty-three, she was beginning to give thought to a chin tuck and doing something around her eyes. Not her nose; that was a little off, but was distinctive, and Evelyn, her makeup woman, thought the imperfect nose might be the key to the authoritative cast of the planes of her face. She would have to cut back on alcohol one of these days, too; it was adding to her caloric intake, and both Edward and the camera liked her angularity. The reminder made her thirsty.

"Really stuck on him, hunh?" Irving kept jabbing away. "Don't let it interfere with his work. I finally got him going down the money trail to finding the sleeper."

In her new emotional state, Viveca hoped she and Irving could cut the bickering and be friendly colleagues. Even Edward admitted the reporter's instinct and information had been right about the direction of the investigation into the currency markets.

"Lookit—" She bit her tongue, noting she was picking up New York speech habits. "I was with Edward last night. He can't call you on the phone, and snail mail takes too long. He needs to know what your Fed contacts say about the meeting scheduled for day after tomorrow on interest rates. Will the interbank rate be cut or not? He thinks Berensky will be going after billions if what you say is true about his mole in the Fed. He wants to parallel the sleeper's trades and try to spot the main broker dealing for Berensky."

"Makes sense. I'm seeing my Fed guy this morning. You'll know by COB tomorrow."

She smiled at his close-of-business initialese. "What's with you and COB?"

"It's business lingo. Women reporters dig it like catnip."

Maybe Irving was a little jealous, absurd as it was; she decided to take it as a compliment. "I'll take whatever you get from the Fed down to Memphis with me after my news spot tonight. You get anything out of the Latvian girl about the Berensky family?"

"Yeah. Tell Dominick there was a letter from a friend of the sleeper's Russian wife to Shelepin that called the kid Masha. That's the girl that was born after Aleks Berensky flew the coop. The name of endearment is good inside stuff, like my mom calling me Irveleh."

"Did your mother call you Irveleh?" She just could not visualize him as a little boy; it was as if Irving Fein had been issued full-blown as a hard-bitten investigative reporter, hurrying and harrying.

"About the Fed, I'll phone your office from a booth." He gave her the code: "Humphrey Bogart means rates go down, Joseph Mankiewicz means no change, and Ava Gardner means I couldn't find out. You'd better jot that down."

"That damn movie must have meant a lot to you. It got panned, you know."

"The contessa was frigid with her shoes on, but when she took 'em off, she went wild. Gotta run." He was off with his usual lunge; Viveca paid the check, slipping her feet into her shoes under the table. Had he noticed she had been resting her sore feet? Unlikely; he had not looked under the table, and she had removed her shoes with an imperceptible motion of her heels. But Irving seemed to notice details and make them work for him.

"Irving, if you know the identity of a person or persons passing inside information to any unauthorized recipient, you are duty-bound as a citizen to tell me." The enforcement man, Hanrahan, was adamant. "That is a violation of U.S. Code 18, Section I forget which, the fraud provision of the criminal code."

"Yeah-yeah. I know the person"—Irving was careful not to indicate a man or woman—"but I want to talk to the person before you pick him or her up. I'm a reporter, remember? I'm not just a fink."

"Very big money is involved here. An egregious betrayal of the public trust. We have a major investigation in process. You cannot just interview the subject for a story, don't you see? He'll bolt. He'll be out of the country in a flash and we'll all look like idiots."

"I know how the KGB agent Howard got tipped off and slipped away from FBI surveillance and got back to Moscow," said Irving, recalling an episode that had embarrassed the Bureau. "Not going to happen here. I got a plan."

"I got a better plan," said Hanrahan, "which is to grab him first and sweat him awhile until he sings and then tip you. That's the American way."

"I got a better way, and I hold the cards here."

"Wait. Wait. What's the basis of your suspicion? What have you got on this guy?"

"I got a message from a CIA source that this is the mole in the Fed."

"That's zilch, Irving. A tip from a spook is not admissible as evidence. It's not even the basis for an arrest. Tell me who the CIA source is, I'll go through FBI channels, maybe we can get some untainted evidence that can be the basis for a court warrant for a wiretap."

"Ah, you see? It's not zilch, it's what you need to catch the mole, whoever he or she may be." Talking in this way—"person" and "he or she"—automatically led the listener to believe it was a "she." He wanted Hanrahan to make the wrong assumption.

"If I were a mole," the enforcement agent warned, "and a reporter flushed me out, I would get a gun and shoot that reporter between the eyes and head for the airport."

"Nobody shoots reporters. Just not done. You ready for the plan?"

"Tell me your goddam plan."

"The mole lives in the Zeckendorf Towers, like a whole bunch of people from the New York Fed nearby. Goes home for lunch every day, almost without fail. I'll show up at the apartment tomorrow, confront the traitor with what I know and pretend I know more, and he or she will panic and blab."

"Lousy plan. She'll plug you between the eyes."

"I don't have to give rights, or hand over a quarter to call a lawyer, or any of that shit. I'll rattle the hell out of him the way I know how."

"What makes you think the mole won't run?"

"Here comes the rest of the plan. You get a few guys who can make an arrest on suspicion of mopery—FBI, New York cops, whatever— and be outside the front of the apartment house and the service entrance in the back. I'll be able to point to you, Hanrahan himself, standing right across the street. The mole will recognize you and know there ain't no hole to run out. Then I'll phone you to come and get her. Or him."

"I cannot be part of a conspiracy to deny this woman her legal rights," said Hanrahan.

"As a civil libertarian, I'm proud of you. Be assured I'll point that out in the story."

"You can be a real prick, Irving."

"The last person to call me that was a woman who didn't know she loved me. Hanrahan, lookit—your way, the mole would read all about it in Moscow and laugh. You'll invite me to your retirement party?"

"We won't need to arrest her," the security man said, preparing a fallback position. "We can request she come to my office for a little chat. If she refuses, I'll figure something out. You'd better wear a wire."

"None of that." Ever sensitive to electronic snooping on himself, Irving prided himself on never stooping to doing it to others. "I'll hold a recorder out in the open, fair and square. I don't go for your sneaky stuff." He recalled the request Viveca had relayed from Dominick in Memphis. "So whaddya think, Charley, you guys cutting interest rates Friday?"

"You a stock tout on the side?"

"I know from nothing about the market." Irving worked out an excuse for prying: "It would be helpful to have the latest scuttlebutt to prod our little mole along."

"They don't tell me and I don't want to know." When Irving kept looking at him, saying nothing, the enforcement officer added, "The scuttlebutt is no, the economy is okay, a stimulus could be inflationary, but what the hell, you can read that sort of speculation in the papers this morning. In fact, that's where most of the scuttlebutt comes from. Don't bet on it."

Mortimer Speigal, hunched toward his computer screen, frowned at the sound of his apartment bell; he was not expecting any deliveries, and the intercom had not announced a visitor. He saved the urgent message he was writing to a floppy disk, quit Windows, waited for the kaleidoscope of After Dark to appear, went to the door, and asked who it was.

"It's Irving Fein with the hot pastrami sandwiches."

He looked through the peephole in the door. It was indeed Irving Fein, a relatively familiar face from Washington parties and recently television, holding up a brown bag whose greasy spots indicated he was telling the truth. The Federal Reserve Board official opened the door.

"I was in the neighborhood and figured you'd be hungry and could help me with some stuff about Chairman Eccles," said the reporter, bustling past him and finding the kitchenette. "You got any beer? I didn't bring any beer. You wrote the bio of Eccles, didn't you?"

"I'm flattered anybody remembers," Speigal said. "There's no beer. Diet drinks only."

"Got any Dr. Brown's Cel-ray?" As he heard the sound of the fridge opening, the Fed Chairman's assistant for international conferences went to his computer, called up the list of files, found "Fkft.tie," and deleted the short message he had just started. "Nah," Fein answered himself, "no celery tonic. Strictly yuppie stuff, kiwi-flavored Perrier. Yecch!"

"I didn't know the great reporter Irving Fein was coming, bearing gifts. Why didn't you call?"

"I never call ahead," Fein said, setting out the sandwiches and drinks on the coffee table. "Puts people on their guard, you know?"

"Should I be on my guard?" He was inclined to think so, but could not throw the man out; it would look odd if all Fein wanted was what he said he wanted.

"Alla time. Financial types want to know what you know about interest rates, so they can steal a march on the Fed." He bit into the overstuffed sandwich. "I lied," he said in a muffled voice, munching. "It's hot corned beef. I swear I ordered pastrami."

Speigal could not help being amused, and relaxed enough to help himself to one of the sandwich halves. The message to the Frankfurt tieline could wait a half hour.

His visitor swallowed, took a sip of the kiwi Perrier, made a face, and slumped back on the couch. "Here's my recorder, saves me taking notes," he said with candor, after pressing the record button and laying it on the table next to the half-eaten sandwich. "Okay with you? Now. Tell me about Marriner."

"What is it you'd like to know about *FDR's Moneybags?*" said Speigal, mentioning the name of his book, which he always thought had deserved a paperback reprint. "I could be more helpful if you told me the nature of your interest."

"Actually, it isn't Eccles that interests me," said Fein. "It's the other Mariner. The mole at the Fed. You and your hidden life."

That was it. Speigal felt suddenly sick. Of all the ways he had conceived he would be informed of the government's discovery of his long deception, this visitation by a reporter was one he had never imagined. "Get out of here."

"No-no. I'm here as your friend. You have no idea how much better it is for you to tell your story to me instead of the gummint, which will be out to get you."

How much did the reporter know? Fein had the code name; could it be he knew and the federal law enforcement agencies were still unaware? Didn't all stories come from prosecutors' leaks—was it possible a journalist could do an independent investigation? He had to find out.

"I don't know what you mean about a 'mole' or 'the other Mariner.' Suppose you tell me what you have, and I'll try to set you straight."

"Gee, I have none of the color. Just the bare bones." Irving Fein seemed relaxed about it, as if it were a dull financial story. "For years, you've been sending the Russkies advance poop on the Fed moves. My sources showed me all the taps and the trades and the stuff about the Swiss bank account. Pretty good story. Not as good as a mole high up in the CIA, like Ames, but pretty good. A bitch to write and keep interesting, with all the figures on the trades and shit about derivatives. Time to 'fess up, Mort, and maybe save your ass, or at least share the blame with somebody else."

He felt faint; this resolutely cheerful Savonarola was going to expose him and put him away for life. Who had betrayed him? The sleeper agent? The Finnish economist? The private Swiss banker before he was killed? The brokers in London? Maybe the control: he should have caught the signal of the failure of his control to contact him recently; the Feds were probably rolling up the entire operation. Mortimer Speigal never thought of himself as a professional spy, but as an insider who stretched the ethical rules to provide financial data beyond the System. It was not a national security matter, nothing to do with military secrets. Only money.

"I admit nothing. Get out of here."

"Whaddya gonna do, Mort, call the cops? Go ahead. Call your buddy Hanrahan at Fed enforcement—he'll come and help you get rid of me."

"How much does Hanrahan know?"

"Hey, are you the reporter or am I?" Long silence. "C'mon, Mort, jig's up. Been a hell of a ride. People all over the world gonna recognize you for the financial genius you are, in my story. I got the dates and the accounts, all I want is some of the color. How'd you get the idea at the start?"

"They came to me," he could hear his voice croaking. "Through a Finnish woman who was an economist I met at Davos."

"Sure, I know who you mean." Fein seemed to search his memory, then snapped his fingers. "Sirkka whatsername. The knockout Finn, married to that stiff Kraut." He did know; the reporter was not bluffing. The "knockout Finn," as Fein derogated her, was capable of anything; she had probably dispatched the banker in Bern herself. Speigal's resistance, like his professional reputation, was crumbling; was there anything he could salvage? "Smart as hell," Fein observed, "but weren't you afraid of her husband, Karl? He's a pisser."

"I have been afraid for six long years, of everyone. I was not cut out for this, but once you start . . ." He could feel tears stinging his eyes.

"Then what? Let it all hang out, Mort. You've been dyin' to tell somebody."

He broke down sobbing for the first time in his life. After a few minutes, he could hear the reporter's sympathetic voice saying, "Look, you're not an ax murderer. You sold the Russkies some poop, now they're our allies. You may wind up with a medal. Tell me about the first piece of information you sent that made 'em a bundle."

"The Chairman's reliance on gold as an economic indicator, starting in 1989." Knowing that, Berensky—whoever the trader beyond the cutout was—could anticipate Fed judgments. "A couple of years ago, when we finally convinced the Chairman to switch to a basket of commodities—mainly soybeans and pork bellies—I transmitted the change in influence to them. Then, for a currency coup last spring, the beginning of the series of interest-rate increases." He could not stop the flow of his unburdening, which gave him a perverse pride. "This year, by tipping them to the Chairman's testimony to the Banking Committee, which I prepared, I was able to make possible another killing in marks and yen."

"What bank did you use?"

"My nominee was given stock in Middlesex Midland Bank. It became the nexus of the empire."

"What brokers did the operation do the most business with?"

"In London, they own Baker, Warr—" Speigal caught himself before he answered. No need to name names. If Fein did not know the currency traders, he did not know everything, and might not know the identity of the cutout or the existence of the sleeper. Why was he confiding in a man who would expose him to the world? "Do you know my contact in Washington?"

"Tell me."

Fein did not know of the cutout's possible middleman in all the dealings with Berensky, though he did know of the fallback contact of Sirkka in Frankfurt. Had either of the contacts talked? Or escaped, and was now unavailable to testify? A shrewder thought came to him: did the government have no real case against him, and was that why they sent a reporter to get him to talk without benefit of counsel?

"First you must tell me who sent you here, Mr. Fein."

"I don't have to tell you a thing, Speigal," said Fein, his breeziness gone and his face turning cold. "You're a fuckin' traitor. You sold out your country to a foreign power for money. Unless you come clean, you'll be a total shit in everybody's eyes, and if you're lucky they'll put you away where your slimy buddies can't knock you off. So talk fast— when did you last do business with your contact in Washington?"

He tried to push back his panic. "Tell me his name and I'll tell you when."

"Don't play games with me! A good American is dead because of your goddam spying! There's blood all over your hands! Who's your handler?"

Speigal blanched and backed off. He had nothing to do with violence and was not responsible for what happened to the profits earned from the information he passed along. But now it was vital for him to find out one fact from the newsman. "I'll get you the file," he said.

He went to his desk and used the combination to open the locked double drawer. He straightened up with a gun in his hand. He had never used a gun of any kind, not even in the Army in the Korean conflict, when he was a company clerk. He had been told by his Washington handler, who had given him the gun, that the .38 was loaded.

"Mr. Fein, do not make me use this." A pistol was heavier than he thought. "I am not a violent person."

Fein did not treat the threat seriously. "Nobody shoots journalists, Mort. It isn't done. Put that damn thing away before you hurt yourself. Do you really want to protect the guy who sold you out?"

Everything Fein said ended in a terrifying question. Speigal had a question of his own: "Does any other reporter have this story?"

"You never know. We don't tell each other, but I'm part of a team, you know?"

"As far as I know, you're alone. And not even the government knows, or they would be here, not you." He raised the gun, holding it with both hands; it was growing very heavy.

"For crissake, Mort, are you gonna take your little misdemeanor and raise it to Murder One? Look out the window there. You'll recognize Hanrahan and his assistant across the street from the front entrance. He's got guys in back, too."

The economist, certain it was a bluff, stole a quick look over his shoulder out the window. It was no bluff; Hanrahan, who had been in his nightmares for years, was there.

"Going crazy is not the answer. Use your head. Give me a little color, get a great lawyer, and you'll never have to serve time. I can turn you into a kind of hero, the man who turned the tables on the baddies."

He raised the gun again and pointed it at Fein behind the coffee table full of sandwiches and pickles and kiwi Perrier. "You don't know much beyond what I just told you, do you?" If it all could only be contained to one nosy reporter—

"You mean about Berensky and the fifty billion stashed away to overthrow the government in Moscow? And about Madame Nina and the Feliks people with their Chechen hitmen who are going to be very angry with you? And about Davidov's KGB coming after you, and—"

Speigal's last hope collapsed, and he turned the gun around, put the muzzle in his mouth, and pushed his thumb against the trigger.

"Oh-shit," Irving breathed. This was turning into some story. Then to the tape recorder he added, "He blew his brains all over the window behind him. I'd better call the police right away." The bullet had passed through his head and broken the window; the cops were surely on their way. He turned the tape machine off.

He sat for a moment, his heart pounding. Then he went to Speigal's desk and poked around for anything resembling intercourse with an international brokerage operation; no luck. The computer was on, showing a screen-saving pattern of moving lines. He touched the mouse; the directory came on the screen. Irving looked down the list, touched the space bar, looked further down to the end; no filename triggered an obvious response. He used a search program to look for the names Berensky and Numminen and Baker and came up with nothing.

Fein figured Mort had had time to erase his current file before coming to the door or while Irving was keeping up a line of patter in the kitchenette. He cleared the screen, went to DOS, and called up the "undelete" program; it showed that three files had been recently deleted and might possible be brought back. He marked down the filenames: "Rates," "ToDo.7," and "Fkft.tie." He worked the "undelete" process and hoped for the best.

"Shit, piss, and corruption!" He got the worst; not one of the erased files could be retrieved. Only the Feds could do that with sophisticated equipment, the way they did with the erased Iran-contra White House files. He jabbed at the button and turned off the computer.

Sore at himself, furious with the dead Fed mole, Irving punched out Hanrahan's cellular number on Speigal's telephone and told him there was a suicide and to come on up to apartment 606. The officer was already in the lobby banging on the button for the elevator. The reporter picked up his recorder, removed the tape, and stuffed it in his wallet; he inserted a blank tape and put the little machine in his pocket in case the police asked for the recorder. He did not get near the corpse; the last time Irving Fein had been in the same room with a body outside a funeral home was in his police days a generation ago. The remainder of the corned beef sandwiches lay on the coffee table. "You never even touched your pickles, Mort," he said to the body of the faithless Fed economist.

A sudden thought occurred: check Speigal's modem for phone numbers, as he had Clauson's. He turned on the computer again, only to get "Error reading Drive A"; that meant a floppy disk was still inserted. He released the floppy inside, and wondered if Mort dutifully did what Irving so often forgot to do: to save to the floppy, protecting against loss on the hard disk. When the C prompt came up, he switched to the A drive and called up the directory of the floppy. No "Rates," no "ToDo.7," but there was "Fkft.tie."

Rap on the door and a furious jiggling of the doorknob. He went back to the modem directory in the C drive, found a "Fkft.tie" entry under frequently dialed numbers, and copied down the number next to it. On the modem directory, among the most frequently used numbers, was "Fkft.tie," and a local New York number. Should he erase it, gaining time on the Feds? No, he was a law-abiding citizen; you destroy evidence, you wind up in the slammer. Besides, it would take the Feds weeks to figure out where to look for what.

The reporter shut down the machine. Looking morose, he opened the door to Hanrahan & Co.

Chapter 41

NEW YORK

At his colleague's not-too-cryptic message, "Get your ass up here," Michael Shu caught the 6:00 A.M. flight up from Memphis and made it to Irving's West Side apartment on 86th Street by midmorning. Fein claimed it was the oldest apartment building in New York, older than the Dakota, and to Shu the quarters looked their age, but the lobby with its high ceilings and ornate moldings had its appeal. However, the elevators, a century-later addition, looked cramped and ramshackle; the accountant chose to walk up three flights of worn marble stairs.

"What's so hush-hush," he asked a haggard-looking Fein, "that we can't trust it to the most secure communications system outside the Pentagon? We don't even go through the phone company anymore—we got our own satellite setup. Not only that, I burn the stuff that comes out of the shredder."

"I need your sharp pencil, kiddo. Had to be now, because I'm going up to Syracuse tonight."

"Liana still up there?"

"It's the last day of her seminar. I brief her tonight on what to plant on Davidov, and bring her to Idlewild tomorrow." Irving still called New York's JFK International "Idlewild," as the tract of land had been known in the fifties; Michael assumed Fein's unwillingness to go along with the name change had something to do with an old political score. "Liana and Davidov go back to Riga tomorrow night via Helsinki on Finnair. Then in a week or so we send Dominick over to stir the pot, if he's ready. That should get a rise out of the sleeper."

"Dominick will be ready." The accountant was proud of the recent breakthroughs. "I have a graphic representation of the Berensky empire on the Macintosh. Still some gaps, but I can pinpoint over fifty billion dollars in assets, with the trading and shipping companies, the front lawyers, the shell corporations in Liechtenstein, a Japanese hotel chain, the two key banks in the Antilles, and another in of all places Biloxi, Mississippi. Mark-denominated securities up the kazoo. We probably got a better picture of the fortune than Berensky himself does."

"Maybe he'll retain you as a consultant when all this is over."

Shu shrugged. "Got any more Fed printouts? They were great. Our big break was our switch to studying currency trading, where the turnover makes it possible to hide trades that take your breath away—"

"Do you have a currency outfit in London begins with Baker?"

"You mean Baker, Warren & Pease?" His Memphis operation had been unable to establish which broker was the sleeper's major London connection; Dominick had acknowledged it was a weakness in their search. "You sure it's them, Irv? How did you find out about that when all the computers couldn't track it down?"

"Shoe leather."

"That could account for—jeez, another ten bil." Shu had taken to referring to billions familiarly as "bils"; he could remember not so long ago when "big ones" were $1,000 banknotes. This project had exponentially expanded his thinking.

"Don't get carried away with the war room shit," Irving cautioned. He tapped his forehead. "The theory of the story is still up here."

Shu nodded; he did have a tendency to get wrapped up in details. "I'll get tracking the Baker firm right away."

"Our trouble is that the sleeper, the real one, has not yet approached Dominick," said Fein. "Hell, he hasn't even approached Liana again, and she's right here in the States. So we're gonna have to shake him up, give him more of a reason to come to us. You know how he never loses his bets? My plan is to give Berensky a big financial kick in the head. His first major reversal, and it's gonna be a beaut. And he'll know it's our doing."

He took Michael to his notebook computer, a cheap monochrome job, outdated, but with a removable hard disk that meant its guts did not have to be left at home for searchers to rummage through. He called up the file labeled "Fkft.tie" that was on the floppy disk he told

Shu he'd lifted from Speigal's machine. At the top was the routing: "@bt/qu:number/sl:marin," which the accountant presumed was the transmission coding to direct the message through the system at the other end, and then a short message: "On your trip tomorrow to the casino in Rhein/Main, would you put one whole chip on black for me. Just have a feeling it could be my lucky day. Reg."

"Doesn't look very mysterious," said the accountant. "Not like one of your *Barefoot Contessa* specials that calls attention to the fact you're using a code. This seems like a pretty straight request to put down a little bet. Who's Reg?"

"This is a transmission that has not yet been sent," said Irving slowly, "of data about what will happen at tomorrow's meeting of the Open Market Committee of the Federal Reserve. Now tell me what you think it means."

Shu looked at the message with new eyes. "Well, Rhein/Main is the name of the military airport in Frankfurt. I suppose that would have to do with buying or selling German marks. If you wanted to trade in the pound sterling on that analogy, you'd use Heathrow, the big airport near London. Or speculating in the yen, you'd say Narita, the airport near Tokyo that costs a couple hundred bucks in taxi fare."

"Okay, so the message is saying to buy or sell marks. Which—buy or sell?"

Shu shook his head. "No way of telling. The 'one whole chip' would be one whole percentage point in interest rates—a hell of a big move by the Fed—but it says the bet is on 'black.' The colors would be black or red. Black could mean rates up, and red could mean down, or vice versa."

"Nobody's guessing the Fed will be raising rates," said Irving. "It's either stay the same or cut. This says a cut."

"Then you're saying, on the basis of this message, they'll cut a whole point. That would weaken the dollar, of course, so if marks is your medium you would sell dollars and buy marks. You could make . . ." He calculated quickly, on a 98 percent margin, with the billions Berensky had available. "Hoo-boy, you could make a killing that would be the mother of all killings."

"That's why I wanted you here, to tell me that. Now, here comes the beauty part. I have a little disinformation scheme in mind. What could I tell them to get them to do exactly the wrong thing?"

"Change the word 'black' to the word 'red.' Simple."

"Too simple. C'mon, think it through. A lot rides on this."

Michael quickly concluded Irving was right, of course. The rate's rising a point, when all the world was speculating about whether or not it would drop, would not only be absurd but would panic the markets. The Fed was not in business to destabilize markets.

"If you changed 'black' to 'red,' " said the accountant carefully—an awful lot of money was at stake here—"you would have to deal with the 'one whole chip,' meaning 'one full percentage point.' You'd have to say 'a quarter chip,' but that would sound like a code, because chips don't come in quarters."

"The disinformation I want to send," said Irving, "is that the Fed will do nothing. You and I know it will cut rates by a whole point; but I want to misinform our gal Sirkka in Frankfurt, or Helsinki or wherever the hell she really is. I want to make her think that the Fed won't change rates at all."

"Then let's drop the reference to a chip completely. Instead of 'put one whole chip on black for me,' make the message read 'bet on red for me.' That would mean 'Fed does nothing to rates—act accordingly.' That would be an order to sell marks on a grand scale, and buy dollars. Berensky would lose his shirt."

"You slants are geniuses." Because the slur was wrapped in a compliment, Shu did not take offense. Irving edited the message on the machine.

"But who's Reg?" Mike asked. "Reginald somebody? Regina?"

"I think he was interrupted as he was writing the sign-off," said the reporter. "That could be the beginning of 'regards.' "

"Regards who? You can't just leave it unsigned, it'll look funny." Shu looked up at the routing code. "It's to 'number' from 'marin.' There's a Marin County in California, big on hot tubs."

" 'Number' should be Numminen, Sirkka's maiden name," said Irving, his vulpine grin returning. "And the signature is 'Mariner.' Now let's see if the tieline works."

The reporter called up the modem's frequent-calls menu, to which "Fkft.tie" and a local number had been added at the bottom. He plugged the telephone cord into the computer and into the wall outlet and hit the button. "Now it should make a noise like a long fart when it connects, if the number works."

When the modem did its discordant raspberry, Michael Shu raised his fists and gave a cheer. "It's connected! They've got it, and now Berensky's brokers will be selling marks and buying dollars like there's no tomorrow. Oh, Irving, somebody is going to be very angry about this when the mark jumps and the dollar dives. The sleeper's whole setup will be in an uproar. Wait'll I tell Dominick."

"Better not. In fact, definitely don't."

"Why not, Irv? We could make a few bucks and cover expenses."

"But if Dominick should win while Berensky loses, the sleeper will figure out it was us who screwed him. Better Berensky should think it was his own people. Disinformation that breeds distrust, and gets people ratting on each other—Jesus, Angleton would be proud of me." Irving looked at his watch. "I gotta get a guy on the *Times* to do me a favor and kill an obit. Then I gotta make a plane."

Chapter 42

SYRACUSE

"How do you like American food?"

"I'm sure it's very nourishing." Liana was guarded in her reply. She did not want to appear a bumpkin by giving an uncosmopolitan opinion.

"That night at Ace's apartment, you must have been on a diet," Irving Fein said. "You were eating with long teeth."

She looked quizzically at him, head tilted; she and the American reporter had worked out nonverbal signals to overcome communication gaps.

"It's an expression, dunno where from, meaning eating because you have to, not because you enjoy it. But tonight we're really gonna tie on the feedbag." He rolled his eyes. "Horses, oats in a bag you tie on their nose. Maybe it'd be easier for me to learn Russian."

"If you speak only Russian," she explained, "even if you have been living in Latvia all your life, you cannot be a citizen unless you learn Latvian. That is the new law to keep Latvia from being overwhelmed by the Russian colonists. I speak both, so I am okay, but it is hard for the half of the people in our country who don't speak Latvian."

She enjoyed feeding Irving Fein facts like that. He sucked them all in, digested them, seemed to forget about them, but up they would pop at the right time, sometimes a little altered to fit the point he was making. Nikolai Andreyevich was not that way; he did not trust her as Irving Fein did. The KGB man would listen to an observation of hers, weigh it to see if he could trust her judgment, then reject it if it did not fit his specific needs. Or so it seemed to her. And if she was not trusted, she had no obligation to be trustworthy.

Irving drove her in his rental car for forty minutes to a restaurant called Krebs, in the town of Skaneateles. The eating place was like none she had ever seen. In a great, rambling house, people were seated at a blizzard of white tablecloths, with ruddy-cheeked waitresses running around the tables ladling out soups and gravies, offering platters of roast beef and roast chicken, buckets of fresh peas and candied carrots tasting unlike any vegetables she had tried in America. Whenever an empty spot appeared on a customer's plate, busboys would cover it immediately with sections of a crumbly golden cake or dark rolls with raisins embedded.

This was "family style," Irving explained while eating prodigiously, with no menu or apparent plan, in an atmosphere of hearty appetites, plentiful servings, and happy diners. Liana did not know if she could say no to the healthy-looking waitresses and kept eating as fast as she could to clear a spot for the next helping. When she reached for the crumbly golden cake, Irving told her not to fill up on the corn bread, to leave room for the great pudding desserts.

"The whole meal is thirty-six bucks for the two of us," Irving announced when the check came. "That's value. In New York City or in Paris, that sort of money won't buy two people a goddam appetizer."

"I am grateful to you for taking me here. This is another America," she said, happily stuffed, ruffling the stubble of her hair. "Not Ace's elegant America, or the dormitory luncheonette America, but Irving Fein's America."

"The white Protestant sauce at Krebs is not exactly my dish of tea. And the earliest seating here lets you out at—" he checked his watch— "not even seven o'clock, which is not yet time for dinner in a real city. But I wanted you to see this, Liana Krumins from Riga, Latvia, because they do good work here, they're proud of their reputation, they make a profit, nobody gets slammed against the wall, people laugh a lot and don't learn to lie to stay in the game." He dropped the white napkin on the clean plate that had held the heaping of creme caramel atop the nutted brownie. "Now let's go back and scheme and plot and connive and otherwise commit journalism."

Though she was staying at the Sheraton on the Hill, Irving took her back to his downtown hotel for a couple of drinks in the Persian Room bar. The memory of the moment of Speigal's suicide weighed on him, but he did not want to burden Liana with that, and besides, it was not one of the three lies he wanted her to lay on Davidov. He was getting deeply into the disinformation dodge now; not only Angleton but Shelepin, master of that game, would have been impressed.

"Are you ever worried about the way we are all using each other?" she asked.

He allowed to himself as how that was pretty insightful for a kid, even one who had been a successful counterrevolutionary in her teens. "What worries me more," he told her, "is you going back to Riga right now." He was glad he'd put his finger on what was bothering him. "Berensky and his bunch, and the Feliks people too, are likely to be pretty pissed next week. Lotta money will be lost."

"Davidov says I should not worry about danger from Berensky."

"Easy for him to say not to worry. He doesn't know what's set to hit the fan." At the tilt of her head, he said, "It's only the punchline of an old joke, and I forget the joke."

"He did warn me about Madame Nina and the Feliks people, but they are the KGB's rivals. And Arkady, who works for Madame Nina, I am sure is a good man."

Why was Davidov worried about Liana's safety with Madame Nina and not with Berensky? Irving could not add it up. On the other hand, Davidov must be wondering what the hell Dominick was doing in that Memphis bank, and might now be buying into Irving's fiction that the Memphis banker was Berensky himself. Liana would have to breathe on that spark of suspicion in the KGB official's mind. "One of these days I'll have to have a heart-to-heart with your boy Davidov."

"I would like to be a fly on the wall," she grinned. That was an expression he had taught her on their long walk down Fifth Avenue, shadowed by God knew how many different outfits.

"You got those three lies in your head that I want you to plant on Nicky-boy?"

She nodded.

"Tell me. I think I forgot one."

"One, that you know why I was chosen by Madame Nina to conduct the search for the sleeper. And two, that I am angry at you for not telling me 'why me.' Three, that I suspect Edward Dominick of Memphis is the sleeper."

"Right. I forgot the last one, and it was bothering me."

What was really bothering him was that he wanted to take this not especially good-looking but—to him, tonight—profoundly attractive young woman upstairs and to bed. But did not want to come on to her, get rejected, and introduce an awkward note in a budding mentor-mentee relationship with a journalistic colleague and altogether nice person who was, as they used to say, young enough to be his daughter. Harassment was not his style. On the contrary, getting ignored and standing aside with his hands in his pockets while another guy made out was his style.

That bleak recollection of rejection caused him to glance at his watch; Viveca's news spot, which he never missed, would be on in an hour. And Liana, who struck him as not the sort who slept around, had already admitted she had something going with Davidov. That left Irving Fein as odd man out again.

"You got a lot of packing to do for tomorrow morning, huh?" All the women in his life had been serious packers.

"No. I bought some jeans and T-shirts here, and some CDs in New York, but I stick them all in the duffel bag. Takes a minute."

He had offered her an excuse and she hadn't picked it up, so he took the plunge: "Lookit, you want to come upstairs and sleep with me tonight? I'd really like that, but it has nothing to do with our working together, so—"

"I would be honored."

He did not quite know how to deal with that; "honored" was not a reaction he had ever experienced after a proposition. "It's not like I was the Pulitzer Prize, kid."

She picked up her heavy bag, slung it over her shoulder, and waited for him to lead the way to the elevator. Inside his room, she sat on the edge of the bed, smoothed her skirt, and seemed to be waiting for him to take the initiative. At the window, he observed a light snow falling and made some conversation about hoping it would not affect their travel plans in the morning.

Irving remembered how he had kissed her hard on the mouth at the Bird Library, but that was an impulse, and this was not a moment that called for a masterful male. She seemed to him more than ever youthful and vulnerable, and he felt guilty already about taking advantage of his position. He reached for her tenderly, and when she asked, "You will be gentle with me?" he found that not in the least cornball and it made him feel more protective than passionate.

She was tentative at first, disappearing into the bathroom to get into a robe rather than let him see her nude. He waited for her in bed in the dark. Davidov, he was certain, must have raped her, the commie bastard.

He liked the feel of her head with its crewcut hair resting gently on his shoulder, a sweetly satisfied kid with an older man who had finally gotten the break he deserved. With his left hand resting lightly on her mons veneris, he took the television clicker in his right hand and thumbed his way to the channel that broadcast Viveca's 9:00 P.M. news spot. He waited through two commercials as Liana sat up and pulled the sheet to cover a bosom that was more ample than Irving had suspected. "This takes only forty-five seconds," he half apologized. "She expects me to watch. She read my last book." Liana, a television reporter-performer from another world and generation, not only did not appear to take offense, but seemed to take a professional interest.

Chapter 43

NEW YORK

"You're going to let her go on like this?" The makeup woman was in the control room, nearly hysterical. "She dozed off in my chair, for God's sake. That's never happened before."

"Thirty seconds to air," the stage manager was saying. "Quiet on the set."

"You all right, Viveca?" The director was frightened; he had never heard a newscaster stumble through a run-through as if drunk.

"Sure, sure," the network newswoman nodded, hair perfect, makeup perfect, eyes glazed. "Hell's wrong with you?"

"Twenty-five, twenty-four . . ."

"Whereza damn paper scrip'? 'Smatter you guys?"

"This is live, we got no substitute." The director, frantic, hissed at the producer: "What'll we do? Prime time, thirty million viewers."

The producer, who had taken more than his share of abuse from Viveca Farr, shrugged. "It's her spot. Star knows best."

On his monitor, the director could see Viveca rolling her head around her shoulders, blinking her eyes like a driver on a dark highway fighting sleep.

"Fifteen seconds."

"Cue up another thirty-second spot in case," the director told the technical director.

"Got none. Only the ten-second for the midway."

"Cue up the last one again, quick!"

"You okay, Viveca?" On set, the stage manager broke the count and looked at her closely. "We can abort. Say the word."

"Outa here! Um fine."

"We can't put her on like this," the director pleaded. "She'll self-destruct. Go to black?"

"You go to black, we all get canned," the producer said. "It's her ass, not ours."

"Five, four, three . . ."

"Roll tape. Come up on one," the director told the TD, and snapped his fingers: "Take one." Viveca's face filled the screen.

"Thiziz News—Newsbreak, Viv'ca Farr 'porting." She squinted at the words on the Teleprompter.

"Back on one," the TD said, "come up on two." A film of rioting in Nagorno-Karabakh appeared over Viveca's shoulder.

"A institoosh . . . inst . . . tooshnal crisis is looming in the UN over 'Gorno Ka'bosh . . ."

"For crissake, she's bombed out of her mind!" the director could hear the stage manager's voice whispering urgently.

"I'm going to black, okay?"

"On your own responsibility, not mine," the producer snapped. "Nobody's ever been thrown off this network yet, and I'm not starting with the VP News's former cookie."

"Ten seconds to midway commercial. Ready to roll two."

"Fill screen with the film," the director told the TD. "At least get her face off."

Viveca reached the end of the news item and stopped, peering at the prompter.

"Go to two."

"Can't, the tape leader is running."

"Go to the numbers, it's better than black. Now!"

As the commercial came on, the director whirled in his chair to face the producer. "We have ten seconds to decide. The talent cannot read the prompter."

"Maybe that'll sober her up."

Over his earphones, the director heard the stage manager suggest, "I have a bulletin on paper."

"Hand her the paper to read," the director ordered. "Better tell her to intro with 'This just in.' "

"Come up on one. Last chance to save your ass, Viveca."

"Thiz jus' in." She held the paper up close to her face. "Federlzerve announced tonight cancellation of the Op'n Market meeting shed—

scheduled for t'morra. No ackshin on rates for the next month, 'cord'na chairman. No 'splanation offered for the un, unyoosual 'sponemint."

She looked up and gave the camera a radiant smile, first time anybody in the control room had seen that joyous an expression on Viveca Farr's always-authoritative face. "Thizis been Newsbreak!"

"Roll thirty-second spot. We'll come up early." Viveca started to yawn, and the TD said, "Go to black for three seconds, three, two, one. Come up on two."

To tape. They all slumped back, the director with his head in his hands, the producer with the frozen smile of a fascinated spectator at the destruction of a career. The makeup woman was crying. All the telephones in the control room started to ring.

Chapter 44

MEMPHIS

Michael Shu, stunned at the news, switched off the television set in the war room at Memphis Merchants and picked up the ringing phone. He knew it would be Irving in Syracuse.

"You see that?" The reporter's voice was strained. "You see her come apart just now?"

"Yes, but I liked that big grin on Viveca's face at the end. Reminded me of Charlie Chaplin in the last scene of *City Lights*. She ought to do that more—"

"Schmuck! She ruined herself. It's all over for her. Her career is shot."

"She did sound a little tipsy—"

"She was sloshed, plastered, and the sharks in her business smell her blood in the water. Where's Dominick? Is he with you or up in New York with her?"

"I have a number to reach him at in San Diego."

"Patch me through fast. If that poor kid is stupid enough to get blotto for all the world to see, she's stupid enough to do worse to herself when she comes to."

The accountant was glad Irving's reaction to Viveca's career catastrophe was closer to sorrow than anger. He dialed the number Dominick had left. As it started to ring, Shu reminded Irving that the patched connection would not be secure and added, "As soon as you finish with him, call me back right away. There's something else we have to talk over."

SYRACUSE

"I saw it, Irving," said Dominick. "We get a live feed by satellite out here. Yes, it was awful. I'm trying to get through to somebody at her studio on the other line."

"She'll be all right as long as she's smashed," the distraught Fein told him, "but when she sobers up and finds out what happened on the air, God knows what she'll do."

"Her job is all-important to her," the banker agreed. "The disgrace will hit hard."

"How fast can you get to her? I'm socked in up here in Syracuse. No plane out till morning, and the train takes all night."

"I'm chartering a Gulfstream from here. Should get to her place by midmorning."

"I'll meet you at her house in the country. Stay in touch on the way, you hear? Use Mike Shu in Memphis as the contact point—he'll stand by the phone. We can't let her out of our sight."

Ace went directly crosstown to the studio as soon as he heard the terrible news from Irving. Viveca, he was told by a red-eyed makeup woman, had been bundled into her limo after the broadcast and had left moments before.

"Is there any actual evidence that she was under the influence of alcohol?" In his youth, Ace had been trained as an attorney; though he had not negotiated her television contract, he wanted to be ready with a contractual defense should the network seek to dismiss her "for cause."

"I didn't see her drinking, if that's what you mean," said the woman seated next to the empty barber's chair in the makeup room.

"You couldn't smell liquor on her breath." His question was in the form of a statement to be refuted.

"She likes wine, you know, not hard liquor. No, I couldn't smell anything. You're really her agent, not from the press?"

Ace presented his card. On the monitor in the makeup room, he watched a rerun of Viveca's forty-five-second broadcast; the technicians were making copies, salable souvenirs of a memorable debacle. "She was obviously not herself," he allowed cautiously, inwardly dismayed at the public exposure of his client's apparent but unproven alcoholism. Ace had always suspected Viveca drank too much, but that was true of many of his clients and was rarely career-ending. Assuming the makeup woman would be sought out for a statement by reporters and network lawyers, he implanted a thought and phrase in her mind: "Could it be plain exhaustion, a mental lapse brought on by overwork and some unexpected stress?"

"I'll say that if you want and it helps her," the woman told him. "But she was pretty woozy when she came in. Fell asleep in the chair, which never happened before. Even when she'd been having a few."

Sounded to Ace more like drugs, which would be worse for her reputation; plenty of good newspeople drank too much, but narcotics was death to reputation and might also be cause for summary dismissal. He came at it another way: "Could somebody have slipped her a mickey?"

She looked at him, uncomprehending. "Slipped what?"

"Mickey Finn" was apparently not in the current vernacular. "Could someone have surreptitiously put something like a drug in her coffee? Someone who did not wish her well?"

"Plenty of those people around here. But if you want the truth, it looked to me that she came in here with a load on."

"You don't know that," he reminded her. "All you've told me you know for a fact is that she exhibited all the appearances of exhaustion, and it seems to me her producer and director were derelict in their duty."

"Producer made a sexist crack in the control room." The makeup woman told him about "the VP News's former cookie" remark, which he commended her for remembering. He suggested she make a contemporaneous note of it immediately. "Where did she go?"

"Home."

"Pound Ridge?"

"I think to her apartment on Central Park West."

Ace marched out of the studio and directed his driver to take him to her nearby pied-à-terre. He recalled her saying that she couldn't stand personal humiliation—that she would rather be "dead or slinging hash in a diner" than be mortified. She dreaded such mortification above all else, Ace recalled. At the time he had dismissed her professed horror of humiliation as showbiz hyperbole, but now her dire phrasing and the rash of recent suicide reports caused the agent concern.

The doorman said she had not returned. From his car, Ace telephoned her Pound Ridge home and spoke to the housekeeper, who said she was not expected that night. Determined to leave nothing to chance, Ace directed his driver to take him to her home. It was a long trip and the hour was late, but he thought her life could be in danger. In the limo racing up the parkway, he phoned his report to Irving Fein in Syracuse, then to various network executives, who showed various shades of shock, along with that guilty thrill of pleasure in another's misfortune that the Germans called *Schadenfreude*. He was glad he had an ironclad contract for her on the book project: that might be Viveca's primary source of income next year, provided she and Irving could deliver a book. Television networks contracted for personal services, but book publishers contracted for a product.

It was nearly midnight when he drew up to the house in Pound Ridge. His driver telephoned in to the housekeeper, so as not to alarm the woman. She came to the door accompanied by an extraordinarily large—and to Ace, suitably menacing—black watchdog, only to report no word from Ms Farr. He reported that on the phone to Irving, isolated and worried in a Syracuse hotel room, who asked him to hang around the house awhile: "When she sobers up, that's where she'll go to ground." Ace agreed and took a nap in the library. At three in the morning, the faithful agent acknowledged he was getting a little old for this sort of thing and he went home.

With Liana in tow, Irving Fein arrived at the Farr estate at a little after ten in the morning, not ten minutes ahead of Edward Dominick.

"We missed her. She's been here and gone," the reporter, pacing around the library, told the banker when he arrived. "Housekeeper says the limo driver dropped her off here at seven in the morning, all hung over. She watched the replay of her performance on the morning shows—it was the big deal this morning—and kind of flipped out."

"Where is she? Do we know?"

"Housekeeper, Brigid, says she went to her strongbox and cleaned it out and packed up and left in her Montero, the four-wheel-drive thing."

"How much was in the strongbox? Does the housekeeper know? If it's not a lot," Dominick said, "she'll have to use credit cards for gas. I can get MasterCard to track her. We'll know her whereabouts at the first gas station."

"Maybe ten grand in cash, she thinks," Irving said glumly. "Plus some good jewelry. She can go underground a long time with that, just crawl away and hole up and make a new life as a total nobody."

"If she wants a life at all," Dominick said.

"Surely she will be recognized wherever she goes," Liana put in. "Hers is a famous face. She is a great celebrity. How can she hide?"

"Ms Krumins, you've never seen Viveca with her makeup off," said Dominick, "and with her perfectly coiffed hair all a mess, and not all crisp and authoritative in a tailored outfit, and not projecting her voice from her diaphragm. Believe me, I have, and—out of context—she's somebody else. She can hide from her shame for as long as she wants to live."

"No. We'll find her," Irving assured Liana with more certainty than he felt. "The Feds owe us one."

"They're not the only ones indebted to us," Dominick said, taking a deep change-of-subject breath. "Let me get on to Mike Shu." He did his call-me-at-the-candy-store routine and reviewed a bunch of rates and numbers with the accountant. Using his subnotebook, the banker dialed into some financial service and jotted down a few numbers, shaking his head in wonderment at the results. Irving noticed he also watched Liana, inspecting the library books, out of the corner of his eye.

"Irving, you know that little trick you played yesterday on Uncle Aleks?"

Fein nodded; apparently the banker had been briefed by Michael Shu the night before on the discovery and suicide of Mort Speigal, including Irving's ingenious changing of the coded message from black to red.

"Yesterday," Dominick said, "that London trader put down some of the biggest trades ever made on the dollar. So did the four other banks and brokers we've been following who have been acting for Berensky. They went overboard on leveraging, betting the farm on the accuracy of the inside information from the mole in the Fed. It's hard to believe, but Berensky's brokers and acolytes may have accounted for ten percent of yesterday's trillion-dollar world currency trading."

"We crossed 'em up," Irving explained to Liana, who deserved to be in on the story. "I wanted Berensky's network to lose its shirt, so his brokers and agents and banks would turn on him and panic him to come to us. So I fixed the message from the Fed mole so they would do the wrong thing. Not bad for a nonbanker, hey, Edward?" He was proud of that financial maneuver and glad that Liana could hear its results from a sophisticated banker like Dominick.

"You probably missed the substance of the bulletin that Viveca read on the air last night," the banker said, "because you were concentrating on the awful thing happening to her."

Irving had not a clue to what Dominick meant. Liana remembered, though: "It was about the Federal Reserve postponing a meeting."

"That's exactly right, little lady. The Fed was planning to lower interest rates substantially. The mole, Speigal, wrote that message to Berensky's brokers. But when the mole was found out, and committed suicide, the Fed Chairman wisely decided to postpone the meeting entirely."

Irving began to feel queasy. "So what happened?"

"Well, if the mole's original message had been delivered correctly, the Berensky group would have lost a fortune—several fortunes, bankruptcies down the line like a row of dominoes, and all furious at being misled by Berensky."

"But I changed the message from black to red," Irving said slowly.

"Which made the message fit the actual last-minute action to postpone taken by the Fed," said Dominick. "You changed the mole's leak; the Fed Chairman did not do what he planned to do; and your signal of 'red' paid off big this morning for those who bought dollars and sold marks."

"Then Berensky came out ahead," Irving frowned.

"Ahead? My God, man, there's never been such an 'ahead' in the history of currency trading. Mike and I figure—on the basis of your ultimately correct 'red' signal—Berensky made a profit of nearly twenty billion dollars."

The reporter stood silent, trying to digest the turn of events. Liana came up to him and put her hand on his arm. "You were able to help the Russian sleeper make twenty billion dollars?"

"Nuthin' to it," Irving said weakly. "You got to know when to hold 'em, when to fold 'em."

Dominick was doing his long, low chuckle. Then he stopped. "Your strategy will still have the desired effect, Irving. I think this coup puts the sleeper at or near the hundred-billion level, a sum that must be getting impossible to conceal. And when word gets out about the biggest currency killing ever, governments everywhere will want to know who was behind it. That means Berensky has to make a decision quickly about the disposition of the fortune."

Irving took that a step forward. "Which means the financial press will be hot on the sleeper's trail, too—now we've got competition. It means it's time for you to get your ass over to Riga, maybe with Our Gal Sunday here."

"Yes. If I'm to play Berensky to his people, now's the time. The sleeper looks like a hero after yesterday's huge coup, and I know all the details."

Irving reviewed the status of the impersonation. "I'm pretty sure we've got Davidov's KGB hooked. He now suspects you may be the sleeper."

"That's so," Liana confirmed. "Nikolai told me to be very careful of what I said to the banker from Memphis. And I will tell him I am sure you are Berensky when I see him next."

"That tracks with what I'm getting," Dominick said. "Our Globocop security people say somebody's been trying desperately to penetrate our communications with a second satellite. The more we frustrate Davidov, the more he thinks our operation is the real thing."

"And we know the Feliks people have plenty of lines into the KGB," figured Irving. "That means that what Davidov suspects, Madame Nina suspects."

"The seed of suspicion has been planted everywhere," said Dominick. "The only one on the other side who knows for sure I'm not the sleeper is the sleeper. Now I must persuade the hunters that I'm indeed the one they're hunting."

"Wait," Liana said. "If you convince them you're Berensky, why won't the KGB or the Feliks people just seize you and torture you until you give them all the money?"

"Not to worry," said Irving quickly, before she took the edge off Dominick's desire to go. "Goose that laid the golden egg."

"He means that the real Berensky is too fragile to touch, Liana. One heart attack and they lose a hundred billion dollars, the salvation of their respective movements, the economic control of Russia. Access to much of the fortune is in his head. Both the KGB and the Feliks people want him to be alive, and to be their agent, not their enemy."

She was not persuaded. "But they want the money, and Edward Dominick, no matter who he pretends to be, does not have it." She pointed this out in what Irving noted was a sound reportorial way. "What happens when you can't put real money on the table?"

"In a short time, I think I'll be able to," Dominick replied. "Focus on the sleeper. Berensky is a financier who always deals through fronts. He now has every reason to use me as his front in dealing with both groups of Russians. With what I know about his mode of operation, I'm in the perfect position to be his middleman, his agent or broker."

"Why?" Irving was glad she'd asked, and looked at Dominick for the answer.

"Whichever group he decides to give the money to, he will make the other an enemy. The rejected party will be out to kill him, and those people are good at that. Berensky will have to remain anonymous all his life. He needs me—the fake Berensky—to be his shield. Bankers call that intermediation."

"Spooks call it a cutout," Irving added. "Our whole object here is to make Edward a player in this game. Berensky will have to play with his impersonator—it's in his interest, he can't avoid it—and we'll have the story."

"Dangerous," Liana said, shaking her head.

"Less of a risk to me," Dominick told her, "than to Irving here, or Mike Shu. Or Viveca. Or you, Liana. Big players don't get hurt; the lives of all others are expendable."

Irving did not express his disagreement with that notion; it was better Dominick thought that way on the eve of placing his head into the jaws of the bear. "So you want to be careful, kid," the reporter told Liana. "You want to get close to Davidov, but not too close, and tell him you're sure Edward Dominick here is really Aleks Berensky."

"He'll ask why I think so."

"Woman's intuition. Reporter's hunch. Whatever. And remember to insist on a trade—that always makes your info more believable. Niko's got to tell you what's the basis of Madame Nina's interest in you. Find out from him why everybody elected little you to be the top banana on the story." Before she could ask, he amended the trope about the banana: "That's the central journalist, my counterpart in Europe."

"Be careful of this Nina woman," Dominick added. "I wish I had warned Viveca to be on her guard, too."

"You think somebody deliberately made Viveca Farr drunk?" Liana got right to the point. "To stop her from finding Berensky?"

"Definitely," said Dominick. "She drinks, as we know, but she's no drunk. I'm willing to bet somebody spiked her drink with some kind of timed-release drug."

"Maybe," said Irving, wishing it so. "But even if that's so, nobody would believe it. Too many people have seen her boozing it up, and too many knives are out for her at all the networks, and not just from the men."

"That is why she wants to crawl into a hole and disappear?"

"She once told me," Dominick said, "that if her career crashed or she was otherwise humiliated, she would either kill herself or pack up and get in a pickup truck and drive to Yucatan."

"Told me that, too. Dunno why Yucatan. Could be the sound of the name."

Dominick said he would head back to Memphis to get his global security people tracking Viveca, and to prepare for his own visit to Moscow and Riga as Berensky.

"I have a detail for you," Liana offered. "Irving said you wanted anything about Berensky's family from his file that he would be expected to know. A friend of the wife that was abandoned wrote to Shelepin. She complained of the pain her husband's assignment had caused herself and Masha."

Irving caught the detail. "The kid's nickname could help, Eddie."

"Many girls are called Masha, and boys Sasha," she cautioned, "not just those with Maria and Sergei in their names. I still turn when I hear Masha; it's the most common endearment of all. But I hope it may help a little."

"I'd have to be careful with it," Dominick said. "Berensky left before the child was born, and might not know what his wife called her. On the other hand, it would be natural for him to check up on them from over here, if only out of curiosity." He thanked Liana, shook her hand solemnly, and suggested she call him at the Metropole in Moscow if any other such information came to her.

When he left, she said, "A brave man."

"He's too old for you."

"He's your age."

"You got it." Irving looked around Viveca's library, feeling slightly uncomfortable. "I'm missing something." He started tapping the side of his head with the butt of his palm, wondering what it was that should be in the library and was not, like Sherlock Holmes's dog that did not bark.

That was precisely it. He snapped his fingers. "Housekeeper!" he shouted, and the woman appeared. "Where's the pooch? My big black dog?"

Brigid told him Ms Farr had taken the animal with her in the car that morning along with one of the twenty-five-pound sacks of dry meal. Irving permitted himself one small sigh of relief; the presence of Spook in the utility vehicle was the most hopeful news he had heard all morning.

Chapter 45

NEW YORK

Walking alone back from the airline gate at JFK where he had seen Liana off on her flight to Helsinki, Irving Fein remembered he had not called his message service for more than a day and a half. Too much had been happening for him to go looking for more communication: man blew his brains out in front of him; Liana came along in his life; billions of dollars were made instead of lost; Viveca disappeared.

"You have six messages," said his permanent sweetheart, the sexy robot's voice that was there for him when all others let him down. "To get your messages, press two." Irving slipped into his automaton mode, doing what he called the dominatrix of the dial directed, except you couldn't use "dial" anymore. "Call answering message at ten-eighteen A.M., Thursday, November eighteen. To get your message, press zero." He obeyed. Message came on that his shoes were not ready to be picked up because they weren't making the plantation rubber soles anymore for his old Wallabees, and would Vibram soles do, and call with the answer; but the shoemaker forgot to leave a number. He pressed star-D and deleted that; a man who could earn $20 billion in a day for somebody else deserved new shoes for himself. The next message announced by the android operator was also from the previous morning, and he pressed zero again to get it.

"This is me." Viveca's voice. "I've got something kind of important that I found out last night. It's—it's something I can't make head or tail out of, but you ought to hear tell about it, might change your whole theory of the story. Can you call me back real soon? I'm at home in the country and the fireflies are out. I can't leave you a hint or anything on this machine; it's too confidential. It has me a little shaken up, to tell you the truth—my judgment isn't getting any better with age. If we miss connections, leave word on my machine that you can meet me in Portofino tomorrow at the usual time. Who knows, you may discover that you have a real reporter for a partner after all. Call back quick, Irving—whoops, sorry, Sam, Harry, whatever your name is. I need you."

The girl robot said, "To save this message, press one. To delete this message, press star-D. To skip to the next message, press the pound key."

He pressed 1 and played Viveca's call for help again and again, every nuance of her worried voice etching itself onto his memory with each repetition. He wanted to believe that she had not self-destructed, that she did not have her weakness to blame. He preferred to think that she was the latest victim of the sleeper, who had swept this particular chess piece off the board without having to kill her. In every instance of protecting his identity, the sleeper played on the weakness of his target: Clauson's passion for arcana amid rusticity led to a seeming accident; Speigal's weakness was the fear of disclosure that led to suicide; Viveca's vulnerability was a horror of humiliation, and she was now running far away, with whatever clue she had discovered buried in her isolation.

He pressed 1 again. "This is me. . . ."

PART THREE

The Sleeper

Chapter 46

VERSAILLES

"The Mirror Gallery was one of the great technological achievements of the seventeenth century," the curator was telling the small group of patrons inspecting restoration plans in the palace of Versailles. "Artificial light was at a premium at the time. The diamonds in the crown of Louis XIV could hardly be seen at dinners."

Karl and Sirkka von Schwebel fell behind the others to be able to confront their latest marital strain. The couple had contributed nearly a million marks toward the refurbishment of the castle and new landscaping in the gardens; they were being solicited again to resilver some of the deteriorating portions of the historic Hall of Mirrors, scene of grand balls, the crowning of a German emperor, and peace treaties ending the war to end wars.

Ahead, the fund-raising curator ambled on. "Candles set in front of polished metal backings doubled the candlepower, but it was not until the development of silvered glass that reflected light could be multiplied many times. Here in this hall, for the first time, great sheets of the silvered glass were created by palace artisans to line both sides of a gallery, bringing unprecedented light to a state dinner and properly showing off King Louis's crown." The heads of his audience angled upward to follow his pointing finger.

"I was assured by the publisher personally," Karl von Schwebel told his wife, "that the magazine would not run the picture."

"You are too trusting, Karl. She was the sensation of this year's festival in Cannes. And here she was looking so adoringly at you."

He had gambled on being with Ari Covair that evening without attracting attention, and lost. The paparazzi's photographs—placing his mysterious-mogul respectability against her Gallic vivacity and deeply backless dress—were taken, sold, distributed, and published. Karl was less concerned at the chagrin of his wife than at the reaction of his moralistic backers at the headquarters of the Feliks organization in Riga.

"I can state categorically that Ari and I are not having an affair," he lied.

"You poor man. Getting all the credit and none of the fun."

"You don't believe me."

"What does it matter to me if you sleep with every woman in your communications empire? But you used to be discreet. That made it easier for us to go out with our friends."

"I harass nobody. This young woman started 'coming on to me,' as they say, at the party in New York. You must have seen how I rejected her advances."

Sirkka's genuine laugh stung him. He asked what was so funny, and she parried it as if his lie were of little importance to her; that made him furious. He demanded an explanation.

"Karl, you were making love to that delicious little string bean all the next afternoon. I'm not a spy, but it was common knowledge at the hotel—"

"You are not a spy, then?" He could not contain his fury. "And at the very moment that you seem to think Ari and I were consummating our relationship, were you not conspiring with the KGB in the Oak Room of the Plaza Hotel?"

That stopped her. Her face ashen, she stared straight ahead at the curator and the group.

"Well?"

"Tell me the rest, Karl."

He caught himself; an atypical loss of temper had caused him to tip his hand. Knowledge of her Stasi past was a useful secret not to be wasted to indulge a sophomoric passion. He turned his interrogation away from suspicion of espionage. "What more is there? Are you having an affair with the handsome Nikolai Davidov? Not that I mind, but it would make it difficult to go out with our friends—"

She looked directly at him. "He told me that you managed to suppress my Stasi file in Germany." He had never before seen tears glisten in those gray Nordic eyes. "Why did you never tell me, Karl? Why did you make me live a lie with you?"

He turned the question back on her. "Why did you never confess to me?"

She shook her head in bitterness. "All my fault. Blame me. You, a German patriot, married a Russian spy."

How much did she know about what he knew about her? Beyond that, how much had Davidov told her about the control of Karl von Schwebel's fabled "vast media empire" by the amalgam of Russian mafiyas and politico-capitalists centered outside KGB jurisdiction in Riga? He had to assume that Davidov knew of his backing by the Feliks people and had informed Sirkka. Because he had to anticipate her using that against him, he preemptively confessed: "I married a spy, and so did you. We are not only man and wife, but we are brothers under the skin."

"You are working for the Feliks people?"

He knew she already knew that. "Capital they siphoned out of Russia provided my initial financing," he said as if he were revealing a secret to her. "Not all their money went to the sleeper agent. Enough went to me to buy control of the communications empire that enables me to harass starlets and secretaries—"

"I should not have said that. I was angry and jealous." He hoped she would say more, and she did: "I don't care so much what our friends say. We don't have real friends." He accepted that as true enough. "It is just that I think I can make you happier—in every way—than any little slut trying to buy your favor. May I be frank? It hurts me when you turn elsewhere for love."

Was she being frank or being a very good spy? He suspended judgment and took her hand. "We are in a unique position, you and I . . ."

Unique was the word.

Against what she presumed were all museum rules, her husband struck a match to light a cigarette. She could see its ever-reflecting image in the mirrored walls disappearing into infinity. He obviously did not fully trust her, nor did she him. "Do you ever wish, Karl, there could be a way of breaking away?"

"You've read *Faust*," he said, shaking his head. "You make your deal with the devil, you deliver up your soul. In our case, you and I made a deal with opposing devils. We cannot deny them their due."

"What about what everybody calls your 'vast media empire'? Your programming can sway public opinion in cities that are a world apart. Why can't you use that power to break free of your mafiya?"

"No more than you can tell Davidov that you resign from Russian intelligence," he said. "We have more in common than we thought, Sirkka. We are together in quicksand, and every move we make draws us in deeper." When she shook her head, rejecting that despair, he stopped her to instruct: "Media power is reputation times momentum. If my reputation is besmirched, that causes me to lose my momentum, to break stride, and I become vulnerable to terminal slowdown."

"Nonsense. You can counterattack and crush whoever criticizes you. You can hire bodyguards to block whoever threatens you. You can reveal the worst about anyone you want. You are invulnerable."

His face took on the rueful, sardonic cast that once attracted her. "Live by exposé, die by exposé. With your fine economic background, Sirkka, you have been led to believe that media power is an amalgam of stations, and publications, and software and programming."

"The synergies—"

"Do not be taken in by notions of 'synergy' in controlling both production and distribution. That's a lot of mechanistic mogul talk to romance the security analysts and bemuse writers of market letters. Do you know what would happen if Madame Nina, or Kudishkin, or one of those nasty little neocapitalists in Riga chose to reveal the dirty sources of my investments, to expose the real owners and creditors of my 'vast empire'? My competitors would trumpet it, legitimate investors would run, governments would start investigations, deals would disappear, talent turn away, credit dry up—the vaunted synergy would devour itself and me. Nobody invests in a laughingstock."

Sirkka Numminen von Schwebel recognized his defeatism as rooted in the same feeling of helplessness that had afflicted her when she was again pulled into economic espionage: the self-destructive step you were about to take was inescapably determined by the terrible steps you took before. Her past had a stranglehold on her future. Spying was irreversible; nobody resigned from the KGB or the CIA, from the old organized-crime mafiya or from the new world underworld; these institutions and "families," more than nations or social establishments or companies, were the last demanders of lifetime loyalty.

Or so everyone said. But that was the mind-set left over from the Cold War, before the information revolution and the collapse of ideology. She stopped, released his hand, took his arm, and squeezed it hard.

"The paradigm has shifted," she told him, knowing he would grasp her meaning. From the start, she could talk in philosophical shorthand to Karl; their minds had always leaped ahead together, bypassing the long conversational valleys traversed by traditional European couples. "Think through, brother Faust, your idea of the opposing devils."

Karl looked surprised. Then his face went into its Germanic blankness that obliterated all expression during financial deals, personal crises, and original thinking. For the first time, Sirkka felt truly married to the man, and allowed herself to be slightly hopeful about their future together.

Von Schwebel was reminded suddenly of his reason a few years before for all the emotional trouble and financial pain in rearranging his marital life. Not for him the sophomoric lust to recapture lost youth with a tall Nordic goddess, nor the self-indulgent desire, felt by so many of his pretentious executive cohorts, for a trophy wife to celebrate his success. The primary reason he had been attracted to Sirkka, as her latest signal reminded him, was her genius for Mephistophelian manipulation.

The old Faustian analogy, when seen in the light of the "paradigm shift" now popular in the literature of fresh thinking, illuminated the tectonic changes in their espionage landscape: if he had sold his soul to the devil of the Feliks people, and if Sirkka had sold her soul to the devil of the KGB—could the doomed couple not find its salvation in exploiting the opposition of the two antithetical devils? A less mythic metaphor came to mind: the two locked-in agents had a breakout possibility in the enmity of their two imprisoning organizations.

"The central question," he posited, "is, who is the sleeper?"

"The immediate question," she countered, "is, who is this Edward Dominick? Is he the sleeper?"

For purposes of exploring this conundrum, he decided to trust her. "I know, from my intimate and complete surveillance of their Memphis operation, that Dominick is a creature of the CIA, run by the journalists Fein and Farr and Shu."

"You're certain of this."

"Sirkka, it's my own satellite they're using. Our overhears and searches show that their method of entrapment has been set up to parallel the real sleeper's trading, to track him down or to attract him into making a deal. That is what I have accurately reported to Madame Nina. She will be ready to confront and expose Dominick when he comes to impersonate Berensky."

"While I suspect," she continued in satisfying symmetry, "from my accurate trading information received from Dominick and Fein and Speigal, that Dominick is the real Berensky. In my construct, all the evidence of your overhears and transcripts is part of a grand deception. I believe that the Memphis operation is an elaborate CIA device to fool both the KGB and the Feliks people in Riga."

Though he gave her outlandish notion no credence himself, Karl saw the attractiveness of Sirkka's construct to a deeply duplicitous mind. But a theory alone did not present an effective dangle. "Nikolai Davidov is not an Angletonian paranoid or a Shelepin clone," he observed. "How are you going to persuade him of your deception theory?"

"With the greatest trading profit in all of human history." Instinctively, she covered her lips with her fingers as she put a profound secret into words. "Three days ago, Speigal sent me a red signal—sell marks, buy dollars. The Dominick-Fein-CIA group transmitted that message. You and I are independently certain of that."

He nodded; his surveillance had intercepted and read the message from the Fed mole, Speigal, just as it was received by her.

"The advance information to me from Speigal, transmitted as you know by Fein, was absolutely accurate," she informed him. "Contrary to the market's expectations, the Fed did nothing, just as Speigal's fax to me said it would do."

He was almost afraid to ask: "How much did the sleeper make as a result?"

"Berensky made over twenty billion dollars on the currency markets. Twenty billion, mainly through London and Philadelphia, the real sleeper's regular conduits." As he absorbed that figure, he was more willing to accept what had at first seemed an absurd theory. "This huge profit, Karl, is the culmination of the sleeper's success. Ergo, Dominick—posing as the fake sleeper—must be the real sleeper."

The scope of the financial coup staggered him; he had had no idea that the Americans were so daring as to let the sleeper accomplish his $100 billion goal. Certainly it gave some legitimacy to the proposition Sirkka was planning to make to Davidov: that what seemed to be the CIA's parallel Memphis operation was actually the real sleeper, Berensky-Dominick, at work.

Her hypothesis could not be dismissed out of hand by the KGB. "Davidov is already prepared to think that Dominick is the real sleeper," he mused, "because the KGB has not been able to penetrate the security of the Memphis operation. He knows that no normal bank is so secure in its communications. He does not know that it is my subsidiary Globocop, not the CIA, blocking his penetration."

"By adding the hard fact of a twenty-billion-dollar profit to his suspicions," Sirkka said, "I will let him come to his own conclusion."

"Don't overplay it," Karl cautioned. At her look, he apologized: "You are too subtle for that." She was. He let himself say what suddenly came to mind: "Why do I have the urge to make love to you right here, right now?"

"Must be the mirrors."

"Sirkka, you will persuade Davidov that Dominick is the real sleeper. At the same time, I will inform Madame Nina of exactly the opposite— that Dominick is an impostor. That will put you and me in a unique position vis-à-vis the gentleman from Memphis."

Her graceful head inclined in a nod. "It is we who will determine if his mission succeeds. If either one of us finds it opportune to switch our position, Dominick is believed, or—"

"Or he is a dead man." Karl von Schwebel took the deep breath of liberation. "We cease to be manipulated by others. We become pivotal players ourselves in the disposition of the world's largest fortune."

He formally offered her his arm. His current duchess probably had a heart too soon made glad, but he could indulge himself in letting her think they could be a married couple in love. Her guard was up in anything to do with espionage, and a natural skepticism permeated her economic analysis, but he suspected a certain sentimentalism might creep into her assessment of their marital relationship, which he could take advantage of.

She took his arm, and they caught up with the group in time to catch the curator's concluding remarks about the enhanced brilliance in the diamonds in the crown of Louis XIV.

Chapter 47

MOSCOW

Davidov marveled at how easy it was for a person to disappear in America.

In the days of the Soviet Union, a fugitive would soon have to produce an internal passport to move about, or to work; now in Russia, such controls were loosened, but it was still relatively easy to track a suspect down. Sooner or later a man on the run would have to produce his papers to work or to find a place to live. He knew that in China, a system of local informing was in place that made it impossible for anybody to hide among more than a billion Chinese.

But in America, a person—even a famous television personality—could go underground and, provided she took care to avoid using credit cards and getting arrested for minor offenses, could go undetected for years, perhaps decades. Nobody had to produce papers on demand; that's why millions of illegal immigrants went undetected. Hideability was a measurement of the freedom Americans enjoyed, though it was also a measure of the difficulties ordinary police faced.

Were it not for the low-tech position transmitter his agent had placed in the dog's collar, and Viveca Farr's curious decision to take the animal along with her into hiding, Davidov would have had no way of knowing where Fein's partner in the CIA's search for the sleeper had gone. The message left by the disgraced telecaster on Fein's voice mail the morning of her drunken on-air debacle indicated no plan for flight; on the contrary, she had left a message for her journalistic partner that Davidov was certain would lead directly to Berensky. That message had not yet been delivered; Davidov wanted to be the first to get it.

He was fairly certain the CIA was in the dark about her whereabouts, because Fein was frantic in his calls about her to friends at the FBI and the Federal Reserve. Nor did the private security agency, Globocop, that so tightly protected the Memphis bank have a lead on the Farr woman, despite Fein's open-wire pleas to Dominick to get that agency to track her down. Only Davidov's directorate of the KGB knew of her location in Sedona, Arizona, two hours' drive north of Phoenix, but Davidov had no agent he trusted to visit her there. The head of his Memphis team, a hero of the Afghan war, had an inordinate fear of large black dogs. Davidov was not about to turn for help to Foreign Intelligence; KGB detractors there would surely cause trouble in the Kremlin if they knew of his unauthorized contact with their Bundesbank spy, Sirkka Numminen von Schwebel.

That woman was an agent he had to see again, and soon, whatever the bureaucratic cost. Sirkka had to have some knowledge of Berensky's colossal coup three days before; he suspected that her Davos Forum friend, Mortimer Speigal, was probably a Foreign Intelligence mole in the Fed. Through an informal channel—an old lover of Yelena's in FI—Davidov had learned that their mole Speigal had broken off all contact since his last transmission, which was accurate as usual. He had not even appeared at work.

"Where is Sirkka Numminen now, Yelena?"

"Still at the Trianon Hotel in Versailles," he was informed, "with her husband. They seem to be having a second honeymoon."

"Arrange for me to see her in Helsinki this weekend." She was a Finn, had family there, and could get away from her supposedly reenamored husband on that score. That media magnate, whom the KGB knew to be financed by the Feliks people, would welcome the time alone in Paris. He made a mental note to see if Ari Covair could be recruited, but as quickly set it aside; nobody worked for ideology anymore, and the economic intelligence directorate did not have the budget to attract a top actress. And if he did not produce results quickly on the sleeper, his directorate would have no budget at all; the Kremlin's pressure to find the sleeper's fortune was growing as rumors spread of a recent $20 billion coup.

"While you were in America, you had an urgent message from Arkady Volkovich in Riga," his aide reminded him. Davidov could not be everywhere, and was afraid to delegate these contacts to potentially disloyal handlers; the man he had inside the Feliks network of criminal authorities was especially vulnerable to betrayal from within the KGB. Arkady, though reliable, tended to exaggerate the importance of his information; Davidov believed the KGB, with its Memphis surveillance, was well ahead of Madame Nina's organization in the search for the sleeper, and he could treat information about her meetings in Riga as not all that urgent.

"What is your analysis of the voice-mail message the woman left on Fein's machine?" he asked. Yelena was good at such evaluation.

"The reference to Portofino was their silly *Barefoot Contessa* code to set up a breakfast at the coffee shop. The only word that might indicate a better code is 'fireflies,' but we have no context for that. 'Hear tell' is an American idiom meaning 'get information aurally' and may be a reference to Berensky's hearing impairment—or not. I think she had specific information about the identity of Berensky. I think the sleeper had somebody drug her and arrange for her public humiliation, knowing she would run and hide or perhaps commit suicide."

"Smart of him. Killing handlers is nothing, but killing reporters is taken very seriously. Would change the nature of the pursuit on the American side." That reminded him of the Latvian reporter so central to the case. "What of Liana?"

"I have a report on her intimate relationship with the CIA's Fein that you don't want to hear."

"Right." Impetuous young woman. He wished now he had never let her take possession of the only copy of the strip-search tape.

"You were certain," said Yelena coolly, "that if she went to the U.S., the sleeper agent would make direct contact with her there. Apparently that did not happen."

"Apparently. Unless Edward Dominick is the sleeper."

That caught his assistant unawares. "You suspect that? On what evidence?"

"First, on the absolute absence of evidence to support that theory." The impenetrability of the Memphis operation, in contrast to the ease with which all other eavesdropping could be conducted in America, troubled him. "Second, have you noticed how everything we do get points to a CIA parallel operation to simulate the sleeper? Everything. It is as if we are being led to the conclusion that Dominick is being trained for an impersonation. Could it be—I'm not saying it is—but could this be a deliberate CIA manipulation?"

The beeper hooked to his belt went off. He looked at the number it registered for him to call: 371, the code for Latvia.

"It's Liana," he said. "I gave her this number in case of an emergency, and this is the first time she's used it."

He pulled his telephone over and punched in the digits showing on the beeper.

One ring and Liana was on the line, sobbing. "Come here, Nikolai, I need you. Now, right away, I don't know what to do. I'm frightened, I may be next—"

"I'm on my way." He motioned to Yelena to arrange an aircraft. "Who has frightened you?"

"Arkady. He's here—"

He wanted to tell her not to worry, that Arkady worked for Madame Nina but was a KGB double agent and would not harm her, but to say that on the open line would jeopardize his life.

"I just got home," she cried. "He's on my bed, and all is blood. He's dead. Nikolai, he's dead. The sleeper will kill me next."

He could not tell the distraught young woman that the corpse on her bed was not a message to her from Berensky, but to the KGB from Madame Nina. The bloody body was not a warning to Liana, but to Nikolai Davidov—that his KGB penetration of the Feliks people would meet the most savage retaliation.

"Get out of that room and go to the Tower café," he told her. "One of my men will be there to protect you. You will not know him, but he will know you and make sure you're safe. I will be there in a couple of hours. Just sit in the café in a table against the wall looking at a newspaper and talk to nobody. Do you hear, Liana? Say yes." She stammered that she would do as he said and hung up.

"The car is downstairs and the plane with two guards will be ready," Yelena said. She held out the phone. "Here is the executive for operations."

He knew how he had to respond to Madame Nina. "You have a location fix on the Chechen who was at the meeting in Riga last week?"

The answer from operations was yes; the chief enforcer of the Feliks *organizatsiya* was in Moscow today.

"Take him into custody now."

"He has bodyguards, Director Davidov. There may be resistance."

"Then kill him. Kill his bodyguards, too, and make sure the picture of the bodies appears in the newspapers. Nothing political—they were killed in a bank holdup. Let us not forget the traditions of this agency."

Chapter 48

RIGA

Liana, still enduring fits of shakiness, bought a *Diena* outside the Tower souvenir shop and stared at the newspaper, without reading it, at her table in the café. Her temporary protection, whose impassive face and cheap coat obviously concealing a weapon marked him as a KGB security man, had wedged his burly frame into a small chair two tables away.

She would give up the apartment; she could never open its door again without looking at the bed for a dead body. What had Arkady done to deserve such an execution?

Liana had told the police part of the truth: that he had been an occasional research assistant and driver. She had not mentioned his work for the woman he had always referred to only as Madame Nina, or to the Feliks organization; they could find that out for themselves. The police treated it as a gang killing and a warning to her to avoid television broadcasts about the Russian mafiya's reach into the near abroad. She was not suspected by the Latvian police, but she was certain she was suspected by Madame Nina. The sense that her life might be in danger, which she had dismissed so airily during the revolutionary days of the late eighties, was no longer a stimulus; it was a weight on her chest.

It was nearly nine o'clock and dark. Whom would she stay with that night? Her mother's flat was out of the question; Liana had not spoken with Antonia Krumins since Independence Day, and she did not want to arrive at that hard-faced woman's doorstep, after all these years, as some sort of scared supplicant. Her men friends in Riga were inadequate to her need tonight. To be alone was out of the question. She decided to stay with Nikolai Davidov, if he asked, as he surely would;

he was strong and she felt his affection toward her. Should she carry out her assignment from Irving Fein about the three lies? Of course; she was a working reporter, not an ally of the spies, and would repay Davidov in other ways, at other times, for being with her at the moment when she was most horrified.

He arrived at last and took her hand for a long moment. Against her wishes, she felt her eyes well with tears; she shook her head angrily, pulled at his silk scarf until he handed it to her, and wiped her face. Long ago she had stopped hating herself for weeping at emotional moments; if it was not the mark of a good reporter, so be it.

She reported what she had seen of Arkady in the apartment and answered his questions about both times the veteran had accompanied her to the files at Lubyanka.

"I wish you could have known him," she concluded. "Good man. A soldier. Faithful."

"I do not meet many people like that." He looked appropriately sad. "If you like, I will look to his burial. As a veteran of the Great Patriotic War, he has some privileges in Russia. Come, let us walk."

"I have a suitcase."

He lifted it, said, "It's not that heavy," and motioned to the KGB guard to carry it, following behind them. He took her hand again. "Do you have any questions for me?"

"That is your way of introducing the questions you have for me," she said, taking long strides, running her free hand along the stubble of her hair, trying to overcome her trembling. "It is your technique."

"While we were in America, did Berensky try to get in touch with you again?"

She paused before answering that, because it involved one of the lies. "Maybe."

"I hoped we could be honest with each other."

"I am not hiding a contact from you. No babushka whispered to me on Fifth Avenue. But I may have met the sleeper, just as you may have. It may be Edward Dominick, the man from Memphis at the party that night."

"What makes you think Dominick is Berensky?"

"Hard to say. You know the English word 'hunch'?"

"That is a word Irving Fein would use. Did he suggest this to you?"

"I told him of my hunch." She found lying to a policeman trained to sense lying was a challenge; but she was moved by Nikolai, and needed him tonight, and felt bad about what she was doing. "As you know, I have great respect for Mr. Fein. He is a world-class journalist, and we are working together on this story."

"Yes, I know."

"And—do you know?—he was the one who recommended the USIA invite me to lead a seminar at Syracuse University."

"Yes, yes, I know that, too. And when you told him?"

She enjoyed his impatience as she told him what she knew he already knew. "He said that hunches were overrated, just as there was no such thing as 'women's intuition.' Irving said to concentrate on details that are sometimes revealing. He is a fine journalist. I learn so much from him."

"Yes. He dismissed your hunch, then."

"Not completely. He said it was possible that Dominick was the sleeper, but I think he said that so I would not be discouraged."

"Do you think he would tell you if he knew?"

"Maybe not. He doesn't tell me everything, which is not fair, because I shared what I learned from the files with him." She looked behind them; the guard was trudging along with her suitcase.

"What is he not telling you? Maybe I can help."

"He says he knows 'why me.' He thinks there is some sinister reason I am the one reporter chosen by the Feliks people and by you to be encouraged to find the sleeper. But he won't tell me what it is, and I am a little irritated by that."

"And what do you think the reason is?"

She stopped and looked at him in as forthright a manner as she could muster. "Because I have the most closely watched television news program in the Baltics, reaching even to Leningrad, I mean Petersburg. Isn't that so? And because I am a good journalist who will not be frightened, even by dead bodies in my bed. Isn't that a good enough reason?"

"Those are two powerful reasons, Liana. But Fein says he knows of another?"

"That's what he says. Do you know of another? He says you do."

"Your program is closely watched, as you say, sometimes even in the Kremlin, on tape." By the way he slid past her question, not lying but not responding, Liana judged Irving to be right: there must be a deeper reason for her being allowed access to the files. Now she felt less bad about lying to Nikolai; he was not telling her all he knew.

"Your hunch," he was saying as he kept up her pace along the waterway, "when did it come to you? At Ace's party?"

"Yes. When I shook hands with Dominick," she said, "it just seemed to me he was more than a banker from America, or Viveca's escort. He looked very closely at me for a second, and I thought—that's him."

"Oh-shit," said Davidov in English, an expression he must have picked up on his last trip to America or listening to taps on Irving. Because that little pretense about her handshake with Dominick apparently hit home to him, she veered off the subject, lest she have to make up more about it.

"Wasn't it awful about Viveca? Irving Fein was quite upset. She is his partner, you know. Do you know—I think there may be more there, too, emotionally. He's jealous of Dominick."

"I wouldn't know about jealousy. It is an emotion I never experience." The tight-lipped way he said that indicated he meant the opposite, which she liked.

She stopped and faced him. Behind them, the KGB man set down the suitcase, the vapor from his mouth in the cold evening air showing him to be breathing hard. "You followed us in Syracuse, too?"

"You know that."

"And you know about our watching Viveca's broadcast together? You had our room bugged?"

"No, but I have a vivid imagination."

"You have no right to be jealous."

"I have no right to be in Latvia."

She touched his face. "I am so glad you are here. If you want to feel jealous, or be possessive, go ahead."

"If you like, we can stay at our safe house."

She looked behind her. "Just the three of us?"

"I will carry the suitcase."

She embraced him; he held her tightly, saying nothing. She was quivering less from the earlier fright than the present cold, and it would be good to be under a blanket with him. "Nikolai Andreyevich, do you have anything to tell me?"

"Liana, I have so much to tell you." That was all he said, implying much to tell of personal feelings, but again slipping away from her probe about the reason for her being chosen. As a result, she was happy to be at his side but not on his side, and did not feel the smallest twinge of conscience about having implanted Irving's three bits of disinformation.

Kudishkin seemed oddly pleased.

"The new KGB responded like my old KGB," he told Madame Nina. "Two of our Chechen friend's fellow Chechens were shot dead, and the third, the Ingush, was beaten severely about the head. Our colleague is now in a cell in Lubyanka, where there are no longer supposed to be any cells."

"We could not allow von Schwebel's report at our last meeting to be transmitted to Davidov," was the woman's firm reply. "Arkady had to die. Your friends in Davidov's directorate must be rewarded for betraying the informer who was betraying us."

The former high official of the KGB remarked that the traitor's body had been put to good use. The chairwoman agreed: it had both frightened the sleeper's daughter and brought Davidov on the run. "Both the KGB and Liana Krumins are now more likely to be deceived," Kudishkin noted, "by the fiction of the Memphis banker being Berensky."

Von Schwebel reported that his wife, Sirkka, was scheduled to meet Davidov in Helsinki on the coming Sunday: she would, he promised, fuel the KGB's falsely based suspicion that Edward Dominick was the real sleeper. "The journalist Irving Fein is selling the CIA's creation to the KGB," he told the board. "Davidov is an inexperienced investigator, no more than an academician with family connections in the Kremlin. Fein has him half persuaded already that the Memphis banker impersonating the sleeper is genuine."

The Group of Fifty executive interrupted to get to what he liked to call the bottom line: "But what of Berensky, the real sleeper? He's now sitting atop assets swollen to one hundred billion dollars. Isn't that getting impossible to conceal?"

"He will allow his impersonator to make the approach to us, as well as to the KGB," Madame Nina replied. "Dominick will be his conduit for the return to Russia of the assets so skillfully invested—through us, or through the KGB."

"That is a very big 'or,' " protested Kudishkin. "The CIA's Fein may be conspiring with Davidov to deliver the fortune to the 'legitimate' regime in Moscow. What are we doing to make certain the sleeper—through Dominick or whoever—delivers the fortune to us?"

All eyes shifted to Madame Nina. "We are well equipped to thwart any diversion to the regime now in power," she said, "and to seize the assets for the future government of Russia and its near abroad. I can hardly wait to meet this Edward Dominick, and through him finally to confront Aleksandr Berensky."

Chapter 49

"I just got off the phone with our friend in the former Dzerzhinsky Square," Ace said from his digitized cellular phone. It was advertised as secure communication, but he put nothing past the predatory nature of his fellow literary agents and spoke as cryptically as he could about Davidov to Irving Fein. "He suggests it may be time for you and him to have a tête-à-tête."

"Hell with him, I got my hands full."

"Irving, I realize you're under quite a strain—"

"Where'd she go? What's with the FBI and that cockamamie Globo-cop? Why can't they find her? Viveca Farr's got a famous face, for crissake."

The agent sympathized; Viveca's disappearance only added to the media firestorm about her public disgrace. After the first news cycle of the daily newspapers and morning TV talk shows focused on her drunken performance, a second wave of sensational coverage crashed over her disappearance in the newsmagazines, supermarket checkout scandal sheets, and TV magazine documentaries. "Dragnet for Boozy Newsie" was one checkout headline that effectively captured the spirit of the search for Viveca Farr. "Abused 'Airhead' Had Hollow Leg" shouted another, pretending to defend her on the grounds that parental abuse had caused her alcoholism and downfall. The serious and responsible press, deploring all the sensationalism and professing to use the Farr episode merely as an example, examined in exquisite detail the role of the communications industry in the destruction of its own personalities.

"You see *Soft Copy* last night?" Fein demanded. "They played that goddam half-minute clip for the thousandth time. Kids can recite the whole thing, like we used to the Gettysburg address, with all the drunken slurring. The damn thing's on T-shirts."

"An abomination. I'm suing one do-gooder for using Viveca's likeness in his antidrug advertising." The agent then directed his attention to business: "Fortunately, none of this craziness seems to have affected your publisher. Not a word from them about cancellation of the book contract or demand for repayment of the advance."

"Aah, they're afraid they'd get hit with a ton of sauerkraut."

"It could well be," Ace agreed, "that our social contact with Karl von Schwebel of Unimedia gives pause to his American publishing subsidiary. Whoever suggested you put them on the party list did you a big favor."

"That poor bastard is dead now," said Fein. "Where the hell is Viveca, Ace? You suppose she's watching everybody who ever knew her dump on her on national television? Does she get the goddam magazines with her face on the cover when she goes to buy food? Is she gonna stick her head in the oven?"

"We can hope she's far away from major media. This will all die down in a few weeks." Ace did not mention the two books contracted on her life by other agents, and the television miniseries based on one of them; a lawsuit to stop that was next week's headache. "But Irving, life goes on. Remember your great story. Surely Viveca would want you to pursue it, and Liana as well." He was reluctant to use Davidov's name on the line. "What shall I tell the fellow you irreverently call Niko?"

"Let him talk to Dominick. Eddie's over in London anyway, getting prepped for opening night."

"No, Irving, it's you he wants to see." He glanced at the notes of his conversation with the KGB man. "Said you could have a late dinner in Moscow and watch the fireflies. I could get you a reservation at the Metropole."

"Not budging out of here till I get a line on Viveca. Let him miss me."

"Should I countersuggest London? You could do it over a weekend." Ace felt the reporter should go; the buzz on Wall Street was rising about the mysterious currency coup of the previous week, and he sensed it had to do with the sleeper. The exclusivity of the sleeper story might soon be in jeopardy. In the long pause, Ace could envision Irving tapping his temple.

"Fireflies?" Fein said at last. "It's practically December. No fireflies in Moscow now, the damn bugs would freeze their asses off. Was that your word or his word?"

"His exact word."

"I'm missing something." The blank spot apparently changed his mind: "Okay, tell Niko I'll meet him in London at the Lawns Hotel, a fleabag in Knightsbridge. None of his taps or bugs. Maybe that's what he means by fireflies. And tell him he'd better be ready for some heavy trading. My time is valuable."

Chapter 50

LONDON

"Put another quarter in the heater."

"Doesn't work on quarters, or rubles," Davidov said. "Do you have any British change?"

Irving, sitting in the room in his overcoat, shook his head; heavy English money made holes in his pockets. He presumed that Niko, as a KGB big shot, had become accustomed to fancy living; proletarian lodging would bring him down a peg.

"Can't the CIA afford better than this?" Davidov looked around in wonderment. "Russia is not a rich country, but we treat our agents to decent hotels on official business. You don't even have a phone in here."

"I don't work for the CIA."

"And I don't work for the KGB. I'm just an epistemologist helping out for a few weeks."

"Lookit—you want to think I'm a spook? Be my guest, but I take that as an insult. Reporting is a noble business and spying is a grubby business. Now put a slug or whatever in the heater and tell me what's on your mind."

"Tough guys like it cold. Have you heard from Liana?"

"She told me how you helped out when she was scared shitless," Fein acknowledged. It bothered him that Davidov had to be the man Liana turned to when in trouble. "I'm sure you took advantage later."

"No more than you in Syracuse. And at least I am closer to her age group."

"Too-shay. Okay, brother-in-law, what do you have to trade?"

"The body in her apartment was that of a double agent. Liana doesn't know that. Arkady Volkovich had penetrated the Feliks *organizatsiya* for us. They have their headquarters outside our jurisdiction, in Latvia. He was killed before he could give me a report on their last meeting."

"So let's make a little Chinese menu of what you want and what I want," Irving told him, taking out his pad. "Item one in Column A— what you want—is the report of Madame Nina's session in Riga."

"No. That would probably just be von Schwebel's account of the surveillance of your Memphis operation, which may or may not be better than ours. I want more than that. I want to know what your CIA has going on in that bank building in Memphis."

Irving wondered which von Schwebel he meant, the husband or the wife, but did not want to show ignorance by asking. "Don't tell me you're getting into Sirkka's pants, too," he tried.

"We'll talk about her later," Davidov said. Irving took that as a no, and guessed that Karl von Schwebel was the one working for the Feliks people; the reporter already knew that Sirkka was being used by the sleeper in America through the cutout of Speigal, the dead Fed mole. Busy couple—he with the Russian mafiya, she with Russia's Foreign Intelligence and the sleeper. He wondered if the von Schwebels compared notes.

"So item one in Column A," said Irving, "is the lowdown on my little operation in Memphis, which you think is a CIA proprietary because you're paranoid."

"Correct. Now to Column B, your intelligence requirements. What do you want to know?"

"Item one is what the hell happened to Viveca, my partner, and where she is now." Irving's priorities were very clear; getting to Viveca came first. "But that's not something you'd know."

Davidov surprised him. "I have half of it, the part about where she is."

"You do? How come? You mean she's been working for you?" Irving's stomach churned; was nothing sacred?

"No, just luck. Back to my Column A," said the KGB man. "Liana says you know why she was chosen by the good Russians and the bad Russians to be the bait for the sleeper. I want to know if you do know."

Good for Liana—she got to him. "That's a twofer," Irving said, then had to explain the Americanism meant two-for-one. "That would tell you if I know, and then what I know, about 'why her?' Come to think of it, it's a threefer—it would also tell you if she's working for me against you."

"No, it counts only as one item. You would not have to get specific about relationships."

Oh-shit, Irving thought, maintaining a poker face. So Liana was "bait," and had a "relationship" with the sleeper, which probably meant a family relationship—it could not be a wife or sister, Liana was too young. Taken together, "bait" and "relationship" meant only one thing: Liana was Berensky's daughter.

Instantly, the vista became illuminated: Liana was the goddam sleeper agent's own left-behind daughter and didn't know it. But Davidov's KGB did, and Madame Nina's rump government did, and the real sleeper did. And now Irving Fein, who had only pretended to know, knew it too. Unless Davidov was playing games, which was always possible.

"Column B, my needs," Irving said, silently absorbing that inadvertent leak and turning to his own questions. "What I want to know is, what do you guys know about the murder of Walter Clauson of the CIA?"

"And what I want to know," the KGB man countered, "is what happened to our mole in the Fed, and why you personally permitted him to send the most valuable information two weeks ago to Sirkka, knowing she would pass it to the sleeper to add to the fortune."

"Twofer."

"I accept that."

"Who's Madame Nina," asked Irving, "and how would she be able to identify the real sleeper?" He would need to get that information to Dominick in a hurry, before he went to see her.

"Twofer," said Davidov.

"Accepted," said Fein. "So let's deal." He reviewed the three items under each column. "You prepared to answer all three of mine?"

"No. I can tell you where Viveca Farr is now, or at least where her dog is. Would she abandon the dog?"

"Never. She loves that dog." Irving fervently hoped so.

"Then I can give you her exact location. On the second item—about our knowledge of Clauson's investigation of the sleeper, and what you call his murder—that's KGB family jewels. I can't trade that. On the third, about the identity of Madame Nina, we just don't know." At Irving's skeptical expression, he added, "It pains me to admit that, but not even Arkady knew, and he was in fairly close. We're working on it, believe me, trying to turn one of the Group of Fifty."

Negotiating, Irving said, "I don't think we can do business." He was prepared to cave, however, to discover Viveca's whereabouts.

"But here's something," Davidov said quickly. "I brought along a printout on Aleks Berensky's early life in Russia, including some photos, which you should find useful if you're really planning an impersonation."

"You're offering one and a half answers." Irving went down the list of three KGB queries. "I can give you the biggie—the lowdown on our Memphis operation. I won't tell you what's with your mole at the Fed or why I helped Berensky make the twenty bil, because that's my equivalent of family jewels. But I can give you my answer to 'why me?' about Liana."

He totaled it up like an old-fashioned grocer with a pencil on the paper bag: "That's more than you're giving me—two full answers to your one and a half—but I feel generous."

"To compensate," said the Russian, "I will open first." He took a large manila envelope out of his briefcase. "This is the essence of the Berensky and Shelepin family files. Letters, little intimacies, a poor photograph of Aleks and Antonia Berensky on their wedding day, a better picture of their baby, Masha. Very little of this Liana has, though frankly she led us to most of it."

Irving opened the envelope and fingered the photographs. "Damn wedding shot is out of focus. Looks like the original, though. He was a foot taller than her." He held up the baby shot and took a small gamble. "Here's the answer to your question about why-me. This kid in this picture, Masha Berensky, is now known as Liana Krumins."

"May I ask, as one professional to another, how you learned that?"

Irving felt his chest constrict in joy at the confirmation; he was sorely tempted to tell Davidov he had figured it out from his questions. "No freebies. And I am not a professional spy. Some say I'm the world's greatest reporter, which I'm too modest to admit, but every now and then, like right now, I think they could be right. Okay, let's stop horsing around—what about Viveca?"

Davidov took out his own notebook. "She has taken a job at the health club of the Vortex Inn in Sedona, Arizona, a resort about ninety miles north of Phoenix. She has rented a small house one point three miles farther north on Portal Lane. No telephone, no television."

"Is she okay?"

"She's not the same woman, I'm told. The dog apparently moves around a lot."

"How the hell do you know any of this?"

"As one professional to another?"

Irving made a face and nodded.

"When the tradecraft stays simple, it works. One of my men attached one of those locator transmitters to the inside of the bumper of her car—they're cheap, you can get them anywhere, people use them to foil car thieves. The device made it possible for us to track her easily to Pittsburgh, where she sold the car and rented another with a cash deposit. That effectively took her off the map."

"So how did you find her in the goddam Grand Canyon?"

"In a burst of inspiration, my agent attached another one of the tiny transmitters to the metal license tag on the collar of Clauson's dog. As long as the battery lasts, and as long as the collar stays on the dog, it will signal the dog's exact location. Then I had somebody go to Arizona to make sure."

"An eyeball check?"

"I am unfamiliar with ophthalmology, or your CIA locutions. The animal has become highly protective of your partner, I understand. Our observer, a retired agent living in the Southwest, was chased for nearly a mile across the desert and refuses to get near the Farr house again."

Irving ached to see the two of them. He focused on an inconsistency: "How come your first man was able to get the dog's collar off to put on the bug?"

"Fresh hamburger. Everybody has his price."

"What kind of job did Viveca take?"

"Says here 'massage therapist.' "

"Are you telling me, Davidov, that Viveca Farr has become a fuckin' masseuse?"

"Shiatsu, to be specific." The KGB man shifted his spine in the seat and looked at the cold heater. "And now to what I want to know. Tell me what goes on behind that extensive security at the Memphis Merchants Bank."

"You think that's where the sleeper is, don't you?" Irving knew his grin was at its most vulpine. "You think Dominick is really Berensky. But I conned you. And that con is what brought you here spilling your guts."

With no little delight, Irving laid out the details of the Memphis impersonation: the plan for a substitute Berensky, the war room to track the real sleeper's trades, the parallel operation operated by Dominick, and finally, with the help of a little purloined U.S. government regulatory data, the ingenious walking back of the currency cat.

Because Davidov had not been forthcoming about Clauson's death, Irving left out the part about his initial contact with the murdered CIA man. And because Hanrahan at the Fed had arranged with the FBI and the New York cops to hold back the news of Speigal's suicide, Irving volunteered nothing about his brief and somewhat embarrassing association with Mortimer Speigal, the mole at the Fed.

"Has your plan succeeded?" the Russian asked. "Has the sleeper agent contacted you?"

"Not yet. We figure that will happen right after Dominick has his little chat with Madame Nina and that crowd. That's when Berensky should contact his impersonator and decide where his loyalty lies— with the old KGB guys who sent him over, or with the new government that split up the old gang. Or he and Dominick could go into business for themselves."

"Much rests on that decision." Davidov adopted a formal tone. "I would think that your government is duty-bound to make sure our government receives its stolen assets and the fruits of that theft."

"You been talking to a lawyer, Niko. I don't work for the gummint. I work for the story. And Dominick doesn't work for the gummint. He's in this for the glory and the money."

"I do not buy that cover for a minute," said Davidov. "I believe you are a front group, a proprietary set up by American intelligence. There is no way your so-called journalistic operation could have come this far without the active participation of the CIA, the NSA, the Treasury, and the Federal Reserve. Part of your job is to deny this, of course, but the denial is not plausible."

"Tell you the truth, we got a little help from little people in most of those outfits, and you left out the Ex-Im Bank. But that's just reporting, Dave." He knew the "Dave" would get under his skin. "This is a strictly private show. I don't give a hoot where the money goes, so long as I can tell the world all about it."

"This is more dangerous than you think, as Liana could tell you. As your partner Farr could tell you."

"Dominick's in danger, I admit. I wouldn't like to be in his shoes in Riga next week, sweet-talking this Nina cookie about how he's really Berensky. But Dominick's no dope—he knows that his safety lies in his usefulness to everybody. To you guys and to the Feliks crowd, he could broker a share of the bundle. To the real sleeper, he could help keep Berensky anonymous for life, and beyond the reach of assassins. Dominick will be superrich and world-famous, and he figures it's worth a little risk. Talk about duty-bound—you're duty-bound to protect him."

Davidov shook his head. "In your scenario, a greedy American banker helps a faithless Russian agent steal our money. Why should we protect him?"

"Edward Dominick is the goose that's laying your golden eggs. He disappears, your bridge to Berensky disappears. You keep Dominick safe, it'll pay off for you." He hoped Davidov would buy that pitch; Irving owed Dominick whatever cover he could provide.

"By the way, how did you come up with Edward Dominick?"

Irving was wary of "by the way" questions; he was a frequent user of that pretense of casual interest to get to the heart of the matter. "Looked around for a six-foot-four international banker, some Russian travel, could fake a hearing problem. Viveca liked the one from Memphis. Good choice, no?"

"Who steered you to Mortimer Speigal at the Fed?"

This guy was sharper than Irving had thought. That made him less certain of his victory in learning of Liana's why-me; maybe Davidov wanted to plant that on him. He brushed that probe aside: "When is it my turn to ask about your sources and methods?"

"Too-shay, as you say," said Davidov. "All I need from you now is a list of the assets held by our sleeper around the world, which you have led us to believe is about one hundred billion dollars."

"Nyet problema, Niko. That list of companies and banks and

mutual funds and whatnot will be Appendix A of our book, which should list for thirty bucks but you can get it at the discount stores for twenty-two ninety-five. And Viveca had in mind running those names at the end of the telecast in what they call a 'crawl,' whatever that means. If you'll spring for a shilling to make that heater do its thing, I'll send you a free copy of the book plus the videotape. A forty-nine ninety-five value."

The KGB man rose and put a shilling in the heater; the filaments reddened almost immediately. He put his hands in his jacket pockets, rocked back and forth on his heels, and made a kind of formal declaration: "I think Irving Fein is a contract employee of the operations branch of the Central Intelligence Agency, which used to be called the 'dirty tricks' division. I think Viveca Farr and Ace McFarland are active agents run by you under Dorothy Barclay's direct command. I think Edward Dominick of Memphis is in fact Aleksandr Berensky of Moscow, and is only posing as an impostor, and has been operating for the past five years as a double agent. I think, finally, that your operation is an attempt by the United States government to destabilize the government of the Russian Federation and to bring about anarchy and further political disintegration." He sat down.

Irving Fein rose to reply. "I think you are jumping on the bones of Liana Krumins and Sirkka von Schwebel simultaneously, and that unbearable pleasure indefinitely prolonged has driven you out of your mind." He drew his overcoat about him and took his seat.

After a moment, Davidov said, "Then I'm half right."

Nice return; Fein took a beat. "You're not making it with Sirkka?"

"She says she's in love with her husband."

"One of those." Irving didn't believe it. "No, you're not half right, Niko. Your conclusions are consistent. You're either all right or you're all wrong."

"Tell me why I am wrong."

Fein would not be suckered into a selling position. "It may be more to my advantage to have you think you're right." Davidov's academic training was in the knowledge of knowledge, and he must be sophisticated in double deceptions, so Irving decided to try a transparent reverse sell.

"My immediate purpose," the reporter said, "is to help Dominick persuade the Feliks people that he is the real sleeper. That would lock him in as the broker and ensure the success of my book. Now: if you think my impostor is the real Berensky, and if your new KGB is shot through with leakers like the kind who betrayed Arkady, then it follows that Madame Nina's inclination to believe the impostor will be reinforced by reports from traitors within the KGB. Ergo—it's in my interest for you to disbelieve me."

Irving held up his arms. "Okay, Niko, I confess: I'm a spook, Dominick is not just playing Berensky but actually is him, and the U.S. is out to grind Russia's face in the dust."

Davidov shifted in his chair to look at Fein's image in the mirror against the closet door. "But you make that case in such a way to induce me to disbelieve it. You want me to think you are not a spook, that Dominick is not the real sleeper, and the U.S. interest in Russia is benign, or is not germane to your journalistic project."

"Yes."

"Why?"

Fein lunged out of his chair and stared in Davidov's face. "Because you're not a schmuck, that's why! Because I started this whole deal, because I know what's true and what's false, and because right is right and wrong is wrong." He extended his arms heavenward. "James, Jesus, and Angleton, save us from all this shit about gray areas and mirror images and spies in from the cold. Moral relativism went out in the garbage with the Cold War. And stop looking at me in the fuckin' mirror."

"What do you suppose she meant about the fireflies?"

Irving could hear Viveca's voice on the recording: *"Can you call me back real soon? I'm at home in the country and the fireflies are out. . . ."*

"That's on my dunno sheet, Dave. Mind if I call you Dave?"

"Mind if I call you Feinzy?"

"Niko?"

"Fine. What's a 'dunno shit'?"

"Sheet. Sheet of paper with what you don't know on it. Like—are the fireflies bugs, and was Viveca saying be careful of the bug on the line? Or maybe it meant nothing except we'll sit on the porch, and we confuse ourselves by overanalyzing."

"You turn almost human, Fein, when you talk about her."

"I'm only telling you this because you won't believe it—but I got a real feeling for that woman." That wasn't the half of it. "You think she boozed herself up, or that somebody did her in?"

"That's on my dunno sheet, too. Right under why Speigal's last message went to Sirkka from your fax machine."

"You only get one freebie. But if you want to make another trade, get Sirkka to get her husband to get Madame Nina to get in touch with Dominick at Claridge's. They ought to take tea together, with those sandwiches the cannibals like."

Davidov made that three-cushion deal with a nod. "I'm seeing Sirkka this weekend."

"Gonna take a run at her?" She was a little on the detached and stately side for Irving's taste, but the cool Finn was at least in his age cohort. Davidov was too young and inexperienced for her. "For your country's sake?"

"I intend to be faithful to Liana. I tell you that because you will not believe it, but it may inhibit your transgenerational lust. Liana worships you, by the way, though of course not physically."

"Yeah-yeah. But you don't tell her she's chasing after her own father. You don't tell her the body on her bed was your agent. That's your idea of fidelity?"

"Either you or I or Madame Nina will tell Liana, but only when she has something to trade."

Irving did not argue; business was business. "You were once an epistemologist?"

"I studied epistemology in university." Irving found that intriguing; Clauson, the old Angleton protégé, had once told him that the discipline of epistemology—the study of the nature of knowledge, and the deceptions that limited it—was essential for a spymaster.

Irving tested him: "You read Wittgenstein on Certainty?"

"Yes."

"You sure? What about Heisenberg on Uncertainty?"

"Maybe."

The heater shut down with a clank, and Davidov left, smiling. Irving paced the room for a while, wondering whether to stick with Dominick in London or head for Arizona right away.

He decided to call Dominick at Claridge's and meet him and Mike

Shu in front of the fiddle players in the lobby to brief him on the big news about Liana being the sleeper's daughter. That would arm the impersonator for the session with the mafiya lady; ignorance of that relationship would have been deadly. Then Irving would take the next plane to Phoenix. That could be justified as business, but business was not always just business.

"Madame Nina would have seen through me in a minute," Dominick said. "Nothing else I've boned up on is as important. Thank God you found out in time."

"Thank Davidov. He wanted us to know Liana is the sleeper's daughter. Planted it on me very skillfully, if it's true, which I think it is. The question is, why did he want us to know it?"

"I guess he wants the impersonation to succeed," Michael Shu offered. "The KGB wants us to fool the Feliks people, their rivals for the money."

Claridge's string quartet struck up a Viennese waltz, and Irving got the time-warped sensation that the Franco-Prussian War was about to begin. "You sit tight here in London," he told Dominick through the protective noise. "I made a deal to get the von Schwebels to deliver Madame Nina here. Be safer for you than in Riga."

"Von Schwebel is in cahoots with the mafiya?" Dominick seemed to be surprised that a media mogul could be so compromised.

"Right. You met him at Ace's party. His publishing house is our meal ticket."

"Wait a minute," said Michael Shu. "Let's stop and think about that. It's a matter of record that von Schwebel owns Globocop, too."

"Hunh?"

"Our security at the bank." The accountant looked worried. "You just told us that the guy who is tied in with the Russian mafiya owns the company we hired to prevent anybody from listening to our phones or monitoring our trades. Riga must know everything."

"Not to worry. The more overhears they rack up, the less they believe us. All those spooks have a looking-glass mentality."

He hoped Dominick would buy that reassurance; the penetration of the Memphis bank by Madame Nina's crew meant that she knew all about the impersonation plan. But when the KGB was told the same thing about Memphis, Davidov believed the opposite—that Dominick was indeed the sleeper. So go figure.

Davidov slipped into the front seat of the Bentley. Yelena was driving, wearing a chauffeur's cap too big for her head, because he did not trust the London station chief's driver. They drove around Knightsbridge and up King's Road through Chelsea for about a half hour as he thought through the encounter with the American reporter. When Davidov was ready, he spoke quickly.

"I tipped him to Liana being Berensky's daughter," he reported, "which he did not know. At least it gives Dominick a chance with the Feliks people. Then I sent Fein to see Viveca Farr in Arizona, because only he can find out what she knows. Ask me questions."

"The firefly message?"

"He pretended not to be able to figure it out, but it's surely what brought him here. Must be a past personal reference, unbreakable as code." He adjusted the seat belt. "Fein sent the Speigal message to Sirkka, that I'm sure of. Means that Fein wanted Berensky to collect one last grand coup. Probably means that Speigal is turned or dead."

"Is Fein CIA?"

"He has a subtle, original, daring mind, and is not a drinker. Definitely not CIA. He uses a dialect of reverse meanings—the word for 'I don't believe you' is a double positive, 'yeah-yeah.'"

"Is this a U.S. government plot to destabilize the Russian Federation?"

"No."

"Is Dominick an impersonator or the real sleeper?"

"Going into this meeting, I could have sworn Dominick was a legitimate fake, though I sent all the signals to the opposite. Now I'm not so sure."

"Who would know?"

"Not Irving Fein. Maybe Madame Nina. Probably Viveca Farr."

They drove in Bentley silence through Queen Elizabeth Gate up Park Lane toward Claridge's. As the car turned into Davis Street, Davidov reached inside his shirt, drew out the small recorder, and passed it, tape and all, to the analyst. "There's a reference on this to sandwiches that cannibals like, I don't get it. See if you can figure it out."

He nodded hello to Roman, the doorman, and trotted up the steps to the lobby. Ahead was a string quartet laboring over a tune popular in the E. Phillips Oppenheim era, and to its left were Fein, Dominick, and the accountant Michael Shu in earnest conversation. He veered off to the elevator and went directly to his suite.

Davidov direct-dialed Sirkka at her private number in Frankfurt. When she answered, he said without identifying himself, "Memphis wants to meet Madame here in London. See if you can get your mutual friend to arrange it. Call me back at Claridge's as soon as you can."

He ordered dinner for one in the suite. Two hours later, Sirkka was back on the telephone. "Madame has declined the kind invitation from Memphis to meet in London. She tells my friend she and her committee will see him next week in Riga if he wishes. However, on the day after tomorrow, her organization will send a representative to meet him at Claridge's for tea in the lobby at four P.M."

"Who is the representative?"

"Her name is Antonia Krumins. It has been more than twenty years, but the one who sleeps will recognize her. If not, she should be able to recognize him."

Chapter 51

"Finger sandwiches, madam?"

Antonia Krumins declined; cucumbers and alfalfa shoots on two inches of trimmed white bread seemed to her all too emblematic of the triumph of Western decadence. She ordered warm scones and thick-cut vintage marmalade with her Earl Grey tea and awaited, in the Claridge's lobby, the arrival of Aleks Berensky or his impersonator.

Would she recognize the husband of her youth? A quarter-century had passed since Shelepin's son had abandoned her, eight months pregnant. Soon after, when the rejected wife was eighteen, she was informed by the KGB that she was to be uprooted from family and friends and sent, alone with her infant daughter, to Latvia to aid in its Russification.

Aleks never said goodbye. She received no letter or any form of communication from him, then or ever. That abrupt and final abandonment engendered an abiding hatred of him that helped sustain her throughout a hard and bitter life.

The KGB's responsibility ended with the arrangement of a marriage to a compliant Latvian, Ojars Krumins. He died some years after serving his purpose of providing a different last name for the wife and child of an agent sent abroad alone on permanent assignment. She felt little animosity toward the KGB, the pervasive presence that had at least bound the Soviet Union together. No; the loathing that permeated her being through the long generation was directed personally at the callous Shelepin and his illegitimate son, her tall and handsome runaway husband, Aleks Aleksandrovich Berensky.

Would he recognize her? For the occasion that she had anticipated all her adult life, Antonia Krumins, the longtime ballet teacher, set aside both the drab costume she wore during most days and the bulky woolen undergarments and grandmotherly dress that she wore on cold, damp evenings in Riga. She chose instead a suit made in St. Petersburg copying a Chanel design, and shoes with heels that accented her lithe dancer's legs. In addition to eyeshadow, she had applied a foundation creme that covered her pockmarked cheeks, and finished her makeup with a daring shade of red lipstick. She had washed and set her hair, cut medium-length as was the fashion, adding an auburn rinse to conceal the strands of gray. The steel-rimmed glasses that partially corrected her poor eyesight were replaced on this day by contact lenses, an extravagance that was her major concession to vanity. She stopped short of using perfume.

She knew her associates outside the ballet school would hardly recognize her. Would Aleks Berensky, after all these years? In her estimation, he probably would. The pretty, smiling girl of their youth had developed into a handsome woman, when she wanted to be, with a permanently stern expression but identifiable on close inspection as the same person. Ballet exercise had kept her body supple. Men who wanted to flatter her during the Soviet days would say that she and her daughter, Liana, looked like sisters.

But would an impersonator—a man pretending to be Aleks Berensky—recognize her? She had been thoroughly briefed, just before coming to London, on the details of a surveillance of a Memphis, Tennessee, bank; she knew that Edward Dominick frequently complained of a lack of photographs of his Russian bride. A Western impostor would probably be looking for the plump and plain stereotype of the middle-aged Slavic woman. On the other hand, she noted no other lone woman waiting at any of the tables in the Claridge's lobby; she was, as the English novelists put it, Hobson's choice—for whoever came in to meet a woman, it was either her or nobody. She kept her eye on the entrance.

Tea was served. She told the waiter she preferred to wait until it became strong and she would pour it herself. In five minutes, she reached for the pot to pour.

"My name is Aleks Berensky."

A suitably tall man was standing over her. The voice was familiar, but not enough to make an identification. She half-smiled up at him and indicated a chair to her right. He told the waiter to move the chair around to her left and sat down.

"I would have known you anywhere," he said in Russian. "You haven't changed."

"Of course I have."

"You dress a lot better, and you make yourself up now, and you're a woman, not a girl. But you look the same to me."

"You have changed." She did not want that to be an accusation or a judgment and added: "You look prosperous. It is hard to think of you as a banker." If it was indeed Aleks, he must have put on fifty pounds over the years; the face was pudgier and he had obviously been in an accident at one time; the eyes, as well as she could make out, were the same greenish gray, but that was a common color. Her own contacts did not let her focus too closely, but she could see that a puffiness around the eyes replaced the sunken, intense look of cruelty she could never forget. The height was right. He could well be the same man; on physical evidence alone, he could possibly not be, too.

"I got banged up in a car before they invented air bags. You didn't have a face-lift and I did." The voice was definitely deeper, but that was to be expected, and his hairline had receded, also predictable. The hair was a little darker than she remembered, but so was hers.

Did he know that the Latvian television reporter tracking him was his daughter? The report and tapes from the Feliks organization's operatives in America showed no awareness by Dominick of his relationship to Liana. "You left behind more than one of us."

"I saw Masha at a party in New York. I recognized her because I've been getting tapes of her broadcasts—frankly, that's all the Russian I hear and why my Russian is so rusty."

"Did you identify yourself to her?"

"Of course not. God, it was awkward, shaking hands with your own daughter after all these years and not being able to embrace her properly. Or even to introduce yourself as her father."

"Especially when she is searching for you."

"She's being used by quite a few people to find me. My job—the meaning of my whole life—has been not to be found." When she chose not to fill the pause that followed, he said, "She's a fine young woman. Your mouth, your cheekbones, your dancer's way of carrying yourself. My eyes, I think; gray, rather than your brown." He noticed detail, as a trained agent would. "We should be very proud, but you especially."

"I am ashamed of Liana. She was a traitor and she has become a whore."

He did not respond directly to that. "And you blame me."

"I blame you for nothing," she lied evenly. "I never thought of you until recently, and then only because a woman of great influence summoned me."

"You speak of Madame Nina. What can you tell me about her?"

"Nothing." In a low voice, she added, "My purpose here is only to report to her if you are the son of the hateful Shelepin."

He pulled his chair closer. "I tried to switch around to give you my good ear, but I missed what you just said."

That had the ring of truth. She remembered his youthful frustration at his hearing loss, and how he would insult her by turning his deaf side to her during an argument. "Is your hearing no better?" She chose not to commit to calling him either Aleks or Edward, and did not use a name. Nor did he, she noticed, use hers.

The tall man, whatever his identity was, dug a flesh-colored device, the size of a marble, out of his right ear. "This is the latest hearing aid, and it helps." He took a small screwdriver out of his pocket, made an adjustment, and put the device back in his ear. "The Americans have a saying: 'Nobody's perfect.' "

So cavalier now, and a cultivated gentleman. She remembered the savage way her young husband had forced himself on her, slapping away her shyness, breaking her resistance to break her spirit. As if in fond recall, she asked, "Do you remember our wedding anniversary, Aleks?" If he was an impostor, he would have been briefed to have that date on the tip of his tongue.

"It was in April, I think. Yes, around the time of the mushroom rains. I'm sorry, it's not a date I have had the occasion to remember."

"And after the ceremony, in Sokolniki Park?"

"The only time I was in Sokolniki Park was as a boy, to visit the American exhibition in 1959. Khrushchev and Nixon argued in a kitchen. Are you testing me, Antonia Ivanov Berensky Krumins?" He had her names correct. "Remember the glorious time we had on top of the Eiffel Tower?" Then he became serious. "Do you really think I am somebody else, pretending to be Aleks Berensky?"

"That is what you say to your CIA friends in your corner office of a bank in America," she said carefully. "I am told that you ask your fellow spies for letters that I wrote to your father, Shelepin, begging for him to let you return." The memory of those early days of enforced isolation began to burn in her again, but she was determined not to let it affect her mission. "You keep demanding some little fact about the sleeper agent's past in Russia that you could use to prove that you were him." She waited for him to refute that.

He heaved a sigh, impressive in a big man. "I have been fully aware that Karl von Schwebel's security company has transmitted to the Feliks people the sound of every flushing of the toilet in my executive bathroom. But you have to remember that every word I said about an impersonation I knew that you and others would hear. In my business, it is called disinformation. You may judge me for a bad husband, but do not take me for a fool."

"Then your impersonation—"

"—is the greatest impersonation anyone can perform. I am impersonating myself. In the grand looking-glass war, I am pretending to be someone else pretending to be me." She bore his disappointed glare. "I would have thought that Madame Nina would tell you that."

She permitted herself a full smile, as she did rarely, and wished that her new lenses permitted her to examine his expression closely. "Let us assume that you are who you say you are, and you are not who you say you are not." She reached for her purse, drew out a sheet of paper with a message typed on it, and read it to him.

" 'We expect you to be prepared to turn over the investment entrusted to you by your father's legitimate political heirs.

" 'You were sent abroad by Aleksandr Shelepin, last of the legitimate successors to Feliks Dzerzhinsky, for a great national purpose. Five years ago, you were given a certain sum by those of us who were driven from communist stewardship by the so-called reformers, followers of the traitor Andropov and his protégé Gorbachev. You were provided intelligence by members of our organization to make this investment of the people's capital grow.

" 'None of those assets are yours,' " she continued to read. " 'Nor can the usurpers presently in the Kremlin make any claim upon them.

You hold them in trust for us, and there can be no negotiation to get them back where they belong.' "

He held out his hand for the paper and read it for himself, then returned it to her. "That may be. But first I must make certain that the Feliks people are a serious political force and not a bunch of hooligans and financial con men and deadwood apparatchiks."

"Is that for you to decide?"

"It is. And I control the money."

The waiter came by with a tray of finger sandwiches. "These are good. You want some?" asked Dominick/Berensky. Inwardly seething at the professed spy's display of insolence, she again declined. He picked up a handful and popped them in his mouth all together.

"Let me pour your tea," she said, emptying a pitcher of hot water into the bone-china teapot and stirring it, "before you choke."

He held out his cup without the saucer—apparently he had forgotten his Russian habits—and said, "You still move like a ballerina. Now I'm sorry I put on all this weight. You're wrong about Masha, though—she may fool around a little, but that's the modern way. And her politics are a young person's politics."

She felt an urge to dash the hot water in his face. Instead, she poured the milk in the cup first, as the English did, and then the strong tea through the strainer, and then a little hot water, and then offered the raw sugar crystals. The ceremony was, as he suggested, a ballet, and she could hear the strains of the tragic theme in *Swan Lake*.

"I am to tell you that a meeting has been arranged of the Feliks organization's politburo in Riga next week," she recited. "Outsiders are never invited, but you are not an outsider, you are considered their agent and financial adviser. At that meeting, you will have the opportunity to ask a few respectful questions about their plans. Be prepared to answer questions about their assets in your care and to cooperate in their transfer."

"Fair enough, and well remembered, Mrs. Krumins. Will I see you again, in Riga?"

"No. I am not in politics. And for me, Aleks Berensky died a long generation ago. Goodbye."

"If there is one thing I wish, it is that I had been given the chance to say goodbye."

That was surely a lie, but she knew it was one her former husband would tell to stir old emotions and solicit undeserved sympathy. She left him sitting there amid the empty teacups and the sounds of the straining string quartet.

RIGA

The heavyset woman with iron-gray hair asked the status of the Chechen being held hostage in Lubyanka.

"They are trying psychological torture," Kudishkin reported. "Playing a recording of a man screaming in the next cell all night. We have gotten word to Leonid, however, that it is just a tape, and to pretend to be terrified. So he won't break; it is a standoff."

"Maybe it wasn't the best idea to kill Arkady and send Davidov's girlfriend the body," said Ivanenko, the new capitalist.

"It was my idea," said Madame Nina.

"I'm not second-guessing," he said hastily, "but it seems to have stirred up the KGB."

Kudishkin rapped on the table. "We are here to find out about the location of our money." He looked to the woman in the center. "What is your assessment, Madame Nina—is Edward Dominick the sleeper?"

"No. Von Schwebel's information was correct," she reported. "Dominick is a CIA fake. An impressive fake, like a well-made counterfeit bill."

"The German puts great faith in his eavesdropping," Kudishkin countered, "but that can be used as a conduit for disinformation if those being overheard are aware of the surveillance."

The woman in the center fixed her gaze on the former head of a KGB directorate through large glasses whose thick lenses made her eyes seem to protrude. "Your intelligence expertise is always appreciated, Oleg Ivanovich. But I do not rely on a single source for my initial judgment. I found Liana Krumins's mother, the woman who was married to Berensky before Shelepin sent him to America. I sent her to London to verify or expose him."

The representative of the Group of Fifty rapped the table in approval. "What was her judgment?"

"She says that, physically, Dominick could pass. Right height, hard of hearing. The face was supposedly in an accident, which makes the more obvious identification difficult. And he is well briefed about Berensky's life."

"What was the giveaway?"

"The real Berensky is his father's son: ruthless, brutal, a little crazy—a perfect agent. But in this man, the Krumins woman saw a softness and weariness that has nothing to do with age. I trust her judgment that Edward Dominick is not Aleks Berensky. Women can tell these things." Madame Nina folded her hands. "The impostor is working for the CIA and probably Davidov as well, to find out about our operation. And so I invited him here for our meeting Friday."

Chapter 52

Arlene Paltz was now her name, taken from a missing person. She had a driver's license issued in Pennsylvania with a vaguely similar face on it, a Social Security number, and a credit reference, all courtesy of a sympathetic used-car dealer. He traded the basis of an identity for $1,000 in cash.

She found Arizona in December to be not at all bad. Although Arlene had planned to keep driving out of the country, through Mexico to the state of Yucatan, she and the car were too worn out after a week to continue. A friendly lady in a pet-supply store in Phoenix, where she picked up a half-dozen extra-large rawhide bones, suggested Sedona to the north. It was a kind of resort for New Age types who believed that Indian spirits and Buddhist philosophies of energy vortexes combined with the clean, dry air to help stressed-out souls find inner tranquillity. She drove up there and found a remote house rental, cheap and dirty, but near a stream necessary for her companion and protector, Spook, who sat half immersed in the cool water much of the time.

She went to one of the many local spas and invested in a massage and a mudbath. The manager needed a clerk-massage-therapist, and a Japanese woman taught her the rudiments of shiatsu. Within a week, Arlene Paltz had an afternoon job to keep her occupied in a world that knew little about television reporting or supermarket tabloids, and nobody gossiped about the delicious downfall of Viveca Farr. She limited her massages to women, who talked mostly about energy vortexes and real estate values. Their conversations neither involved nor threatened her, and she found the kneading of flesh and digging into muscle a help in forgetting who she was and what she had done.

In the mornings, she sat on the red rocks or with her feet in the stream with Spook and grieved. She did not pass an hour without at least one stretch of sobbing that left her chest sore and throat raw. To relieve this, the runaway from celebrity sought comfort in the available pot, learned to drink cheaper wine, and counted her resentments until she achieved the respite of a midmorning streamside nap to make up for the hours lying awake at night. Frightened of an unrelenting future, she filled her time retracing in bitterness the systematic way every person in her previous life had let her down.

She kept asking herself what she had done, or not done, to deserve such a savage, gleeful, and universal rejection. No civil libertarians came forward to prevent a rush to condemnation, not even the regular counter-condemners who find exculpatory root causes in the actions of ax murderers. It seemed that everyone was eager to believe the worst about a woman who had had to claw her way up by herself and had come "too far too fast." Her network colleagues distanced themselves from "a good presenter, but no news person." The ferocity of the attacks in the media and the paucity of understanding among her associates were incomprehensible to her; she had not risen all that high to be brought so low.

Mired in the misery of the aftermath of so public an embarrassment, she found release in tearful anger much as the masterless Newfoundland found solace in the wetness of their stream. Above all, Arlene Paltz did not want anyone from her previous existence—family, friends, lovers, so-called fans and colleagues—to find her, to attack and hurt her again with their mocking laughter. She felt certain that would happen the moment she surfaced again as Viveca Farr, the industry's favorite object of pointed fingers and even more pointed refusals to comment in her defense. When her eyes were not tearful, they were frightened; the effect of what she had inadvertently learned and what she had subsequently done was overwhelming.

A van from the spa drew up to the porch and was met by a barrage of deep-chested barking. The driver eyed the wet dog and did not get out. He called to her that a group of businessmen had arrived and wanted massages that night. Arlene went up to the van window and reminded the driver she didn't do men and didn't work at night. When told the manager said her job depended on her showing up, she shrugged and quit. She had her hiding place; she was not yet so low on money as to have to smile when hassled.

Two days later, staring blankly at what remained of a woven Sioux wall hanging in her living room, Arlene Paltz heard another car engine approach and tires slide to a stop in the dirt driveway behind her own vehicle. A short bark from Spook in the stream behind the house, and another as the dog raced around to the front, was followed by silence. That drew her to the window. She parted plastic-backed curtains that blocked the harsh sunlight and looked out through a narrow opening at the visitor.

The Newfoundland was moving forward cautiously, her tail slowly wagging. A man in a disheveled suit and tie, obviously from far outside the area, was struggling to emerge from a compact car. With a mix of irritation and guilty pleasure, she recognized the familiar, lurching form of Irving Fein.

He said, "Hiya, pooch," and then, as the approaching sodden Spook gave an indication of a coming event, the reporter held out his hands in horrified supplication. "Don't shake! Stay back! Don't shake!"

Spook shook herself as only a shaggy 130-pound Newfoundland emerging from a muddy stream and comfortable with his surprise company was capable of doing. She gleefully unburdened her thick coat of moisture. The man in the suit, backed against his car, bore the full brunt of the spray. When it was over, the dog crowded up to him, rubbing her ears on his pants, licking up at his chin, delightedly smearing his shirt and tie with huge front paws. The man gave up trying to protect his clothes, took out a handkerchief, and wiped droplets of mud from his eyes.

Viveca had her first good laugh since she became Arlene. In bare feet and a terry-cloth robe, she went out on the sunlit porch and squinted at the man in the uniquely decorated outfit.

"I'm a guest at the Vortex," he called out in one of his prepared openers, "and I want to know why you don't give massages to men."

She went inside to put on jeans and a T-shirt. She was not pleased to see anybody from her Viveca life, because it meant her privacy had been pierced, but better Irving than anybody else. She brought out a Coors, which was all anybody around there drank, and handed him the can along with a paper towel.

"Fridge is broke—it's not cold." He exuded gratitude anyway, gulping and blowing away foam, which Spook licked up. "All right, tell me how you found me."

"I'm the world's greatest reporter, what'd y'expect." He took a long, quenching guzzle and hung his jacket on a chair. "Thanks. Nobody hides from Irving Fein." He punctuated his pride with a belch.

"No, seriously, I have to know. Otherwise I'll have to start running right away. I can't face anybody."

"You look great," he said irrelevantly. "Your eyes are all red and there's a splotch on your forehead, but otherwise you look great. The big towel you were wearing for a bathrobe makes a statement. And I like your hair better this way, mousy and messy. Hated that frozen lacquer look."

"Tell me how you found me." She had to know. "Can I expect a parade of photographers now?"

"Nope, you're safe for a while. Here's the guy who ratted on you." He pulled Spook toward him and took off her collar, inspecting it closely. He reached in his pants pocket for a tool—Irving was the kind who carried a Korean knockoff of a Swiss army knife, not caring about a bulge in his pocket—and pried something off the license tag. "This is the little bugger," he said, holding a device between thumb and forefinger. "It's a transmitter that people use to track car thieves. One of Davidov's boys planted it on your car and on the pooch. You dumped the car, but thank God you didn't get rid of the dog."

Her heart sank; it had been such a lot of trouble to establish a new identity, and she was beginning to like Arizona. "So the KGB knows I'm here."

"The question you should be asking," said Irving, ever the determined instructor, "is, if Davidov knows, how come he told Irving Fein? And the follow-up—why is Fein burning his source, which he never does without a reason?"

"I'm just too tired," she told him. So what if it made her sound like a dolt: information-trading, with its conniving and lying and testing and sparring, was no longer a game she was prepared to play. She had come to the conclusion that dead-serious journalism, with all its delicate probes and brassy intrusions and highwire footwork, had never really been her line of work, and a straight presenter afflicted with investigative pretensions could get badly hurt in the interplay of interests. It was true about being worn out; she was bone-weary all the time, often lacking the energy to prepare food or go to the diner. Only the responsibility of feeding the dog reminded her to eat, and that was once a day.

"You look a little bushed," Irving agreed, "like you're on a diet. You're down to fighting trim, but you don't need to lose any more."

"I've read a little Greek mythology lately," she said, ignoring his observation about her weight, "because I don't buy the newspapers and thank God there's no television in the house. You know the story of Icarus?"

"I covered that story when I was a cub on the *Albany Times-Union*," he said. "Hotshot kid from Troy, in the tri-city area, flew too near the sun, wax melted, wings fell off, into the drink he went. The trick is to be Daedalus, the old guy in the story who knew better and jumped for Joyce."

"Irving knows everything," she said to Spook, panting and slavering between them. "He is the reincarnation of Daedalus, and he taught me all I know about reporting."

"Taught her all she knows, but I didn't teach her all I know," he replied through the dog. "More to come."

Arlene Paltz, resolute nonentity, shook her head. "I don't even want to know all I already know. I took a run at heavy reporting and it almost killed me. Certainly ruined me." She walked back into the kitchen for a warm Dr Pepper. Irving followed her, Spook lumbering after him. She led the parade back outside and down to the stream, the drab rental property's most appealing feature.

Irving deposited his rear end on the stony bank. "These pants have had it," he muttered. "And all I brought was a ditty bag."

"That's all you need; you're not staying." She pointed to a looming red rock formation in the distance. "If you're into meditation, that's the place."

"Vortex central?"

"Don't knock what you don't know. It may be that energy flows through the mind and the meridians of the body, the way they say. I may study it."

She wished he would explore that philosophical vista with her, but true to his nature, he followed a news lead. "Tell me what it is you know that you don't want to know. The thing you say ruined you."

She could not control an eddy of fear, and shuddered.

"I'm sorry I made you shudder. Sump'n has you scared shitless. That's not like you to have the shakes when you're not even hung over."

She had the sudden desire for escape in a drink or a joint but did not want to make the trek back to the house. She turned on him: "Being scared has always been like me. What do you know about me? What do any of you care? I've been running scared all my life."

"I thought you were pretty sure of yourself, the way you rolled over people."

"I was not the complete bitch that some people made me out to be." She let a deep sigh raise and lower what little was left of her bosom. "Aah, who cares. All over now."

"Not true. This is just a little dip. You'll get over it and be back on your feet in no time."

She reached down and patted Spook's head. "Don't you worry, sweetie, everything's gonna be just fine. It's all in your head."

"I didn't mean it that way, Viveca. I just wish I could cheer you the hell up. Okay, you took a shot, but you gotta be an optimist. You can come back."

"That's been your experience. It's not been my experience. You're a big man, with a reputation like some kind of invincible gunslinger. People help you because they're afraid of who you are and what you can do. Me? They look at me and want to kick me, and now they know they can."

His face grew stony, and he shut down communication. She let him stew, but soon felt bad about that; he had come far to find her, and maybe only partly out of book deals and other selfishness. After a long silence, she asked the question she knew he wanted her to ask: "If Davidov knows where I am, how come he told Irving Fein?"

"Insightful question." He didn't answer right away, probably sulking about being lumped together with everybody else who wanted to kick her. Or maybe he was just noodling things over, the way he often did, seeming to commune with a handler on a distant planet. She could sense the saucer of his mind scouting Arizona, its little green men circling around looking for a place to land. "Excuse me, I was sucked into the vortex for a minute. Davidov? I made a deal with him: I'd tell him the truth about Edward Dominick if he'd tell me the whereabouts of Viveca Farr. Frankly, I didn't think he knew, but he did. Those guys are better than I thought."

"You traded Dominick for me?"

"I'd trade anything I got for you."

"I don't believe that for a minute."

"You're right." He took out his Swiss army knife knockoff, looked at it fondly, put it back. "Not my knife. Anything I got except that."

That was Irving backtracking from his blurting out of a human feeling; she knew him well. His intensity rubbed off on her enough to stimulate a question about her old life: "Irving, what did you tell Davidov about Edward Dominick?"

"Like I said, the truth. I filled him in on the Memphis war room, the parallel sleeper operation, the impersonation."

She was too fearful of reinvolvement to try to figure that out for herself. "Why? That was our big secret."

"Stirred the pot. Besides, Eddie's big target is Madame Nina and the baddies hanging out in Riga. And you know what? I got some inside family poop out of my new buddy Niko that will blow your mind. It'll help Dominick make his pitch there."

"Go ahead, blow my mind."

"Like Liana is the sleeper's daughter. That's why she was picked by the KGB and the Feliks people to be the bait. How does that grab you?"

She let herself look surprised and impressed. She thought about Liana's fine features and poor skin, and of Edward's slightly scrambled features and poor skin; they did not look alike. The eyes were the same, a cool gray, but the expression around the eyes, usually the telltale of a family resemblance, was different—his canny, hers defiant. They shared no mannerisms because they had never been together. She probably took after her mother.

"And she never told us."

"She doesn't know," Irving said.

"Least you should do, Irving, is to tell her. That girl has eyes for you."

"C'mon, Viveca, be serious. You left a message on my machine that's been driving me crazy. Musta played it a hundred times. What is it that you learned that's buggin' you?"

She turned the information about Liana's lineage over in her mind, and it brought out a rueful smile. "If we had only known what was going on at that party."

"Sometimes the best question is no question at all," he said, as if instructing himself. "I'll just take my shoes off and roll up my pants and wiggle my toes in the water. Move over, pooch."

"Irving, I became emotionally involved with Edward."

"Yeah."

"He was very much the gentleman, and I threw myself at him. And on the night of November eighteenth, in one of those huge corner suites at the Plaza Hotel in New York, we went to bed together."

"Bottom line, please. Spare me the details."

"No I won't, because the story is in the details, you once told me that." That was becoming painful to her, and it would be to Irving if he was in any way stuck on her, but he had come all this way and was entitled to hear it all set out.

"We got in that canopied bed and we made love. Edward was very tender, and then very passionate, and I never opened up to a man like that in my whole life. It was more than sex. We became one person. I cried afterward, it was so beautiful."

"Yeah."

"And I lay there next to him, and I wanted to—to serve him, in an intimate way, so I murmured in his ear did he want me to bring him a washcloth. He didn't say anything. I supposed he was half asleep. After a few minutes he pulled me on top of him—"

"Hey, come on—"

She motioned to him to shut up. "And after we made love again, Edward pulled me over to his other side, his right side, and I lay there for a while again, exhausted, thinking he needed a younger woman. I whispered again did he want me to bring him a washcloth. And this time he said what a great idea, that no woman had ever said that to him before, and he lifted his arm to let me out of bed."

"As my punishment for renting one porno flick, I have to listen to all this from—"

"There's a point to what I'm telling you, Irving."

"So what's the point?"

"He's deaf in his left ear."

"But he's supposed to be, same as Julius Caesar was. We got him the hearing aid to fake it—"

"He's not faking it! Don't you understand? Later on, I tried it again. I snuggled into his left side and lay there for a while and whispered to him that I loved him, which I did, more than any man in my life, ever. Nothing; no reaction. Then I got up and went to the little bar under the television that you open with a key"—she rose and bent over to demonstrate—"and got out a little bottle of Grand Marnier, he likes that, and came back to bed on his other side. And I snuggled in again and whispered I loved him into his right ear and he responded immediately and kissed my head and said he loved me, too."

"Brother. You sure the hearing aid wasn't in his left ear—turned off—making it hard for Dominick to hear on that side?"

"The hearing aid was on the night table between his watch and the open package of condoms."

"You're allowed to edit some stuff out, Viveca. But if he's really deaf in his left ear—"

"Then Edward Dominick is really the sleeper." She had to drive it home to him, as the realization had been driven home to her. "He is both Edward Dominick, our impersonator, and Aleks Berensky, the real sleeper. One and the same man."

"Oh-shit." He looked blank for a long minute and then started bumping the butt of his palm against his forehead. "Where'd I get him from? From Walter Clauson at the CIA. Clauson and he were in cahoots."

"Then the whole deal was a CIA plot, using you and me. Your friend Dorothy Barclay double-crossed you, Irving. You've been a cat's-paw for the spooks."

"Maybe. Maybe." She watched him blinking and thinking; he reminded her of a slot machine, its lever just pulled, with the apples and oranges and lemons whirring in independent windows before coming to a stop and paying off with a torrent of coins or not. "I can't believe Dorothy would do that to me."

Viveca/Arlene wasn't finished. "So we were lying there in bed."

"No more, for crissake. If you tell me he got it up again, I'm going to lie facedown in this stream and drown myself."

"I couldn't sleep knowing he was really Berensky, and that he was lying to us, and only playing with me. But he couldn't sleep either, and I had a hunch he suspected I'd discovered his secret. Maybe I shouldn't have tried to double-check, but then I couldn't be sure."

"You didn't say anything to him, confront him or anything?"

"No. Frankly, I was afraid he'd kill me. We finally got to sleep, and the next morning, he seemed to forget about it. He put the thing in his ear natural as pie and could hear fine, the way Dominick did. When he went into the bathroom and the shower started running, I called you."

"I got that message the next day."

"I knew you'd catch the signal about the fireflies—remember the assassination beetle you told me about, from the Angleton days? Dominick was our assassination beetle, the phony firefly, our fake impersonator."

"Sure," he said in a smaller voice. "I got that immediately. But I checked my service a day too late, after your show. Davidov heard your message too, on his tap. He didn't know what the fireflies meant, the dumb schmuck."

"But there was a phone extension in the bathroom, and I think now Edward was listening. But he never let on, and I was less sure when he came out all hard and ready and—" At Irving's dismayed look, she skipped ahead lest he lie down in the creek. "The rest of the day we spent together, at the Met Museum, in the park, dinner in the grill-room of the Four Seasons, and then he delivered me to the studio for the broadcast. I was feeling a little woozy, but I thought it was just the two glasses of wine, and I could always handle that."

"He drugged you." The Fein judgment admitted no other possibility. "He slipped something in your food or wine that would hit about nine o'clock."

"I think so. I wish I could say for sure."

"It's for sure. Get that? No equivocation, no ifs. The sumbitch commie agent drugged you, knowing what it would do to you on the air, and knowing what a disaster it would be for you." Irving was adamant and getting angry. "He caught you in the act of exposing him, and he wanted you out of the way. Murder would have been the hard way, and your message was already on record, on my machine. He took the easy way, which was even more effective in wiping you off the board, because it didn't also involve a homicide investigation."

"That's what I think," she said tentatively, "and what you think, because you're my friend. But are other people ever going to give me the benefit of the doubt? Not going to happen, Irving. The sight of me falling on my face—Ice Maiden dead drunk—gave too many people too much of a thrill. No excuses."

"I can give public opinion a swift kick in the head," he said with supreme confidence, "and turn it the hell around. Come back with me now. We can strategize with Ace about how to handle it."

She shook her head, no. "My name is Arlene Paltz. I'm safe here. No media conferences, no backstabbing, no pressure. You can write your book and keep all the proceeds. All I want from you, my dear friend, and that's what you are, is protection of my privacy. Can you make that part of your deal with Davidov?"

"Only if you let me put the transmitter back on Spook's collar." He was not joking; he seemed very firm about remaining in touch, and although she would never trust anyone completely, she decided to trust Irving for a while. "I have to be the one who knows where you are. Gotta be some connection. Otherwise, so help me, it's the *National Enquirer* and—" he groped for a headline—" 'Boozy Newsie Turns Massage-Parlor Floozie.' "

That pulled a smile out of her. She extended her hand for a formal shake on the deal, the way they had in Ace's office eons ago. He held out his arms and she reached her arms up around his neck, holding on without hugging. Irving Fein was not part of what she was running away from; in his perverse way, he probably loved her. "Ain't nobody's fuckin' cat's-paw," she heard him murmur in her hair, which was, as he said, mousy and messy, the way she wanted Arlene Paltz to be.

Chapter 53

HELSINKI

Sirkka Numminen von Schwebel sat in the private computer lounge of the Helsinki airport between two men to whom not telling the truth might have serious consequences.

"If you lie to me," said Nikolai Davidov in a measured voice, "I will have you arrested by the Finnish police out in the hallway and extradited to Russia by the Moscow prosecutor. You will be convicted of stealing tens of billions of rubles from the Russian Federation and you will never see the outside of a prison camp for as long as you live."

"And if you lie to me," said Irving Fein, who seemed to her more excitable than the KGB man but trying to be equally menacing, "I will do a series on your meal-ticket husband that will trigger Congressional hearings that will be telecast by his competitors all over the world. He'll be sued by every stockholder in every company he corruptly controls. You will see, Sirkka baby, what happens when the media turns on one of its own—there'll be SEC suspensions, Fed freezes, Interpol exchanges, and criminal prosecutions in a half-dozen countries. Blood all over the floor."

Davidov's threat she took more seriously. "It will be hard to break a habit of a lifetime," she told them as coolly as she could, "but you have made clear that it is now in my interest, and my husband's interest, to tell what I believe to be the truth." She had worked out with Karl the night before in Rome what truth she should tell to the KGB and CIA-Fein, and what truth he should tell to the Feliks people. "Further intimidation of me would be counterproductive. Let us proceed."

Davidov came at her first. "What has been your relationship with the Feliks people?"

"Nil," she said, which was the truth. "They know I have been working with you. Karl's business empire, as you know only too well, is entirely under Russian mafiya control. Madame Nina and Kudishkin have warned my husband about me and ordered him not to reveal to me his knowledge of my Stasi or KGB work."

"But he did."

"No," she lied safely. "It was you who told me he knew, Nikolai. That is why I cannot trust him." She and her husband were allies, however, an island of self-interest interfacing Davidov's KGB, Fein's CIA, and Madame Nina's Feliks people in the search for a percentage of the sleeper's money.

Fein broke in. "How are you in cahoots with the sleeper in America?"

With her command of languages, Sirkka presumed "cahoots" was related to "cohort" and alluded to conspiracy among those of like interests. "Only indirectly. Through my work for Russian Foreign Intelligence, as Director Davidov knows, I became friendly with Mortimer Speigal of the Federal Reserve. We meet every year in January at the World Economic Forum in Davos, Switzerland. I am his channel to FI."

"He sends you inside stuff about the Fed's plans," asked Fein, "and you pass it on to the KGB?"

"In recent years, it has been to Russian Foreign Intelligence," she corrected him, because Davidov would know, "now separate from the KGB. I also handle the Russian payments to Speigal, in cash personally in Davos, as well as by transfers to his Swiss bank accounts."

Fein again: "Then is Speigal working for the Russian government, or for the sleeper in America?"

The reporter she assumed to be working for the CIA was getting to the heart of the matter; she could not safely deceive him with Davidov present. Nor could she deceive Davidov, with the CIA's Fein present, about her connection to the rogue operation in America run by the CIA mole Clauson and the sleeper. Her usual lines of duplicity were closed; it was smart of the rival agencies to join forces to elicit what she knew.

Sirkka took refuge in the truth: "Mort is working for both," she answered. That was the first time she betrayed a fellow agent, but she had no choice, because the KGB, by Davidov's presence at this interrogation, approved; he would have to fight the bureaucratic battle with FI. "Speigal was originally recruited by the KGB in the mid-eighties. Ever since, in one channel, he has been a useful source about the economic plans of the American government to Soviet and then Russian planners."

"Tell us about the other channel," Davidov ordered. "Outside the KGB."

She tried to buy a little time. "Why not ask your CIA friend here? Mr. Fein knows all about the other channel."

"Don't play games," said Fein, jet-lagged eyes burning into her. "You're right on the edge of public exposure. Answer his goddam question and answer it straight."

She shrugged. "We now come to the CIA's cooperation with the sleeper Berensky to build the fortune."

"I thought so," Davidov said, giving Fein a cold look.

"I was contacted by Walter Clauson of the CIA just after I married Karl, in 1989," she said truthfully. "It was in Washington. Clauson knew of my Stasi and KGB work, and I thought at first he wanted to turn me, have me report back to Russia what the Americans wanted sent back. But he had somthing more complex in mind than making me a double agent."

They waited. She was puzzled by the reporter's interest, which did not seem feigned. Did the CIA's Fein not know this already? Perhaps it was compartmentalized and he was not in the compartment. She looked to Davidov: "You are ordering me to tell him about Walter Clauson?" It would mean betraying a second agent.

At Davidov's nod, she said, "A nod of the head is not sufficient. I am sure you are recording this, and you will have to say your order out loud."

"What did Clauson say to you when he made contact?"

She felt his verbalization to be a small victory, although he could cut it out of the tape. "Clauson revealed himself to me as a Soviet agent inside the CIA."

"Oh-shit," whispered Fein. He looked at Davidov: "Is she telling the truth?"

"About that, yes." Davidov told her to continue.

"Clauson said he knew of the Soviet sleeper agent in America who had been given three billion in gold to invest. He also said he knew—

either through the KGB or the CIA, I don't know which—of the Soviet mole in the Fed, Speigal."

Davidov wanted to know if the sleeper and the Fed mole—Soviet agents in the U.S.—knew the other's identity; she said no, which was true. "Clauson was the only bridge between the mole and the sleeper," she said. "And he said nothing to the CIA or KGB."

"A double double cross," said Fein, still shaking his head as if all this were news to him. She assumed the reporter's thunderstruck demeanor was all a charade. "Beautiful. So Clauson had this great idea to make a bundle."

"Walter Clauson had a daring plan to set up a separate operation—a rogue operation, if you will." If their intent was to test her reliability, she would surprise them with the truth. "Speigal at the Fed would supply the inside information on the American side. I would supply the economic intelligence from the KGB side. And Berensky, the sleeper, would use the data to invest the Communist Party money to generate one hundred billion dollars in assets."

"And who would get the jackpot at the end?" Fein asked.

"I always presumed it would be you, the CIA," she said with care. "Or split up among the CIA and FBI and KGB and FI, which would fund their operations for years. But I don't know the arrangement Clauson and Berensky made among the agencies."

Fein asked if she had heard from Speigal lately. "Not since he sent me the fax that made possible our coup on interest rates," she replied. "I suppose he's entitled to a few weeks off."

"And Clauson?"

"Sometimes months go by and I don't hear from him." Why was he asking this? Had they been turned? If so, what were they saying about her?

"And the sleeper?"

Time for a lie, not checkable. "The first time I met him was with the both of you, at the literary agent's dinner party." She remembered watching the quick, casual encounter of the sleeper with his unknowing daughter and shook her head in wonderment at the memory. "That was some party."

Davidov's turn. "Did you exchange any words with the man who called himself Dominick privately that night?"

"No." True.

"Hard to believe. You were his colleague in a rogue operation for years, and when you find yourself in a room together, you gave no hint of recognition?"

"Of course not, Nikolai. The KGB rule is never to speak unless spoken to by an undercover superior. You're trying to trick me. I cannot be tricked because I am sticking to the truth."

"You told me before," said Davidov, "that you believed Edward Dominick was not just pretending to be Berensky, but was actually him. Did you ever deal directly with the sleeper?"

"No. Clauson is my cutout."

"Has Speigal of the Fed ever met him?"

"No. The only person who deals directly with the sleeper is Clauson." She turned to Fein. "And recently, you. You dealt with him all the time, in his role as Edward Dominick. And you forwarded the message to me from Speigal—that fax I passed on to the sleeper's brokers—and it led to the biggest currency trading profit ever. Isn't that the truth?"

"I know what I know," the stone-faced Fein replied. "I want to know what you know. And I don't like the way you've been diddling us."

"What means 'diddling'?"

"It means to gently raise and lower the male genitalia."

"Very colorful." She decided the moment had come to take offense and push back. "The truth, gentlemen, is that I have been working for the KGB for nearly a decade on a penetration of the Federal Reserve. You, Davidov, know that. At the same time, I have been working with the CIA since the fall of the Soviet Union on its profitable operation with the traitorous sleeper to finance the Agency for years to come. You, Fein, surely know that."

That was the truth as far as it directly affected each of them and their organizations; her separate activity with her husband in Riga to get a cut of the fortune was strictly the private business of the von Schwebels.

She heard the public address system voice in Finnish and told them coldly, "They are calling the Riga flight. Because your two agencies have decided to work together, you have been able to force me to betray two men I deeply respect. I have given you Walter Clauson, one of the great minds in espionage, and Mort Speigal, who has become my good friend. I hope you are satisfied."

"I presume you intend to warn them they have been compromised," said Davidov. "Do not."

"They have no place to run to," Fein added. "I will conduct their interrogation and we will see how much of what you told us is true."

She picked up her pocketbook and pulled her rollaway bag out into the corridor without a bon voyage. They had squeezed her hard, and she had been forced to reveal much, because the combination of KGB and CIA interrogators was like a nutcracker on a double agent. At least they did not associate her with the death of the private banker in Bern.

She wondered if she should try to get a message to the sleeper; perhaps Berensky/Dominick could warn Clauson and Speigal, or put them out of their misery.

"Class act," said Irving.

"Lies with a nice intricacy," Davidov replied, "like a fine oriental rug."

"You ever tie into that, Niko?"

The context made the American's colloquial meaning clear, and Davidov replied obliquely, "We were friends once." Not so; Finns were tough for Russians, even as fellow agents; he had tried to breach that Mannerheim Line and been thrown back with such adroitness and good humor that he was unsure to this day if he had been permanently rejected. "The man who has dominated her life has been the sleeper, and it is difficult to imagine they dealt with each other only from afar. I would put that on your dunno sheet, along with the true identity of the sleeper."

"Lookit, I understand if you don't trust me. I gave you a bum steer on Dominick last time. I have since found out from Viveca that my boy Eddie is damn well Berensky, and I was a horse's ass."

To confirm his suspicion about Berensky's self-impersonation had been Davidov's purpose in providing Irving with the address in Arizona so valuable to him. "How did Viveca find out?"

"The hard way. Nibbled the wrong ear."

A slipup at an intimate moment; Davidov was surprised that the sleeper had let himself get caught that way. "At least he didn't kill her, the way he did Clauson." The death of the CIA official had not been announced, and apparently Sirkka thought he was still alive, but Davidov's Washington sources were alert. "I liked the way you let Sirkka continue to believe Clauson is among the living." He concluded his compliment with "Even if you had to confirm you are a CIA operative."

"Confirm, conshmirm. Believe what you like."

"I take it that Speigal is also no longer working for Russian Foreign Intelligence."

"No freebies," said Fein. "You got something to trade? Like—was Clauson really a Soviet mole in the CIA? Or is Sirkka von Schwebel making it all up?"

"Walter Clauson was a KGB mole in the CIA for more than twenty years until Berensky killed him last month."

Long, head-in-hands take by the reporter. "Twenty years. Then he fooled Angleton, even. Our own little Philby."

"He fooled you, too?"

"Suckered me to a fare-thee-well. I came to Clauson, a pretty good source over the years, with a lead on the sleeper story. Who knew he was a mole? And not your run-of-the-mill mole, but one who had gone into business with the sleeper in a little private project to rip off the whole world?" Irving looked slightly ill as the extent and import of his gullibility sank in. "So when I gave him my great idea for an impersonator, he protected his operation by sending me to the sleeper himself. They had total control."

"Don't flagellate yourself," Davidov told him, tending to believe his story. "It happened to be the luck of the world's greatest reporter to have as a source the world's greatest double agent, who happened to be in business with the world's greatest sleeper agent. Of course they penetrated your operation and turned you without your knowing it. It was second nature to Clauson. And Berensky has been a splendid actor all his life."

"Gotta find out why Dominick—Berensky, that is—killed old Walt. That's a loose end."

"A fundamental difference in motivation, of course." Davidov enjoyed being the instructor's instructor; the world of rational journalism could never keep pace with the world of empiric espionage in epistemological constructs. "Clauson set up the rogue operation for the straightforward purpose of making an enormous fortune, to be shared with the sleeper, with a small percentage to Speigal and Sirkka. But Berensky was in the plot to assemble a fortune for a political purpose and to justify his life's work. The essential interests of the two men were in conflict from the start. In the end, one had to kill the other."

"Yeah, but Clauson was the go-between for leaks from the Fed. Berensky didn't know Mort Speigal from Adam. Clauson was the cutout, which was his life insurance policy."

Davidov made a guess. "There came a moment when Berensky made a direct connection to Sirkka, and through her closed his circuit to the mole at the Fed, Speigal. At that moment, Clauson was a dead man."

"You're only guessing," said Fein, "but you're a good guesser. When I get back to Langley, I'm going to have a little chat with the DCI and maybe arrange for her rapid retirement."

"Too bad. You respect Dorothy Barclay, I take it."

"Lookit. I know it looks like I am in the CIA's pocket on this, and they jerked me around pretty good, but I'm not an agent or an asset. I was hooked in by Clauson."

"How did he hook you?"

Irving gave that some thought. "The blind tip that started me on this, left on my message machine. Said I should check with one of the old Angleton types. That drew me to Clauson, because he was the only logical one I'd call. He sent me that tip, to get me to call him. I was suckered."

"That is believable."

"It doesn't mean there's no wall between spooks and reporters. Do you believe me about that, too?"

"I do."

Fein squinted at him. "Why?"

"I am, as your dossier on me explains, an epistemic logician. Your employment by the CIA makes so much logical sense that it becomes illogical. Real life is rarely so symmetrical."

"Cut the shit, Niko. Why do you believe me?"

"Because I am not authorized to deal with the CIA directly on this matter. But the Chief Directorate authorized me to deal with the press. By accepting your protestations that you are a pure journalist, not a

CIA agent or asset, I protect my bureaucratic position back home." If anything would have the ring of truth to it, that would.

Davidov listened to the airport loudspeaker making a last call for the plane to Riga. "This has become a conversation all in Column B, for your benefit," he said. "Now for me—what's become of Mortimer Speigal?" He suspected the FBI had caught the Fed mole and the CIA was blocking a prosecution in the hope of turning him. Davidov could not allow his newly expanded economic counterintelligence unit to appear to be misled by disinformation.

"I shook him up with a few questions," Fein replied, "and he blew his head off with his handy-dandy .38. Didn't like publicity or something. Then I changed his message to Sirkka from a buy to a sell. I thought that would cost Berensky a bundle, but the Fed Chairman changed his mind at the last minute and so the message I sent along made megabucks. Gigabucks."

That was like a shortwave burst from an agent behind the lines. Davidov permitted himself to blink. After he separated out its dramatic components, the Russian considered the implications of Fein's revelation. With Speigal dead, and Sirkka blocked, and his cutout Clauson removed, Berensky was cornered. Very rich and thus powerful, the sleeper was no longer anonymous and no longer the possessor of the infallible crystal ball. The flushed-out spy would have to make his decision and cast his lot with either Moscow or the mafiya right away.

The KGB man judged that illumination by the reporter to be a fair return on his investment in Irving of the information about Clauson's molehood. "What bothers me," Davidov said to his fellow traveler on the journey to the fortune, "is that Berensky now has a clear field in Riga. All he has to do is prove to Madame Nina's politburo that he is who he is, and show good faith by turning over a sample of his assets. Then he'll be able to take over the major criminal authorities in Russia and most of the near abroad, along with a large part of the KGB and Foreign Intelligence. And if he promises to pay the army veterans a pension with a piece of his billions, Berensky could move right into the Kremlin."

"I say we accompany Sirkka to Riga."

Davidov produced two tickets. "That has been my plan."

He had no plan, only several options dependent on the sleeper's state of mind, which he hoped was undecided. Perhaps he could appeal to the practical side of Berensky's patriotism, advocating the investment in a vital capitalist infrastructure. Or there might be a way of driving a wedge between Madame Nina and Berensky, assuming a natural rivalry for the leadership of the Feliks people. Failing that, Colonel Nikolai Andreyevich Davidov had been invested from the start with the authority to terminate the longtime KGB sleeper operation with what the Americans once were said to call "extreme prejudice," a nice euphemism for execution. The best outcome of his quest was to return the fortune to the treasury of the legitimate Russian government; the fallback goal was to deny it, at any cost, to the force that would use its vast resources to oust the present government and perhaps destabilize the world.

They nodded cheerfully to a surprised Sirkka on the plane and squeezed into a pair of seats three rows behind her.

Irving, fastening his belt, startled him with "You got the hots for Liana, huh?" Davidov did not react, which did not stop his seatmate. "Lemme give you some advice. She's a reporter. You ever have the hots for a girl reporter before?"

"No," the KGB man replied, careful to give little away. "I have never had the hots for a woman journalist."

"You can insult 'em, you can run 'em ragged, you can browbeat 'em, you can steal 'em blind. They lap it up, makes 'em feel like one of the guys." He wriggled around. "How do these commie seat belts work?"

Davidov reached over and clicked the Russian-made buckle into place. When Irving seemed to lose his train of thought, Davidov said, "They lap it up."

"Yeah. But double-cross 'em on a story and you're a shit in their eyes for the rest of your life. And they'll keep after you till they run you into the ground. Now here we are, you and I, with the knowledge that Liana is the sleeper's daughter, which she doesn't know."

"And we are now certain that the sleeper is Edward Dominick, which she also does not know."

"She's gonna find out pretty soon, maybe from her pappy himself, because she's hungry, like a reporter has to be. And then it'll hit Liana that we knew all along and didn't tell her. That's gonna piss her off at me—which is too bad, I like the kid—but it's gonna knock you clean out of the ring, if you get what I mean."

"I take your point," Davidov said, familiar with the boxing metaphor. He resolved to inform Liana at the first opportunity, or at least to use the sleeper's daughter in such a way as not to let her think he had betrayed her trust, such as it was. "From your generous advice, I take it that your own hots are directed to the woman in Arizona."

"That murdering sumbitch loverboy Dominick broke her spirit, that and the way everybody in her miserable fucking world of backstabbing bastards piled on." He concluded his outburst with a sigh. "No family loyalty, the way print reporters have, or used to. I think about Viveca a lot. I think about her all the time, for crissake."

Davidov, who still discounted much of what Fein had said, and had been unable to get an explanation of the "fireflies" reference out of him, detected a note of sincerity in that. He would have felt sympathy for the man defeated for the affection of his beloved by a skilled seducer, were it not for his rage at Fein's almost casual conquest of the woman Davidov thought about constantly. "Surely Viveca Farr was encouraged by your visit."

"When I tried to tell her to cheer up, she went into a deep funk. Here's some good advice about handling depressed women, Niko: never tell 'em to cheer up. Never offer a smidgin of optimism, because they take that as proof you despise their beloved despair."

"Maybe she isn't cut out for the reporting busines," Davidov offered.

"She's not. Not everybody is. But she's still entitled to a life." His head back and eyes closed to take a nap, the American asked out of the blue, yawning: "Was Nosenko a dangle?"

Davidov recalled what he had read about that defection of thirty years ago. CIA counterintelligence worried that Yuri Nosenko had been sent over as a false defector to reassure the Americans that the KGB had had no part in the Kennedy assassination. Davidov had pulled that file out for possible sale before being visited by Ace McFarland in Moscow; in it was a statement that of all defectors, the one Director Andropov most wanted to see dead was Nosenko. Now, that would suggest that Nosenko was a real defector, handing over damaging information about the KGB; but the other possibility was that he was a successful dangle and the KGB Director was worried he might some-day be broken. Such limits to certainty were at the heart of epistemology, mankind's sustained attempt to push the envelope of knowledge about knowledge.

"No freebies," the KGB man parroted. A few minutes later, as Irving began to snore, Nikolai said, "The files contain proof that Nosenko was a real defector, not a dangle." He could not be sure that Irving's snoring was not a deception, but he presumed that the reporter—if aware and falsely snoring—could not be sure the KGB official was not aware of that.

Chapter 54

"You need an ally," Karl von Schwebel told him. "You cannot go into this alone."

"I always like to have allies," Dominick responded cordially. "I'm a born coalition-builder."

"Be serious." The media baron—a bogus title to which he never objected—saw an opportunity to position himself near the center of the largest financial arrangement in history. "First, I have to know—are you actually Berensky, as my wife believes? Or are you a remarkably skillful impersonator, as I believe? Or are you both, if that's possible?"

"My name is Edward Dominick. I'm a Memphis, Tennessee, banker, and I'm told you own the company I hired to protect me from snoopers. The way I figure it, that means I have no secrets from you."

"You are telling me that you are indeed the impersonator," said von Schwebel, trying to fix a position without losing momentum, "working with Fein and probably the CIA to find the assets the real sleeper has amassed."

"You're free to draw whatever inference you like, my friend." Dominick, seated comfortably in his hotel suite, was giving nothing away; von Schwebel, who came equipped with an electronic device to jam any transmitters or recorders, was not to be so easily put off.

"You don't seem to realize that your life is hanging by a thread." The German let that statement lie there unadorned.

After a moment, Dominick—Berensky/Dominick—said, "You've got my attention, Karl. Who's out to get me?"

"Both sides. The Feliks people headquartered here, if they come to believe you are an impostor, are prepared to kill you. There is some talk of trading you for the chief Chechen murderer, now being held by the KGB, but frankly Chechens are cheap."

"You said both sides."

"And Davidov of the KGB is prepared to order your elimination—if he believes you are the real sleeper about to transfer the assets to what he calls the mafiya."

The visitor from Memphis smiled, impressing the German as a man who enjoyed the most perilous predicament. "Then I could sure use an ally, as you say. What can you do for me?"

"Provide you with information that might save your life. Of equal importance, I can support your bona fides as the sleeper to the Feliks organization. That will help you make your deal." He noted that the Memphis man had dropped his pose of nonchalance and was at last showing a serious interest. "That involves considerable risk to me, as the fate of a fellow named Arkady Volkovich shows. When I take such a risk, I expect a handsome return."

"Tell me first who is saying what about me here."

Von Schwebel was prepared to put a sample on the table. "I have reported to Madame Nina, and to the board that calls itself the politburo, that you are an impostor, that your operation is a CIA front. That puts you in danger with them." With some relish, the media owner revealed the range of his usefulness: "My wife, Sirkka, with whom the sleeper has had contact through an intermediary, believes you are the true Berensky, and has so informed Davidov. That puts you in danger from the KGB, because it convinces them that you can deliver the fortune to whomever you choose."

"You married well. It's helpful when a husband and wife can agree to disagree, and work both sides of the street. On your side, what other reports are coming in to the Feliks people about me?"

"I take it you want to know what sort of an impression you made on your first wife at Claridge's."

"That would be valuable to me," Dominick acknowledged.

"More than valuable," the German pressed. "It is central to your credibility. If she has reported you are her husband, you must appear contrite at leaving her. If she has accused you of being an impostor, you must recall to the committee her hatred and jealousy."

"Do you know what she played back to Madame Nina?"

"Yes."

"And you are prepared to vouchsafe that to me?"

"If you make my wife and me your junior partners."

"How junior?"

"Five percent, if you are the sleeper himself. Or five billion dollars, whichever is larger. For the active help of the two of us."

Dominick did not blink at that. "And what if I am not Berensky?"

"One-third of whatever brokerage you get from the real sleeper. I presume your take would be a large fraction of the sleeper's assets."

"Three percent of the first, if I am the real sleeper, or one-fourth of the second, if I am the impostor-broker," the Memphis man offered, maintaining the mystery of his identity. Then he added qualifiers: "Payable when and as I make the transfer, provided I am alive and free. And nothing in writing; you'll have to trust me, as everyone always has."

The German extended his hand, and Dominick or Berensky shook it firmly. "That gives me a great interest in your continued good health." He did not know which name to call him, so he used neither.

"Here's what I need, Karl. Get Sirkka to change her story to Davidov. Get her to shake his present certainty that I am Berensky, and to at least allow for the possibility I am not the real sleeper. That may require Sirkka to get very close to Davidov, and quickly."

He was issuing orders to employees; von Schwebel, with the price right, understood and accepted that. "I will leave her means to accomplish that mission to her discretion," he replied; his wife would do what an attractive female double agent sometimes had to do.

"Now tell me what Antonia Krumins reported about her meeting in London with her former husband."

"This will surprise and displease you," von Schwebel reported, now that his loyalty ran to a new center of power. "Madame Nina reported she debriefed the woman herself. She told the board last night that Mrs. Krumins said you were not—repeat not—Aleks Berensky. That you came well prepared with family secrets, and some of your physical characteristics were well rehearsed, but that you were an actor, not her husband."

That seemed not to surprise him. "You're sure? Maybe Madame Nina's lying."

"That's possible. But nobody's going to challenge her."

"You will. I am positive that damned woman was certain I was Aleks Berensky."

"Maybe she was, but lied to Madame Nina. Woman scorned, and all that." After turning that possibility over in his mind, von Schwebel rejected it. "Madame Nina would see through that. She's a shrewd judge of character, and dominates the board by her command presence. Nobody dares lie to her." He was prepared to do precisely that, but the reward was enormous.

"What could I have done wrong?" Dominick shook his head, irritated at himself. "I'll just have to turn it around tonight. Will you be there?"

"I'll be consulted beforehand, in the wine cellar where the meetings are held. It is vital that you and I keep our stories coordinated. You and I had this meeting today. I am asking you about your holdings in the media, as a test to see if you are the real sleeper. Can you give me a sample?"

"You found out I own a shell in the Antilles that controls the Dresdener Creditbank, which holds all the mortgages on the properties of Satellvision."

Von Schwebel had been trying to buy that multinational and knew its considerable assets in stations and production facilities. "That company even owns the best television station here in Riga," he noted.

"I know. I wanted to make sure nobody blocked my daughter Liana's career."

"Then you really are the sleeper?"

"If I answered that, brother Karl, would you believe me?"

Von Schwebel shook his head no. "I have a firm principle, which has guided me to a position of great power in the world of international business. I firmly believe what it is most profitable for me to believe at any given moment."

Dominick—von Schwebel still thought of him as that—consulted his watch and asked him to stop in the bar downstairs and send up Liana, who was expected about that hour. The media baron could not remember the last time he had been dismissed and sent on an errand by anyone other than Madame Nina, but the prospect of a payoff perhaps in the billions induced even in him the sweetest humility. He now had two bosses, but that clash of interests could not last long.

Liana finally had the answer to Irving Fein's why-me. She ordered a black balsams and sat nursing the Latvian drink, trying to digest the personal revelation that Nikolai had just given her.

Did Irving know, too, that she had been chosen by both the KGB and the Feliks people as the favored reporter because she was the daughter of Aleksandr Berensky, and was not, as she had believed all her life, the natural daughter of Ojars Krumins? Davidov would not say. He, at least, had a reason for keeping the secret from her; she was his "bait." But she felt strongly that Irving, if he knew, should have trusted her; they were working on this story together.

She shook off that minor resentment, a ripple in the roiling emotions churned up by the revelation. One fact was that she was a Russian, on both sides, not half Latvian, half Russian as she had always believed. It might affect her citizenship status. An even more important fact to deal with was that she had a living father.

She had met him and not known it; how could that be? At Matthew McFarland's dinner party, the man who went by the name of Edward Dominick had never approached her for a direct talk, though he must have known her relationship to him. She had seen no physical resemblance; she had felt no sense of kinship. That struck her as incredible; a person should get some kind of strange feeling, a premonition or sixth sense of family, in the presence of a natural father.

Beyond that new fact of paternal presence was its terrible political circumstance: he had been working all his long adult life for a regime she had been working all her short adult life to defeat. He was even now dealing with the apparatchiks and criminals who would end democratic reform in Russia and perhaps reannex the Baltics and all the other near abroad.

She had to reexamine who she was. Liana Krumins, Latvian nationalist, anticommunist dissident since her early teens, discovered herself to be the granddaughter of Aleksandr Shelepin, last of the old-line internal security chieftains, a bloodily repressive line that had begun in Lenin's time with "Iron Feliks" Dzerzhinsky. She knew she should be politically ashamed of her lineage, but she could not help feeling a curious new sense of pride in those rapacious roots. Why had her good-communist mother said nothing all these years? Had she so despised the husband who had deserted them that it had become an obsession corroding her life and ultimately her attachment to her daughter? She felt a new rush of distaste for the unsmiling woman who had frozen her daughter out of her life, reviled Liana's revolutionary ardor, and cruelly withheld the truth about her parentage.

She was startled out of these thoughts when the stuffy German media magnate—the one married to the brilliant Finnish economist whom Liana had admired at the dinner party—came up to her in the cocktail lounge, reintroduced himself, and said that Mr. Dominick awaited her in his suite. She hoisted her leather backpack and went to what she knew would be the most significant interview of her life.

"Now let me really look at you." His hands gripped her shoulders. His gray eyes were more familiar to her, now that she knew who he was; like her own eyes, but his face was not. "You are fortunate, Masha. You look more like your mother than me."

"Who are you?" she demanded. Davidov's opinion was one thing; Liana wanted to hear the news from the source.

"I am Aleksandr Berensky. Your father."

She started to cry, which was not the reaction she had had in mind at all. Mortified at her display of weakness, she looked away and started to rummage in her knapsack for a handkerchief or a notebook. He touched her stubbly hair but did not embrace her.

She brought herself under control quickly and asked, "Are you the sleeper agent that the KGB says you are?"

"I have been a Soviet agent in the United States for more than twenty years, yes. I am proud to say I have served my country well."

"And what of the man who was supposed to be helping my journalist friends find the sleeper by impersonating him?"

"That was a trick. An undercover colleague, a man named Walter Clauson, who was for many years a Soviet mole in the CIA, sent your friends to me. By the device of impersonating myself, we were able to keep full control of the pursuit."

"I suppose you are proud of that, too."

"Masha—may I call you that?—my assignment is my life. I gave up everything for it—your mother, you, my life in Russia, my real identity. I pledged my life to my father, Shelepin, your grandfather. And now his vision, and my sacrifice, has given us an amazing opportunity."

"Us? Whose side are you on? What do you represent?" She reminded herself she was a journalist and this was a world-class story, and wondered if she would inhibit him by taking notes. She decided not to; she would write down all she could remember when she left.

"That is what I have been trying to find out," he told her. "I was sent to America by my father—your grandfather, I repeat—the last truly visionary chief of the KGB. I was later entrusted with three billion dollars in gold by strong communist leaders when they saw the apostles of weakness and division taking over. I created an operation to run that up to a massive fortune for worthy political purposes—to stop the Kremlin's slide into chaos, to bring disciplined central government back to Moscow, and to recapture the lost territory of the Soviet Union."

"Including independent Latvia." He was the enemy. "I will expose you and fight you." Though his ideas were frightening, as a person he did not strike her as a hater and a bully.

"I told you my purposes. That was a few years ago. Now, before I deliver this economic power, I must make a new assessment." He seemed sincerely concerned about the impact of his actions. She reminded herself to be wary, but to keep an open mind about him. "I want to hear your opinion about the near abroad. And I want to find out firsthand, from Madame Nina and her colleagues, how they would use the assets I hold in trust. I am not turning them over to a group of greedy capitalists allied with street gangsters, if that is what the 'Feliks people' really are. What do you know, for example, of Madame Nina?"

"She is a mystery. Arkady, rest his soul, said none of them knew her background. She appeared at the beginning of the breakup of the Soviet Union and began rallying the underground antireform forces. He said she rules by the power of her personality and by her ruthlessness—even the Chechens and the Ingush don't cross her."

"Is she a political leader, or our own Russian brand of mafiya godmother? That would make all the difference to me."

"Mr. Dominick—"

"You may call me Father, if you wish."

She veered away from her question to set him straight: "No man who deserts his wife and unborn child deserves to be called Father."

"Aleksandr Aleksandrovich, then," he amended quickly. A patronymic was neutral and not formal. "So, then—you are as angry at me as your mother."

"I can never forgive you for putting the State before your own flesh and blood. It is brutal, inhuman. Your former wife is right about that."

"I saw her last week."

"Don't tell me about it. I have no interest in Antonia Krumins at all."

"I notice you don't call her Mama. Why does she call you a whore?"

"She hates my politics, and my style of life, and me."

"And you feel the same way."

"I pity that woman."

"But not enough to reach out to her."

That was exasperating. "Who are you to preach family loyalty?"

He gave the short, stifled laugh best described as a chuckle, which to her was his most endearing sound. "You're right—I have no credentials as a husband and father at all. Still, it seems to me that your abandonment of her and her disgust with you are not all that different from my desertion of the both of you. At least I had a patriotic motive."

She changed the subject. "Why did you want to identify yourself to me after all these years? You must have a selfish reason, or what a professional spy would call a patriotic reason."

He rose and went to the window looking across the river and park toward Latvia's Freedom Monument. "To business, then. First, do you have any doubt in your mind that I am your father, Aleks Berensky?"

"I have a feeling you are," she answered truthfully; his eyes now reminded her a little of what she saw every day in the mirror. "But I can't say for certain. Only your former wife"—the words "my mother" did not come naturally to her—"would know that."

"That is precisely my problem. Your dear mother hates me, Masha, even more than she despises you, which is to say a lot. We have that problem with her in common, you and I." He looked at her and added, "Just as we share a certain inner toughness."

"I will do nothing for you, Aleksandr Aleksandrovich."

"Yes, you will. Not because I am your father, but because I have a great story for you. One that will astound Irving Fein and Viveca Farr and all the journalists in the world. But you will have to earn it."

Liana felt a surge of anger at his treatment of her as a child. "What would I have to do?"

"Here is the deal, daughter of mine. I will supply to you a complete list of the assets, nearly one hundred billion dollars, of the sleeper operation. I have prepared a step-by-step account of how it was amassed. It's in a diary I placed in your name in a bank box, the number of which you will need. Complete with the sort of anecdotes and twists and human-interest revelations that all you journalists hold dear."

She waited for what he wanted from her; if it required the betrayal of her country, she would walk out and never see him again.

"What I want of you is the truth from your mother. She knows full well I am myself; she has no doubt I am Aleks Berensky, her husband. But out of that perversity and hatred that consume her life—and you are well aware of that, Masha—she has lied to Madame Nina. She has told them I am an impostor. This will make it impossible for me to find out about their operation, to judge for myself if the Feliks people are worthy of the fruits of Shelepin's vision."

"Her lie will also endanger your life," she pointed out.

"That, too. And if anything should happen to me, tonight or years from now, call Michael Shu at my Memphis bank immediately. Sometime after you met him here, I confided in him, and now he's the executor of my will." She had liked the innocent-appearing Shu; could he have been seduced by the sleeper's billions to betray Irving Fein? Perhaps her father was lying to her. "But focus on this," he was saying. "I am asking you to go and confront your mother. Demand from her, as you did from me, the truth about your parenthood. And then find out why she is lying about me to the Feliks organization."

She knew from experience with Davidov, another man who professed to feel close to her, what the spy had in mind. "And here in my amber pendant," she said, fingering the jewelry once used to invade her privacy, "you will place a tiny transmitter."

He appeared surprised at her espionage sophistication, and nodded. "I am not asking you to lie. Get the truth from Antonia Krumins. In return, you will get the full truth about the sleeper from me—including a justification for necessarily violent acts."

"Like murders, you mean."

"Acts of self-defense in an affair of state. What is being a good reporter, Masha, but getting all the facts and putting them together into the truth? Irving Fein—a reporter I have come to admire even as I duped him on a grand scale—will be both jealous and proud of you."

Liana knew that she was being manipulated by her father. But how could getting the truth be wrong? And why should she be any less demanding of her mother than her father in finding out her true parentage?

But that was thinking like a daughter, not a role she relished. Thinking like a reporter, she asked herself what she would tell Irving Fein of this interview, and tried to anticipate his criticism of the questions she had failed to ask.

She tried one that she thought would shake her father's composure. "You mentioned acts of self-defense. Did you kill your handler in Barbados?"

"No. He blew himself up with a bomb he intended for me."

"Did you murder Walter Clauson?"

"Yes." The response was unhesitating. "For the same reason I ordered the killing of a banker in Switzerland. Both tried to take control of my operation for their own ends. To them, money became more important than country, and I had to retain the power—the fortune—to achieve my purpose. Clauson told me the impersonation scheme was necessary to control the journalist who had come to him with a tip about the sleeper agent. I suspect Clauson arranged to place an anonymous tip in Fein's ear, knowing Irving was likely to check it out with him."

"Irving Fein is not going to be happy to learn of that."

"In a way, he will, just as Angleton was entranced as well as embittered at the way Philby manipulated him. Clauson had a brilliantly deceitful mind. When I discovered he was manipulating me, contesting control of the fortune, I had no choice but to arrange his death." He breathed deeply. "That is on 'deep background,' as Fein likes to say. Never attribute it to me."

She thought of the night in Syracuse, watching with Irving as a woman reporter working closely with him ruined her career. "Did you drug Viveca Farr?"

"Yes." With these terrible admissions, he was earning her trust as he was turning her stomach. "She found out after a moment of passion that I was truly hard of hearing, and she suddenly knew I was the real sleeper, not an impersonator. But Viveca loved me and I did not want to kill her. I put a chemical with a timed release in her wine at dinner before taking her to her studio."

"You knew how her life would be ruined by the public humiliation. It was a horrible thing to do."

"But she's alive. It effectively took her off the board at a critical time. I hope to make it up to her one day." He seemed suddenly irritated with himself for his long-windedness in justification. "Well, then. As your grandfather would say, the house is burning and the clock is ticking. Get the truth about me from your mother. And to be useful," he said, attaching the usual device to her amber pendant, "that truth has to come from her lips within two hours."

"I have not seen Mama in five years. Does she live at the same address?"

She ran the three blocks to the Tower café, where Irving and Nikolai were waiting for her.

"He killed Clauson and drugged Viveca and will give me all the details on the fortune if I can get my mother to tell the mafiya tonight that he is really Berensky." She was out of breath.

"Full disclosure is hardly in his interest," said the KGB man.

"If you help Berensky sell Madame Nina on his bona fides," Irving explained, "and he makes a deal with them, he'll double-cross you in a minute. And it's goodbye to Baltic independence."

They did not feel her sense of revelation and did not understand the urgency of her father's need. "You're both wrong. He is tired of all this, and he won't betray his own daughter."

"You cannot be sure of that," from Nikolai.

"He's using you, kiddo," from Irving.

"So what?" She gave Irving Fein a quick lesson in Latvian journalism: "I'll get a part of the story at least, and he won't kill me or drug me. I will have the names of the banks and the companies and the buildings he owns, and you can write your story after you hear it on my program." She turned on Nikolai. "Your eavesdropping truck—can it pick up this transmitter from Mama's apartment?"

The KGB's representative nodded yes. She grabbed her knapsack and ran out.

"You suppose she'll turn her old lady's opinion around?" Irving was doubtful; if he had been a wife left high and dry with a hungry brat, he would want to stick it to the errant spouse when he came crawling back asking for a big favor.

Davidov shook his head no, and tapped a finger on his cellular phone. "Antonia Krumins is not at her apartment. Left an hour ago. Didn't go to the ballet school, either, which will be Liana's next stop."

"Where'd she go? Your guys follow her?"

"Of course. The woman is right here, in this restaurant. Either upstairs, in one of the private rooms, or downstairs in the basement, where the Feliks politburo will interrogate Berensky. Where Berensky thinks he will cross-examine them."

Irving licked his lips in satisfaction; the exercise of running around aimlessly would take Liana down a peg. "I'm still pissed off about Mike Shu," he said.

The reporter was against eavesdropping in principle, but could see why lawmen and spooks swore by it. Fein and Davidov had been unable to hear what von Schwebel said in Berensky's hotel room—Davidov said the German was probably carrying a jammer—but the sleeper's subsequent conversation with his daughter had come through loud and clear. And the words that shook up Irving Fein had to do with his right-hand man: "If anything should happen to me . . . call Michael Shu. . . . I confided in him, and now he's the executor of my will."

Now that was a hell of a note. The one person Irving Fein trusted in the world was not his mother, his lawyer, his agent, or his partner on this story wandering off in the desert—but his accountant, Mike Shu. They'd been through the media wars together. The young Eurasian knew exactly how much Irving had cheated on his expense accounts a few years ago, and when the IRS audited, Mike had kept his lip zipped at no little personal risk. He was straight that way. This was the man who had been "confided in" and had become the executor of Berensky's estate in the sleeper's will? That meant he might have been working for Dominick all along, and maybe for Clauson before that. Was Mike a wide-eyed innocent who had been corrupted by avarice toward the end, or was he a bit player on the wrong side from the start? Irving felt the sand shifting beneath his castle of loyalties. He owed this Berensky bastard a few hard shots in print.

"Don't assume your accountant colleague betrayed you," cautioned Davidov. "Berensky must suspect his room is bugged. He may have sent back disinformation just to rattle you."

"Yeah, but he knows we know that. At this stage of the game, he can't think he's dealing with a couple of hayseeds who don't know from disinformation."

"That's just what he might expect you to be thinking, unless he thought you would anticipate that."

"James, Jesus, and—hey, look who's here," Irving said to the life-long commie so steeped in Ping-Pong deception he couldn't tell it was costing him his girl. He pointed to Karl and Sirkka von Schwebel, standing at the maître d's lectern, waiting to be seated for dinner. "Shall we blow their minds by asking them to join us? He can pick up our tab."

"It might be amusing. At some point, take him aside on some pretext and let me talk to Sirkka alone."

"Oh, Christ, look who's at that table in the back waving to us," said Sirkka.

"It's an opportunity," said her husband quickly. "Let's join them. You have to change your story to Davidov to protect Berensky."

"I absolutely convinced him two days ago that Dominick is the real sleeper. It's going to be hell to turn it all around."

"You won't have to. Just plant a seed of doubt, enough to give him pause in case he plans to take Berensky out. I'll do the opposite with Madame Nina after dinner, to protect our client with her." He pretended to look for the maître d'. "I give you permission to promise your old friend and colleague anything."

She froze inside.

"Jealousy is not in my nature," he went on quickly. "Throw yourself at him if you have to. Turn him around on Dominick. Nothing is more important."

"Thank you, Karl." The feeling of two-against-the-world in the hall of mirrors had been based on foolish sentiment; she despised herself for ever forgetting she was always destined to act as someone's agent.

Sirkka feigned surprise at seeing the Russian with the American. She waved, mouthed hello across the room, and said to her husband, "How are you going to separate Davidov from that boor so I can make my promises?"

"I'll think of something."

"And then we'll have to extricate ourselves to get downstairs to the meeting."

"We'll leave together and come back to the café later." They worked their way through the tables. "Ah, Nikolai," the media baron boomed. "We've caught you giving the KGB's secrets to the world's greatest reporter."

"Curious how they both wanted to go across the street for a cigar," Nikolai Davidov said to Sirkka Numminen von Schwebel. He marveled at her participation in the rump operation set up by Clauson and Berensky, even as she was officially an agent for FI. That did not make her a double, working for the enemy and subject to summary execution, but an agent engaged in what Americans colorfully called "moonlighting." He presumed Sirkka's primary loyalty still rested with Berensky, who had apparently enlisted her husband to help him establish bona fides with Madame Nina.

Davidov further speculated that Sirkka's present assignment was to protect the sleeper from harm. She could accomplish this in either of two ways: first, by getting her admiring acquaintance Nikolai to assign his KGB operatives illegally in Riga to intervene in any mafiya attempt on Berensky's life, should Madame Nina decide he was a fake. On the other hand, if Berensky appeared to be turning his assets over to the Feliks people, the resourceful Sirkka would be ready with a fallback position: somehow to prevail on Davidov and his KGB agents to refrain from killing a faithless Berensky. Of all the attitudes in the *Kama Sutra* of espionage, Davidov observed, none was as attractive as the fallback position.

"Irving Fein doesn't smoke," he said. "Does your husband?"

"Rarely. Cigars make him sick."

"Romantics, then. They wanted us to be alone together."

"Karl has urged me to promise you anything—my body, my soul—to plant a seed of doubt in your mind about Dominick being Berensky."

"You can keep your soul."

"My husband just showed me he does not think I have one."

Davidov had intended his remark as banter and was surprised at her flash of bitterness; an agent as experienced as Sirkka was not supposed to be afflicted with romantic notions. On the other hand, he was aware that his own feelings about Liana affected his handling of this case.

"You and your husband are working closely together," he observed, "to affect the outcome of this meeting tonight. Does Madame Nina think Dominick is an impostor?"

"She has every reason to. If Dominick were really Berensky, he would represent a threat to her control of the organization. The prodigal son returns and takes over. He has the money, and with the Feliks people, money is power and power is all. As I should never forget."

"What about the testimony of Antonia Krumins?" he asked. "Is she telling the truth in denying Dominick's validity as the sleeper? Will their politburo believe her?"

"I think she is telling what she thinks is the truth. I think they will believe the wife's opinion that he is an impostor, despite our testimony that he is the authentic sleeper. And that disbelief is what Madame Nina wants."

Davidov put himself in the Feliks people's shoes and made a judgment. "Then they will decide Dominick is an impostor, and hit him before he gets to the airport tomorrow. Or before he gets back to his hotel tonight."

"Isn't that what you would do, if you were the threatened leader? If you want Berensky's money for Russia, Nikolai Andreyevich, you'd better grab him while he's still alive."

Skillful. That was designed to protect the sleeper from KGB retaliation. He had wondered how Sirkka would accomplish her assignment from Berensky of protecting him from the fury of the Feliks people.

"First Berensky must see for himself that the Feliks apparat is just another underworld mob," Davidov said, just to make her job difficult. "If I took him in before that—assuming, as you say, Berensky and Dominick are one and the same—I would have a prisoner who would never talk. Another pauper in a Lubyanka cell. To transfer the tangled assets, the former sleeper must be ready to cooperate with us actively. Only he knows where everything is."

"You have his daughter."

"You don't know this man, Sirkka, though you have always been valuable to him. He is not merely focused, he is messianic. He would see his daughter die in agony before being diverted from his purpose."

Irving chewed on his unlit cigar and watched the multimedia mogul and his economist wife leave. "Where do you suppose the happy couple are headed, Niko?"

"Around the block and in the back way," the KGB man said. "The pre-meeting meeting is to start soon."

"You got it all rigged so we can listen right here?"

"No. Von Schwebel knows his tradecraft—sweeps, jamming, the electronic works. With Arkady dead, we have no way of knowing what is going on downstairs."

Irving frowned; that probably meant Davidov had a line in and didn't want to share the information with his trusted American comrade. He brightened when Liana came running in, her breath coming in gasps.

"Mama's not there. The neighbors didn't know where she went."

Davidov asked, "What about the dance studio?"

"Not there either." She sucked in air and ran her hand along her hair, back and forth, angrily. "I don't know where to look, and it's getting late. Irving, help me."

Forthright begging was the last, best refuge of a journalist; Irving was pleased that she turned to him. "She's right here in this building, kiddo. Been here all along. Your pal Niko here didn't want to tell us." That little jab was in payment for Niko's holding out on the surveillance.

"You're an evil man," she flashed at Davidov and ran for the stairs in the front of the restaurant.

"That was foolish," the KGB man told Fein. "Remember what happened to Arkady."

"She's the love of your life. Go save her. I'll watch your jacket."

That cost Davidov his cool. "You're a meddling idiot. You were fed a tip by Clauson and he reeled you in. You accepted his choice of an impersonator because you were too lazy to find one of your own. You danced to Berensky's tune for months, wasting time following blind alleys he suggested. You let Berensky turn your researcher, Shu, because you underestimate the seductive power of money. You let Berensky ruin your partner because she didn't return your hots. If you're the world's greatest reporter, God help journalism."

Irving contemplated the dry end of his tobacco lollipop. "But I'm here with a stringer upstairs getting the story. And you—big-shot spymaster, with goons at your disposal all over town—are sitting here, passive, not playing to win but only playing not to lose. You're praying your damn counter-jammer works and you're stupidly refusing to play ball with the one person in this whole deal who's not doubling on you."

The reporter was satisfied with his riposte, but Niko's shot about Viveca went home. Why hadn't he competed for the girl with Dominick from the start? He knew why: his assumption that he had no chance with her had driven him to make certain he would have no chance with her. That timidity had led to her needless endangerment. Irving wanted to make that up to her, and to himself, if she would let him.

Liana tried all the doorknobs in the upstairs rooms. Waiters were setting up for dinner, and some nail-biting British management consultants were placing charts on easels for some gathering of the Group of Fifty. In the ladies' lounge, a heavyset woman with iron-gray hair and thick glasses was sitting by herself, facing a faded lithograph on the wall, intently smoking a cigarette. Liana whirled, and setting her face grimly, barged into the men's room. This intrusion interrupted what she supposed was a homosexual liaison and she hurriedly slammed the door. Behind another door with an EMPLOYEES ONLY sign was an empty closet. Antonia Krumins was nowhere to be found.

Liana ran down two flights of stairs to the basement, but two swarthy guards—she supposed them to be Chechen or Ingush—barred the way. Offering them money did no good. She took the stairs up to the restaurant on the ground floor two at a time, but saw that Nikolai and Irving were gone. She felt suddenly helpless, having failed her newfound father, and knowing firsthand the abiding spirit of bitterness and lust for vengeance in her mother's heart.

She knew that at this stage neither Nikolai nor Irving would let the other out of his sight. They would be somewhere together, watching if they could, only listening if they had to. One had a need to know, the other a need to tell. The heartsick television reporter walked through the streets around the Tower, banging her fist on the back of every windowless van until she found the surveillance vehicle containing two of the three men in her world who meant most to her.

Karl von Schwebel squinted to see the figures in the half-darkness. His wife seated at his side, he faced the panel across a farm table: Kudishkin on the left, a nameless member of the Group of Fifty on the right, Madame Nina in the center, a bearded guard—apparently a lieutenant of the leader captured by the KGB—standing, arms crossed, against the wall.

"I have never had to do this before," he told them, "but I want to correct my evaluation of the Memphis operation. When I stated to you at our last meeting that Edward Dominick had mounted a detailed impersonation of Aleks Berensky, I was disinformed."

"Your judgment now?" Kudishkin was impassive as ever.

"Dominick is Berensky. He is also playing the role of his impersonator. A classic double game, in the Shelepin tradition, and I was taken in. I apologize to the committee."

The capitalist wanted to know what had made him change his evaluation.

"Information supplied by my wife, Sirkka. I will let her speak for herself." He hoped she could bring it off; the truth, with its gaps and inconsistencies, was now what she had to tell, and it was never as believable as a well-crafted legend.

"I am an agent of Russian Foreign Intelligence," she began. "Before that, I was an active informant for Stasi in Germany."

"We have long been aware of that," said Kudishkin. "And we noted the cordiality of your dinner upstairs tonight with Davidov of the Ministry of Internal Security and Fein of the CIA."

"Which we made no attempt to conceal," her husband interjected. "To refuse their invitation would have aroused suspicion."

The Russian dismissed that as obvious. "And why, Madame von Schwebel, are you now offering your services to us?"

"It suits my financial interest, sir." The sallow Group of Fifty capitalist slowly clapped his hands in applause at her refreshing honesty, and Sirkka acknowledged the mockery with a nod.

"I have been doing two jobs," she said. "Not a double agent, pretending to work for one side while working for the other; more an agent working simultaneously for two noncompeting parties."

Kudishkin nodded understanding; the Chechen against the wall stirred uncomfortably; the capitalist looked blank; the lenses of Madame Nina's glasses magnified her eyes out of all readability.

"Working for Foreign Intelligence," Sirkka continued, "I maintained contact between Moscow and its penetration agent in the American Federal Reserve System, as well as its mole in the CIA."

"Their names?" asked Kudishkin.

"I would prefer not to say."

"The names," rasped Madame Nina.

"Mortimer Speigal of the Fed and Walter Clauson of the CIA's counterintelligence branch."

"Continue."

"Soon after the sleeper was activated in 1989, Clauson set up what I believe to be an independent operation—not Russian, not American, but private—with the sleeper and Speigal of the Fed."

"Who activated the sleeper?" asked Kudishkin. "The KGB or Foreign Intelligence?"

"Not Foreign Intelligence. Clauson told me not to discuss it with FI. I presume it was a part of Federal Security, but not the part of the KGB that Davidov knows anything about."

"Did anyone mention an 'inner KGB'?" Kudishkin asked.

"No. But whoever it was had three billion dollars to invest."

"Could Clauson's independent operation, as you call it," the former KGB official pressed, "could it be run by the CIA?"

Sirkka paused. Her husband put in: "Are you suggesting a triple agent—a Soviet agent pretending to be working for the Americans and actually working for the U.S.?"

They all turned at the sound of the Chechen sliding down the wall to a sitting position, his gun in his lap.

"If the mole were caught," Kudishkin continued, "—if an Ames, for example, betrayed him—it would be just as easy to turn a double agent as any other."

"No," said Sirkka. "Clauson controls Speigal at the Fed. And last week, Speigal gave me the information about Fed plans that Berensky was able to use to make twenty billion dollars in currency trading. The biggest financial coup in history. And Berensky came here, to make arrangements for transfer of the money to you."

"Running an enormous personal risk," her husband added. "Davidov has a dozen men in this city and is prepared to kill Berensky if he finds out the money is going to you."

"The greater risk would be the CIA's if it were a CIA operation," said Sirkka. "If they did make all that money, and then put their agent in enemy hands and lost it all, the American Congress would put the Agency out of business forever."

"It is one thing to lose a dozen agents," added Karl, sharpening his wife's point, "but losing a hundred billion dollars is a serious business. No, Clauson's loyalty does not ultimately run to the CIA. To construct a brilliant defense, Clauson set up a parallel operation with the reporters Fein and Farr, sending them to the sleeper for him to impersonate himself. Truth and falsehood in one man. Breathtaking."

"You may go now," said Madame Nina abruptly. The couple rose, Karl smiling confidently. Leaving, von Schwebel was certain he and his wife had accomplished the mission they had undertaken for their client. Berensky's bona fides had been well attested to; his persuasive appearance before the board would put the icing on the cake.

"You believe them?" asked the Group of Fifty representative.

Madame Nina looked at Kudishkin for reply.

"He's working for the sleeper, she's working for Davidov, and both are betraying us," the former KGB man said. "With that clearly understood—yes, I believe them."

Madame Nina came as close to smiling as the new capitalist had ever seen. "Tell him why."

"Berensky's operation is a replica of the Shelepin Plan of 1958," said

Kudishkin. "An inner KGB to disinform and manipulate the enemy, an outer KGB to engage and be captured, never knowing the strategy. Parallel organizations that are one and yet not one. Just the sort of thing Shelepin's son would do. He's Berensky, all right."

"And you discount the testimony of Antonia Krumins, Berensky's wife?" The capitalist was uncertain. "She says he's not Berensky, and she should know."

Kudishkin looked to Madame Nina, who shrugged and said: "Could be just a jealous woman."

Berensky/Dominick did not know if Liana had made contact with her mother, to persuade her to change her story of disbelief. Nor did he know if the von Schwebels had been successful in persuading the Feliks organization leadership that their switch in judgment was genuine. He knew only that, in the end, the success of his lifelong mission rested on his own shoulders, in his own capacity for creative duplicity, which was as it should be.

Before he could form a judgment about the worthiness of the Feliks people to receive the fortune, Berensky knew, he would first have to persuade them that he was not the instrument of a reformist culture or a foreign power. He would weigh them and they would judge him; if either fell short in the other's estimation, the disengagement would turn ugly.

The irony, however, was not lost on him: after a lifetime of pretending to be someone else, and after a strange, dark interlude pretending to be someone else pretending to be that pretender, he would now have to assert the reality of his identity and hope it would be believed.

A guard at the foot of the basement steps brought him into the room, darkened and chilly for human contact but suitable for the preservation of the wall of wine bottles. An elderly, pale woman in a bulky Russian peasant's dress, magnified eyes noticeable in the murkiness, spoke first.

"I would like to interview this man alone," Madame Nina told her colleagues in a hoarse whisper.

"That is irregular," said the man the sleeper presumed to be Kudishkin of the old KGB.

"Go home, both of you," she said, flicking them away with her hand.

Kudishkin and another man, dressed in jacket and tie, whom Berensky took to be the representative of the Group of Fifty, left together. That was a nice assertion of power.

She nodded to him to sit across the table from her and told the armed Chechen to wait outside with the two guards.

"Before we begin," she said with great authority, "I want the name of the private bank, the name and number of the original account, the basis of your trading."

Berensky interpreted that as a demand for a chip to put in the pot to begin the game; earnest money. The sleeper gave it to her. "The Sennenhund Bank in Bern. Feliks Edmundovich Dzerzhinsky. Account number 456345234—easy to remember. Three billion, all in gold, of course not bearing interest." He had replaced the original stake in that first account. He repeated the number and she jotted down the information on a yellow pad. He did not have to repeat Iron Feliks's full name.

She walked heavily, with a slight limp, to a cabinet, opened it to reveal a small box of electronic equipment, and flicked a switch. "The jammer will fade. Your friends trying to listen in the truck down the street can soon hear clearly."

For her to characterize Fein and Davidov as his friends was disconcerting; perhaps the von Schwebels had failed, and Liana had not been able to reverse her mother's testimony.

"Why do you banish your own colleagues," he asked, "and broadcast to the competition?"

She did not answer.

"I established my bona fides with a small contribution," he said. "In return, Madame Nina, before we begin—who are you?"

Bowing her head forward slightly, she took off her thick lenses and laid the spectacles on top of her yellow pad. She reached behind her head, pulled a couple of pins out of the knot at the nape of her neck, and slowly pulled off an iron-gray wig. The short hair beneath was auburn. She looked up at him. In the dim light, he was able to make out, stripped of makeup, the same face he had seen in London one week ago and in Moscow twenty-three years before that.

"Nina," he said.

The diminutive of Antonia; how, in all his memory-searching, could he have forgotten the name of endearment he had called his young bride? Perhaps some unadmitted guilt of his abandonment repressed all recollection of the simple detail. The naked face wrenched him back to the reality of his own past, unleashing memories that the tarted-up persona of the woman he had met a few days before in London had failed to evoke.

The sleeper felt a perverse surge of delight at being the dupe of so delicious and extended a deception. For him, the sudden knowledge that the wife of his teens, the mother of his Liana, the embittered daughter-in-law of Shelepin, was the woman at the head of the Feliks people opened a field of trails for walking back the cat.

He began to calculate rapidly what she knew of the sleeper's operation, when she learned of his duality, why she used their daughter as bait, and what Nina's prior knowledge of Dominick's dual identity meant for the disposition of the fortune.

He opened with a compliment. "You fooled me. The Americans have a saying, 'Never kid a kidder.' But you did, successfully. I am well and truly flummoxed."

She did not accept his invitation to savor her victory. "What is the extent of the assets you control in our behalf?" Her voice became the clear voice of the woman at Claridge's.

"I calculate close to a hundred billion," he replied truthfully, "including the original stake of gold I have just turned over to you. My accountant is more conservative and says eighty-five billion because most of the assets are not liquid." Berensky then employed the technique he had learned from Irving Fein, never to end a statement without a question. "How would you and your Feliks organization propose to put that to use?"

"That is not for you to judge. My esteemed father-in-law sent you to America to be ready for a great task. We assigned you that task five years ago. We gave you the capital and gave you the information needed to multiply the capital. Now all that remains is for you to transfer the assets with your usual skill."

"If I so choose."

"Not a matter of choice. It is your duty."

"I am the one to interpret my duty, Nina. I will decide what government commands my loyalty. Is yours a government? Is the Feliks organization capable of maintaining the sovereignty and sway of Greater Russia? Or are you a giant gang, interested only in gaining the power to enrich yourselves?"

"Was Feliks Dzerzhinsky a gangster?" she countered. "Were Beria or Shelepin or Andropov gangsters?"

"No. They were rulers. They made possible the consolidation and expansion of the state." Perhaps not Andropov, who began the weakening of the KGB, but this was broad-brush argument, not the time for close analysis. "Those men controlled the criminal element, they were not controlled by criminals. They were a force against the tendency of Russians toward anarchy. Can you say the same of your Feliks people?"

She placed the glasses in her hand on the table, using her sleeve to wipe strained eyes. "I will not stoop to justifying the purposes of this organization to an agent. Perhaps your stay in the United States has turned you toward democracy. Perhaps you now disapprove of the kind of criminal democracy that served Russia so well for seventy years." She looked directly at him as she never had as his wife. He felt the force of her glare. "Your reformist notions are of no importance. We want a schedule from you on the transfer to our authority of the assets you hold only in trust."

"First I must see your table of organization and meet your key lieutenants."

"You are in no position to bargain."

"I am in an excellent position. I have the money."

"We have you. We have your daughter."

"She is your daughter, too."

"I would snuff out her life in a moment, as well as yours."

He took that as a transparent bluff. "You would throw away a hundred billion dollars merely to indulge your personal bitterness? I don't believe that. And if you did, your own people would tear you apart."

"It would be interesting to determine," she said, "to what extent I have control of this organization." Her coolness in assessing the possibility of such a gamble struck him as the mark of a potential dictator. She would have to be irrational to test her strength by losing such a fortune, but rationality was never the central characteristic of the strong leaders of Russia. Historians would later see it as a bloodily defining moment, and the fact that it was even a prospect made Berensky begin to see why she was able to dominate the leadership of the Russian mafiya. The thought formed in his mind of heading a Shelepin-style KGB in support of an authoritarian woman leader.

She interrupted his rush of revisionary thinking to observe, irrelevantly, "You never said goodbye." He was forced to think of her back then—a whining, pregnant, clinging child, inviting his abuse by threatening his future.

Nina brought a large pistol out from under the table, held firmly in both hands, and leveled it at him in a way that suggested she knew how to use it. "Now you can say goodbye."

Berensky shook his head, no; it made no strategic sense for her to kill the potential financier of a grasp for national power. Yet he could not set aside the possibility that something as primal as a desire for vengeance could upset the work of his lifetime. The gun was clasped in steady hands.

He began to think of what he could say to pique her curiosity about the fortune or their daughter, but Nina's ominous serenity persuaded him he had no time for such delay. Better to gamble on a physical move than a mental game. The room was badly lit, her eyesight was bad, her glasses were on the table. He remembered how, when they were married, she would flinch at his threatening gesture. All he needed now was a moment's flinching.

In a slow, natural move, he raised his hand to his ear, inserted his fingertip, and took out the hearing aid, saying, "There is one more thing you have to know before the banker will give your messenger that money." As that notion caught her attention, he flicked the tiny plastic device to his right; it made a pinging noise when it hit a wine bottle, distracting her for an instant as he lunged across the table to slap away the gun. The last thing the sleeper saw was the whitening of her finger as it squeezed the trigger.

The roar of a gunshot caused Irving, in the truck, to rip off his earphones. Liana pressed her hands to her head and wailed, subsiding into sobs. Nikolai said into a transmitter, "Grab the woman in the basement and leave the body behind. Three guards—kill them if necessary. Assemble at the plane."

"I gotta get some film of this," Irving said aloud, then to Liana,

"Come on, get with it, you hardly knew the guy." He was no camera-man, but the only way his book would sell was as an adjunct to a tele-vision show, and the video camera he had lugged along now had to do its stuff. He wished he could count on Liana, who was taking the murder of her long-lost father by her estranged mother personally. He wished even harder he had Viveca around, intense and sober, to take the video dimension of the coverage off his hands.

Davidov, gun in hand, was first out of the truck parked behind the Tower, racing around the corner, across the street into the café, Irving close behind, Liana trailing. Down the stairs to the locked door of the basement; urgent time wasted shooting out the lock and breaking through the door jammed by an iron bar under the handle.

Inside, no guards; no body; no anybody. They were at the scene within five minutes only to find no scene; Madame Nina must have been premeditating this murder for years. In a moment, Davidov's KGB men appeared and began feeling around the walls of the wine cellar for the hidden exit. Irving filmed them but could not be sure there was enough light. "Bring down a goddam lamp," he told Liana. "There's got to be traces of something—a bullet, blood, whatever—unless we were tuned in to a radio program."

Minutes later, one of the KGB searchers, feeling around the bottles, found a lever that enabled a rack to be swung back; the concealed door-way led to an alley where a car must have been waiting. Liana came down with a standing lamp and the restaurant manager, who was expostulating in rapid Latvian. Liana as interpreter said he'd heard nothing and was demanding to know what they were looking for in his wine cellar.

"Tell him to show us the plug for electricity or I'll break every bottle in this joint."

The manager plugged in the lamp, and the reporter panned the room with his camera.

"Slow Eddie didn't have a chance," said Irving, filming, to Davidov, on his knees examining an item on the floor. "Whatcha got there? Hold it up in the light."

Through the lens, the reporter could see a small device that Dominick had once shown him: the hearing aid to simulate an attempt to improve the hearing of an ear that—in reality—did need a hearing aid. But back then, when Dominick was preparing to play the sleeper, who knew?

"Show it to Liana, Niko." She moved into the frame, her cheek wet, to inspect the only remnant of the great impersonation. "Yeah," said Irving, both director and cinematographer, holding the camcorder as still as he could. "This could be the Rosebud shot."

While his companions were focused on the shot of the hearing aid, Davidov was plotting the likely course of the pistol shot that had killed Berensky.

He assumed Madame Nina had been seated in the middle of the table, with the sleeper agent in the single chair facing her across the table, his back to the wall. The cement floor behind the chair was wet and smelled of a strong detergent, suggesting that blood had been spilled there and had been efficiently mopped up moments after the shooting. On a line past the chair and the wet spot was the opening to the alley; he rolled the wine rack back into place and started pulling out and examining the bottles.

On the shoulder of a bottle of Bordeaux he found a small blob of brown-red material, still freshly wet; he scraped it off with a credit card and put card and blob into the only container he had, a plastic floppy-disk protector. Davidov felt around in the rack behind the bottles and plucked out some splinters of what seemed to be bone, which could be skull fragments. He found no bullet.

As Irving swung his camera around toward him, Davidov slipped the plastic wrapper into a pocket of his jacket and shook his head. "No bullet. They must have picked it up, or it's still in the body." To distract the reporter, he asked, "What is a Rosebud shot?"

"Take too long to explain," Irving said. "You have to be part of the culture."

Epilogue

RIGA

This was not the style in which Michael Shu expected the world's newest multimedia star to be living.

The living room was what his tidy Vietnamese mother would have denounced as a mess, with books and tapes piled in corners and files stacked on the couches. In the larger bedroom, the accountant could see the back of the man the star was living with, hunched into a computer, a television set blaring the news nearby. The door to the smaller bedroom was closed, but the wail of a baby demanding to be fed or changed could be heard.

"Here, you can spread out all your papers," said Liana Krumins, rearranging the stacks of printouts and mail on her desk by sweeping them into a basket. "Did you see the show? Did you like it?"

Shu decided it would be prudent to keep all his documents in his briefcase and work from his lap. "The program was a great success, Liana. The ratings were amazing for a documentary, and all the hype beforehand was only a part of it."

"The network went all out," she admitted, ruffling her hair, which was getting longer. "But did you like it? Was it good journalism? Is Irving proud?"

"Irving Fein hasn't talked to me in a year," he said sadly. "But the reviews—well, you saw them, it should win every prize they give. I spoke to Viveca, in California, and she's grateful for the way you and Irving made her the heroine of the whole story."

"You spoke to her? You're the only one who has. Was it okay, the re-creation of the bedroom scene, where she discovers he's the real Berensky? And it wasn't painful for her to see the replay of the drugged newscast?"

"She thought the way you set it up beforehand, showing how the sleeper drugged her to stop her from exposing him, restored her reputation. Made a lot of network brass feel guilty as hell, which is one reason they promoted the show, to rehabilitate her." Shu thought Liana's personality—an admixture of old-world mystery and youthful enthusiasm—enhanced the program. Viveca would have been her cool self, and she would have had to be at least apparently modest about her role in finding out the secret of Dominick/Berensky. At any rate, Viveca's refusal to return to television and Irving's insistence that Liana be his narrator and star had worked out well all around.

"Wait till they read Irving's book," Liana said. "He credits her with brains and bravery and just about everything. Not objective. Do you suppose he loves her?" Without waiting for an answer, which Michael did not have, she ran to the baby's room, shushed the kid, and came back. "Ace was on the phone this morning, says he has the book clubs in a bidding war. I love the title."

"*The Return of Iron Feliks* will be a best-seller," Shu was certain. "The videotape of the program will be in every journalism class at the Newhouse School in Syracuse, as you wanted. The CD-ROM, with all the money-transfer data and use of derivatives, will back up a Harvard Business School case study, as your late father wanted." He snapped open the lid of his briefcase and contemplated the well-organized accordion files. "Now you and I have some work to do."

She adopted a serious look and folded her hands in her lap.

"As sole executor of the estate of your father, Aleksandr Berensky, also known as Edward Dominick," he said formally, "I have the fiduciary obligation to give you a preliminary accounting of the estate's assets, and his last will and testament's disposition thereof, one year from the date of his death."

"Today is the anniversary," she said. "I didn't forget."

He drew a breath. "I have the privilege of informing you that you are the major beneficiary of your father's estate. As your television program indicated, the value of the estate is in the neighborhood of eighty-five billion dollars, pretax. Since most of the assets are held outside the

United States in various tax havens, I estimate the after-tax corpus to be about sixty billion. Half of that goes to you."

"Half?"

"Thirty billion. Liana, you are a very wealthy woman." He cleared his throat to utter a sentence that would sound like hyperbole but was a simple statement of fact. "You are the wealthiest person in the world—not just that but you have more assets in your name than anybody has ever had in the history of the world." The accountant was overwhelmed by what he was saying. "What this means is, you're richer than hell."

"Good. I promise to spend it wisely."

"You'll need an accounting firm, legal advisers, investment advisers—"

"I want you to meet my chief adviser."

She gestured toward Nikolai Davidov, brushing his jet-black hair, shirt open to the waist, standing at the bedroom door. "How much?" he asked Shu.

"Thirty net to her."

"What we figured."

Shu, who had been able to buy a major accounting firm with part of his bequest and his anticipated ability to direct the award of great chunks of long-term accounting business, suggested that the adviser would have a full-time job, ultimately employing hundreds of people full-time.

"Niko's unemployed," Liana explained, as if that settled it. "Fired the minute Antonia Krumins was appointed Minister of Federal Security. Irving faxed us a draft of his chapter on how the Feliks people took over the KGB in Moscow."

"Three billion in gold helped Madame Nina," Davidov added. "The President in Moscow was plenty sore at me for failing to stop her seizure of the gold. I was lucky to be fired instead of being prosecuted."

Mike Shu thought fast of a way to keep him occupied. "The second major beneficiary of the will is the Shelepin Foundation, fifteen billion to provide pensions to veterans of the KGB and the old Red Army. Liana was given the power to appoint the board. You could be chairman. It would be a post of enormous power and prestige."

"We'll think about it," Davidov said. "You're right about hiring the best advisers. Liana has in mind funding a Berensky Institute of Epistemology in a new University of Riga."

"The most modern university anywhere, multilingual, multinational, multicultural, multimedia, multi-everything." She did not hide her excitement. "And a huge fund to help Russians in Latvia who are unhappy here to build houses in Russia. And—"

"You'll need an accountant who knows where all the bodies are buried." Shu bit his tongue; that might not have been the best figure of speech.

"I'll ask Irving," she said brightly. The accountant cleared his throat; that was not a reference he wanted checked. "Come see my baby, Michael. Fourteen weeks old today."

At the door to the tiny nursery, Shu ventured to whisper, "Davidov's?"

"Um," she answered. He could not tell whether that was yes or no.

"You two going to marry?"

"I would like to. Niko is thinking about it."

"Be sure to make a marriage contract first," he advised. "Your husband, especially as the father of your child, would have a claim on billions." He looked down at the red-faced, sandy-haired, kicking baby in the crib, swinging a tiny fist at the mobile overhead. The accountant started, swallowing hard, as he saw what he could swear was the infant image of Irving Fein.

FRANKFURT

"That damnable, libelous program has all but ruined me, Mr. Shu," Karl von Schwebel fumed. "The lie that I am backed by mafiya money has been perpetrated by my media enemies, and they are legion. You are the executor of Berensky's estate?"

The accountant nodded.

"I have a substantial claim against it," the media baron declared. "I was his silent partner. It was solemnly agreed between us the day he was murdered by that Nina fanatic."

"You have a contract in writing?"

"Of course not. Sirkka here, who was his closest colleague through-out the earning of his fortune, who was indispensable to him, is my witness to our verbal contract."

"Meaning no disrespect, we have a saying in America that a verbal contract is not worth the paper it's written on."

"We shall see, in court if necessary. Why have you come?"

"To see your wife, sir. May I talk with her in private?"

"No. We are a team. We have no secrets from each other." He turned to Sirkka Numminen von Schwebel, seated quietly at a writing desk in the couple's library.

The tall, slender woman, with what struck Michael as the most intel-ligent violet-blue eyes he had ever seen, agreed: "My husband's inter-est and my own are inseparable."

"That's admirable, ma'am. But I was directed by Mr. Berensky, as he was preparing his will, to deliver a message to you privately before discussing his bequest. I must carry out his wishes to the letter." To take the sting out of what might be construed as an insult to her husband, or to avoid his nascent suspicion, the accountant added, "For all I know, it may be a coded security matter."

"Ah, then," said the husband. "Take him into the garden, darling, where there is no possibility of being overheard."

Shu reminded himself that overhearing was a specialty of Karl von Schwebel's, who had penetrated the elaborate security of the "war room" at the Memphis bank by owning the company that set it up. The Finnish woman led him out to the formal garden, where Shu figured directional microphones were hidden in every bush. He insisted to Mrs. von Schwebel that they talk in his rental car in the driveway. She acceded without argument.

"How much?"

"Five hundred million dollars to you, with an 'if.' "

"Though the sleeper sleeps, he does not rest," she said. "What must I do?"

Good way of putting one of Berensky's final manipulations, the accountant judged. But despite her sardonic smile, she appeared ready to do whatever was required.

"Mr. Berensky evidently had the highest respect for you, but not for your husband. The bequest will be made available to you, specifically not subject to any joint ownership agreement you may have with your husband, in the form of securities that will be acquired in a holding company in the Antilles that controls the parent company of Unimedia."

"The stock of which has fallen through its low because of that terrible, though quite accurate, television program by the brash Mr. Fein."

The accountant nodded; that low price made the purchase of control all the easier. "Mr. Berensky wanted you and another person to control that media empire. He wanted the decision to be yours—whether or not to keep Mr. von Schwebel in management or terminate his services."

"Who is the other person?"

This woman did get right to the heart of the matter; Michael could see why Berensky had such a high regard for her acumen. "I'm not yet at liberty to say, but it's a person with experience in the media, who has been bequeathed similar resources. The testator believed your experience would complement each other's. Between the two of you, control of the Unimedia holdings will be removed from the Feliks organization."

"Who did Aleks have in mind as my partner?" she pressed.

"I will inform you of that as soon as I have a meeting with that person."

She nodded reluctantly. "I take it by your frequent use of the word 'person' that it is a woman. So be it. And one billion between the two of us would be enough to control a five-billion-dollar empire. Do your duty, Mr. Shu."

The accountant had a personal note to add. "I was with Aleks Berensky when he was drawing up the will in Memphis. He wanted you to know that he appreciated your fine work over the years, and that—these are his words—he was 'drawn to Sirkka Numminen more than to any other woman I ever met.' I suppose that's why he wanted you to have your independence. And for what it's worth, he also sympathized with you as a dog owner for having to follow a veterinarian's advice to put down your mountain dog."

She sat still for a long moment. "I was useful to him. There came a moment when I was vital to his plan."

At first, Michael Shu presumed she meant the grand currency coup, but that was too obvious; he reminded himself to think like Irving at moments like these. Perhaps Sirkka was alluding to the killing of the

Swiss banker in Bern; from Berensky's remark about putting down a Bernese mountain dog, the accountant suspected the woman from Helsinki had arranged for his accidental death or done the deed herself. That would have been really useful.

"Aleks knew the risk he was running, going to see them in Riga," she said. "He wanted to be sure the fortune was used to rebuild a Russia capable of defeating the West. That called for discipline and patriotic intensity, not the Russian mafiya's corruption and greed."

"He was disciplined, all right."

"Curious, isn't it, Mr. Shu—Shelepin's purpose in creating a sleeper was defeated by an enemy he created, without intention, at the same moment. In the end, the husband and wife canceled each other out." She put her hand on the door handle, and said with affectionate detachment, "I hope Aleks was given a moment to appreciate the irony of that before he died. The mafiya and its allies are taking over in Moscow without his fortune. His life—all those years of self-denial—turned out to be a waste."

The future media baroness opened the car door. "You said 'drawn to' me was the phrase he used?"

"Those were his words."

"And I to him. I have been useful to Stasi, useful to the KGB, useful to FI, useful to my husband. Of all those I have served, Berensky alone gave me the sense that I was not merely 'useful.'" She walked, head thrown proudly back, into what was—for the time being—her husband's mansion.

NEW YORK

"I appreciate your bringing us together in your office, Mr. McFarland," said the accountant, drawing his chair up to the desk. "May I call you Ace?"

"Tell him to call you Mr. McFarland, the disloyal creep." Irving Fein was lounging on the couch.

"I used to disapprove of that racy nickname," said the agent, "but age is mellowing me. Irving here finds your transfer of allegiance to

Berensky in midstream reprehensible, which is why he prefers to deal with you through me."

"I can't blame him." Shu produced two envelopes. "You, Mr. McFarland, are entitled to a copy of the will because you are mentioned in it"—he handed a manila envelope across the desk—"in reference to the document on these disks." He handed over the smaller envelope containing Berensky's twenty-year diary and memoirs.

"I am to represent his estate in the sale of this book?"

"Actually not. The diary is his bequest to you, as is stated on page forty-seven of the Berensky will, in recollection of a dinner party in your home at which he met his daughter. The royalty is all yours."

"Smart bastard," Irving called across the room. "That way, Ace, you'll knock yourself loose to get the biggest advance; that'll force the publishers into a big first printing, making them advertise like crazy to get their nut back. And Berensky will get his message across to the biggest possible public, making that murderous commie bastard look like a victim and a hero."

"That's substantially what my client had in mind," Shu admitted.

"I have represented villains as well as heroes," said Ace with solemnity, "in line with my lifelong dedication to the principle of free speech." He ignored the loud noise imitating the sound of regurgitation coming from the couch. "Mr. Shu—why did you ask me to persuade Irving to come here today? Is he in the will, too?"

"No. I wanted to explain to him my seeming betrayal."

Fein was instantly on his feet. "Seeming? Seeming? You sold out, you little shit! He put ten million bucks in your name in a secret Swiss account not two months after you went to Memphis—on an assignment I sent you on, and paid you for. You were working for two opposing clients at the same time, and I'll have you up on an ethics charge and drummed out of the satisfied public accountant's dodge for the rest of your life. Y'unnerstand? And what piece of the estate do you get as an executor's fee—the usual five percent? Five billion for your sellout?"

"The will specifies one-tenth of one percent, or ten million, whichever is greater," Shu acknowledged. Irving would find out sooner or later.

"A lousy ten million. You were a cheap buy. You're rich, all right, but you'll be dead meat in the eyes of every bean counter in the world.

No matter how you try to buy respectability, in your obit it'll say 'traitor to accounting and journalism.' Just try to enjoy your blood money, big shot—I'll dog your steps for the rest of your double-crossing life."

Shu closed his eyes and took the abuse from the man he respected so much, comforting himself with the thought that at least they were in direct communication again. When Irving subsided, Michael said only, "I didn't sell out."

Irving then went into another long fulmination, replete with facts and dates, evidently drawn together for a follow-up story on the sleeper's subornation of a greedy and ungrateful Vietnamese-Russian-American. When the reporter wound down, the accountant told his story.

"Remember the time, after Clauson's death, you went to see Dorothy Barclay at the CIA?"

"Listen to that weaseling 'after Clauson's death.' You mean after your client murdered him, don't you?"

"Right. I don't know it for a fact, and neither does anybody, but it's a fair assumption that Berensky killed him."

"Thank you."

"Anyhow, remember when you went to Langley? And the Director of Central Intelligence gave you the brush-off?"

"Yeah."

"Well, you must have shaken her up. She turned the whole Clauson file over to the FBI Director right away quick, so she wouldn't get hit later with an Ames-type delay. And that's when the FBI agents came to me."

Fein said nothing, listening. Ace was the one who said, "Go on."

"They wanted me to work for the Bureau while I was in Memphis with Dominick. They said it was my patriotic duty."

"But you were on retainer to me, to a private U.S. citizen, and nobody suspected back then that Dominick playing Berensky was really Berensky playing Dominick."

"You're wrong about that, Irv. I think Director Barclay was tracking the sleeper, maybe starting after she walked back the cat on Walter Clauson. Something fishy was in the file about Clauson and Dominick working together on a trip to Kiev a few years back. She gave that to the FBI, and the FBI leaned on me to arrange a tap on von Schwebel's tap. And I gave them our encryption code. I figured—it was the FBI, right? They're on our side."

"They're on the side of the law. You were supposed to be on the side of the truth." Irving, as ethical Savonarola, was unrelenting. "You had a CPA's obligation to come to the client who was your meal ticket, kiddo. That was me."

"Did I? I don't know. They were very insistent that I tell nobody, especially not you, because you were getting cozy with Liana in Riga and Davidov of the KGB. The FBI guys—and your friend Hanrahan at the Fed was right with them—wanted me to seem to get closer to Dominick and further from you."

"The FBI's idea was to entice Berensky to try to suborn Michael Shu," Ace said to Irving, as if he needed further explanation, "which would require him to reveal to Mr. Shu that he was not Dominick. Good plot device. E. Phillips Oppenheim, I think, used it in a novel written right after the First World War. *The Great Impersonation*."

"Cut it out, Ace." Irving glared at the agent for his life-follows-art routine, but was no longer looking cloaks and daggers at Michael Shu. "So when did Berensky pop your hymen, Mike?"

Ace started to object to the sexism in the phrasing of the question, but Michael thought it was an apt enough reference to his loss of professional virginity. "Just before the last all-out currency coup. Clauson made his bid to take over the operation and was killed. Berensky needed Sirkka over there, and some way of getting to Mortimer Speigal at the Fed over here. Clauson was always Speigal's cutout; Berensky needed somebody here to complete the trading circuit, and that somebody couldn't be you, Irving, you're too—I don't know, incorruptible?"

" 'Incorruptible' is a good description of Irving Fein," said Ace. "Occasionally deceivable, often disagreeable, but never corruptible."

"So when Berensky made his pitch to me, and revealed himself as the real sleeper, I reported that to the FBI. Right then and there they made me promise not to tell you. The agents said it would be unauthorized disclosure of confidential government information to a private interest and I'd lose my license."

Irving licked his lips. "And Dorothy Barclay was in cahoots with them in this? She was part of the plot to use my information and my researcher against me?"

"She was jerking you around from the start. I wouldn't trust her," Shu said, hoping to position himself on Irving's side in some way. If Irving got Liana to contest his appointment as executor, calling into question his fidelity to Berensky while working for the FBI, it would cost him a bundle in lawyers' fees to hang on to his executor's fee. "And about that business about her being a lesbian? An FBI guy told me it's a cover story. Claims she's as straight as you and me."

"There's an exposé for our times," Ace offered mildly, writing the headline: " 'Top Spook Revealed as Closet Straight.' "

"Your FBI bosses told you Dorothy got suspicious of Clauson after my visit to Langley," Irving said. "When I had the dog in the car."

"It wasn't until then that she called them in, they told me," Mike reported. Why was Irving focusing on that detail? "The Bureau's agents were miffed that she didn't suspect Clauson. They thought she should have called the FBI in much sooner." He added, in case it was relevant, "They didn't know about the dog."

"You have a headache, Irving?" Ace asked. The reporter was slumped forward on the couch and was banging his head, slowly, with the palm of his hand.

"He does that when he's thinking," Mike explained. "So do you forgive me, Irving? Our friendship and your good opinion are very important to me."

"You bet I'm important to you, buster," the reporter said, back among the living, "and friendship's got nothing to do with it. One word from me, and Liana and Niko' not only will knock you out as executor, but won't hire you to manage their thirty billion bucks. And if you controlled that business, you could complete your takeover of the biggest accounting firm in the world. So don't play me hearts and flowers about friendship and good opinion."

"If I thought you were a practical businessman, Irving, I would offer you a cut of my cut. But you're an idealist. You'd throw me right out that window."

"Damn right. You can stick your commie payoff right where the sun don't shine and—"

"Wait-wait, let's not be hasty," said Ace. He shot Irving his let-me-handle-this glare, and Irving, to Mike's surprise, shut up. "Mr. Shu, although you have been in this office before as an employee of my client, as you know I have never represented you. I represent Mr. Fein, an artist who is not to be bothered by crass commercial considerations like perfectly legitimate finder's fees." Mike, catching the hint of a deal, nodded agreement; Ace's cut of Irving's cut of Mike's cut would amount to a tidy sum.

The agent turned to his client, who seemed to have suddenly lost interest in unfairly berating his faithless associate and was looking at his watch. "Irving, you made a big point to me earlier about having a reservation on a plane to San Francisco. I will buzz my driver, who will take you to—which airport?"

"Idlewild."

"He tends to bear a grudge," the agent said to the accountant. "I don't know what he's got against the Kennedys." To Irving, he said, "The driver will take you to JFK International. Good trip, Irving; give her my love. No, Michael, sit-sit. We have much to discuss."

Shu waited for Irving's Parthian shot; the reporter never stalked out of a confrontation without some final, heart-stopping pop.

"Funny you were able to get a will probated so quick without a body," Irving threw back over his shoulder.

The accountant winced. "It was a bitch getting a death certificate," he allowed. He shook his head in despair; Irving was on to it.

LANGLEY

Irving had told Ace's driver to take him to the Marine Air Terminal at La Guardia for the shuttle to Washington. He used Ace's car phone to change his flight to California to later that day from D.C.'s Dulles. Then he called Dorothy Barclay at CIA.

"I'm coming down on the Delta shuttle that arrives at eleven-thirty," he told her. "It should take a cab about ten minutes to drop me off at that little park on the river near the Agency. Meet me there, then, alone, and tell your driver and your guard to pick us up again in twenty minutes."

"There's a White House lunch I have to be at, Irving," the DCI replied cheerily. "What about breakfast tomorrow at my apartment?"

"You go to that lunch instead of seeing me, Dotty, it'll be the last time they let you in there."

"That sounds like a threat."

"I never threaten. I can write like a sumbitch, though, when I've been snookered. This is an open line. Be at the little park named after the chief of staff of General McClellan at a quarter to noon." Fort Marcy Park was the customary place near the Langley headquarters for intelligence officials to meet sources away from official grounds and bugged offices. "I'll be leaning on the cannon."

She showed up at the assigned time, and her car pulled away, as agreed. "Isn't this the park where—?"

"Laid out right over there," Irving answered. "Never found the bullet."

"I watched your program last night. Everybody at the Agency is talking about it. Kind of gives us a black eye, what with Clauson being our second mole, but it could have been worse. Can hardly wait for your book."

"That's where the rest of the story is going to be."

"What's troubling you, Irving? What couldn't wait?"

"The FBI is getting set to dump on you, kiddo. Their story is you didn't tip them off about suspecting Clauson was a mole until that day I was in your office." That was the information he had beaten out of Mike Shu; he then made his educated guess. "But you knew about it two months before, when you were briefed by your predecessor."

She did not deny either part, which half-confirmed his guess. "DCIs have to take a little heat from Congress," Barclay said. "That's what they pay us for."

"But it gets worse," he said. "Your agency didn't tip the FBI to catch your mole for at least a year, long before you got appointed. And you continued the cover-up."

"Why would I do that." It was not in the form of a question, more of a playing-out of a dialogue she expected.

"Because going after the second Russian mole in the CIA would have loused up a bigger operation you had going, to catch the sleeper."

"You have evidence of that?"

"You bet. Eyewitness. Me. You used me in the final stages of your hunt for the sleeper. Suckered me to a fare-thee-well. Now I'm going to pay you back."

"I didn't sucker you, Irving. Walter Clauson did. I couldn't stop him, because—as you say, we had bigger fish to fry."

Fein played his hunch. "I need the dates of the two findings. One from the last President, one from this."

She betrayed no emotion. "You know I can't give you either date."

That gave him plenty. If the Director of Central Intelligence was going to refrain from reporting knowledge or reasonable suspicion of a federal crime, that would be against the law—unless covered by a written "finding," signed by the President, that such withholding of evidence from the Department of Justice was in the national security interest. When a new President came into office, he would have to sign a new finding to protect the new DCI. With her refusal to give Irving "either" date, Dorothy Barclay had confirmed that there were two findings, and that the CIA had put higher priority on its search for the sleeper than on having the FBI close down the mole. That was the meaning of "bigger fish to fry."

But Irving was well aware that he was dealing with a shrewdie; Dorothy knew what she was doing with her "either date" in tacitly and deniably confirming his guess. He sensed there was something she wanted him to know, and could not tell him, which would justify her agency's year-long withholding of evidence from the FBI. The reporter assumed it had to do with an answer to his charge of cover-up, which he had told her he got from a Bureau source. He gave it another little push.

"What pisses the Bureau off," he said, arm around the McClellan chief of staff's cannon, "is that counterespionage within the United States has always been their baby. The FBI is going to protest that you spooks didn't have any right to search for a sleeper agent in Memphis."

"True."

"That would mean you had no reason to get a finding from the President to refrain from informing the FBI about a suspected mole in your agency." But of course that did not add up. Presidents don't sign nervous-making findings, which sooner or later have to be shown to a few overseers in Congress, without a very defensible reason.

"Unless," she said, and said nothing more.

He was closing in on it, he could tell. He wasn't there yet. Unless? Unless the reason for not informing the FBI had to do with counterespionage not inside, but outside, the United States. Which meant the finding had to do with a CIA agent who was conducting that counterespionage as part of his spying mission.

Irving felt he had a corner of it: the CIA was using a spy in a most sensitive and dangerous position abroad to find out about the sleeper in America. That spy had to be so high up and so central to the success of this particular mission that the Agency could persuade two Presidents that his identity should be known only to those with an absolute need to know. Not even the molehunt for Clauson was to be allowed to compromise this overseas agent, which was cause for the FBI to be cut out for nearly a year.

Irving suddenly relaxed; he had it. He ran his hand lovingly along the nubbly black iron surface of the Civil War cannon. But first he would have a little fun with the DCI, who had been manipulating him so skillfully from day one of this story.

"Antonia Krumins," he said. "You helped put her in at the top of the Feliks people, and you hired her to entice her former husband over to Latvia and to rub him out. Nasty business. I thought there were laws against assassinations. But I suppose you had to do what you had to do, Dorothy. And you paid her off with three billion in gold, and now you have her as your agent at the top of the KGB. Brilliant. Tops Philby. You won't be the first to write a great memoir from jail."

"I hope to hell you're only kidding, Irving. You are, aren't you?"

Fein let her sweat out the possibility he might be serious for a moment, then smiled. "In the Army, when the artillery gets the range wrong and fires on their own troops, you know what artillerymen say to take the edge off the horror of friendly fire? They say, 'Fuck 'em if they can't take a joke.' "

"You asked me to come here on no notice for a reason," the DCI said, unsmiling. "I'm here. What is it you want to know?"

"How come Mike Shu and his lawyers were able to get the Berensky will past the probate judge with no corpse on hand?"

When she did not immediately reply, Irving added, "Ordinarily, no body, no payout for seven years—maybe more in the case of the richest will in the world. How do we know for sure Berensky is dead?"

"He's dead, all right. There was proof. Enough to convince a panel of judges."

Not a single probate judge, but a panel. Irving figured that meant the panel of appellate judges in Washington assigned to deal with high-security cases.

"Now you're going to tell me what that proof was, Dorothy."

"Part of Berensky's brain stem was spattered against a wine bottle on the wall. The cells were clearly identifiable as being from that part of the brain, and nobody could live with that part of the brain destroyed."

That locked it in. "You know the next question," Irving said.

"Sure I do, but I'm not doing your work for you."

"How do you know the piece of the brain you scooped up was Berensky's?"

The Director of Central Intelligence looked almost proud of her interlocutor. "Because the DNA of the brain cells found on the wine bottle matched brain cells the hospital was able to extract from his daughter, Liana Krumins."

Fein's mind flashed to the cellar in Riga, with Nikolai Davidov poking around the wine bottles, sneaking away—unobserved, the KGB man thought—with some evidence in a plastic envelope. Evidence that wound up in the hands of a panel of judges in Washington specializing in secret CIA matters. That evidence, provided by Nikolai Davidov, led to a decision awarding the money to Liana and some Russian do-good charitable institute—and denying the fortune to the Feliks people, which had been the goal of the U.S. government all along.

"The CIA had a sleeper all its own in place in a Moscow university," Irving said. "You activated him for the big operation—to find the Russian sleeper in America with all the dough that could upset the government in Moscow. You were able to get him appointed to head the directorate of the KGB that was assigned to find Berensky." He remembered the moment, with the President on Air Force One held hostage by a hijacker, when Dorothy was willing to give Irving the home number of a top Russian, but not Nikolai Davidov. "And your own sleeper, Nikolai Andreyevich, or whatever his American name is, damn near brought it off."

"I cannot confirm any of that."

"I don't need you to. I was there when your boy scraped the brains off the bottle, remember? But tell me, Dorothy—after it was over, how did you get him out of there?"

She leaned back against the cannon, took a deep breath, and let it out. "We didn't have to exfiltrate this agent from Moscow. When Davidov failed to get the money back for the Russian government, they fired him for incompetence. He left the country in disgrace, with the KGB's good riddance, and nobody knowing about his working for us. Irving, how long have you known about—about this theory of yours?"

"Some theory." He was not about to tell her he had just figured it out. "It was a goddam masterstroke, Dorothy. All your people at Langley, and around the world, are going to be very proud. And over on 9th Street, the Bureau will shit a brick."

"The Russians will kill him, you know."

"What do you mean?"

"That's why I came here when you called. Why I told the White House I had something more important to do." She stepped closer to him. "If you include your theory about Davidov being our sleeper in your book, he's a dead man. We'll do our best for him in the Witness Protection Program, but Madame Nina is now running the KGB, and she will put out a contract on him that won't quit. Nick is not going to want to live his life in hiding, and sooner or later they'll gun him down."

"Baloney. They wouldn't kill one of our spies. It's not done."

"He was born there, didn't come here till he was a teenager. They'll treat him as a Russian traitor, not as our man, and the Russians execute their traitors. It's their way, their discipline. They cannot fail to do it."

"And you're telling me that I have to save Niko's ass by keeping him under cover forever. By spiking a great story, one that makes you guys winners for a change." He didn't want to end on a statement. "How many people know about him already?"

"Six. My predecessor and me; the last President and this one; Nicholas David; and you."

"And when the Congressional committees get shown the Presidential findings in timely fashion?"

"Our agent, his post, and his assignment are not readily identifiable from the findings. If asked, the President and I will make it a point of honor and hang tough."

"And if I go with the story?"

"Our man's blood will be on your hands. And we'll never give you any cooperation again. If you get a lead on the white-slavery racket that goes to the highest authorities in the Pacific rim, and could topple two major governments, don't come to me for two thick folders I have in my desk."

"I'm way ahead of you on that. Centered in Japan." In truth, her tip was news to him, but logic suggested the Japanese would be in on it. "But let my power to burn Niko be a lesson to you—never fuck around with the press, Dorothy. Got it?"

"I swear to God, never again."

"There's your car. I want to think this over." He would not give her any guarantees. One day, in a few months or so, he would tell Niko that his secret was safe, if the countersleeper who turned out to be a noncommie nonbastard made an honest woman out of Liana. Niko would, of course; the CIA wanted a handle on all that money being handed out in Russia.

He used his pocket phone to call a cab and spent the waiting time looking around in the grass for a bullet, not expecting to find anything, just browsing. His brain, having just sprinted the hundred in nine seconds flat, kept trotting along past the finish line. If Liana's DNA proved the brain that was blown out came from her parent, who was to say it was her father and not her mother? In that case, Madame Nina would be dead with some CIA dame impersonating her in Moscow, and Berensky would be alive playing King Lear to his loyal daughter. An Angleton type would lap up that possibility.

"Nah," Irving Fein said aloud, "you gotta have closure." Nina shot Berensky; the bulk of the money went to Liana; its disposition would be guided by Niko—Nick—still working for the Agency but no longer as a sleeper. That was the story, half of which he would write.

To the Civil War cannon pointed out over the Potomac, Irving Fein said aloud: "This park is named after William Marcy, who was not only McClellan's chief of staff in the war, but later became the general's son-in-law. Nobody knows that little fact but me." He looked back over his shoulder and barked an order to the imaginary cannoneer: "You may fire when you are ready, Gridley."

PALO ALTO

Irving looked at her in sweater, jeans, and running shoes, with a lawbook in her rucksack, and said, Stanley-like, "Joe College, I presume."

Viveca took his arm and squeezed it with what seemed to him to be genuine affection. "I loved your show. You brought the best out of Liana. I told her you'd be like a master teacher."

"I brung you the bound galley of *The Return of Iron Feliks.*" He stuffed his book in her bag, which made it fairly heavy, and she handed the whole rucksack to him to carry. "What you need, kiddo, is a schlepper."

She didn't get the Yiddish word. "Did you say I need a sleeper?"

"No. No-no-no. A sleeper penetrates, but a schlepper never makes it. He's just somebody who follows you around schlepping, carrying things, handy to have around, but at the end of the day—just a schlep. How's our pooch?"

"Spook's protecting the house. I rented a place off campus with a backyard and a pool and his own room to sleep in. That dog of ours is costing this scholarship student a fortune."

He took "ours" as a good sign. They sat on a bench facing the law center. It twisted him inside just to look at her again after a year apart, so he lightened up. "I could understand you becoming a massage therapist, that's an honorable profession. But a lawyer?"

"Don't start with the lawyer jokes or I'll give you a slap upside the head. I'm good at this, getting high marks at the best law school in the country. Should have done this ten years ago, but it wasn't too late. At last I'll have credentials."

Because she was sincere rather than bantering, he took a serious tack. "Must give you a lot of satisfaction. When you pass the bar, you gonna do pro bono stuff, civil rights, help the homeless, like that?"

"Not me."

"Criminal law, then," he guessed. Viveca Farr for the defense; she'd be terrific in front of a jury. "Public defender, maybe?"

"Forget it. Corporate law for me. Underwritings, mergers and acquisitions. What made you think I was a bleeding heart? You never really knew me, did you?"

"You never let me. You fell for the wrong guy." When her expression turned bleak, he recovered with "You'll need your corporate legal-eagle training. Keep your eye out for talent here. You may have to hire the whole graduating class."

"I don't need any help. I can make it on my own."

"You sound like a teenager without a cause. Actually, you look like a teenager. Matter of fact, you look like a goddam dream. You had a face-lift, or what?"

"Clean living, no more booze. I think you meant that as a compliment, so thanks, they come so hard to you. Now what is it you came out here to tell me?"

"First, I miss you."

"You miss the combat."

"No, I miss you."

"I hope so." Noncommittal, but not a rejection.

"Next, I wanted to be the one to give you the good news."

"If it's a television offer, Irving, save your breath. I'll never get in front of a camera again."

"Well, it is and it isn't. That sumbitch Berensky must have felt guilty about what he did to you, so he tried to make it up." Ace had briefed him about the will on the airplane telephone because Irving was a newsman and this was news he wanted to be the one to break.

"He left me some money? Good, I can use it. The mortgage on the house in Pound Ridge is a drain, not to mention the extra room here and the pool for the dog."

"What the sleeper really left you is clout. Power that nobody can ever take away. You know Karl von Schwebel's Unimedia? The stations, the network, the software, the on-line publisher, the music company, the movie studio, the works?" Irving paused for dramatic effect. "He's left you and Sirkka the dough to buy control of the holding company and kick the old Kraut out."

It took Viveca a moment to digest that. "Sirkka Numminen is one smart lady. But buying control—that would take a bundle of money."

"Nah, between your five hundred million and her five hundred million, and what you already know about corporate law, you could swing it easy."

She swallowed. "Irving Fein, this isn't just you teasing?"

"Check it out with Shu of the FBI. He'll be along tomorrow with the details. A good kid at heart—his firm could help you two with the bean-counting." He had squeezed his nutcracker as hard as he could to extract from Mike the delicious kernel about the wedge between the FBI and CIA that had inspired his guess about the findings, and had led to his discovery of Davidov as the countersleeper. Fein would go easy on the accountant once Ace made the deal.

She stood up. "Walk me to the co-op. I need a book for a class tomorrow."

He slung her sack of heavy books over his shoulder, the way he had seen Liana airily do it once, but they banged into his spine and made him wince.

"You know, Irv, nothing's going to stop me from getting a law degree."

He shrugged. "Be an idealist. Get your credentials. I hear you."

She moistened her lips. "But when I take over that holding company, and become a big player in the industry, there's a bunch of guys whose asses I want to see fired and never hired again anywhere."

He liked her evil glint. "That's unworthy of a distinguished attorney."

"Yeah."

"The possibilities kinda get you in the old vortex, don't they?" He stopped to shift the book burden. "Now. You're wondering why I really came out. I got a tip about a Pacific-rim prostitution ring, Tokyo-based, corruption right up to the top in at least two nations. Makes Lucky Luciano look like a piker." She wasn't old enough to remember Lucky, and he had no more from Dorothy Barclay as yet to flesh the story out, so he hurried on. "As you know, I'm a Unimedia author."

"Sorry, I can't be your partner in the story."

"Who needs a partner? I need a publisher with deep pockets. When Ace calls you, and pitches my project, you'll deliver?"

She stopped walking. "Oh, Irveleh, you can have anything you want."

That sweeping commitment hung in the air. The reporter felt he had reason to hope "anything" meant more than any assignment he wanted.

"You're not one of those phony fireflies," she added, "that prey on the real lightning bugs, are you?"

He took that to be freighted with every meaning in the book. "I'll need an office setup in San Francisco," he noted briskly, "in that building comes to a point on the top. And an expense account up the gazoo. And a place to live near the pooch, where I can take her for long walks and work out the theory of the story."

Slouching toward the co-op, the sharp corner of the book bag digging into his back with every long stride, Irving reflected that some detractor could claim that both the world's greatest reporter and the American sleeper agent once thought to be the rising star of the KGB wound up as a couple of glorified gigolos. But in the episodic adventure that was his life, he had taught himself that on rare occasion, in dependence was independence.

"You can move right into the room with Spook," Viveca suggested. "Save you on expenses. And I could use a schlepper."

ABOUT THE AUTHOR

WILLIAM SAFIRE is a Pulitzer Prize–winning *New York Times* political columnist and the author of two best selling novels, *Freedom* and *Full Disclosure*. As the *Times*'s Sunday word maven and author of *Safire's New Political Dictionary*, he is also the most widely read writer on the English language. He lives in Maryland.

ABOUT THE TYPE

This book was set in Galliard, a typeface designed by
Matthew Carter for the Merganthaler Linotype Company
in 1978. Galliard is based on the sixteenth-century
typefaces of Robert Granjon.